Margin of Error

Also by Paul Henissart

Wolves in the City
Narrow Exit
The Winter Spy

Margin of Error

Paul Henissart

HUTCHINSON

London Melbourne Sydney Auckland Johannesburg

Hutchinson & Co. (Publishers) Ltd

An imprint of the Hutchinson Publishing Group

3 Fitzroy Square, London W1P 6JD

Hutchinson Group (Australia) Pty Ltd
30–32 Cremorne Street, Richmond South, Victoria 3121
PO Box 151, Broadway, New South Wales 2007

Hutchinson Group (NZ) Ltd
32–34 View Road, PO Box 40–086, Glenfield, Auckland 10

Hutchinson Group (SA) Pty Ltd
PO Box 337, Bergvlei 2012, South Africa

First published 1980
© Paul Henissart 1980

Printed in Great Britain by The Anchor Press Ltd
and bound by Wm Brendon & Son Ltd
both of Tiptree, Essex

British Library Cataloguing in Publication Data
Henissart, Paul
  Margin of Error.
  I. Title
  823'.9'1F   PS3558.E4958H/   08111317

ISBN 0 09 140720 6

for Sylvie
with love and gratitude

Part One

*In today's world no one is innocent, no one is a
neutral.*

> —George Habash, leader, Popular Front
> for the Liberation of Palestine, at
> a 1970 symposium on revolutionary
> strategy organized by the North Korean
> Workers Party in Pyongyang.

Chapter One

Guthrie

GUTHRIE EMPLANED at Dulles Airport on the evening of August 1. Traveling under his own name, he was returning to Zurich, where he had vice-consular cover.

The cover tended to be transparent. One of his colleagues had remarked, "A fellow who's of a certain age and still halfway down the list at the Consulate, who isn't promoted and doesn't get transferred: you can figure out what that means if you're in the business." Guthrie's name had turned up twice recently in the papers, where he had been identified as an intelligence agent; it was a nuisance, but it didn't matter really. He reacted by telling people that he had assassinated no one in at least a month.

In the departure lounge, his clear, skeptical eye fell upon a billboard on which a national-circulation magazine was advertising its latest issue; the lead article was titled "How Women Can Get Along Without Men." Women without men was a tragic concept. Women with men was another.

Guthrie was over thirty-five.

He had sandy hair and an Irishman's mobile mouth and

rosy neck. He was chunky and possessed an amiable, oblique smile which he did not feel inclined to use as much as in the past. An inexorable New England stamp was on him of winter-tempered foresightedness and prudence. His brother Joseph was a detective first grade in Boston's Police District Two, in Roxbury, which is not considered a showplace of gracious living. Guthrie himself could have been cast in a television series as an incorruptible silver-badge had not the role been preempted once and for all by Telly Savalas, who was bigger and burlier and bald.

Guthrie had spent his home leave fixing up his uncle's saltbox in Marblehead, sailing a Sunfish up past Nahant and Swampscott into cold inlets remembered from his boyhood and pursuing an affair with an auburn-haired girl photographer whom he had met at a small party in Cambridge. She was a Boston University graduate with hair that smelled fresh, and she had invited him to move in at the end of their third date. Darkroom and bedroom—business and pleasure—were interchangeable, he discovered, as she insisted on his taking imaginative poses of her which were intended to grace *Penthouse*.

As far as she was concerned, he was employed by the State Department. She had a vague idea that he issued visas and helped strung-out American college students stranded abroad. Whether she believed this nonsense or not he didn't give a damn. For a moment, when it almost became serious between them, he had worried about telling her. Then it had all been over and the problem was resolved by default. After a while she had said without rancor, "You told me when we met that you like the unpredictable. I found that was wonderful at first, but eventually a girl expects something else." To which Guthrie had replied that his former wife had taxed him with the same failure to provide the predictable.

On their last night together she had mocked him fondly. "So now back to your breathtaking job at the Consulate?" In fact, on the following day, he had been down at Langley listening to a provocative if not entirely enlightening précis on international terrorism by Emmett White.

White (Kent School, Princeton, Christ College, CIA old guard) was now in charge of the Agency's task force on antiterrorism and liaised with State; it was by no means a promotion, quite probably the contrary. Anything was possible these days at the Agency. Guthrie had found Langley badly mauled, suffering from a plethora of Directors and a lack of direction. Officers blown in Madrid, The Hague, South America; a former chief writing up the Agency in *TV Guide*; a McCarthyite Irishman in Paris who had dumbfounded the Embassy by his abysmal misevaluations. Disgruntled chiefs of station were retiring to live on a combination of government pension and private income in the horsy country of northern Virginia (one of them declared bravely: "I'm not bored. I'm sailing boats, screwing girls— doing all the things I looked forward to"). At Headquarters there was far less money available, and there were far more regulations about its disposal. The debate continued unresolved with State over an ambassador's right to approve clandestine action and see the station files, which contained operational details. "We haven't reached that point," White said. "If we do, we might as well fire everybody and close down the factory. Let them get a few neutron bombs and some more cruise missiles and handle it by themselves." There were acrimonious hassles with the Equal Opportunity Office over the recruiting of minorities; but as somebody had long ago noted, the Agency was in one respect, at least, an equal-opportunity employer—it had both geniuses and idiots on its payroll.

In the midst of this, White participated joyfully in the rarefied social feuding that enlivens CIA. He belonged to a prominent Boston maritime-insurance family whose members two decades earlier had snubbed his deputy's parents. White was not above reminding his deputy of this. He was also not free of flamboyance: as Chief of Station in Bangkok he had packed a pistol around the Embassy whenever a

11

Congressional junket appeared, although the nearest Communist guerrilla was forty miles away.

Guthrie found him aging in the way apples and movie producers age, his skin a maze of shallow, meaningless wrinkles. "Emmett, you never looked better," he grinned malevolently.

White folded his arms behind his head and grunted. "The same to you, you Irish ignoramus," he said, and with these *politesses* out of the way he got down to specifics.

"Terrorism . . . the ambition of every police force is to stop it; of every intelligence service, to find out how it functions—communications, funding—and who's behind it.

"There are at present some two hundred known terrorist networks in the world—big and small, smart and dumb—and clearly we cannot be interested in them all. Let's forget the woolly-minded amateurs and self-destructive charlatans for the moment. The major networks interface: the Red Army Faction, the Red Brigades, Al Fatah, the IRA—"

"That provable?"

"Is your heart bleeding for the Provisionals, Guthrie?"

"Not especially, provided that Catholics get a crack at the same salaries as Protestants in Ulster. There's nothing like apartheid to make a terrorist of a man."

It was the sort of glib comment he immediately regretted. White, however, showed no reaction and went on. "Most governments instinctively want to sweep terrorism under the rug, get rid of it as an embarrassment, especially if it wasn't committed on their territory. As a result, cooperation hasn't been what it should be. Some Western countries cooperate more than others. Everybody has a reason, when it suits him, for failing to take a stand."

"There's none to speak of in Communist countries," Guthrie noted.

"Naturally. The KGB by definition is against disorder and abhors showboat operations, but things are different if a specific target is of interest to Moscow. At any rate, terrorism is worth somebody's while, to judge by the funds being poured in. Terrorists have credit cards, put up at Hilton hotels, rent Hertz cars and jet first-class around the world. Obviously Libya can spare a million dollars for an operation without batting an eyelash. In Western Germany, *Rote Hilfe*, the radical groups' umbrella organization, raised half a million dollars in eight months by illegally publishing books about subversion and selling them off cheap. . . ." White paused. "Well, what are we doing about all this? Take the Germans, for example. Since Schleyer's murder, they program every possible scrap of information pertaining to known or suspected terrorists—voiceprints, blood types, sex habits, dental history, favorite restaurants. The Bundeskriminalamt in Wiesbaden is as good as, and probably better than, the FBI at information analyzing. Still, the whole act has produced not one really top-level arrest."

Guthrie stirred in his chair.

"Which brings me to you. We have to find out more: you're to talk to the British and French on your way back. There's an inspector named Moreau at Sûreté headquarters in Paris who occupies himself with urban guerrillas; he claims to know a few interesting things. The idea is to establish a spectrum of options—"

"You want a report?" Guthrie asked, dumbfounded.

"The new Director wants it," White rectified aloofly. "A report on world terrorism and what's being done about it: the latest antiterrorist procedures."

Who would read it? Guthrie thought.

Night was deepening over the Atlantic, but Guthrie was wide awake.

Not for the first time, he was recalling how he had got into all of this. Before his parents made some money and moved to Belmont, he had grown up in shabby, peeling Lynn, where his cousin still lived in a sprawling five-bedroom, gambrel-roofed wooden house with a stick-style porch on Prescott Road. The success in the family was his uncle Paul, who had been elected a state senator. Guthrie had vaguely thought of following his uncle into politics, but in his mid-twenties he had received a small grant to study political science at the University of Freiburg in Germany. There he had promptly been recruited by the Agency. Given his wary, elusive character, the offer made eminent sense. His uncle Paul, however, had expressed some doubts about his chosen career. "You can't be an intelligence officer without lying like a Romanian. You'll make colonel, but you won't be able to afford cheese," he had opined in his loud, nasal bray. But were basic conditions really so different on Beacon Hill? Guthrie had wondered.

While in Europe he had met a dark-haired girl from Santa Barbara who swiftly shared his enthusiasm for living together. They were married within six weeks and received enough money from her father to pay for a long honeymoon or buy furniture. They had chosen a month of bumming through the islands off the Dalmatian coast. Returning to his post in Frankfurt, Guthrie had settled down to his bride and job. That was in 1965. His roving imagination temporarily stabilized, Guthrie had looked upon his life as a workable, occasionally splendid proposition.

Two years later he had been assigned to Vietnam. He had arrived for the Phoenix program, and he had seen what happened at Quang Ngai when submachine-gun–toting irregulars in berets and Levi's who were failures back home rounded up Viet Cong prisoners and herded them off to Provincial Interrogation Centers. At the time, he had no idea of the full number of victims, but long before reading the secret reports at Langley he had found the goings-on barbaric and stomach-turning. Phoenix was a form of terrorism too. After one tour of duty he had requested a transfer and, to his surprise, got it.

His wife had waited for him in Hong Kong and Bangkok; then, like other CIA wives, she had become bored and returned to Washington. When he came back, she divorced him, they split their property and he went back to Europe, where, in truth, he felt freer. In Zurich he ran a modest operation and reported to Ditweiler, who ran the whole show out of Bern. Ditweiler most of the time was glad to have him in Zurich, though on some days Ditweiler hated everybody.

There were one or two tight assignments—running a Swiss businessman into Estonia, outmaneuvering an Iraqi revolutionary in Geneva—but for the most part Guthrie's duties were routine. He had made GS-13 seven years ago —early for his age—but since then he had been vegetating. He was an oddball, tolerated but unacclaimed. Not too high in rank, not too low in age, that's me. Each time I shlep down to Bern I think of how the world gets on and Guthrie stands still. At this stage of his life, his unsung, unspoken hero was Giuseppe Tartini, the composer who had lived in Padua one hundred and fifty years earlier: that inventive Italian spirit, while writing sprightly concerti, had managed to make an acceptable living teaching the refinements of swordsmanship, and as the years passed his fencing school had flourished while his musical reputation waxed. Guthrie thought of him with generous envy.

Which brought him up to the present. His friendly heart ached for the lost auburn girl, but not intolerably so. He was going to have a few days' per diem calling on the merry men of DI-6 in London and their counterparts in Paris. A Cook's Tour of Western intelligence—the first would provide gin and clever chatter; the second, food and sophisticated shrugs. Being thankful for small blessings, he felt content, and softly he started to hum.

The stewardess who came by smiled. She didn't get many aloft who sang when they were sober.

Chapter Two

The Two Inspectors

IT WAS Europe's hottest summer in years. All week, record highs had beset the Continent, but it was Paris that suffered most, a city temperamentally attuned to drizzle and darting damp breezes, prudent skies of conservative gray. During the burning days Paris suffocated and sunset brought no relief, for no wind rose and the air remained dry as cinders.

Just past seven o'clock on that evening, two police inspectors arrived at a building on rue Chateaubriand in the Eighth Arrondissement. The elevator was out of order, so both men walked up to the fifth floor.

Two days earlier, a solitary gangster had held up a fashionable jewelry store on avenue Matignon when it opened for business. He had put a gun on the owner, told him which stones he wanted, pocketed them and fled. The owner gave the police the thief's description, and it appeared in the newspapers. The description included the fact that the bandit was left-handed and spoke with a marked Provençal accent. Two days had passed; then police headquarters had received a telephone call from a concierge on rue Chateaubriand, who reported that a man resembling the wanted gangster was staying in the apartment of a young woman tenant who was herself absent.

Moreau, one of the two inspectors, was older by ten years than his colleague, Vigy, and longer on the force. He had recently been detached to Division B-2, on international terrorism, of the Direction de la Surveillance du Territoire, but his training and experience—hence instincts—were rooted in the Brigade Criminelle's procedures.

Both inspectors were armed, and they approached the apartment with caution.

Vigy flattened himself against the corridor wall and got ready. Moreau rapped on the plywood paneling, then quickly stepped aside and fingered the grip of his service-issue 9mm Parabellum.

They heard footsteps within, the click of a bolt, and then the door opened wide.

A man in a short-sleeved navy blue Lacoste shirt stood on the threshold frowning and squinting into the corridor's stingy light.

"Police," Moreau barked, and moved forward, poking the gun barrel into the man's stomach.

The man in the doorway backed off and stared at them out of light blue eyes clear and chill as an alpine pond. He had cropped straw-blond hair and was in his late-thirties.

"Identity papers!" Vigy snapped, entering and covering the other doors in the living room.

Utterly motionless, the man studied them with neither anxiety nor defiance, his breath issuing in shallow, placid exhalations only a few inches from Moreau's face.

Vigy repeated the order, but the man ignored it and watched him thoughtfully.

It was then that the thought crossed Moreau's mind that there was something wrong about the man, about his un-intimidated stare; something akin to the deceptive passivity of one of the medium-sized cats padding back and forth in its cage at the Vincennes zoo. Only the feral odor was

17

lacking, though Moreau could have sworn that he caught a whiff of that too. "What is your name?"

"Schilling—my name is Bruno Schilling. What do you want here?" he grumbled. To Moreau's vexation, there was no doubt of the foreign accent, like a slight but inextirpable blemish on his tongue. He might have known. Paris was full of foreigners. Moreau could feel Vigy's deflation.

Deflecting the gun barrel, he said, "Let's have a look at your passport."

"It's in my jacket." The blond man addressed Moreau. "In the hall."

"Get it."

Calmly—too calmly, to Moreau's way of thinking—the man retrieved a green passport from the interior pocket of a crash-linen sport jacket draped on a clothes peg and handed it to the senior inspector. As he began to leaf through it, Moreau was aware that Vigy too had remarked the man's way of submitting it with his right hand.

It was an Austrian passport made out fourteen months earlier to Bruno Schilling, thirty-eight, domiciled in Linz, hair: blond, color of eyes: light blue. The photograph pasted on page three was unmistakably that of the apartment's occupant. The following pages contained random frontier-post stamps of non–Common Market countries: Switzerland, Sweden, Yugoslavia.

"There is no date of arrival in France," Moreau observed mildly.

"The police seldom stamp passports any more at Common Market frontiers."

"I am asking you when you entered."

"Two days ago."

It occurred to Moreau that were the blond man lying, he would have specified any date other than the one on which the holdup had taken place.

"How long do you intend to stay in Paris?"

"A few more days."

Moreau understood people who shifted their weight and

blinked under questioning; he was uneasy with people who stood their ground, neither cooperating nor refusing to do so, allowing their antipathy to seep through their reserve like dirty water backing up in a sink.

For the first time a trace of annoyance sharpened the Austrian's voice. "May I have my passport back?"

"In a moment. What exactly are you doing here? Is this your apartment?"

The man said with unshakable patience, "A friend lets me use it while she is away."

"Away where?"

"In Switzerland—on business."

Moreau, who was originally from Marseille and still invariably drank pastis in hot weather, was not drawn to this frozen Nordic type. "You can account for where you were at nine thirty A.M. two days ago?"

"I arrived in Paris at four P.M. and came straight here." He gave back stare for stare, his blue eyes betraying no feeling save for that fleeting gleam of dislike. "I am beginning to think you are confusing me with someone else."

"You have a pen or something to write with? I want you to sit down at that table and write out your name for me."

Frowning, Moreau waited while Schilling complied; then he took the sheet of paper and compared the thick-stroked, Central European signature with the one in the passport. They matched, and this time Moreau, looking up, met Vigy's gaze and sighed faintly. What was important was less the signature than the fact that Schilling was truly right-handed. Vigy was clearly wondering why they did not drop the matter then and there and make their exit, pausing below to lecture the concierge on the need to avoid wasting the police's time and energy with false denunciations based on unfounded suspicions.

"You watch him," Moreau addressed Vigy. "I'll just have a quick look around the place before we go."

Schilling exhibited sudden resistance. "Where is your search warrant?"

To transient foreigners Moreau felt no duty to explain anything. "If you want to make an issue of it," he said equably, "we'll take you with us and get one."

It was bluff, of course, and Schilling probably realized it, but he said nothing as Moreau went toward the door at the far end of the living room.

The bedroom was small and square, and the pale summer dusk revealed little. Moreau switched on the light and felt ridiculous. He realized that he was inspecting the apartment on the basis of animosity, which was not a respectable motive. He did not expect to discover any of the stolen jewels here. Schilling had had nothing to do with a holdup committed by a French bandit. But there was something unpleasant and disturbing about Schilling—a cold, repellent quality beneath the aloof facade which Moreau associated with Germans during the Occupation and which caused his neck hairs to bristle. However, you couldn't book a man because you objected to his manner or the untamed glimmer in his eye. Moreau, being modest, did not unreservedly trust his instinct. He was thinking that once he checked out the bedroom his duty would be acquitted and he would please Vigy by skipping the rest of the apartment and calling up Headquarters to report that they were on their way back. . . . He tapped his chin thoughtfully and was astonished to discover that he still held Schilling's passport in his hand.

He put it in his pocket and looked about the room. The single window was tightly shut, the day's accumulated heat boxed into the small space. The room was stuffier than Police Headquarters. Moreau wondered if Schilling slept without opening the window. Was he the type who was impervious to his own odor? Methodically Moreau noted the handwoven Indian coverlet and plaid throw pillows on the bed, the plant hangers strung by jute twine from the ceiling, the wallpaper in contrasting bold stripes of tan and sand, the aluminum-framed nonrepresentational prints, the Art Deco chaises—the female tenant of this Right Bank apartment had resolutely opted for contemporary Left Bank styling. On a white Finnish vanity stood aligned her array of flacons, atomizers and hairbrushes. Then Moreau's glance traveled to a navy blue vinyl tennis bag resting on the bed. It was the only object in the room that possibly belonged to Schilling rather than his girlfriend. Moreau picked it up and found it heavy. He unzipped it. A Beretta 7.65mm pistol, its new blue-black finish gleaming dully, lay in repose like a beautiful and dangerous snake on top of three brand-new, greased Czech 9mm Makarovs. Refraining from uttering a sound, Moreau stared at the automatics, noted that the safeties were on, thrust them carefully aside and began to forage inside. The bag contained, in addition, four spare magazines with full clips, two boxes of ammunition, six electric detonators, a half-kilo of plastic explosive and four lightweight Dutch V-40 fragmentation grenades, which can be thrown twice as far as an ordinary grenade. As Moreau inventoried the mini-arsenal, he was so dumbfounded that he forgot a basic precaution he had learned years ago. "Vigy," he shouted, "come here and . . .!" only too late realizing that by doing so his junior partner for a split second was turning his unguarded back on Schilling.

Chapter Three

The Network

". . . WHAT HAPPENED then we may never know, because they're both dead," Ditweiler declared sixteen hours later at the American Embassy in Bern. He sat in his second-story office and contemplated Guthrie, bent not on eliciting a comment but on providing him with facts.

"The concierge of the building is the source of what comes next. She was in her kitchen getting dinner ready and minding her own business, she claims—which shows you how much Paris has changed—when she heard gunshots. However, they were faint, and she thought they were probably not real shots at all but part of the action on someone's television set playing overloud with the window open. Nothing else happened—no call for help, no further commotion—so she decided that she was mistaken. But immediately afterward she heard someone—a man, to judge by the noise—racing down the staircase, the elevator apparently being out of commission. She hurried into the hall, where she found the front door ajar; then she rushed out into the street, but saw no one: whoever had come pelting down the stairs had already disappeared around the corner. So the concierge ran back indoors and marched up to the top floor with the intention of methodically checking each apartment and working her way down. She was worried that a summer burglar had got into an apartment and been surprised in the act. The police, you see, hadn't co-ordinated their raid with her.

"The door of the first apartment she came to on the fifth floor—it was where the tenant she suspected of being a holdup man was staying—the door was wide open, so she began there. A man's body was sprawled face down on the carpet in the middle of the living room. That was Vigy, the younger of the two inspectors, and he was dead, shot in the head at close range. The concierge is a tough old biddy; she got hold of herself and then noticed the second corpse lying face up in the doorway of the bedroom beyond. It was Moreau. Left behind were handguns, grenades and detonators. What would have happened if he hadn't searched the bedroom and discovered them? In all likelihood nothing, and no one the wiser as to what the temporary tenant was really up to." Ditweiler paused to run a fingernail meditatively over the opaque black report cover on his desk. "After another look at the mess, the concierge beat it downstairs as fast as she could to alert Police-Secours . . ."

Ditweiler was a thickset, muscular fiftyish; he jogged two miles each morning, and on summer weekends he played tennis with his secretary or, when he could not get out of it, the Ambassador. Under the usual Political Section cover he was in charge of the Agency's large station in Bern. He drank abstemiously, read everything and was of Swiss ancestry on both sides, which facilitated his relations with parliamentarians and Government department heads in the capital, who appreciated this heavy-boned, stinting American so like themselves.

". . . The first thing the police found," he resumed, "was a stack of leaflets and brochures on a bookshelf—'Lies

23

about the Palestinian struggle for Liberation,' 'Angola's anti-imperialist victory' . . . so their thoughts turned naturally to radicals and activists. Then, reinforcing this impression, they found an Austrian passport still in Moreau's pocket. It turned out to be one of a dozen blanks stolen two years ago by a suspected Soviet agent in Vienna. The data in it are, of course, pure fantasy: the Austrians have no record of a blond-haired Bruno Schilling born in Linz on March 14, 1940."

Guthrie had returned to Zurich the night before from his fact-finding trip to London and Paris, which had yielded only picked-over bones. His appointment with Moreau had been canceled at the last moment without explanation. Then Ditweiler had called first thing in the morning and suggested a meeting in Bern before noon, which was their standard arrangement whenever a situation arose that could not be handled on secure lines. On the new Autobahn the driving time from Zurich is little over an hour, but in his Audi 80 Guthrie had reduced it considerably. He had arrived in the Embassy parking lot on Jubiläumstrasse at eleven fifteen. And now, as he sat in Ditweiler's sunny office, the first slight, unpleasant intimation tingled like an early warning through his body that his report on terrorism was going to uncover more than he had bargained for.

He shifted in his seat and said succinctly, "Fingerprints?"

"Plenty of fingerprints all over the apartment; Schilling wasn't making a secret of being there. But whose? The French police lifted them and went through their records of known lawbreakers, terrorists and undesirables. Negative result. They queried the Austrians and Germans through Interpol. Same result. So what do we have? This character, whatever his real name, sitting with a tennis bag of automatics in that apartment when by chance two police inspectors turn up looking for someone else. They're careless and let him out of their sight for a moment. He has, apparently, a nine-millimeter Beretta stashed away, which he turns on them without a second's hesitation. Each one is gunned down with a single shot." Ditweiler said reflectively, "Expert job. No panic, no indecision. And then he takes off—he had only one block to run to disappear on the Champs-Elysées—and he hasn't been seen since."

"The guns he left behind?" Guthrie prodded him softly.

"Swiss—we're all over the place when it comes to arms." Ditweiler stated it almost with pride. "Part of a lot intended for shipment to a Third World country. Pilfered from a warehouse at Winterthur, the 7.65mm Beretta was used four months ago to assassinate the deputy police chief of West Berlin." Ditweiler paused. "What was he waiting for in that apartment? Where is he? And when you get right down to it, *who* is he? The French don't know, the Austrians don't know and more to the point, we don't know."

Guthrie stirred. "Al . . ." He always addressed Ditweiler by his first name; the Ambassador did, everyone at the Embassy down to the cafeteria cook did, in spite—or possibly because—of his pompous bearing. "Al, why do we care? Isn't it the French police's problem?"

Ditweiler nodded his massive head and again tapped the report lying on his desk. "In fairness, I know you haven't read this. It's been kicking around awhile, getting fatter. Let me summarize the contents.

"Bruno's name has turned up on the terrorist circuit before, but always very circumstantially, never verifiably. A German woman schoolteacher, Uta Eisenberg, who belonged to the Baader-Meinhof gang and went on a hunger strike in Frankfurt prison, mentioned the ringleader of a certain 'Aurora' network; the Krauts noted it, checked it out and got nowhere. At the time of the Munich Olympic massacre, one of the captured Palestinians declared that a blond code-named 'Bruno' had supplied the arms for the attack. The Palestinian gave the address of a boardinghouse in Schwabing; the Bavarian police went around, and the landlady confirmed that she'd had a blond lodger registered under that name, who had left twenty-four hours earlier without a forwarding address. So that lead petered out too."

Bit by bit, Guthrie reflected, they were getting to the point. He had learned not to try to speed up Ditweiler; in

Switzerland everything, including CIA, proceeded at a deliberate, imperturbable pace.

"Back home, they're interested in Bruno. We didn't know, of course, that he was in Paris: we'd never have picked up his trail without the shoot-out. . . ." Ditweiler surveyed Guthrie critically. "I said he vanished, but still there are *some* leads. The girl who lent him her apartment is in Zurich." He had cast another glance at the evidently lengthy report. "Her name is Marie-Christine Lemarchand, and she runs a boutique on the Left Bank in Paris. It's apparently quite successful. Two days before the shoot-out she flew into Zurich to attend a fashion show. . . ." The blond August light glinted becomingly on Ditweiler's thick gray shock of hair, no doubt in the way his expensive barber had promised: Ditweiler was vain about his personal appearance, a fact that cheered Guthrie. "The Swiss interrogated her early this morning at the French police's request. Her story is that Schilling, a former boyfriend, turned up in Paris just before she left. It was she who proposed his moving in: empty apartments in Paris during the summer are easily burglarized, so she decided it would be better to leave someone in the place."

"No known radical connections?"

"None."

"*Former* girlfriend, did you say?"

"Yes."

Guthrie thought it over. "Why didn't she fly back to Paris after the shoot-out?"

"Insists she's uninvolved. Incidentally, she's staying at the Baur au Lac."

Guthrie watched the rotund, overdressed figure behind the laminated walnut desk. Ditweiler, it occurred to him, had a sort of battering-ram intelligence that occasionally —not consistently, but every so often; enough, at any rate, to keep Langley happy—drove home to the truth by dint of sheer perseverance.

"Look at it from this angle. If you were a Swiss policeman"—for some reason the notion seemed to charm Ditweiler—"how deep would you dig? Did the shoot-out occur on their territory? Were any Swiss nationals killed? The answer to both questions is no. We can assume the Swiss police conducted a routine interrogation for the benefit of their French colleagues, telexed their findings to Paris and passed on to more pressing matters. That's why I see some point in your talking to the girl. It's possible that some lynx-eyed Zurich sleuth overlooked something." After a moment Ditweiler said, "We'd like to get a fix on Schilling before the others."

"Before the French, that is."

"The French are unlikely to take him alive. They want to balance the books—one dead terrorist for two murdered inspectors. We, on the other hand, are interested in letting him tell us about the funding and communications setup of Aurora. That's our stake in this." Guthrie was already rising. "Just to keep any egos from being bruised, you'd better coordinate it with Huebli. And, Guthrie"—Ditweiler smiled thinly—"do me a favor: let me write a passing fitness report on you. It reflects on me, after all."

"All right. I wouldn't want you to be tarnished by my incompetence."

"Why are you in such a hurry?"

"I'm looking forward to meeting a high-fashion terrorist."

Chapter Four

Marie-Christine

MARIE-CHRISTINE OPENED the door and stood composedly, watching her two visitors out of green, exquisitely thoughtful eyes. She was a slender honey blonde with silky legs and a fashion model's fluid movements, which she probably could turn on and off at will. A couturier's joy, Guthrie decided, assessing her Kelly green silk shirt, contoured white slacks and embroidered espadrilles. For all her high grooming, however, it was the vestiges of a finishing school's discipline that fascinated him: not a strand of blond hair, not a pleat of slacks fabric was out of place; her well-kept hands did not flutter. Guthrie thought, What have we here if not a French Catholic version of my once-upon-a-time wife? Marie-Christine was a girl whose teeth, posture, pastimes and friendships had almost certainly been subjected a few years back to unrelenting surveillance by worldly nuns. And beneath the tidy package of ladylike surfaces? Even the nuns could not always control that.

Guthrie studied her. She seemed totally at ease, serenely unimpressed by their presence. Then he recalled that she had already been interrogated. Practice makes perfect. The Baur au Lac, with its fresh flowers in the lobby, its nonchalant rhythm, its splendid garden before which Rollses and Ferraris idled, was the right hotel for her. Probably, in view of her moneymaking boutique, she was keener on defending than on destroying the system . . . which rendered her role all the more intriguing. Guthrie grinned crookedly, as always when he was undecided about the terrain ahead.

Huebli—Kommissar Emil Huebli of Zurich's Kriminal und Sicherheitspolizei—had just introduced him. "With our authorization, my colleague from the American Consulate wanted to put several questions to you which our police may have omitted to ask."

Marie-Christine looked at Guthrie and withheld comment.

"If you want to bring over those chairs from the corner," she said, choosing for herself the two-cushion sofa facing the color television set. She had already been questioned by two detectives and interviewed by reporters of three newspapers. Never having been questioned by either before, she had emerged from both experiences considerably relieved: the police were as superficial and predictable in their inquiries as the newsmen.

"Only a few questions," Guthrie specified amiably, starting slow. "When did you find out about the shooting in your apartment?"

"At seven in the morning the police woke me up to interrogate me." Her clear gaze on him was steadfast. "I still don't believe Bruno did it."

Huebli stirred, and Guthrie asked, "Why is that?"

"I'm not saying that he is innocent, but I have only the French police's word—and that slow-witted concierge's—for what happened. A friend of mine is accused of two murders. My reaction is to hope he had nothing to do with it, that a mistake was made." Her first impression of him was ambiguous: this vice-consul in his late thirties, with ruddy skin almost imperceptibly freckled, was probably clever, certainly scrappy. She judged men by their eyes, their manner, to a certain extent their interest in her. The American's blue-gray eyes weren't bad, she conceded.

Guthrie frowned. "There's no mistake about the guns he ditched—one of them was used in another terrorist attack."

"Perhaps not by him. He never mentioned any political opinions to me."

"How do you account for the literature he left behind together with the guns?"

"I can't account for it," she said.

"Incidentally, Bruno Schilling isn't his real name."

"It's the only name he used with me," she said promptly.

"And how long did you know him?"

"On and off over two years. Whenever he came to Paris I saw him."

Huebli intervened unexpectedly. "Came to Paris from where?"

"This time? Geneva, he said."

Her answers were too pat, too standardized, too dry as she described a two-dimensional relationship, Guthrie thought. The interview so far reminded him of an act out of French classical theater: ceremonious and standoffish, Cartesian, spare, bereft of song. So what was she holding back?

He had an irresistible urge to shake her up. "I have the impression you didn't know him very well."

Marie-Christine allowed herself an inward-directed smile. "Pretty well."

"What does that mean? How long was he your boyfriend?"

She took it in stride. "For a few months. I didn't mean a great deal to him; he had plenty of girls. . . . So—*d'amant il est devenu mon ami*, nothing more, and it remained that way," she concluded firmly.

It was just possibly true, Guthrie thought. If he lived as

long as his uncle Paul, he would never outgrow a sense of wonderment at sleek, lithe girls like this who were attracted to men like Schilling who kept squads of others waiting in the wings. His own accomplishment along those lines wasn't negligible, but it wasn't record-breaking either.

"You knew him pretty well but had no idea whatever that he might be a terrorist?"

"No." She was beginning to wonder how far she could go without plunging over her head into evident contradictions. "Do you have any more questions?"

"Not more than a hundred."

She shook back her blunt-cut honey hair automatically. "I can believe it."

Marie-Christine did not smoke, he noticed, and seemingly did not even yearn for a cup of coffee. She was also apparently dissatisfied with the way she had described her relationship to Schilling. "Bruno was a small part of my life . . . do you understand?"

It was the first sentence she had uttered with a ring of complete truth, but it threatened to lead off into areas he didn't want to explore just now.

"What did he claim to do for a living apart from illegally transporting arms?"

She smiled at him. "A *few* questions, you promised. He said he was an information specialist. . . . He had stories about his associates. Incredible stories."

Huebli had not opened his mouth again. God only knew what he was thinking at this stage.

"Did you meet any of those unbelievable associates?"

"No. As a matter of fact, his life-style was so erratic—he traveled a lot, Europe, the Middle East, airports were where he passed his life—that I couldn't believe he had a serious career. Once or twice I took him to parties; my girlfriends thought he was nice but too sure of himself and so very playboyish: here today, gone tomorrow. . . . So I decided he was an adventurer who was doing something not altogether honest—"

31

"Obviously that didn't interfere with the friendship."

Marie-Christine opened wide her admirable green eyes. "No, of course not. He had a certain raw-edged charm, if you see what I mean. I fell for him. He was interesting and offbeat."

"Where did he stay when he wasn't using your apartment?"

"With other friends. I was looking for someone to babysit my apartment, so when he arrived in Paris I immediately offered it to him. He accepted—more, I had the impression, to do me a favor than because it really appealed to him. He came by with his bags, as we had agreed. I saw him for about fifteen minutes. I gave him the key, showed him where everything was in the kitchen, and then I had to run to catch my plane." Marie-Christine grimaced. "Now I'm sorry that I gave the key to anybody."

"Was he planning to stay until you came back?"

"Yes. He told me he would be in Paris about a week."

"And where was he going after Paris?"

"He didn't say."

Guthrie looked at her, and Marie-Christine said reluctantly, "He made trips often to Germany." For the first time her cheeks flushed. "Why do I have to repeat everything? I've already told the police that I haven't the faintest idea where in Germany."

Guthrie grinned. She reminded him increasingly of Ditweiler in Bern; what a pair they would make!

His next question took her by surprise.

"What nationality did you take him for?"

"Austrian. It was one of the first things he told me about himself."

"Which you bought?"

"Of course. Why shouldn't I?" Nothing about this American, she thought, was simple or obvious.

"By the way, how did you meet him?"

Marie-Christine blinked rapidly, realizing that both men were suddenly watching her. "At a swimming pool—Piscine Molitor. If you don't know Paris, it's hard for me to explain where it is."

For a self-assured blonde, Guthrie thought, Marie-Christine kept smoothing her hair back over her ear remarkably often.

"I go there sometimes in summer—well, he was there too and we just happened to begin talking." Guthrie continued to grin, but by this time Marie-Christine was aware of the danger—he couldn't be as much of an imbecile as he wanted to appear; that uncritical good humor did not prevent him from trying to set tiny, invisible traps. Rattled, she added superfluously, "Later we went to a café nearby, La Frégate. It has a sidewalk terrace I like."

Abruptly Guthrie got to his feet. Marie-Christine appeared astonished by the sudden end of the questioning. So did Huebli.

Guthrie placed a visiting card on the writing desk. "You can reach me at either number," he said briskly.

"Why should I want to reach you?"

"*Qui sait?*" Guthrie allowed himself a moment's fun, his eye resting appreciatively on her figure. "How long are you going to be with us in Zurich?"

"At this point I'm not sure," she said with sudden lassitude.

Once in the hotel elevator, he turned to Huebli. "Is that true about not setting a return date to Paris?"

"She's made it clear that she's in no hurry to undergo further interrogation in Paris."

"Well, that's understandable."

"What did you think of her?"

"Quite a pepper pot, probably, under the ice. Is she under surveillance?"

Huebli stared hard at him. "For what reason? She's committed no crime. She knows Bruno, but wasn't in Paris when the shooting occurred. She maintains she knew nothing about his activities, and it is hard to prove otherwise. Her status here is essentially that of a tourist." Huebli was well meaning, but his allegiances never swerved. "Do you know how much surveillance of a single person costs? You do, of course. The expense has to be approved at the Ministry; we Swiss are not nearly so rich as you imagine. We questioned her as a service to our French colleagues, but that is the limit of what we are prepared to do."

It was all developing along very Swiss lines. Ditweiler knew whereof he spoke, Guthrie thought.

As they crossed the lobby he said, "I'd like to check out one detail with the hotel telephone operator."

"Why not?" Huebli was cooperative as long as no expense was involved; parsimony not only dictated policy in Switzerland, but was esteemed a virtue. "She works in the telex room behind the reception desk. I've got information from her once or twice in the past on other cases."

Huebli led the way past marble-topped tables and framed oils to a small windowless room where a portly woman with a black cashmere sweater over her shoulders sat before a switchboard. With Huebli she spoke in Schweizerdeutsch, then turned to Guthrie.

"I would like to know whether direct-dialed calls go straight to the rooms," he asked.

The operator had a soft, querulous voice. "Direct-dialed calls come to the switchboard and are then connected to the guests' rooms."

"Did Mademoiselle Lemarchand in Room 220 receive any long-distance calls two nights ago or on the following morning? Can you tell me that?"

Another middle-aged woman had just entered the room and deposited her handbag on the table.

"I wasn't on overnight duty, but Frau Lent was," the switchboard operator said, indicating the other woman.

Frau Lent, who had been listening to Guthrie, nodded. "Room 220? She received a call from Paris shortly before midnight."

"What makes you remember that so well? You don't keep a record of incoming calls, do you?"

"No. The reason I remember is that Room 220 didn't answer at first; however, the man at the other end of the line insisted that I keep ringing, as it was important. The night concierge had seen the lady return a short while before and pick up her key at the desk. I tried the bar, but it was shut; the barman said she was not in the discotheque downstairs. So I kept ringing and finally she answered—she said that she had been asleep."

"How do you know the call originated in Paris?"

"The party said so when he asked me to keep trying her room."

It was only when they stepped out of the lobby that Huebli spoke up. "Perhaps the call had nothing to do with the shooting? Perhaps she wasn't lying about only learning the news the following morning?"

"Anything is possible," Guthrie said politely.

Together they struck off in the direction of the lake. Along the shore everything was placid and freshly painted; the trees, lush with foliage—catalpas and copper beeches —seemed to have been pruned by a benevolent banker. In the lingering heat of the August afternoon, groups of tourists were assembling at the pier waiting to board the sightseeing boats; the siren sounded of an incoming steamer from Kusnacht making for the landing stage. The long lake gleamed smooth and lavender as far as the eye could discern between prosperous slopes. It was a clear day, and they could see down its whole length to the snowy alpine summits of Scheerhorn and Mythen.

"As a matter of fact, Marie-Christine is lying in her teeth about that and other things too," Guthrie said calmly.

"Other things?"

"She mentioned La Frégate. I'm acquainted with that part of Paris better than she assumes, and it happens that La Frégate was torn down six years ago. She's known Schilling much longer than she cares to admit."

"Is that why you got up and left?"

"I was getting pissed off with her. That girl has the arro-

35

gance of amateur liars and is convinced that men are so busy admiring her looks that no one will spot the inconsistencies in her story."

"I still don't think the Ministry will approve an order for surveillance," Huebli said.

Chapter Five

The Forest

HE SPRANG down from the delivery van and waved farewell to the driver who had brought him this far. The vehicle made a wide U-turn and was soon out of sight on the highway leading back westward to France.

The marketplace of the Luxembourg town of Echternach was busy as the bell struck 11 A.M. in the fifteenth-century Town Hall, and none of the street sellers or their customers paid the hefty blond man attention as he strode toward the far, northern end of the square. Without referring to the folded map in his pocket, he followed a succession of narrow streets and found an asphalt promenade flanked by silvery poplars and fragile willows which curved beside the winding Sûre. Next to a filling station was a café flying the blue-white-and-red Luxembourg flag; cars were parked before it, and from a half-open window escaped an odor of *frites*. A main eastbound road led across an old stone bridge into Germany. On the near side, two green-uniformed Luxembourg gendarmes with field glasses were intently watching for illegal crossers downstream.

He put the bridge behind him and continued along the promenade until he reached an outlying area beyond which open country began. After the hot, rainless summer the Sûre was running low; it was less than forty feet in width, and the current was not markedly rapid. It certainly wasn't a barrier—he could swim it in two minutes, or perhaps wade it; but he didn't dare. Someone was perhaps observing and might report him; in wet clothes, anyway, he could be conspicuous. On the opposite, German, bank two boys were fishing, invisible in the tall reeds except when they cast their poles. Two other youngsters came down the river paddling clumsily in a rubber boat. He thought of enticing them away by sending them on a paid errand and then stealing their boat, but he decided it was too complicated. Germany was tantalizingly close and very clear—it seemed he could almost reach out and touch the rank riverbank vegetation. Farther on, a few isolated houses stood in the midst of trim apple orchards, cars sped along a secondary road, then the land rose abruptly toward towering granite cliffs. In the sky a glider soundlessly banked and returned westward.

Meeting no one, he kept going as far as a beechwood. It was eleven thirty by now; the sun was high; the air smelled fresh, with a hint of developing summer warmth, and the grass and chickweed in the fields were dry, the dew long since evaporated. Ideal walking weather. Beyond the beechwood, dark, coniferous slopes formed a tight semicircle around the valley. At the near limit of the wood was a camping site where tents were raised beside Volkswagen buses and trailers with German plates.

A German family—parents and two lean children, all in short pants and hiking shoes—marched toward him. "Hola!" Bruno responded as the parents came abreast and greeted him. Throughout Europe, Germans on holiday assumed that any walker they met was also German, and often they were right.

Presently he stopped at a bend in the path and consulted

his map. It was a detailed, large-scale camper's guide to the facilities in the area, and it indicated rambles on both sides of the German frontier. The footpath he was on bisected the wood at first, then skirted a rock outcrop and finally, less than one hundred yards from the meandering river, abruptly plunged back into the forest and zigzagged for a while until it ended at a surfaced motor road that proceeded northward to the Luxembourg village of Weilerbach; from this junction another, unmarked trail indicated merely by a hairline branched off and came eventually to a footbridge across the Sûre. It was the first border-crossing point—open during daylight hours only for pedestrians—upstream from the stone road bridge. That was the way it appeared on the map. Whether the map could be relied on was another matter.

The sun was directly overhead now, and its warmth was on his back as he trudged steadily in the beechwood. The neckband of his shirt was damp, and he loosened his collar, but he could not remove his jacket without revealing the 9mm Beretta jammed into his waistband. The gun shifted slightly to the rhythm of his gait, and every so often he paused to stick it like a rebellious shirttail back into place. He removed his faded golfer's cap and stuffed it into his pocket beside the map.

The wood was very still at midday save for the flitting of midges and fluttering of birds high in the heavily foliaged beeches. A steady, purposeful pace would bring him to the footbridge in forty minutes; there was absolutely no need to break into a run. The sun penetrated deep into the wood at this hour, carpeting the glades he passed in blond light; it hadn't rained in more than a month, and the brittle undergrowth bunched beside the path rang and crackled like glass whenever he brushed against it. The last time he'd had a drink of water was in Paris, six hours ago. Once, with his Foreign Legion regiment in Algeria, before taking off on a search-and-destroy mission for FLN *fellaghas*, he had forgot to refill his canteen; after landing in the drop zone they had made immediate contact with a rebel patrol and run into automatic-weapons fire. During the brief, intense battle that followed there were other problems than thirst; then he had been separated from his platoon and found himself stumbling with his machine pistol under the African sun across an eroded, waterless plain; finally he had reached his lines at twilight. That was in the Nementcha mountains, where the thermometer rose in August to over 120 degrees and sunstroke felled almost as many paratroopers as did the enemy's patient snipers. When his men found out how far he had marched with an empty canteen, they had named him *le chameau magnifique*.

He was deep in the forest now. The far-off whish of cars had died out; a brook sluiced impetuously down to the Sûre past tree stumps and stones permanently mossy in the shade. He came upon a vacant weekend lodge ringed with discarded beer bottles, then no other human habitations. The beeches were succeeded by oaks, then European larches, *mélèzes*, which grew fifty feet straight up before putting out branches. The breeze made a sound like surf in the swaying treetops, and the trunks creaked as though in protest. He felt quite safe, and suddenly he was reminded of boyhood, of the piny-smelling woods where he had withdrawn and escaped temporarily from the authority of his foster parents. They had lived in an austere working-class neighborhood of Bremen, and in their house he had spent a thin, emotionally unnourishing adolescence that was like weak gruel. Boyhood is an ordeal you outlive. He recalled the house's inexpungible stench of failure and meanness, pettiness and brutality, and those years as a tunnel through which he had advanced cautiously, convinced that in the end he would find his way out into light.

He shook his head irritably. Long since, the house had been torn down; he had forgotten landmarks and probably could not even have found his way back; his foster parents had died, their motivations forever fathomless; those faint echoes which still reached him from the past, less and less recurringly, had diminishing power to torment—all that survived the awful early disappointment with life was a residue of pain walled up in consciousness and memory.

Suddenly his thoughts swerved to Marie-Christine's apartment in Paris. It was so stupid, so unforgivably careless to have left the bag even for a moment in sight on the bed! The two Frenchmen had mistaken him for someone else—whom exactly he had no idea, but he had foreseen that they were about to admit their error, give up and get out—surlily, not with apologies, to be sure—when for no specific reason the older, more skeptical inspector had gone toward the bedroom. He had stood rooted where he was in the living room, fury flooding through his flinty body, his ear cocked for the inspector's exclamation when he discovered the tennis bag's contents. And it had happened just that way, except for that experienced Frenchman's unforeseeable blunder in summoning his partner, which had left him, Bruno, momentarily unguarded in the vestibule, where his jacket hung on a peg so that all he had needed to do (he had done it even as the thought formed in his mind) was grab at it and snatch the Beretta from the inside pocket, releasing the safety just as the younger inspector, realizing his error, had whipped furiously about, presenting a solid, easy target, beyond which the older man's figure had materialized abruptly in the bedroom doorway, thus also becoming vulnerable, the younger one fumbling desperately to bring up his weapon as he, Bruno, fired two rounds from a distance of no more than seven yards at the pair. Then, the first Frenchman falling harmlessly sideways and rolling over onto his face, the other toppling backward, taking longer to crumple but still with no more resistance than a window dummy; after which he was hurtling down the stairs, dimly conscious that he'd flung on his jacket and slipped the Beretta back into his pocket without knowing how he'd found the presence of mind to do either, and out unchallenged from the building before the concierge came from her *loge*, and fast around the corner . . . on that

41

sticky August evening the street was deserted and then, two blocks away, on the Champs-Elysées, where he had stopped to draw breath and decide what to do next, it had been just the opposite—the sidewalk crowded with perspiring tourists trudging with the faith of pilgrims up to the Arch of Triumph in the warm, polluted air. He had plunged unhesitatingly into that purposeful horde and let himself be borne toward the George V Métro station, surfacing a half-hour later in a safer part of Paris, near the Gare du Nord, at an antique dealer's shop.

The shop had been closed for the night, but Pierre Rubinstein, the owner, rented an apartment on the floor above and had been at home. And it was then, once safe inside, the door bolted behind him and the radio turned on, that he, Bruno, had dumped himself into an armchair far from the window and checked himself for emotions like a doctor searching for symptoms of a disease and found only a sediment of impatience and resentment. Those snooping Frenchmen! He wasn't even sure they were dead, but recalling the damage a 9mm Beretta could inflict, he assumed so. They were responsible for their own deaths: with their senseless prying they had forced his hand.

"The contingency plan?" He glowered at Rubinstein. "How long will it take to organize?"

The old man disappeared into another room and returned with an envelope, which he wordlessly handed over, that contained a green-gray West German passport, one thousand D-marks in small denominations and a map. Rubinstein and his son were the only Jews in the network. Though visibly shaken, the old man was behaving magnificently under stress.

"At least you chose a propitious month," he said.

"You think so?"

Out of faded gray eyes Rubinstein contemplated him. "This is August—millions of German, Dutch and Scandinavian vacationers driving across France bound for the Mediterranean, millions of others returning northward home. Even if the police wanted to, they couldn't check all those cars for just one man. Tourism grosses millions; therefore it is more important than catching a murderer. That, in a sense, is the philosophy of the Common Market." His irony subsided. "The Luxembourg border is your best hope. It's never closely watched. I'll call Jean-Charles."

A quarter-hour later, Jean-Charles, Rubinstein's twenty-nine-year-old son, arrived at the apartment. He was slim and dark like a gypsy, with a trace of his father's weary skepticism about the eyes. He had parked his Citroën delivery van in the courtyard of the antique shop and brought up a spare poplin Windbreaker, shirt and trousers, and a faded checked golfer's cap.

"What's this supposed to be for?" Bruno asked, turning the cap over in his hand.

"It's a gift. I was going to throw it out. You may need it."

As he changed clothes, Bruno regretted that he did not have a dozen Jean-Charleses in the network, instead of the asses Bauer had recruited.

"We can be in Luxembourg in five and a half hours—six, allowing for heavy traffic," Jean-Charles said. "If we leave right away—"

"Be smart. They'll expect Schilling to get out of Paris at once, so there'll be roadblocks on every road leading out of this city. But by daybreak they'll get tired of it and the roadblocks will have to come down to keep all those tourist cars moving without forming twenty-mile-long bottlenecks. It's light before seven A.M. We'll leave then so as to pick up the heavy eastbound traffic still within Paris." He turned to the old man for confirmation. "You're right; it might not be possible at any other time of the year."

Rubinstein *père* nodded, and so the decision was taken to wait till dawn. "With a German passport in another name, you stand a reasonable chance of getting through—"

"Of getting out of France, but not entering Germany. It's a stolen passport, isn't it, like the Austrian one? The number could be on a list at German frontier posts."

"Then use the map I gave you. There's a footbridge few

people know about in that region." Rubinstein had been traveling to Luxembourg for years to buy antiques.

Another matter abruptly occurred to him, and he turned to Rubinstein's son again. "Go out, find a café that is open and direct-dial this hotel number in Zurich," he instructed Jean-Charles, scribbling it out. "Ask for Room 220 and a girl will answer—this is her name; make sure that you talk to her and tell her to sit tight. She has to realize that the police will be around to interrogate her. When they do, she can invent any sort of story provided she makes no mention of the envelope I left in her office safe." He reflected for a moment. "And tell her to expect another call tomorrow or the next day."

Later, the old man had lumbered off to bed, and he and Jean-Charles had alternately stood watch by the window, napping at intervals on a couch. He had dozed without nightmares (the only dreams he feared were of the house in Bremen), and he had awakened impatient to set out. As the sky warmed over Paris' severe slate roofs, they had slipped downstairs and departed.

The midsummer traffic was dense from the moment they got on Route N33, the main highway leading eastward. Everywhere families seemed to be on the move across the rolling countryside. Everywhere there were cars—at gas stations, bridges, rest areas. In villages, cafés were running short of ice and beer, restaurants seemed to be doubling their prices, tempers snapped. The immobile air was like cotton. Bruno reflected that of all those tens of thousands on wheels, probably he alone welcomed the overcrowded roads. Then, approaching Audun-le-Tiche, only a few miles from the frontier, he glanced at Jean-Charles and saw how stark white his complexion and knuckles were.

"I'll take the wheel if you like. The frontier police generally take less interest in the driver than in the passenger."

Jean-Charles said nothing.

"Stop the car on that shoulder. What's eating you?"

"We can't get more than a hundred and ten kilometers an hour out of this pile of tin—"

"Here. Should anyone start to ask questions, shoot him in the face." Jean-Charles gaped. "I'm going through: no one is going to stop me."

He placed the Beretta in Jean-Charles' lap and drove off down the road, watching out of the corner of his eye as Jean-Charles concealed the gun in the van door's side pocket. Hurling paving stones at the riot police, feinting at their flanks, darting down side streets was—as he had demonstrated during the disorders of May '68—Jean-Charles' style. Crashing a frontier post was not. Still, Bruno was sure that if it came to the point, Jean-Charles would unhesitatingly open fire.

They approached French Customs and stopped. An Opel from Frankfurt was waiting in line before them, and a Citroën with a Parisian number behind. The beefy Security trooper on duty at the Passport Control booth waved all three vehicles through; beyond, a policeman in an unfamiliar green uniform and kepi stared past them incuriously . . . and that was how, Bruno thought, six hours after having fled from Paris, he came to be taking a walk in eastern Luxembourg.

Ahead, two men's voices murmured indistinctly. He moved quickly off the footpath and froze behind a copse that lay in shadow where the path descended a stony slope. He had glimpsed the border guards' uniforms just before they emerged from the wood. Stopped not far away, they were conversing in Luxembourg dialect. They would miss him if they resumed their diagonal patrol. If they came back up the path, however . . . He sank carefully to a crouching position on the litter of pine needles and, rocking gently on his heels, waited.

A faint aroma of cigarette smoke drifted toward the copse, and he realized with anger that the two guards were taking a break. Squatting, he withdrew the Beretta from his belt, released the safety and clenched the grip in both hands. His blue eyes protruded slightly and he knew they were almost transparent, and that his smooth face was drained of recognizable feeling save intent, animal-like

45

watchfulness. If the two guards came too near, he would kill them, like the Frenchmen, with no compunction whatever. *Der Deutsche ist unmenschlich im Krieg*—the German is inhuman in war—an officer in his para regiment had said. Well, this was war; war of a subterranean nature, but no more ignoble than the other. De Wrendt, the man who had started him on the guerrilla's road, had insisted on that interpretation . . . De Wrendt, who had first sensed that he was at home nowhere, yet—with his matted blond hair, strict taut body and voice that was nothing special, an almost metallic scratch—plausible, hence operational, anywhere.

The voices abruptly ceased, and after a moment he heard boots crunching down the slope. The guards were heading toward the river.

He waited ten minutes to be sure, then rose and left his hiding place and began a retreat through the beechwood. Clearly he was mistaken to attempt to cross into Germany by day: the Luxembourg patrol surely had a counterpart on the other side of the river. It did not prove that they were searching for him in particular, but it indicated that the frontier was more closely watched than he had been led to believe.

Eventually he reached the spot he was looking for: a loggers' trail that wound upward to the rock outcropping and the evergreen-splotched elevations beyond. Somewhere up there he would wait for dusk.

The broad ledge protruded from a sandstone bluff formation and offered a panoramic view of a wall of firs and pines stretching toward dun hills on the horizon. He lay sprawled on his back, his jacket folded alongside, and did not stir. Up here the air was marvelously clean, the best he had breathed in months. A Boeing droned high overhead, and soon its contrails blurred in the August sky; the last he saw of the metal speck, it was still on the same northeasterly course. He thought it might be the Lufthansa morning flight for Cologne. Had things worked out differently in Paris, he would have unobtrusively boarded the same Boeing with his Austrian passport. However, if escaping from the police and getting to Cologne meant a tramp through the woods, that was all right—it wasn't the first time he'd been on his own in hostile countryside. His unused Lufthansa ticket was still in an envelope he had confided to Marie-Christine, along with other things, the money and the notes. Up to now he had avoided thinking about the envelope. Fortunately, no one would suspect its existence unless Marie-Christine blabbed.

A muscle in his neck fluttered. He knew her vulnerable side. She was a girl who had a firm and touching belief in the obligations of friendship, but would her loyalty buckle if the pressure grew? It was inevitable now that the police would try to intimidate her, so there was only one solution. Marie-Christine was going to stay in Switzerland longer than she guessed.

As he thought of her, he perceived himself objectively at this moment, here in a forest in Luxembourg, in the heart of Western Europe, hiding out on a rock shelf. Most people would condemn him as one more vicious asocial terrorist skirmishing bloodily but pointlessly with the law; but how could they tell that there was an enormous gap between what had happened in Paris, which was abject and mediocre, and negative to boot, and what he was about to force to happen, which would be more ambitious and far-reaching in its way than the mishandled Munich massacre or the theatrical Vienna OPEC attack? . . .

He awoke with a start and rose swiftly to his feet. In the interval nothing had changed except the sun's position; it was much lower now, almost ready to set behind the circus of dark featureless hills near Echternach. He had slept longer than he expected; he would have to hurry now.

Twenty minutes later he approached the Sûre. It coursed gray and opaque in the last light of day. According to his map, the footbridge lay around the next bend. Leaving the trail and slipping through the gloom of the woods on tiptoe, he reconnoitered the surroundings with care. There it was —a small concrete span resting on posts that emerged from the shallow water at either shore. On a pole by the water's edge, a sign warned, DÉFENSE DE BAIGNER. Another said that transport of merchandise across the river was prohibited at this point. There was not a human sound. It was obviously not a major crossing point, but a facility for pedestrians of the region which they were not supposed to use after dark; it was unguarded. He edged forward out of the trees and then, bracing himself for a shout or a light, he strode rapidly over the footbridge and reached the other side. In the starry light, the land beyond seemed neither unfriendly nor welcoming.

The first village he reached lay in a hollow encircled by vineyards that mounted steep terraced slopes which blotted out the countryside beyond. Thatched houses were huddled around a stone church whose spire sliced the night mist. It was not yet nine o'clock, but the village was already dormant, shuttered. The only light filtered through the curtained windows of a corner inn where singing could be heard within. Above the door was a weathered signboard in faded black letter. His pulse was beating somewhat faster. He was back home—home: an indefinable combination of odor, architecture, household decoration, women's features and mannerisms. Suppose he had been born elsewhere than in that foggy North Sea city, in this cold, brooding country of doomed heroes and unrelenting struggle? He was a German who felt out of place in Germany; he wasn't alone. The inn door banged open and an elderly man smoking a pipe passed into the road.

Bruno took a chance and grunted, "I have to go to Bitburg."

"*Mensch!*" The old man drew on his pipe and slowly removed it from between his teeth. "*Der letzte Autobus fährt von der Ecke sofort ab!*" He waved down the road.

Without thanking him, Bruno raced to the last house in the village. A bus stood parked in shadow, its engine idling for the last run of the evening. Inside there were only two women passengers who were traveling together. He paid the fare and chose a seat in the darkened rear where the driver would find it difficult to scan his features through the rearview mirror. He was in Germany, all right—he had heard it when the old man opened his mouth and now heard it again in the women's thick Rhenish accent.

A half-hour later the bus reached Bitburg, where he changed to another bus, which deposited him in front of the squat railroad station at Erdorf. There was a train to Cologne at ten twenty, which he took.

It was past midnight when he reached Cologne. Beside the station, the giant cathedral reared up, bathed in the ghostly phosphorescent light of rows of projectors. Only a few groups of tourists were sedately strolling about. From a public phone booth in the terminal he dialed a local number. He saw a couple of policemen sauntering through the main hall checking out drunks and foreign workers without papers. He crossed the esplanade and ordered a beer in a café that was still open from which he had a view of the empty station parking lot.

Twenty minutes later, a Ford Taunus with city plates drove up and stopped. It was driven by Hans-Peter Reindorf, a twenty-seven-year-old free-lance journalist who with mounting nervousness had been awaiting Schilling's arrival to begin the first phase of Grand Slam.

Bruno went toward him.

Chapter Six

An Area of Danger

THE SECOND call came in the evening when Marie-Christine was alone in her hotel room.

A man's voice speaking in French enunciated distinctly with painful slowness into the mouthpiece. "Your friend is safe now—Mademoiselle, can you hear me clearly?"

"Who is this?" Marie-Christine interrupted.

Stubbornly taking no notice, the voice went on, mouthing one word after another with stilted precision as though —this suddenly became a certitude for her—its owner knew the language but had not used it in a long time. "May I suggest that we meet?"

Marie-Christine said nothing, but her sense of security promptly faltered.

"He is safe but you are not. The police actively suspect you of belonging to a terrorist network—"

"Are you trying to scare me?"

"I am trying to aid you. A development has occurred that will prove embarrassing for you in Paris."

"I can't think of any." She was favorably impressed by the firmness in her voice.

"Nevertheless . . ."

Marie-Christine was thinking rapidly. "If you want to see me, you know where I'm staying."

Abruptly the voice grew unfriendly. "It is out of the question for me to come to your hotel. In an hour and a half I'll be at the Café Malta on Seefeldstrasse. Do you have that right? I'll wait twenty minutes for you, no more. There is just one condition."

"What?"

"Arrive alone. I don't want to see any Swiss plainclothesmen trailing you."

"I doubt that I'll be there."

"Whether you decide to come is entirely up to you. But bear in mind that it is in your interest."

She hesitated. "If I come, whom will I be looking for?"

There was the briefest of silences; then the voice resumed: "Mademoiselle, I shall recognize you."

After hanging up, she sat down dismayed and glanced distractedly through a picture magazine. The man who had just phoned spoke French poorly with an unmistakable German accent, he sounded middle-aged and the call itself was almost certainly local, since he had proposed a meeting in Zurich in just ninety minutes' time. She was sure that he was not the same man who had called in the middle of the night from Paris. The wise decision was to shun contact with all of Bruno's shadowy comrades, sympathizers or whatever he termed them. However, the more she thought about the conversation, the more her curiosity grew. The man plainly took it for granted that she would not alert the police, and he was right: the police were unlikely to be satisfied with the simple truth, because it would not lead them far, and it would end with her being more suspect in their eyes than ever. Hastily she looked up Seefeldstrasse on a street map. The Café Malta was in a busy neighborhood, and at 8 P.M. enough people would be about to obviate any danger. If someone attempted to coerce her, she would simply get up and leave. It probably made sense to

51

find out more before she faced the French police: to be informed was to be forearmed.

She waited an hour, then slipped on a coat and left the Baur au Lac confident that she had not been seen.

By eighty thirty no one had appeared. Disappointed, Marie-Christine ordered a second brandy and studied the café's patrons. A noisy family of five occupied one corner; next to them sat two bearded young students who were intently debating a political issue she didn't recognize in their hideous, throaty Zurich dialect. Only Swiss Germans could gibber in that way—a throat disease, they aptly called their sublanguage. Nearby, a fat, pallid man in his late forties labored silently over the crossword puzzle in the *Neue Zürcher Zeitung*; he had been absorbed in the paper without lifting his eyes since she entered the café. Her attention focused on him, then moved away. At her right, a teen-age couple were preparing to leave. Beyond, an old woman in a crumpled felt cloche nursed a tall glass of beer and murmured incomprehensible imprecations. The anonymous contact's failure to show up meant—Marie-Christine was not at all sure what it meant, except that she had wasted her time.

But then, as the teen-agers disappeared into the street, the fat man abruptly folded up his paper, rose and approached her table. With a formal nod he said in stiff French, "I am sorry to keep you waiting, Mademoiselle," and plumped himself down opposite her.

Close up, she saw that he had small, shrewd hazel eyes embedded in blubbery folds of skin, a small, wet, womanly mouth, dewlaps as gray as cement. She also noticed that his hands were as big as a butcher's and his nails very clean. To her surprise, he sported a chaste and distinguished platinum-link watch bracelet on his wrist.

"You were waiting for the couple to leave before you came up," Marie-Christine observed.

He shook his head. "No, I was making sure no one followed you inside." His voice was sonorous and ecclesiastical, with unexpected dips and trebles. She looked at him narrowly this time.

"I don't particularly like to sit and talk to a man whose name I don't even know," she said.

"What is the point in giving you a name? This is likely to be our only conversation, so who I am doesn't matter. We have a mutual friend; that is what brings us together for this brief meeting."

The waiter had approached their table. The fat man spoke to him in Swiss German and put enough money down to pay for the glass of tea he still had left as well as the two brandies. Without comment Marie-Christine watched him pocket the change. Apparently, as he had said, it was not going to be a protracted session.

As soon as the waiter had gone, he said in a furry murmur that was inaudible three feet away: "Have you mentioned to anyone the envelope Schilling left in your care?"

"No," she said, surprised, then quickly regained her wits. "What's in it?"

"That doesn't concern you. Is it still in the safe?"

"Of course."

Marie-Christine experienced relief. Was that the potential embarrassment in Paris? When Bruno had handed her the envelope, she had placed it well to the rear in the boutique safe, then forgot its existence. She had given it no thought until she was reminded of it by the first telephone call from Paris.

"Has anyone mentioned it to you?"

"Only the man who thoughtfully called the other night to report the presence of two corpses in my apartment. Your colleague?"

He ignored the question. "It seems an assistant is running your boutique during your absence. What about her?"

"What do you mean?"

"She has access to the safe. Is she likely to open the envelope?"

Marie-Christine stared at him incredulously. "That

53

woman wouldn't dream of opening my personal belongings."

The fat man pondered her reply and appeared satisfied. "How long do you plan to stay in Zurich?" he asked.

It was the same question the American and the Swiss police had put to her. Everyone apparently was dissatisfied with her presence in this city.

"It's none of your business," she replied shortly, "but I'm flying back tomorrow."

"It would be preferable if you stayed. . . ." He made the suggestion ingratiatingly, almost avuncularly, but she noticed that his clever hazel eyes sized her up without friendliness.

Suddenly the reason for his interest seemed plain. "You're afraid that when I return to Paris and the French police interrogate me, I'll mention the envelope. That's what you want to avoid, isn't it?" To her annoyance, she was mimicking him and murmuring too.

"Possibly. Can you put off your departure for a few days?"

"Why should I?"

The fat man gave an irate jerk of his massive head. "It would be better for all concerned."

"No, I can't. My assistant becomes nervous when I'm away too long." It wasn't true, but his manner had antagonized her. Marie-Christine sipped the brandy and set down her glass. "Now *you* tell *me* something, since you put me to the trouble of coming here. Where is Bruno? Did he kill those two policemen?" she whispered. "Why? What possible justification did he have?"

The gaze that met hers was grim and intolerant, and the man seated opposite her seemed to be bursting at the seams with spite. "The justification which repression and violence always generate," he growled.

She was infuriated by the complacency of his answer. Keeping her voice down, she said sharply, "I'm surprised that Bruno has friends like you."

A rosy splotch spread through the fat man's thick features, and she wondered whether he was going to turn insulting; but with visible effort he twitched his lips in a sort of grotesque attempt at playfulness. "I am going to take you to see your friend. He will provide answers to all of these questions better than I possibly can."

Marie-Christine stared at him, her astonishment complete. "Do you mean what I think? Is Bruno in Zurich?" It was the one contingency she had not anticipated. "Why didn't you come right out with it?"

Confused, she preceded the fat man into the street, but once outside the café she had a moment of doubt as to whether to follow him.

"I can't believe it. Are you telling the truth?"

"Come or not, suit yourself."

Having come this far, she thought it would be ridiculous to back out now. The fat man beside her, after all, was simply an underling who carried out Bruno's orders and represented no threat as such. If Bruno was in Zurich, it was essential that she see him to find out exactly what had happened in her apartment. Still, she felt a pang of fright at the prospect. His hold on her was weaker than in the past, but undeniably a claim on some part of her emotions persisted. He had always been adept at swaying her, against her better judgment, with his faintly superior yet engaging and even vulnerable air. When she had referred to his charm before the American, it had been no exaggeration.

She stopped short on Badstrasse under a street light whose anemic glow accentuated the fat man's hard traits. "Where are we going?"

"We have to drive, but it's not far."

Before a darkened pharmacy, she saw a parked BMW sedan with Zurich plates. It was the only car on the near side in the short block, and she surmised that it belonged to him. She had sat in the café almost an hour: it was already nine o'clock, and in Zurich that made a difference. No one else was about—even in summer, pedestrians and traffic disappeared off the streets puritanically early. The fat man swiftly opened the back door and nudged her forcefully toward the unlit interior. Almost simultaneously, she made out another man's indistinct figure at the wheel.

Impulsively Marie-Christine stepped back, but the fat man blocked her way; she caught the gleam of his owlish protruding eyes and felt his mealy breath on her face. She panicked, realizing that she was being kidnapped, that it was happening to her just as it had happened to other men and women, silently and efficiently, without explanation or warning. Terrified, she squirmed aside, clawing at the clamp on her elbow. Nimbly the fat man wheeled and raised his heavy fist to smack her, but he was a fraction of a second too late, and her left hand flailed out, the long-trimmed nails gouging a loose fold of skin close to his cheekbone. As he swore, wincing with pain, she arched toward him, hopelessly shoving with all her force against his dense body.

The pressure on her arm infinitesimally slackened. She found herself free and tottered away. The fat man lunged, trying to snatch her by the waist, but she cried out and darted out of his reach. Starting to stumble away on her heels, she saw at the corner a group of people watching, then breaking into a run in her direction. Behind her, she sensed the fat man's indecision. The car door slammed loudly and the BMW sheered away from the curb. Trembling, she stood paralyzed as the car screeched down the street.

Five people surrounded her, and Marie-Christine recognized the Swiss family who had been so strident inside the café. The mother, a plump blond woman in her thirties, burst out, "That man tried to force you into his car . . ." and reached out instinctively to steady her.

Marie-Christine understood what she was doing and shook her head. She felt empty, cold and vulnerable, but not dizzy, not about to faint; she plunged her icy hands into her coat and shivered less.

The couple's three children were regarding her with intense expectation.

"*Kommen Sie mit uns, Fraülein, zu der Polizei,*" their father said heavily. He was a large, gray-haired man with cauliflower ears.

"I'm all right," Marie-Christine insisted. "I don't want to go to the police; it is not necessary."

"We saw him do it!" the two elder children chorused. "We saw the kidnapper!"

The husband addressed Marie-Christine. "Fraülein, I memorized the license number. ZH 303507. A gray BMW. You must report it to the police; it is your duty."

"He is my fiancé. We had a dispute as we left the café." She scanned their faces, and the parents' disbelief was plain. "The argument was my fault—it was about nothing."

"He hit you several times." The mother's indignation was sincere and unbounded. "I saw everything. You almost fell to the ground. . . ."

Marie-Christine was looking over the children's heads toward Seefeldstrasse, and with relief she spied a lighted taxi that was rounding the corner. The driver saw her upraised hand and stopped.

"*Vielen Dank für Ihre Hilfe,*" Marie-Christine stammered. "Please don't worry about me."

The mother's expression had changed from solicitude to disapproval as she shepherded her children from the curb; her husband continued to stare belligerently in the direction of the vanished BMW.

"The Baur au Lac," Marie-Christine murmured to the driver, sinking back against the seat rest. As she began to comb her hair into a semblance of order, she thought about her next move. For a moment she had been tempted to go with that stolid, outraged family to the nearest police station, but to report what exactly? It meant explaining the calls at her hotel and relating a great many intertwined enigmatic facts, all of which would cast suspicion on her. She had never heard of a police force whose first instinct was not to suspect a foreigner who got into trouble and caused a bother. It was preferable to keep her mouth shut, be grateful for that Swiss family's opportune arrival at the street corner and flee as soon as possible—on tomorrow's first flight—from Switzerland and its unforeseen, nasty subsurface stirrings of intimidation and violence. She would take her chances in Paris; at least, it was home, with all that the word connoted reassuringly in the way of friends and potential assistance. Meanwhile, all she wanted was to barricade herself within her hotel room. But then with a sinking feeling of helplessness she recognized the weakness in this reasoning. Suppose both of the BMW's occupants had correctly gauged how she would react and had driven straight to the hotel? The fat man knew where she was staying, even had her room number, and he was plainly not the sort to give up without another try.

The taxi was heading up Dufourstrasse through a lighted neighborhood where restaurants and bars stayed open late. She didn't know Zurich well, but was sure they were almost at the Baur au Lac. If only, she thought, there were someone in this impersonal nighttime city whom she could call on for help—someone apart from the police. The exhibitors at the accessories salon with whom she had dealings were hopeless; they were eager businessmen but, when it came to rawer challenges, mild citizens whose first instinct would be precisely to summon the police.

It was then that she recalled the sandy-haired American from the Consulate who had put so many terse questions to her and departed in such a cloud of foul temper. Before leaving, he had given her his card. . . .

"Stop at the next corner," Marie-Christine said.

She dug into her handbag and discovered the card beside her coin purse and handkerchief, where she had automatically stored it the afternoon before. In addition to the Consulate phone number, there was a second number scrawled in pencil. If she was lucky it was his home number, and if she was luckier still he would be there.

"Do you want to get out here?" the driver asked her.

"I want to make a phone call, but I'd like you to wait."

"You can make the call from that booth." He indicated a public phone ten yards from where they had stopped.

She was still shaky—drained of willpower—and her finger was unsteady as she dialed the number. After a minute someone answered, and she recognized the American's calm voice. He listened without comment while she spoke, then said, "Don't let the driver go away under any circumstances. Sit in the taxi and wait for me. I'll be there in ten minutes."

Nine minutes later, an Audi 80 stopped beside the phone booth. Marie-Christine, walking swiftly across the street toward Guthrie, thought that it was like a furtive assignation with a married man.

As she sat down beside him, he studied her face for signs of panic, then put the car into gear and made a U-turn.

"You came awfully fast," she remarked.

"I live close by." He did not specify where. "Why did somebody want to kidnap you?"

"I don't know. To keep me from returning to Paris, I think."

"Why is your presence undesirable in Paris?"

Marie-Christine hesitated, and he made no attempt to hurry her up. Finally she said, "The other day I omitted to tell you some things."

"I know that," he said equably.

"I don't like to lie."

"You're not particularly competent as a liar. After our meeting I spotted flaws in your story and asked the Swiss to put you under surveillance, but they refused."

"I wish they had. Put me under surveillance, I mean."

He was humming a tune she found maddening. "Some other time; do you mind?"

"I'll sing it for you. You'll like it. It goes like this:

When I was a bachelor, I lived all alone.
I worked at the weaver's trade. . . .

"It's a college song. Fraternity brothers sing it."

"May I please tell you now," she said wearily, "what I should have explained in the first place?"

"It will save us the trouble of putting you on wire-and-mike." Marie-Christine seemed puzzled. "An idiom meaning electronic eavesdropping."

As they neared the lake, Marie-Christine told him about the two telephone calls and the fat man's questions. "It was all an act," she blurted, "so that I would follow him to his car. He couldn't drag me out of the café, so he invented that rubbish about taking me to Bruno. And then the other man was waiting in the dark. . . ." Her voice rose, almost out of control. "I keep wondering what would have happened to me if that Swiss family hadn't come down the street."

"But they did," Guthrie said unsentimentally.

"They memorized the car number. Do you think they'll go to the police?"

"They won't have much to report without your name. Remember, nothing actually happened, so the police will be polite but uninterested. What was the tag number?"

"ZH 303507. A gray BMW. I didn't think I'd remember it."

"I'm glad you did. It seems to be the only lead we have."

"What about his description?"

"There are a lot of fat men in Zurich. Too much *geschnitzeltes Kalbfleisch mit Rösti*. And most of them speak lousy French."

After a moment Marie-Christine said, "He wanted to make sure no one knew about the envelope that Bruno left in my safe; and he was prepared to kidnap me to prevent me from mentioning or opening it once I got back to Paris."

"That makes sense, maybe. Any idea what's inside?"

Her profile was unperturbed and memorable in the dashboard's pallid gleam. "I swear to you that I don't. No lie: Bruno said, 'Keep this for me in your office safe for a few days.' I wasn't suspicious; I didn't ask what it contained. He was going to take it back on the day I returned to Paris."

"Who has the safe combination besides you and your assistant?"

"No one."

"Incidentally, when are you thinking of returning?"

"Tomorrow. I never thought I'd be so happy to see Paris again."

They had reached Bellerive-strasse, but instead of continuing to the hotel Guthrie swung left and parked at the foot of Klaus-strasse, along the lakefront, where they could not be seen under the trees by passing traffic. Through the open car window a moist light breeze moved in from the inert body of water. The light of a buoy winked green far out. The neon signs over the Tonhalle and Kongresshaus were mirrored in the black shimmering water like multicolored oil stains. Closer in, a couple of swans still hunting for food at this hour glided regally up to the embankment while others slept, their long, aggressive necks curled into their tail feathers.

In the stillness Guthrie said, not loudly, "I'm not sure why you phoned me for help."

"I had to talk to someone. But I couldn't see myself standing up to another round of questioning by the police."

He smiled faintly. "I omitted something too. I'm with the Agency."

She frowned. "Why should I care? What agency? Didn't you say that you worked at the Consulate?"

"Marie-Christine," he said, using her name for the first time, "you're too naive to be true. Let's set the record straight. By Agency I mean CIA."

"It has a very bad reputation in France," she said simply. "I wonder what I'm getting into with you. Can't you just see me safely back to my hotel?"

Her reaction was the way it should be, Guthrie thought —a salutary indifference which the people at Langley ought to be aware of for their ego's necessary chastening: many persons scrambling to determine his affiliation, but so many more not caring a damn. The CIA's existence and crises were by no means their principal concern.

"*Voilà*. I've told you all I know," she said.

His tone changed. "If you want help, you'll have to learn to level with people. You're still holding back info. For example, you've known Bruno longer and better than you claim. I want his real name, nationality, past history, likely present whereabouts. You persist in going out of your way to protect him; it's time you decided which side you're playing on."

"I'm on no side."

"As long as he's at large, you're in danger. I would have thought you'd realized that tonight. It wasn't very smart, by the way, to go to that café alone without telling anybody."

"What happens to him if I tell you?"

"What he deserves," Guthrie said with sudden harshness.

She remained silent.

"You don't have to tell me anything. We'll drive back to your hotel and forget about it. But what happens afterward to others may be your responsibility. And if you get into further trouble, it's strictly your show."

"All right," she said. "His real name is Dieter Koenig; he's a German and comes from Bremen. You won't believe it, but I met him when I was barely fifteen, toward the end of the Algerian war. He was a paratrooper in the Foreign Legion then. Dieter came to Paris on leave—a young German fighting for France. My parents, my friends, everybody I knew in Paris considered the paras heroes. He had no family and seemed lonely. . . . I thought he was very different from anyone I knew, and, well, he seemed to breathe adventure. At that age, what girl isn't silly? I wrote patriotic letters to him when he returned to Algeria. Later we heard that he had deserted to join the OAS; there were no replies to my letters afterward, and he dropped out of sight completely. By then I was studying hard seven days a week, and people were beginning to criticize the OAS as cold-blooded murderers. I thought about him less and less except to wonder, not very often, what had become of him.

"Eight years later I saw him again. He walked into my

boutique and asked for me. We were both—well, at that age you change a lot, to say the least, and neither of us would probably have recognized the other. One thing different, too, was that he no longer called himself Dieter. He was Bruno now—which made sense if he didn't want people to associate him with the OAS. . . ."

Guthrie smiled in the dark. "Was that his explanation?"

"He said that he had a right to wipe out mistakes, so he had a new name—"

"And a brand-new nationality?"

"Yes, he was using an Austrian passport."

"And you saw him again?"

"In many ways I liked him better than before."

"Did he stay in your apartment each time he was in town?"

After a second's hesitation, Marie-Christine nodded.

"It was useful cover," Guthrie suggested. "No hotel registration, a respectable address, a girlfriend with no known affiliations to any terrorist movements . . ."

"It wasn't his only reason for seeing me," Marie-Christine commented serenely.

Guthrie looked her over carefully. "I thought you claimed he was no longer your boyfriend."

"Shall I tell you something? He wasn't overwhelming as lovers go. But he was nice in other ways. He gave me advice when I was having trouble with a man; the advice was good."

"That's why you were lying in his behalf? All that fiction about meeting at a swimming pool . . . because he's a friend?"

She nodded again.

Guthrie decided that he had reached a point where he knew something pertinent about Bruno, but certainly not everything. The background remained murky, and the foreground was out of focus; the middle ground, as in some photographs, was sharply edged but led the eye away disturbingly to fuzzier areas. "You still haven't drawn him for me. Make an effort, Marie-Christine. Strong points, weak points?"

"He's quick, ambitious, determined. Boastful. Brave. Not very well educated, in spite of what he thinks. Playboyish, but it's just an act. He has an antisocial streak and is fundamentally lonely."

Guthrie remained silent, and she sat beside him in the dark and he heard her light, regular breathing. The night was almost breezeless, satiny. Pedal boats with pole lights mounted in the stern circled on the lake like fireflies. Nearby, the anchor chains of sailing dinghies moored to a jetty strained softly. In the untroubled dark there seemed to be only couples whispering and rustling up and down the shadowy embankment. Finally she said, "I wanted to think there was a reason, an excuse for what had happened . . . but after tonight it's not so easy, because obviously he ordered them to try to kidnap me."

"Did he ever level with you? Tell you that he was involved in terrorism?"

"Never."

Guthrie glanced at his watch. It was past midnight. She saw the gesture and shivered slightly. "I don't want to go back just yet."

"Let's go and have a drink someplace, then."

"What for?"

"Do you want to come to my apartment?"

"No."

"Tell me why you don't want to return to your hotel."

"That odious man may be waiting for me."

"Let's hope so," Guthrie said.

"It's not funny."

"He's not dumb enough to stage a return engagement tonight. At any rate, we'll have someone watching your room. You're in no danger; otherwise I wouldn't be taking you back. Tomorrow I'll check up on the BMW's number. Till you hear from me, I don't want you to step out of your room. That means canceling your flight reservation."

"I can't keep postponing my return. Zurich is expensive —I can't justify the cost of staying on for no particular reason."

"I'll explain the reason when I see you tomorrow. *D'accord?*"

After a moment she said with reluctance, *"D'accord.* And thank you."

When they stopped before the Baur au Lac, Marie-Christine hurriedly got out of the car and went straight up to her room and double-locked it. She thought of Guthrie's invitation and the way he had put it. Once in bed she lay awake listening to the ever-lessening noises in the streets below. The noises were peaceful and remote, but she was starkly aware of an area of danger into which she had accidentally ventured this windless evening—through Bruno, the fat man, even Guthrie—that began just beyond the security of her opulent hotel and spread across Switzerland, France, Europe and perhaps even other continents.

Chapter Seven

Paris by Dark

GUTHRIE SET two green-gray American passports on the writing-desk. "We'll be traveling with these."

"We?"

"You want to fly back to Paris, don't you? This way, no tiresome interrogation by French policemen when you land. Do you mind flying as Mrs. Barry Carpenter of Santa Barbara? I'm Mr. Carpenter, lucky fellow."

"What is this all about?" Marie-Christine looked suspiciously at the passports and two Air France tickets. Through her hotel window she saw gulls swooping lazily over kayaks and pleasure boats of all sorts on the placid water. The morning's dapper blue was mirrored in the lake. People were walking dogs beside a broad sweep of greensward, and even the pigeons were mannerly. Zurich at midday no longer harbored the slightest hint of menace.

"We're going to open friend Bruno's envelope. It *must* contain something interesting to warrant a kidnapping attempt; hopefully, it will justify our air fares. Visit Paris and its friendly folk on an all-inclusive tour sponsored by the

U.S. Government. Take in traffic jams on the boulevards, breathe in the tourists' perfume at the Place de l'Opéra." In one of his abrupt transitions of mood, Guthrie said coldly, "It's in your interest to know that envelope's contents before you come up against Sûreté interrogators. And to get out of this town won't hurt either."

"I don't believe any of this. You know I couldn't pass as an American."

"Don't be such a snob."

She turned away from him. "Have you traced the car registration?"

"Not yet. I'm giving priority to our trip. Just pack an overnight bag—you'll be gone less than twenty-four hours, after which you return here with no one the wiser, pick up your belongings and resume your original travel plans. Incidentally, in return for Mrs. Carpenter's passport, I'll need yours temporarily—you don't want to be caught in an airport body search carrying two passports."

"When did this idea occur to you?"

"Early this morning." He did not bother to mention that at the crack of dawn he had resolutely awakened Ditweiler to obtain his grudging authorization. Ditweiler's parting shot had been: "You have a brilliant operational brain, Guthrie, but I still worry about you."

Marie-Christine watched him doubtfully. "I can't believe you're serious."

"Of course I am. We're leaving on the eighteen-fifteen flight, which puts us into Orly seventy minutes later. We don't want to break into your boutique before the staff are gone. I'll come by at four o'clock and we'll depart the hotel through the side exit. Meanwhile, call the desk and tell them you're keeping this room another day. Make sure that enough of your clothes and toilet things are left scattered about so that when the chambermaid comes this evening to turn back the bed she's convinced you're still occupying the room. The fat man or one of his friends may decide to bribe her to find out your whereabouts."

"You want me to travel to Paris with you, yet I don't know the slightest thing about you—except what you told me last night."

"Let's see. I usually vote the Democratic ticket, and I like white wine . . ."

"Never mind, forget it," Marie-Christine said.

"I'll bet you want to know whether I'm really married."

"Are you?"

"I was."

"I was sure of it. I don't even know your first name."

"Sure you do. It's on my card. James . . . James Michael Thomas. The saints are well represented."

She looked down pensively at the passports and suddenly smiled. "After all, why not?"

"Marie-Christine, you're my favorite doll."

"*Une pépée?* Am I? At least, traveling with me you won't need to break into my boutique: I have a key."

A tanned American in a linen blazer who couldn't have been much more than twenty-six was waiting for them beside the Passport Control gate at Orly. As soon as they were waved past, he shepherded them to his car. Marie-Christine learned that his name was Starkey, and she gathered that he would be with them throughout their stay.

By the time they reached the Boulevard Périphérique, it was dusk—one of those lingering Parisian summer dusks as pungent as penny violets that seem reluctant to end. At the Porte d'Orléans, the café terraces were dense with people roaming in search of unoccupied tables. Restaurant lights sprang out in the deepening mauve evening, but no one would think of sitting down to dinner for another hour.

"You're untypically silent," Marie-Christine said. "No jokes about Paris?"

"Probably I'll collapse laughing at the contents of that envelope," Guthrie said drily. "What about the burglar-alarm system?"

Marie-Christine's cheeks became rosy. "We canceled the policy this year. I decided to economize."

Starkey had left avenue du Maine and was heading down boulevard Raspail. It was dark now. For the first time during the drive he spoke. "The police staked out the place around the clock, then lost interest. Before picking you up, I ran a final check."

They were in a neighborhood that was fractionally too far from Saint-Germain-des-Prés to attract nocturnal tourists and window shoppers, Guthrie noted with satisfaction. Chez Marie-Christine was located on a staid side street, near the corner of a larger thoroughfare. It was flanked by a stationery store and a framemaker's shop, both already shut. Farther down the street was a tiny Vietnamese restaurant, before which was an empty parking space.

They alighted and, meeting no one but a couple who were entering the restaurant, walked back to the boutique. Its twin windows were decorated with Art Nouveau mirrors, chrome poles and swivel spots on an overhead light track. Silk squares, canvas summer bags, a collection of lacquered bangles and a single stunning bikini were arrayed in geometric patterns on maroon velvet panels.

"This place all yours?" Guthrie asked.

"All mine," Marie-Christine said tersely. She inserted a key into the lock, the front door yielded and they quickly stepped inside. The boutique was narrow and deep, and the glow from the street did not penetrate to the rear. In the obscurity Guthrie made out more mirrors, glass counters, fragile chairs. Confidently Marie-Christine picked her way to her office at the back, while the two men followed her, the moquette muffling their steps. Guthrie heard her fumbling for the switch on the wall and clamped her hand.

"No one out front can see the light," she whispered.

"No," Guthrie said.

Starkey was running a flashlight over the small windowless office; the beam discovered a steel safe that stood against the farther wall.

"It's a baby safe," Guthrie said.

"No need for it to be bigger. We don't have millions to deposit in it each night, you know."

She was motionless beside him, and he smelled her petal-fresh eau de cologne. "I feel rotten," she said. "He entrusted that envelope to me. . . ."

"Well, the ball is now in your court, Marie-Christine."

She gave him her bag to hold, and while Starkey held the light on the safe door, she spun the dial clockwise, then counterclockwise, drew the steel door open and without hesitation removed from the back of the top shelf a rectangular business-size buff envelope, which she handed to Guthrie.

The envelope was sealed at the flaps with plastic tape; it was not heavy and bore no inscription.

Guthrie began to tear it open, then changed his mind.

"We get out of this place now before some one else turns up," he said.

Outdoors, a group was entering the Vietnamese restaurant, but otherwise the street was empty and silent, as tranquil as a provincial lane. "Where are we going?" Marie-Christine asked as she got in beside Guthrie, but neither man bothered to reply.

The car stopped at Porte de Saint-Cloud before a rust brick building constructed in the thirties to provide housing for medium-grade civil servants on the site of turn-of-the-century municipal fortifications. When Guthrie picked up her overnight bag, Marie-Christine started to say something, but then thought better of it and followed him indoors. She would find out about the envelope's contents first, then tell him what was on her mind. Starkey preceded them to the elevator and pushed the sixth-floor button. She glanced at him more carefully, wondering whether they were going to his place; she had still learned nothing about him except that he had unflappable, thoughtful manners, was a bit reserved with her and was evidently subordinate to Guthrie.

The apartment was small, and its clean but anonymous atmosphere gave it away: it served as courtesy quarters, a furnished sublet that remained vacant for long periods and was occupied by transients the rest of the time. The cream-papered living room boasted a sofa, a floor lamp, a writing table, a few framed prints worthy of an unsuccessful chiropodist's waiting room, but not a single photo. Photos betrayed relationships, and so there were none. Marie-Christine watched Starkey going about fastening the window shutters and checking that the telephone was connected: it was clearly not his apartment, but it occurred to her that possibly he paid the rent.

As soon as Starkey had finished, Guthrie brought out the envelope, slit it open lengthwise with a penknife and slid the contents onto the desk top. There were a yellow Lufthansa flight ticket, a bunch of Swiss franc and German mark bank notes clipped together and a sheet of ruled paper torn from a notebook. To Marie-Christine's disappointment, that was all.

"The money is self-explanatory—at a rough estimate, I'd say we have seven hundred dollars here. So is this," said Guthrie, leafing through the ticket booklet. "One confirmed reservation on the Paris–Cologne morning flight of August 5; let's see, that was yesterday: obviously he was in no position to use it. Which leaves us with this. . . ."

There were three scribbled notations in a broad, slashing Central European script on the sheet of paper.

"Is it his handwriting?"

Marie-Christine nodded.

Guthrie read the notations aloud. "August 7, eleven hundred hours—Domplatz. August 9, twenty-two hundred —Seeblick. August 21, ten hundred—Rosenthalerstrasse. That's all: three items, no more. Any notion what they're about?"

She shook her head.

"The three place names are German," Starkey observed.

"The first notation—Domplatz—means Cathedral Square. He planned to fly to Cologne on August 5. Germany's biggest cathedral is in Cologne. Perhaps—it's not entirely unreasonable"—Guthrie said, glancing across the desk at Starkey—"perhaps he plans to be in the Cathedral Square of Cologne tomorrow—August 7—at eleven o'clock. It would account for the first date, wouldn't it? Cologne is only four hundred kilometers from Paris, and he vanished three days ago. He didn't need this ticket after all to get there. Perhaps he flew on a second passport with a different ticket; perhaps he made it another way: it's no big deal when you have help to cross the frontier." He reexamined the sheet of paper. "The other notations don't tell us much for the time being. *See* means both sea and lake; Seeblick, therefore, is a common name for seaside or lakeside hotels, boardinghouses and bungalows, not only in Germany but in Austria and Switzerland as well: it crops up as often as 'Pineview Lodge' in the States. Rosenthaler-strasse is a street name that exists in virtually any German-speaking city—the question is, which city?"

Marie-Christine couldn't conceal her chagrin. "Probably I made a mistake and misled you about the envelope's importance: we made this trip just for a few travel notes. . . ."

"Who says they're just travel notes? From what happened in Zurich it's plain his network was eager to prevent anyone from obtaining the envelope, eager enough to kidnap you. They didn't go to those lengths to recover a relatively small amount of money and an expired ticket. It was this sheet of paper they were worried about, because the notations refer to something significant or represent a breach of security. If things had proceeded normally, of course, he would have taken back his envelope when you returned to Paris, said Thank you and flown to Germany. But instead, he had to break and run." He considered Starkey again. "The beauty of it is, he's unaware we have the envelope, so he won't be scared off—for example, if he really plans to turn up in Cologne tomorrow."

"Do you want me to contact the station in Bonn?" Starkey asked.

"Move, man!"

Starkey was already dialing from the phone on an oval

table beside the door, and Marie-Christine gathered that he was calling a night duty officer at the Embassy.

Reaching for her handbag, she said, "Now that's all settled, I'm going to enjoy the luxury of sleeping in my own bed for a change."

Guthrie shook his head. "The French police are still staked out at your apartment."

"You never mentioned anything about that being a problem before."

Guthrie was scarcely paying attention to her. "I'm not sure he'll be in Cologne, it's not even probable, but it *is* possible—and it's the only lead to his whereabouts we have."

She began to sense what was coming. "I assume we're flying back to Zurich tomorrow, as you promised?"

"Could you identify him positively in a crowd even if he'd changed hair color, was wearing eyeglasses—sunglasses—that sort of thing?"

"Probably. But my part in this is over. Flitting around Europe wasn't in our bargain."

"You could identify him, however?"

"I'm not going to Cologne, if that's what you had in mind."

"What's wrong with Cologne?" He was genuinely astonished by her attitude.

"I think I've done enough; perhaps more than enough." Marie-Christine foresaw that this was not an argument that would impress him. Upon reflection, it was better to be honest. "I'm afraid. Isn't it obvious why? Anybody but you would understand."

"The last person he expects to encounter in Cologne is you; he's the one who will panic. But to tell the truth, it's unlikely we'll find him. I'm gambling on an outside chance simply because I can't afford not to."

"I can identify him only close up, and I don't want to get close," Marie-Christine said firmly. "He tried to kidnap me no longer ago than last night. You seem already to have forgot."

"No, I haven't forgot."

"Or you don't attach any importance to that."

When Guthrie met resistance, she had observed, his attitude became markedly cooperative. "All right, we'll keep you out of sight, then."

"It's not my affair," she said stubbornly.

"It is now."

"You have a strange talent for making me feel like a totally different person than I really am. I fly into Paris on an American passport, am met by a CIA agent, can't go to my own apartment . . . I want to return to *my* life."

"What does that mean?"

She began to answer, then stopped. "You wouldn't understand." It meant, she was thinking, the agreeable chore of ordering the new season's styles, going to a movie on the Champs-Elysées when it rained, gossiping with her hairdresser once a week, picking raspberries at a friend's millhouse near Gisors on weekends, visiting her father in the *residence* where he now lived alone, attending the windsurfing course she had signed up for to improve her balance, although it was a sport that didn't appeal to her in the slightest.

"Whatever it is, it can wait," Guthrie said implacably. "This lead should be followed up even if it involves momentary minor inconvenience for you."

Starkey had finished his call.

"Phone Lufthansa," Guthrie said to him, "and find out whether they have a late flight to Cologne tonight. If so, book three seats."

"Bruno is too smart for you. He won't be in Cologne tomorrow," Marie-Christine said furiously.

"That's the first thing you've said with feeling. You're becoming involved, *ma jolie*."

"Poor, unliberated, browbeaten Mrs. Barry Carpenter. I pity her."

"Think of the strain if you were really married to me. *Mon Dieu!*"

"There is no late-night flight to Bonn-Cologne," Starkey said, interrupting them. "Lufthansa has a nine-oh-five morning flight. I reserved three seats—two in the name of Carpenter—the tickets to be picked up no later than eight o'clock at the airport. You'll have to clear my trip with the Paris station," he added.

"And advise Bonn of our landing time." Guthrie glanced at his watch and turned to Marie-Christine. "Better get some sleep. There's a bedroom back there you can have for yourself."

She did not stir from her armchair. "I'm not tired."

"I don't want you collapsing with fatigue when I need you tomorrow."

Marie-Christine rose. "Bruno will recognize me—it works both ways. Too bad you didn't think of letting me collect a few items for camouflage while we were in my boutique."

"We'll get you a new Saint-Laurent scarf at the duty-free shop. And you might think about combing your hair in another style. With women that's always a near-perfect disguise."

"I'm sure that I'll manage an appropriate hairdo as your wife. I wish the rest were as simple." She was still miffed.

"Your part in this is."

"Really? *Bonne nuit*, Starkey," she said, and closed the bedroom door, not gently, behind her.

"Can you depend on her?" Starkey asked a few minutes later.

"She came to me with the information about the envelope. We wouldn't have an inkling about Cologne without her cooperation. I go through this job putting trust in people, and sometimes I'm rewarded, fantastic as it may seem."

"If we run into her former boyfriend, how will she behave? Is she going to panic?"

"She's bent on demonstrating that anything I can stand

up to, she can cope with at least as capably, so she won't faint away. I'm beginning to fathom what goes on beneath that surface Parisian haughtiness."

Starkey was looking at the shut door. "I'll bet she isn't haughty all the time."

Chapter Eight

A Ripple on the Surface

In the late evening, Hans-Peter Reindorf returned to his flat in the south end of Cologne. It was located near the Köln-Süd rail yard, in the woebegone industrial district that flanks the tracks just before the cabbage fields begin. In the distance through the summer haze the soaring spires of the cathedral were visible—that was perhaps the flat's sole distinctive feature, certainly its only attractive aspect. Three years ago Reindorf had worked on the *Koelner Stadt-Anzeiger* and been fired, an event that had not impaired his self-esteem but had nullified any immediate prospect of shifting to a better neighborhood.

Hans-Peter was an easily excitable study in paradox. Like many contemporary young Germans, he cultivated, with his trim beard and soulful countenance glazed by indomitable melancholy, a possibly deliberate resemblance to nineteenth-century Russian nihilists. He had a lofty, receding mottled forehead which created a misleading impression of braininess and an agitated mouth that spilled out a cataract of complex sociopolitical terms which only the other *Genossen*, or comrades, grasped without effort. However, while looking too thin and too pliant and too underpaid, he sported his mediocrity with undeniable bravura.

He had spent the preceding two hours at his favorite occupation in bed with Margit Steinbock, a shy, toneless woman of forty who was employed at the Jordanian Embassy in nearby Bonn. She had managed to leave her office an hour early and had hurried back to her studio apartment, where, by prearrangement, Hans-Peter was waiting for her. They had been meeting regularly in this fashion for the past month and a half. She was the senior of two German secretaries attached to the Ambassador, and at the time of her appointment a security officer from Amman had carried out a CBI, or complete background investigation, and cleared her, reasoning that this unmarried, reticent woman with lusterless brown hair was not the sort to become involved in potentially compromising off-duty liaisons. The security officer was an indifferent judge of human nature.

Margit had met Hans-Peter when he called to interview Wadi Khalef, the Ambassador, for an article about German commercial interests in the Middle East. The Ambassador, a peevish and ill-organized man, was running behind with his unrealistically long list of appointments that day, and Reindorf was cooling his heels in the outer office. At one point, Margit observed that this sportily dressed, voluble journalist was eyeing her bosom. When Reindorf emerged at last from his interview and paused to chat further, she remarked, looking him straight in the eye, that in the event he needed additional assistance he could call her at work or home, at any time, day or night.

Reindorf became her lover the following week. He was unattached and perennially out of funds, a free lancer who contributed to three obscure Socialist weeklies in the Rhineland, one of which provided him with the free use of a desk and a telephone, items that made a considerable difference in Hans-Peter's budget. He omitted to mention that he belonged to an action-minded splinter branch of the JUSOS, or Young Socialists, and militated on behalf of still more obscure political groups with cryptic and ferocious goals. Margit's own motivations were simple and forthright: on these redolent summer evenings she was restless to distraction with returning unescorted through Bonn's crowded streets to her solitary apartment. Other women did not return home alone; why should she if there was any fairness left in the world?

A rotund, middle-aged woman with a predilection for certain types of sexual experimentation was by no means repugnant to Reindorf's taste. As long as it cost him nothing, he took what came in that line, and when it coincided with other objectives, he was all the more gratified.

That evening he had actually enjoyed the lively foreplay with his current partner, but when he entered his apartment, relocked the door and found himself confronted by Bruno's pale blue, slightly protuberant eyes, his high spirits instantly slumped. His houseguest's humor was generally as chill as a blade.

"Wadi Khalef is definitely flying back to Amman tomorrow evening for consultation. His return date is open, so tomorrow is the last feasible date for the operation."

Bruno considered him dispassionately. It was a trick of his—to let his aqueous eyes linger over people prolongedly and very carefully before giving them the benefit of his opinion. "I know that. What is his timetable tomorrow?"

"At eleven thirty he calls at the Bundesinstitut für den Nahosten, the Federal Institute for the Near East." Reindorf rubbed distractedly at his unironed shirt collar. "That's all you're interested in, isn't it?"

"Did she specifically state that he will be arriving at eleven thirty A.M.?"

"She confirmed it."

"Is she suspicious at all? She should be—you've been putting so many questions to her lately."

Reindorf hesitated. He had not intended to refer to the

tiny seed of uneasiness that had been planted in his mind that afternoon, but before the other man's unwavering, sharklike stare Hans-Peter always had the impression that it was in his interest to spell matters out with utmost exactness. I'm no match for him; he knows how to see through me, Reindorf thought with cheerfulness. "When I asked about the schedule, she was reluctant to answer. Not suspicious of me, mind, but just concerned that the information might get into the wrong hands."

"What did you say?"

"I convinced her that my editor is making unreasonable demands on me. Listen, these worries about being indiscreet flit through her mind, but when we are together she immediately sets them aside and has other interests. She trusts me. However, it would be unwise to let things dangle too long."

"They won't." Suddenly Bruno grinned, showing strong, prominent teeth. "I'll be glad to get out of here tomorrow. Your apartment isn't the sort of place one wants to stay cooped up in for long." He waved at the cracked lampshade, the undusted books, the drab curtains. "Why don't you fix it up properly?"

"All it is intended for is sleeping." From another standpoint too it had served its purpose, Hans-Peter thought— an unremarkable flat in a lower-middle-class neighborhood, an incurious concierge: an ideal *Absteige*, as the *Genossen* these days called a hideout. "The *Hausmeisterin* asked me as I came in how my 'cousin from Hanover' is enjoying his stay. I said very much. She lacks the imagination to make a connection between a nice, quiet blond German like you and the Bruno of Paris. Fortunately too, your passport photo in the papers resembles you only in the vaguest way."

"I saw the papers," Bruno said with distaste. "They whine about my negative influence on the young, which is typical of the press's idiotic superficiality. The last thing we want is kids wet behind the ears enrolling for a cram course in skyjacking. That's Bauer's idea of revolutionary warfare."

Reindorf uncapped a bottle of beer and gulped from it without using one of the glasses beside the sink. He was debating how to break the unpalatable news he had to his snappish guest. "Bauer bungled the kidnapping in Zurich; the girl put up a fight and got away. Rubinstein phoned me at the office and relayed the message; he paraphrased everything, but the gist was clear."

Bruno wheeled around. He sat down in the only armchair in the room and said with sudden clear fury, "That overfed, wheedling pansy! Acquaint him with the facts, give him simple instructions, set up a situation, hold his hand and stroke his balls for him, and he still manages to fuck things up." His anger subsided without a trace except for the paleness around his mouth. "How is it Rubinstein waited till this afternoon to contact you?"

"He tried earlier when I was out of the office."

"Did he say anything else?"

"The girl evidently still hasn't returned to Paris. Jean-Charles is keeping an eye on the boutique, but the assistant is still in charge. Bauer later checked her hotel in Zurich and was told she is still registered there."

"So much the better. By giving her a good scare, perhaps we've achieved our objective anyway—with no thanks to Bauer. Marie-Christine is too rattled at this point to face the French police." He pronounced her name as though it were an abstraction that existed only in files.

"She could blab to the Swiss police? . . ."

"Blab what? An abortive kidnapping attempt?—the Swiss will shrug it off unless she provides firm identification, and even then it's not the same as if she'd really been held against her will. Information about me? My real name? If she'd done that, it would already be spread over the papers." An indulgent smile softened his face. "The point is, Marie-Christine is a strong believer in old friendships."

"Doesn't that cut both ways?" Hans-Peter could not resist putting the question.

"I can't afford friends," Bruno declared impassively, perhaps as an afterthought. "Did Rubinstein say whether Bauer escaped last night without being identified?"

"That's what Rubinstein said. Of course, Bauer didn't give his name when he contacted the girl."

"Then," Bruno said detachedly, "everything's all right, and I'll assassinate the Ambassador tomorrow."

"Is each detail clear in your mind? No questions? No misgivings?"

Three-quarters of an hour later, they were still seated before a 1:2500 street map of Cologne laid out on Reindorf's kitchen table. A transistor radio beside the coffee maker was relentlessly bawling the top tune on the German hit parade. Hans-Peter rose and switched the set off.

Watching him, Bruno said mercilessly, "Let's run through your timetable a last time."

Perspiring, Hans-Peter repeated with mechanical accuracy: "I leave here exactly twenty minutes after you and drive to Schildergasse, where I park. Then I return on foot to Domplatz, arriving in front of the cathedral at eleven. We meet; by this time we have ascertained that neither of us is running into opposition interference . . ." (it was one of his favorite terms). "Then we separate and I return to the car, while you go to Frankenwerft and the Institute headquarters. This should not take more than fifteen minutes. At the end of those fifteen minutes I start out by car and drive to Heumarkt: another ten minutes. It is now eleven twenty-five. Wadi Khalef will arrive at the Institute at eleven thirty. He will be driven in the Embassy's Mercedes by his chauffeur, who dislikes him and flaps easily, therefore will think of saving his own skin when—"

"We're not reckoning with the chauffeur's cowardice," Bruno interrupted, "but simply with his presence. Did she confirm that he will be on duty—it's not his day off? he hasn't fallen sick? No foolishness of that sort?"

Reindorf felt that his collar was choking him as he sought to breathe. As lately as three weeks ago, Grand Slam had been like a newspaper story he might have suggested in which no editor had shown interest; now suddenly there was a deadline, real and inescapable. "No change of plan is necessary," he emphasized gloomily. "I went to the Jordanian Chancery this morning to collect the extra background material I requested, and I saw that monkey of an Arab in the garage simonizing the Mercedes. He isn't sick; he's on the job. Whatever free time he has accrued he will be allowed to take only after Wadi Khalef flies to Amman. All right? To resume: shortly before eleven thirty you are waiting outside the Institute entrance. At eleven twenty-seven I will drive slowly up the Rhine along Frankenwerft from the south, making sure that I reach the square not later than eleven thirty-one. Once the operation is finalized . . ." Hans-Peter swallowed back the saliva forming alarmingly in his mouth. "That is—I mean to say—"

"*Finalizing the operation* . . ." Bruno's piercing blue stare raked him without pity. "Did you pick up that cheap journalese in a newsroom or a bordello? Are you out of your mind? What you mean is: once I shoot the Ambassador. Spit it out. Say it!"

Hans-Peter felt the sweat prickling his forehead. "Once you *shoot the Ambassador*, you'll start toward the south end of the square. I'll pick you up and we get over the Deutz bridge. . . . We have from eight to ten minutes before the police send out a priority *Grenzalarm* by teletype; another ten minutes and they start to set roadblocks in place at Autobahns, bridges, major intersections, one-way streets—"

"Meanwhile you have to change cars; then we double back. . . ." Bruno considered him fixedly. "The first police to arrive on the scene won't do much, you understand. They can't make a decision; they are not senior enough for that. Their authority does not extend, at any rate, beyond the city limits. Are you feeling better?"

Color mounted into Hans-Peter's sallow cheeks. "I don't know what to expect. It's different for you; you're accustomed to this sort of operation. . . ." He couldn't avoid, he realized with despair, resorting to euphemisms.

"How is it you were picked to help me?"

"I am the best driver available," Reindorf said hollowly, without a trace of pleasure.

"For God's sake, relax. You're lost at the start if your nerves dominate you. Don't you play a competitive sport? Think of this as a match against an opponent full of foxy tricks and it will help you. . . ." Bruno's own body seemed all at once to secrete intolerable boredom. "Do you know why I am going to assassinate Wadi Khalef tomorrow? Have you ever wondered about the real reason?"

Reindorf stared at him in astonishment. Why was he asking such a question? More than two weeks ago, Rubinstein had made a special trip from Paris to inquire about Hans-Peter's availability and brief him on the operation's imperative causes. If the briefing had been less than persuasive—the thought flashed through Hans-Peter's mind with the velocity of a pistol shot—he would never have consented to be a party to the attack. "Because Wadi Khalef represents a reactionary king who attacked the Palestinians once and will do so again if it suits him. Because by staging the attack here we embarrass the Bonn Government, which is overfriendly with Israel—"

"Those are two of the reasons," Bruno conceded without enthusiasm.

"Wadi Khalef personally is a shit—a crook and a liar who participated in the Egyptian–Israeli negotiations."

"I have no interest in him as a person but purely as a symbol. Get that into your head. In Algeria we bushwhacked *fellaghas* not as individuals but as embodiments of an enemy cause. Well, this is war too. . . . George Habash said in Pyongyang a few years ago with reference to direct action: 'In today's world no one is innocent, no one is a neutral.' I was there when he said it." He brooded for a moment. "Your error is to consider this an isolated operation. In itself it is not important. Wadi Khalef's death is a mere softening up, a prelude to a much bigger action."

Reindorf was observing him with interest. "Rubinstein didn't mention that."

"Rubinstein doesn't know everything. Listen to me: what we are going to bring about is a basic upheaval in the Middle East. Why do you imagine I risked my neck to come to Cologne? To eliminate a fat, dishonest Arab diplomat? Any thug or fanatic could do that." He realized abruptly that he was talking too much. "You'll be told more when and if it concerns you." He closed out the conversation with deep-rooted, persisting distrust.

Distractedly Hans-Peter rose and switched the radio on again. A different combo was playing a catchier, lighter tune on the hit parade, but he paid no attention. He understood why his stomach was churning wildly. Perhaps it was true that tomorrow's operation was of little significance, but he was not prepared to cope with that aspect of the attack. His attention span was not superior, and he had to make a serious effort to steer his mind away from the stream of thought where it was tempted to drift. He foresaw Grand Slam, whether significant or not, as succeeding, but at his expense: he—Hans-Peter—was fated to be a victim left lying bleeding to death in the gutter. And there was nothing he could do to forestall the onrush of events. . . . He clawed at his collar fiercely. He needed to stretch out, but the apartment's stickiness was intolerable; he'd always had trouble getting so much as an hour's rest in the stifling bedroom.

"What's eating you now?"

"I can't stand this hot box."

"I gave you some good advice. Relax—if you don't, you'll be a dead man tomorrow."

After Hans-Peter had crept off to bed, Bruno lay on the dilapidated sofa in the living room, hands clasped behind his head, knowing that sleep would come in time. He regretted having mentioned Grand Slam's major objective to that pasty-faced, panic-prone newspaperman. Why had he done it? Because at the close of this suffocating summer evening, in a city where he didn't know a soul, he was overwhelmed by an excruciating need to shatter the silence and incomprehension in which he labored and hint aloud at his dangerous faith. For that was what it was: an unwavering belief, as staunch as an early Christian's, in the underground struggle's ultimate outcome. Terrorism was a mere transient means, not an end; whoever lost sight of this rule drifted perilously off course, away from reality. Terrorism was a ripple on the surface of a profound historical process of change. In Czarist Russia terrorists had thrown bombs, but they had not brought about a revolution; however, they had acted perhaps as a fuse, and this was still their true role. When a rotten underlying situation persisted, someone had to act, make the first violent move and take the lead in revolting. Indignation wasn't enough. Terrorists were, in a sense, prophets, and their attacks were the first tremors before an earthquake. Grand Slam's scope, for example, was uncommon—its impact would affect Palestinians encamped thousands of miles away along the Jordan's banks. His part was minor: merely guiding a rifle barrel toward its predestined target, a small action that came as the crystallization of a cause, a hope, an anger. And then there was Europe. The Right pretended that Europe had to be defended from the Soviet Union. It was far more imperative and estimable to defend the West from its own worst instincts. Look at what had happened in the thirties. It had taken him a while to grasp this simple truth.

Bruno paused in his thoughts. He fancied that he could hear De Wrendt's dry, mocking voice in Zurich. "And so when a Palestinian State is created and Europe is liberated from the technocrats and oligarchs, you will be appointed Minister of the Interior to safeguard order, *mon cher* Bruno? Someone will have the wit to draw upon your intimate knowledge of conspiracy. A classic example of hiring a barbarian to defend the gates of the city."

He moved his blond head slightly, protestingly in the quiet room. That wasn't what he expected, though De

Wrendt might believe so. One of the basic differences between them was that De Wrendt operated within a corrupt, weak-willed society to undermine it, whereas he had always stood outside to attack it. He didn't have to be a militant. He wasn't in this for adventure. Nor for money. One was a shallow motive, the other sordid. But gradually his perception of what was at stake had expanded, and so too an insistent sentiment of responsibility. To hell with it; I'd better worry about Wadi Khalef and make sure of tomorrow's business, he thought. A vision of that fleshy, petulant Jordanian Ambassador caused him to clench his teeth. The symptoms were always the same, whether it was a paratroop raid in Algeria or an ambush in a German city. On the eve of an attack he always felt inner anguish and mounting anger with his intended victim.

Chapter Nine

Cologne at Noon

AT THE Bonn-Cologne airport next morning they found a tall, graying man named Danielson from the American Embassy waiting for them in the hall.

"We're having a powwow with the Teutons in forty-five minutes at the Interior Ministry," he said to Guthrie. "I have my car waiting outside."

Guthrie's watch read 10:10. "I'd prefer to go straight into town," he said. "Are the police already at Domplatz?"

"To tell the truth, there's some skepticism in Bonn about your information. The friendly natives' attitude is 'Our security boys haven't turned up any leads to this particular terrorist's presence in the Federal Republic, so what proves the CIA isn't playing games with us again?' That's why I figured you'd want to come to the strategy meeting and sell your case."

"Sell it? Are you telling me Bonn is dragging its heels on this?"

"Not exactly. Look around," Danielson said.

Marie-Christine did and noted a heavier-than-usual concentration of riot police with machine pistols slung from their shoulders around the ticket counters and flight gates.

"They've got an armored car parked by the taxiway in case anyone is planning trouble there," Danielson went on. "The Interior Ministry has quietly passed a warning around to all ministries, Government departments and foreign embassies that Bruno may be in the neighborhood. The Lufthansa city terminal and other airlines are being guarded."

"What about the railroad station? Bus terminal?"

"I don't know. There's a limit to the cooperation we can obtain. As the political people in Bonn point out with some truth, we've come up with a flimsy lead, and their police are stretched thin as it is. However, there'll be prowl cars near Domplatz, and the State Police are detailing three plainclothesmen who will make contact with you outside the Dom Hotel's main entrance."

"Has anyone verified the bio info on Bruno I telexed?"

"Whoa! No one in Europe works that fast, not even Germans."

"I provided the material more than twenty-four hours ago."

"And we immediately tossed it to the Bundeskriminalamt, who telexed it to the Landeskriminalamt in Niedersachsen, who transmitted it to the Bremen police department. A decentralized state has advantages, but drawbacks too when it comes to coordination."

"I'll be damned if I lose time making a presentation to some tight-assed bureaucrats; while the man we're after comes and goes, everybody pretends he's somewhere else or not for real."

Now that he had landed, Guthrie felt closer to his quarry. He had a gut conviction that Bruno would emerge abruptly into view, in the way an animal is drawn mysteriously and irresistibly across a hunter's sights. "When I get to Domplatz I'll call you, and Starkey will go over to Bonn for the conference if I can spare him."

Danielson looked at each of them in turn. "How are you fixed for weaponry?"

"Don't need it. Let the Germans handle the fireworks."

"As you like." Danielson nodded. "It's your war party. No one back home suggested that you *had* to show at Kraut headquarters. Matching notes with the brass is a time waster, I admit, but we who labor and liaise here have no choice."

He smiled affably and left them. Not bad, Marie-Christine thought, watching him go down the airport's concrete passageway. A lesser official in his position would have stood on his rank and embroiled them in a ridiculous dispute.

"Do you want coffee?" Starkey asked Marie-Christine.

"No, I'm fine."

"Let's get moving," Guthrie said. Outdoors, he looked at the silky sky. Today was going to be another scorcher, he thought.

Bells pealed clangorously in the gusty air as a strong wind blew downriver across the flat Rhenish orchards, and pigeons flapped down from the cornices where they perched onto a fountain that dashed spray on passersby. The fair weather had brought tourists out in force at Domplatz. American Express and Toureuropa buses disgorged brilliantly plumaged groups, and multilingual guides shepherded them briskly into the iron-gray cathedral. Did hot summer days also attract terrorists? Guthrie wondered. And for what purpose? Around the vast tiled quadrangle, which was as thronged as it must have been during the Middle Ages, stood aligned the white, cubelike Roman-German Museum, sidewalk cafés whose orange parasols made splashes of color against the dull soaring stonework, and the municipal tourist office; none seemed like a terrorist objective. As Guthrie's eye roamed over the square, his skepticism grew. Quite probably they had flown to Cologne for nothing.

He stood directly facing the cathedral beside a reconstructed arch of the ancient Roman North Gate. In a gardenlike enclosure laid out with trees and lawn, teen-agers with sleeping bags were gathered listening to a guitar player. Guthrie strolled over and joined them. None was old enough to be Bruno. From here he had an unobstructed view of the north and south transept entrances, where he had posted Starkey and Marie-Christine. Among the crowd constantly on the move around the colossal stone structure, they were inconspicuous. Bruno, he reminded himself, had never set eyes on Starkey. As for Marie-Christine, she wore a new scarf about her honey-blond hair, aviator sunglasses and jeans; thus got up, she was virtually indistinguishable from most of the other identically clad women tourists. There was something to be said for the universality of blue denim on Europe's streets.

From time to time one of the three German plainclothesmen crossed Guthrie's line of vision. One of them had a walkie-talkie. The arrangement was that while sauntering about the periphery of the square, they were to keep an eye on him and be ready to intervene in the event he spotted Bruno first. He noticed that they were straying farther and farther afield. Probably they considered it a wild-goose chase. Probably they also resented being involved in an American-inspired operation. At any rate, by their aloofness they were making it clear that they were unhappy. Their attitude infuriated Guthrie. Surveillance when one wasn't even sure the subject would turn up *was* dull work. But wasn't it their work? What were they doing otherwise in Domplatz?

A quarter-hour passed. It was 10:58.

He had posted Starkey at the north transept, where a metal staff flew a West German flag that whipcracked tirelessly in the boisterous wind. Beneath, an unending parade of visitors formed and re-formed patterns as ingenious and complex as the cathedral's lavish tracery. This sector was the most troublesome to patrol, but Starkey moved about uncomplainingly in the monumental buttresses' shadow, and so Guthrie, knowing that he could be relied upon, turned his attention to Marie-Christine. She was stationed by a secondhand bookseller's under the arcades of the Dom Hotel, and she was beginning to show signs of impatience. He couldn't blame her—she hadn't, after all, chosen to come to Cologne. He went over with the intention of letting her take a break and found her hovering by a souvenir-and-postcard shop.

"No one's come by." Her eye strayed to a twelve-story-high scaffolding along the south transept where a group of workmen were making repairs.

"It was built mostly in the thirteenth and fourteenth centuries. It's one of the loveliest Gothic churches in the world," Guthrie said.

She looked at him surprised. "You seem to know a lot about it."

Whatever reply he intended to formulate was interrupted by her sharp intake of breath. A trio of Italian tourists beside a revolving postcard rack blocked his view.

"Where?"

"He's wearing a jacket and a golfer's cap I don't remember. I'm not sure it's him," she murmured.

Guthrie saw two men conferring before the main west portal, who had not been there an instant earlier. He had not seem them approaching the cathedral. . . . He realized they must have emerged from it together after entering separately through the side entrances.

"Yes, it's him," Marie-Christine whispered.

The blond man in the poplin Windbreaker and checked golfer's cap was sturdy and slim-hipped—smaller than Guthrie had anticipated: not more than five feet five; he looked crisp and pugnacious, like a bantam drill sergeant or, if you knew his background, a paratroop jumpmaster. Was this Marie-Christine's taste in lovers? By contrast, the second, white-faced man was tall and weedy.

Instinctively alerted, Starkey had crossed the quadrangle

and joined them. Automatically, Guthrie looked around the edges of the square for the roving plainclothesmen. He swore: they had momentarily vanished. They were armed and could arrest Bruno and they weren't there when they were needed.

The straw-blond's terse conversation with the taller man was over, and with his cocky paratrooper's walk he was striding quickly off, making for the wide shallow flight of steps beside the museum which led down in the direction of the Rhine.

"Glue yourself to *him*," Guthrie barked at Starkey, indicating the tall man, who was departing westward from Domplatz. "When you can, contact Danielson."

Impulsively Marie-Christine had already struck off across the quadrangle, on a diagonal track that would bring her to Bruno as he descended the steps. Guthrie caught up with her. "Hold back a little; don't crowd him." He bitterly regretted being unarmed. "We'll have to try to take him where he can't pull a gun."

Almost reluctantly, it seemed, she slowed her pace.

The tall man ahead was making his way purposefully down a pedestrian mall crowded with late-morning shoppers, past cinemas, sex shops and pavement displays of leatherware, ceramics and silver ornaments. Starkey wasn't familiar with Cologne, and he hadn't a clue where his quarry was bound. He had not expected to be separated from Guthrie; it had happened too swiftly for concertation, but upon reflection he had decided that it was nothing he couldn't handle. A surveillance was the same everywhere: it was, above all, a matter of persuading the subject, if he became suspicious, that you had a plausible destination. Starkey imagined himself proceeding to a luncheon date with Marie-Christine in a garden restaurant—it was an agreeable reverie, and he decided when he was back in Paris to make it come true. Meanwhile, he was sensitive to the city's atmosphere. He strode near the towers of still another church in this formerly Latin city of churches, crypts and Roman fragments. It was all a bit like Paris, at least that part of Paris on the Ile de la Cité around Notre Dame: Cologne too attracted hordes of tourists captivated by the water traffic, the profusion of restaurants in minuscule squares, the pale, sleepy morning washes.

Abruptly the tall man struck down a commercial side street, accelerating his stride. Starkey crossed to the other side, where the pedestrian zone ended. The street curved to the left, and the tall man had vanished. Starkey swore but didn't stop—stopping, like looking about or turning back, was the surest way of losing him for good. Automatically he noted the blue-and-white sign above an optician's at the corner: Pipin-strasse. He did not relish having to return empty-handed and announce that he had fumbled his surveillance within several hundred yards of Domplatz. Then his eye fell on a cream-colored Fiat with a Kiel license plate parked before a meter, and to his immense relief there was the tall man inside adjusting the side mirror. A taxi was approaching, and Starkey hailed it as the Fiat drew away from the curb.

With growing concern Guthrie hastened down the street toward the Rhine embankment, just managing to keep up with the fast-moving, vaguely military figure ahead. It was a figure that didn't excite interest; its potential destructiveness was quite invisible, Guthrie thought, like Siegfried's sword. Bruno might not have much height to boast about, but he surely had a gun, and it evened the odds. At his side, Marie-Christine kept her thoughts to herself. Just once Guthrie cast a curious glance at her, wondering how she was reacting, but then his attention reverted obsessively to his quarry. He had led them down Bischofsgarten to Frankenturm, then Bollwerk—Guthrie noted the meaningless names out of habit—and now they were pressing onward past still another flamboyantly sculpted church: modern Cologne was a restless, unresolved pastiche of monumental stone and stark concrete, belfries and office towers. They passed a beer garden from which a young policeman in summer uniform emerged, but Guthrie glimpsed him too late; while they attempted to explain the situation to him, Bruno might take alarm and bolt, or a misunderstanding could trigger a gunfight among the street crowd. Guthrie's forehead glistened with sweat in the midday heat. Now that the wind had died, the heat was as bad as in Paris; unusually close for a German summer, it harbored a mugginess that portended a destructive storm later on. He wondered where Starkey, who spoke no German, was at this moment—into what trap he might inadvertently stray. All this was happening because of the three plainclothesmen's failure to be where they were supposed to be when needed. Why in hell had the police assigned three goldbricks to Domplatz? Obviously because they had put no stock in the Agency's information. Who trusted the CIA these days? Yet the superterrorist the European press had been splashily publicizing all week was there, a scant two hundred yards from them, at liberty, and the only thing left was to pray that he did not escape again while they followed him docilely till they could catch him off guard or seek reinforcements.

"Wherever he's going," Marie-Christine observed, "it's a long way on foot."

Guthrie had no answer. Bruno had turned up at Domplatz to meet the tall man—that was the first notation's meaning—but apart from this simple fact, his reason for being in Cologne remained mysterious. To hell with the reason, Guthrie thought furiously. He'll spell it out for us once we get introduced.

Two blocks ahead, the figure in the Windbreaker and golfer's cap paused before a winehouse. They saw him glance at his watch and move off southward along the waterfront at a slower pace.

"I know what he's doing. I've done it myself. He has another meeting and he wants to arrive on the dot," Guthrie said. "Long live the punctual revolutionary."

The racket of long-haul-truck traffic on the broad embankment nearly drowned his words. Turning southward too, they caught the shallow stink of diesel fumes floating off the Rhine—the sparkling legendary river was reduced to an insignificant polluted backdrop in contemporary Germany by the relentless rumble and surge of Common Market vans and refrigerator trucks thundering along Frankenwerft toward profitable destinations.

"Come on!" Guthrie shouted above the uproar, and grabbed Marie-Christine's arm.

As they drew up before an alley into which Bruno had just ducked, Guthrie saw that it led between old taverns repainted in pastel colors; dives where they sold Koelsch, the local brew; jazz cellars that flaunted posters for nightly guitar music. There were sham eighteenth-century signboards, wrought-iron grilles and authentic stone statues of saints in corner recesses, but at this hour the only activity was a woman mopping a doorstep and a truck unloading beer. Ahead, Bruno was already exiting into a wide, cobblestoned square. Without waiting for Marie-Christine, Guthrie struck out alone down the passageway, but as he reached the square he froze, nonplussed. He had been prepared for several eventualities: Bruno entering a waiting car, dodging into a building, continuing on his puzzling lengthy walk or even retracing his steps. In fact, in the doorway of a camera shop on the square's far side, hands planted in his jacket pockets, Bruno stood motionless, staring intently straight ahead at a large sepia Renaissance-style building that had a brass plaque bolted beside the entrance. At the foot of tall windows were boxes of blood-red geraniums. Guthrie dropped back into the shadow of the passageway and waited for Marie-Christine to join him.

After a moment, two men in dark, elegant suits with the punctilious bearing of senior German officials came out of the building and waited on the front steps. Mechanically Guthrie glanced at his watch: it was precisely 11:30. Whatever had drawn Bruno to Cologne was about to unfold in this slumbering, sun-flooded square. Marie-Christine was frowning, engrossed by the immobile enigmatic figure in the shop doorway.

For the tiniest fraction of a second, Bruno's attention was diverted by the couple who had debouched from the passageway but come no nearer. The sandy-haired man was unfamiliar, but the slender girl in sunglasses and jeans bore a certain unsettling resemblance to Marie-Christine. Bruno squinted in the midday glare but couldn't discern the girl's hair color under her silk head scarf. He resumed his solitary rapt surveillance of the target site opposite. The likeness, in any case, was mere illusion, for Marie-Christine was securely in her Zurich hotel, two hundred and sixty miles away. The couple's sudden arrival was a nuisance, but it would be all over too quickly for them to describe much. On the steps of the Federal Institute the two-man reception committee was waiting to escort Wadi Khalef inside. At upper-story windows office workers occasionally appeared and glanced down—more potential eyewitnesses who would rush to phone the police as soon as they collected their wits. He wasn't worried by their presence; he could hold all those bureaucratic sheep at bay indefinitely with a gun.

Three official cars were parked in authorized spaces near the Institute's main entrance, but otherwise almost no traffic troubled the square's drowsy calm. There was not a policeman in sight; the Federal Institute was a low-budgeted, relatively unexciting commercial-and-cultural documentation center that could lay no claim to special police protection. At Bruno's back a lone salesman was rearranging photographic equipment on a shelf in the quiet shop. Once Bruno met his inquisitive stare, but broke it with his own chill blue inspection; the clerk was curious, but he wouldn't come out and ask questions.

In the clarity of the August light, each detail in the square leaped out in stark focus. A short way off, around a fountain with carved statues, children of elementary-school age were practicing with a soccer ball while their supervisor talked with another woman. The inchoate stone mass of Grosse Sankt Martin church soared in the near distance. Bruno was lucid about what was going to happen shortly when the shooting began; he was ready and excited. Bizarrely, he was reminded of what it felt like when he was about to take a girl: a conviction that no force on earth could stop him short of stunning him insensible or squashing him to death, a minute backwash of disappointment at the pursuit's approaching end. By touch he found the safety slide on the barrel of the 9mm Beretta in his jacket pocket and pushed it over to Fire, hoping that the schoolchildren would not get in the way.

A smell of cement dust and excavated foundations lay over the warm, contented day. The throb of a drill subsided; a worker came down a ladder propped against an adjoining shopfront and went away to lunch. The children's exultant cries had died out too; they were gone with their supervisor. Promptly on the half-hour, a black Mercedes 600 with Diplomatic Corps plates and a Chief of Mission's flag swept into the square and braked before the Institute. The chauffeur sprang out and opened the rear door for the single occupant within. Elegantly attired and portly, Wadi Khalef, the Jordanian Ambassador, dismounted slowly as though he suffered from arthritis. As the welcoming committee moved forward, Bruno, right gun hand stuffed into his pocket, was already racing toward the group.

Twenty feet short of the Mercedes and to the left, where his line of fire was unimpeded, he dropped into a crouch, gripping the Beretta with both hands as he took aim. He was bitterly aware that the six-foot, muscular chauffeur did not correspond in the slightest to Reindorf's description of a "tiny monkey." At the same moment, the blinding thought crossed his mind that the tourist couple weren't in the passageway by coincidence either, that by some improbable twist of events the girl *was* Marie-Christine . . . but it was too late to recoil. Across his sunny vision, a line he had read which had impressed him at the time passed like a banner of exhortation: "Don't make a mistake, Razumov. This is not murder—it is war, war." ·

The chauffeur/bodyguard had whipped around and realized immediately that he was being attacked. With a violent exclamation he shoved Wadi Khalef back into the car and brought up a gun in his large fist.

Bruno leaped aside, then squeezed off two rounds. He thought he saw the two German officials flinging themselves without shame to the pavement, where they lay gasping like boated fish.

The chauffeur's gun fired harmlessly in the air and he lurched back, scowling. Then all of a sudden he collapsed, striking his dark head against the open car door. Out of the corner of his eye Bruno spotted the sandy-haired stranger charging across the square. He pivoted, fired and with satisfaction saw the man dive for cover behind one of the parked official cars.

He rushed up to the Mercedes and stared down. The bodyguard lay inert on his back beside the rear wheel, his gray cloth tunic pierced twice, his eyes blank and now uninterested. Hearing another, different sound, Bruno looked up sharply and saw the cream-colored Fiat with Hans-Peter's pallid, strained face behind the windshield slamming across the square right on schedule. He realized that he was running behind. Stepping over the motionless chauffeur, he peered interrogatively into the Mercedes' interior. Wadi Khalef was drawn up into a small, clumsy ball inside, an expression of wild, intense awareness on his clay-colored face; his elderly body was jerking uncontrollably with terror, and his colorless lips were forming incomprehensible fragments of Arabic words. Bruno stared at him, then frowned as he sniffed the stench of shit on the rear-seat leather. As he raised his gun to align it with the ear, Wadi Khalef uttered a little bleating cry. Infuriated, Bruno bawled into his quivering face, "I'm doing this for better people than you!" and fired twice, point-blank. Then he found himself unable to stop and kept pumping bullets into that pampered, unprotected skin until the Jordanian Ambassador's round head seemed to explode in the car.

As Bruno withdrew in disgust, he heard no sound except the roar of the Fiat's motor. No answering gunfire spat from behind the parked car; the sandy-haired man must be unarmed, as he had thought. At that moment a taxi raced incongruously into the square, and a youngish American in a linen blazer leaped out and dashed toward the Fiat. Reindorf's hand flew up, pointing a small, dark pistol through the open side window. A shot cracked out and the American doubled up, clutching his stomach.

Backing away from the Mercedes, Bruno heard a furtive movement, wheeled and fired at the second of the parked cars, missing the blur. The sandy-haired man had lunged forward and taken cover behind the nearest car, fifteen yards away. Hans-Peter had spotted him too and in a frenzy of aggressiveness was aiming round after round at the car's chassis; suddenly the windshied shattered, spraying slivers of glass onto the cobblestones. A nameless rage possessing him, Bruno covered the building entrance with his Beretta. If he couldn't discourage the intruder, he could vent his frustration on the two German officials lying doggo on the pavement. He breathed jerkily and took careful aim at one of the two prone figures. When he was in battle too long, unpredictable, irrational urges overtook him. Then, abruptly, he had had enough and lowered his gun without depressing the trigger. Crouching and weaving, he dodged back toward the cream-colored car and leaped in beside Reindorf, who cast him a flurried glance as though he were a stranger before he slammed the car forward. Bruno strained around for a last look at the square. The sandy-haired man was stooping beside the stricken American's side; the girl in flare-legged jeans was nowhere in sight. As the Fiat tore down the embankment, Bruno sat panting, unable to say a word, benumbed and incoherent like Wadi Khalef.

Marie-Christine stood rooted in the passageway, where she had witnessed the attack from start to finish. She loathed what she had seen, but couldn't move. She found it hard to credit that physically Bruno had been there, so near in space, yet so remote from her. Suddenly she shuddered with a passionate hatred of him far worse than she had felt on the nighttime streets of Zurich. Bruno was the enemy, and she had never thought of him that way before. Each time, it was becoming clear, like a killer cyclone he came and went furiously, without reason, leaving in his stormy wake a trail of wreckage: the corpses in her Paris apartment, the ambushed Mercedes' two matt-skinned victims. But this time, in addition, decent, considerate Starkey lay sprawled lifeless on the round cobblestones.

Chapter Ten

The Flight Back

"SAY SOMETHING."

Guthrie stared through the plane window at the dark, featureless plateau that materialized intermittently beneath the clouds and which was Germany or perhaps already Switzerland. With only ten minutes to spare, they had barely managed to board the last night flight to Zurich after Guthrie had met with Danielson, cabled his report from the Embassy and attended to the bleak final administrative details concerning Starkey.

"What do you want me to tell you? He was twenty-seven. From Rhode Island. Paris was his second post. I never should have sent him after a suspected terrorist without a gun."

"You didn't have a gun either."

In the Boeing 727 most passengers were dozing, and only a few overhead reading lights were on. Marie-Christine said gloomily, "I can't help feeling that if I had warned you earlier about the envelope, everything might have worked out differently."

Guthrie said nothing. Perdurable skepticism about postmortem recapitulations, sorrow and anger, a recognition of checkmate left him dour and incommunicative. He was nauseated by the recollection of Starkey's death and the acrid smell of Wadi Khalef's bowel contents in the trapped car.

The Swiss stewardess stopped on her way forward and considered Marie-Christine with concern. "Are you all right? Can I get you anything?"

"A strong double Scotch would help."

"Make that the same for me."

When he had the drink before him, Guthrie said, "Did you see the way he kept firing at Wadi Khalef? Now I understand what happened in Paris. He can't stop. That will trip him up finally. He has to be put down—not next month or next year, but now. I'm going to nail that blond swaggering bastard."

"It's no longer in your hands."

"Yes, it is." Inwardly, he wasn't so sure. The Jordanian Ambassador and his chauffeur were dead, so was a valuable officer of the Agency and the prey had flown. Ditweiler's reaction wasn't hard to foretell.

Marie-Christine cast a sidelong glance at Guthrie. Most people were probably forever being taken in by him. But scratch the surface and the glad-handed Irish-American act collapsed. She had seen and sympathized with his eruption of cold fury when Starkey crumpled and the cream-colored car sped away with impunity. The fury was spent now, but surviving was unyieldingness, an underlayer of determination, an implicit single-mindedness. Anybody could make bombastic declarations about stopping Bruno, but if somebody could actually bring it off, it might be the man beside her.

As though guessing her thoughts, Guthrie said, "Before, I wasn't personally involved."

"Is it wise to be?"

He smiled with no warmth at all. "They don't always give you a choice."

Marie-Christine finished her Scotch and looked away. "Was the Fiat's license number of any use?"

"The Fiat turned out to be registered in the name of a two-bit lawyer mixed up in radical causes who left for East Berlin last week and hasn't surfaced since. Let's admit it, I blew my opportunity—Bruno outsmarted me. Not only me. Bonn is offering a hundred-thousand-dollar reward for him; they don't part lightly with that sort of money—it's to atone, I suppose, for being made to look so awful. But it probably won't help."

"Why not?"

"Because the leads are nonexistent—he could be anywhere by now." Guthrie swung around and faced her. "He —his network—*had* to have help inside the Jordanian Embassy to get Wadi Khalef's timetable. *That's* the only worthwhile lead, provided the Germans can get cooperation from Amman to investigate the Embassy staff. Do you realize that the Jordanians were one of the few foreign missions who took seriously the alert we sent about Bruno and assigned a security man in place of the chauffeur to drive Wadi Khalef? Well, it didn't stop Bruno. Then Starkey turned up on the scene in the taxi, and that didn't stop your trigger-happy boyfriend either."

"*My* boyfriend?" She rounded on him at once. "That's a cheap shot. You know better than to say that."

"I'm sorry. I could do with ten more drinks." The afternoon papers the stewardess had handed them upon takeoff carried the available printable photos of the assassination spread over the front page. There were no gruesome close-ups of the damage to Wadi Khalef's head, which the police had photographed with strobe lights; those shots wouldn't get into the papers, which was perhaps a pity. "Look at the way the German papers are playing him up: 'Europe's unstoppable superterrorist.' If it's publicity for a cause he's after, he's succeeding with a vengeance. Still, why did he want to assassinate that fat, unimportant ambassador? Wadi Khalef wasn't worth the risk, I'd say."

"Perhaps simply because he was"—the words sounded weird, yet relevant in her mouth—"available to be shot?"

"There was nothing spontaneous or accidental about Wadi Khalef's murder: each detail was carefully planned and rehearsed." He whacked the newspaper against his knee. "It's the list in the envelope that bugs me. If there was ever any doubt about the authenticity of that timetable, what happened today dispelled it. The two other notations probably also refer to attacks. The second notation is—"

"Day after tomorrow." She voiced aloud his worry.

"Not a hell of a lot of time to figure out what Seeblick means. Maybe it doesn't matter. He's realized by now that we—you and I and Starkey—weren't in that square by accident; ergo, there was a leak: somebody had access to that envelope. He'll be doubly careful and will probably revise the entire scenario. Seeblick may already be obsolete. But I don't think he'll just give up and go teach a seminar in revolutionary warfare at the University of Pyongyang for the rest of his life."

"Have you ever asked yourself what makes him a terrorist?"

"I'm sure there are fine, compelling, psychologically valid reasons."

"He believes in what he's doing."

Guthrie looked at her fixedly and then said something that nonplussed her. "Do you know that if I thought he could contribute anything positive to purging this fat-cat society we live in, I might join him? But he hasn't proved that."

"You're becoming so involved that your perception of him is wrong."

"No, I'm not wrong."

"You keep wondering where and how he's going to attack next. But he's part of a network. He doesn't necessarily decide."

"Who does, then?"

She had no answer to that.

"Theory," Guthrie scoffed.

"I know him and you don't."

"I know his track record."

Marie-Christine was pursuing her own line of thought. "Bruno isn't an organizer," she said stubbornly, her oval face profoundly alive with an indefinable expression of grief and reproach. "He exploits situations; he doesn't create them."

"I really need another drink," Guthrie said, and caught the stewardess' eye.

The thought occurred to Marie-Christine, It's his world, not mine, of agents and terrorists and sterile strategy sessions with blasé police officials in various uneasy cities. I would like to return to *my* Paris—and suddenly she was inconsolably homesick for shabby bistros where the wine was sometimes sour; for shoestring art galleries run by youngsters; for the sharp-tongued, chic women customers who came into her boutique and complained of the merchandise, and the foreign workers lining up on Saturday to buy *tierce* tickets, which was their only hope of ever making it; even, absurdly, for the zoo stench of the Métro at rush hour; in short, for a secure world where no underground tug-of-war raged without end.

But in the same instant she realized that this was a romantic illusion: her world was potentially as merciless as any other; further, the basic assumptions of her life had drastically changed: being witness to Bruno's deadly gunplay in the square had driven home certain truths, which she had managed to overlook till then. I thought I'd done my part and could return safely home, but apparently I was mistaken. She had a premonition that it would be a long, intricate and thankless struggle.

As the plane banked for the descent and the seat-belt sign flashed on, Guthrie said, "There's a safe house outside Zurich. . . . I phoned ahead."

When she said nothing, he insisted. "You won't really be safe elsewhere. Bruno must have recognized you in the passageway. And next time his friends come to see you, they won't bungle it."

"I don't want simply to hide."

"I understand that."

"Can't I do anything to be of use?"

"You're one of the few people who knew him before he turned terrorist; that's important."

Marie-Christine was silent, weighing his proposal.

"Where I have in mind, you'll be all right. The safe house won't be for long. . . ."

But that was the first thing he had said during the flight which she could not bring herself to believe at all.

When they landed, it was still incontestably Guthrie's world. In what appeared to be a macabre replay of the scene at Orly only the day before, an unfamiliar American was waiting handily with a car. She gathered that he was there to escort her to the safe house.

"How did you know I would agree?" she asked Guthrie.

"I didn't."

After thirty-six hours spent uninterruptedly in his company, the prospect of going off on her own left her feeling dizzy and lonely.

"I'll come by tomorrow. Meanwhile, don't brood about what happened in Cologne."

"Starkey was so nice. I had the feeling he was going to ask me for a date."

Barely listening, Guthrie spoke to her escort and gathered up his bag.

Before he started toward the taxi stand, Marie-Christine said, "Bruno once mentioned a man who was the single biggest influence in his life—a friend who taught him all he knew about his career . . . career was the word he used."

"You didn't mention that in Zurich."

"I didn't recall it then."

"No idea who he was—nationality? occupation?"

She shook her head. "It may have been boasting for boasting's sake. Bruno's like that."

"While you're at the safe house, try to remember anything more Bruno said about him."

He waited impassively for her to leave. As Marie-Christine walked away, she turned back once to make a slight gesture to him. She was in no way as self-sufficient as she pretended, Guthrie thought; she needed to be reassured, like everybody else. A bond had been created between them by Starkey's murder. Bizarre notions of time, death, love and friendship merged in his mind: the four seemed oddly inseparable and complementary. And God knew, she was attractive. Then why was he so remote with her? Perhaps because he couldn't overcome a certain foreboding about her: she was the sort of girl, it occurred to him vividly, who by her very qualities would always spell trouble, most of all for herself. But maybe that wasn't it at all and he was still simply gun-shy of girls who smiled, walked and tossed their hair like his former wife. The answer would have to wait, and meanwhile he had to face Ditweiler's wrath.

Then, impulsively, he went down the hall after her. At the sound of his step she turned, her face lighting up, and slipped her arm through his.

Ditweiler could wait.

Chapter Eleven

The Contact

DITWEILER WAS back from a quickie trip to Washington to testify at a closed-door session of the Senate Intelligence Committee. His deposition (in favor of broad guidelines rather than specific restrictions on clandestine operations) had persuaded solely those committee members who wanted to believe and turned off many others.

"How was Washington?" Guthrie asked.

"Fucking awful, and vice versa. I wasn't fired, which is a novelty these days. You can't run an intelligence service out in the open. It's a basic contradiction. But everybody on the Hill backs away from that." Being a CIA loyalist to the bitter end and conscious of his lack of success as an emissary from the field, he was tense and his mood was wintry in Zurich, where he had stopped en route to Bern. Guthrie's briefing on the Cologne fiasco had not ameliorated matters.

"We blew the operation and lost a man." Ditweiler was trying scrupulously to avoid being unfair. "The Krauts let us down in the crunch—I'll concede that."

"It was my decision to go unarmed."

"You were right about that. Do you think we're supposed to promote gunplay in the street? I've just been talking myself hoarse in Washington assuring those pudding-heads that our role is intelligence gathering, period period period —we spot a terrorist and pass the word to the local authorities. If they can't clip his wings, it's their lookout—"

"Ours too, in this case."

Ditweiler, shadows under his eyes after his night flight from Dulles, sipped from a cup of coffee that Guthrie's secretary had prepared. He said, "I'm listening."

"Part of the Aurora network you ordered me to investigate is in Switzerland. The shells that killed Starkey came from the same lot of ammo found in Bruno's tennis bag: it was pilfered from Swiss Army stocks."

"You're jumping to conclusions again," Ditweiler barked.

"It's not the only link. Marie-Christine was nearly kidnapped here in Zurich—not Paris, or Cologne: right here. I asked the Swiss, without mentioning the reason for my interest, of course, to check out the car number she furnished. When I got back last night, the answer was on my desk."

"Well?"

"The BMW belongs to a Zürcher named Franz Bauer who has an antique shop on Neumarkt. I have a CBI on him from Huebli. Fifty years old, unmarried; his business is sound. He's a deacon of a nondenominational chapel on Friedheimstrasse in Oerlikon. No known political activity, but he's a fund raiser and recruiter for the Swiss Third World Committee—that's the private group that runs an operation parallel to the government Catastrophe Corps: they dispatch volunteer doctors, nurses, relief workers to Africa whenever disaster conditions exist—drought, earthquakes and so forth. Bauer's a big wheel on the committee. You get the picture?"

"I do."

"His file is as pure as Snow White's."

"I'm happy to hear it."

"But he fits Marie-Christine's description of the hood who tried to shove her into that car."

"Are you trying to put the finger on a Protestant deacon, for God's sake? Guthrie, what ever happened to the sharp, promising Irish son of a bitch who was assigned here to help me, *not* hinder me, five years ago? Did he resign without telling me?"

"It could be a coincidence if you believe in neat coincidences."

"Are you telling me furthermore that this dude social worker/antique dealer used his own car, which could be easily traced, for a kidnap attempt? No one is that stupid."

"Whoever it was—Bauer or somebody else—expected Marie-Christine to go willingly with him to meet Bruno. There was no reason to expect the ploy to backfire."

"Let Huebli tackle it," Ditweiler said with finality.

"On what basis? Heubli knows nothing about the kidnapping attempt."

Ditweiler had drawn up his broad shoulders and withdrawn almost literally into a hedgehog attitude of prickly resistance.

"Al, I may be on the verge of finding out more about the Aurora network. Is it still any of my business?"

"Possibly." It was Ditweiler's standard evasive response, the dilatory tactic he used with the Ambassador, his co-workers, even his wife whenever he was pressed for a binding commitment.

"Wherever Bruno is holed up at this point, he's had time to think—and wonder what a sandy-haired man and a girl with a marked resemblance to Marie-Christine were doing outside the Federal Institute for the Near East precisely when he opened fire on Wadi Khalef. He'll check back with his network here to determine where Marie-Christine was on that day. Now assume that Bauer belongs to Aurora and I supply him with a hint."

"Where is all this hocus-pocus supposed to lead?" Ditweiler asked irritably.

"To Bruno or whoever's in charge."

"Bruno gives orders in the Aurora network."

"Marie-Christine recalled Bruno mentioning another man who had influence over him."

"Are you starting to believe all that that slippy French broad says?"

"Her information hasn't been wrong yet. The German police finally confirmed the background data on Bruno she gave me. They have a record of a Dieter Koenig who grew up in Bremen in the fifties: his parents were killed during a wartime bombing raid a month before the Reich collapsed; he was raised by a foster family, dropped out of school and eventually enlisted in the Foreign Legion during the Algerian war, when the French needed mercenaries. Paris, for its part, confirms that they had a Dieter Koenig in a Legion paratroop regiment who rose to the rank of *sergent-chef*, which is higher than most foreigners normally reach—the dates, physical description and other details correspond to Marie-Christine's story. Koenig deserted in March 1962 and joined the OAS when it was machine-gunning Arabs on street corners and generally running amok in Algiers. He was sentenced to twenty years' imprisonment in absentia by a French military court. Later, De Gaulle amnestied most members of the OAS, but Koenig had dropped out of sight permanently after being last spotted in Marseille among an evacuee group from Algeria—"

"That's interesting as past history, but where do we go with it?"

"I forgot to mention something else. Koenig's fingerprints in the Legion files, which the French reluctantly supplied, match those found in Marie-Christine's apartment."

"That's useful, but it doesn't help us track him down."

Guthrie got up and went to the Consulate window, where he looked down on Zurich's chaotic traffic, a barometer of its affluence and frustrations. Switzerland was no longer an oasis sheltered from other countries' afflictions; the outside world's contemporary woes were relentlessly pressing in.

"The OAS was good training for Bruno, since it dabbled in an early, primitive form of international terrorism," he said. "But some of the puzzle is still incomplete: how—and why—did he switch from far Right to radical Left? Perhaps he's conning us?"

Ditweiler smiled fiercely. "He's conning himself." Forever unable to part willingly with information, he said with almost pathological misgiving, "While I was at Langley I spoke with Emmett White. NSA* has been picking up traffic between Moscow and the Soviet Embassy in Bern with reference to Bruno—nothing to sink your teeth into, but intriguing insofar as it points to a connection. Back home, the task force can't absorb enough about Bruno: at this point he outclasses all the other entries in the field." As ungraciously as he could, he added, "I was thinking of assigning someone else to the case, but you'd better stick with it."

"Then," Guthrie said, "this is what I'd like you to authorize. . . ."

He had no trouble finding Bauer's antique shop. It was located halfway up Neumarkt, a narrow street that wound back on itself between prim four-story houses on the steep slope back of the Limmat River quayside. The twin windows were decorated sparingly with a few overpriced-looking objects: a framed ormolu mirror, a pair of upholstered chairs, several old prints of Zurich. A sign in gilt lettering read OPEN 10–3 AND BY APPOINTMENT.

Guthrie pushed open the door. It was early afternoon; the neighborhood, the street, the shop—all were drowsy on this languorous summer day, and he was the only customer inside the deep showroom, which suited him.

At first no one appeared, and Guthrie sauntered patiently past lacquered escritoires and Chinese screens, halting mo-

---

* National Security Agency, at Fort Meade, Maryland, which monitors communications throughout the world.

mentarily before a pearl-gray Compagnie des Indes plate with a mythological motif placed on a Directoire mahogany side table. There were sounds of typing in a back room.

Then a corpulent man of about fifty in a lustrous silk suit materialized from the rear and examined Guthrie neutrally without uttering a word.

"What period is it?" Guthrie asked in German, indicating the plate.

"It is Kien-Long."

"And what is the price?"

"Five thousand francs." The resonant tone was unencouraging. There was no traditional *Gruetzi* with which Swiss shopkeepers welcome customers, no attempt to supply additional information or make a sale.

The dealer weighed at least two hundred and forty pounds, but the weight was evenly distributed over his bigboned frame, and the muscles in his neck were strong. Quite possibly two decades earlier a competent athlete had inhabited that strapping body. In the squarish, unaccommodating face, the liveliness of the deep-set hazel eyes startled.

"Are you the owner?"

"*Ja.* Why?"

"I am looking for something specific, but my German is not very good. Do you speak French?"

"When I have to."

"I was in Cologne yesterday and saw a plate *en grisaille* like this, but it was already sold. I'm looking for a pair with mythological or floral motifs of the same period." He knew enough about porcelain to scrape past. "Do you have two matching plates; or if not, could you obtain them for me?"

An idea had clicked in the recesses of that impassive head.

"How long are you staying in Zurich?"

"A week—perhaps longer."

"And you are American?"

Without emotion Guthrie noted in passing that the fat

man's French was halting and heavily accented. He remarked also, with interest, an unhealed ragged scratch mark recently gouged in the dealer's fleshy cheek.

"I'm at the Hotel Baur au Lac," he said. "I'll give you my room number. Perhaps you could call me if you manage to locate a second one."

The dealer's thick-lidded, observant eyes lingered a second too long on Guthrie, who thought, That's it, Fatso, you've made the connection; don't let that busy *blitzschnell* brain miss a trick; memorize each detail about me, including the shade of my hair. Does a sandy-haired American interest you, who was in Cologne twenty-four hours ago and is now at the Baur au Lac?

Distinctly less eager now to terminate the conversation, the fat man lifted the plate and turned it over fondly. "I would like to see you acquire the pair while you are in Zurich," he rumbled. "Through my supplier I am sure that I can find a matching plate." It was a programmed reply; every antique dealer made the same response to that question. "In the meanwhile I'll set this one aside for you—with no commitment on your part, of course." A platinum-link watch bracelet glittered on his thick wrist as he brandished a crocodile-skin wallet. "Here is my card. I shall try to be of all possible service during your stay."

Observing the fat man's rosy-gray skin, his foppish dress, his fondling of the plate with those incongruous, powerful bear paws, Guthrie realized what he should have grasped at the outset, though Marie-Christine had not remarked upon it: the antique dealer was, as the saying went, so bent that he couldn't even sleep straight in a bed.

"Ask at the Baur au Lac for Jack Garrison." It was a cryptoname Guthrie hadn't used in years. "In Room 220."

The sunken hazel eyes measured him with affection. Give the old overweight sod his due, Guthrie reflected: he knew his trade well. It was as though Bauer had never in his life heard the number of Marie-Christine's room.

Less than a half-mile away, Emil Huebli entered an office in the Justice and Police Department building of Zurich. A slim, prematurely gray-haired major from Basel waved him into one of two chairs.

"I wanted to talk to you about the forthcoming visit of our eminent guest Mr. Salah," he said. "It's been decided in Bern to entrust you with the security arrangements for his stay."

Huebli cracked his knuckles. "Salah? Rather unimaginative as a cover. Which publicity-shy Saudi sheikh is it this time?"

"Now that you're part of the security team, we can dispense with that charade. Listen closely and brace yourself. I don't spring surprises like this every day. Mr. Salah is listed as a cotton broker from Alexandria, but his real name is Anwar Sadat." The major's voice was laced with a curious, cold intonation, a trace of suppressed intensity.

It was one of the few times in Huebli's career that he experienced a feeling of utter powerlessness. He had been prepared for almost anything but this. "I can't believe it."

"I assure you that it's quite true." The major looked at him sympathetically. "I know what you're thinking."

"I'm wondering how do I protect a man like Sadat?" Into Huebli's mind flowed a vision of a lethal terrorist attack upon Egypt's controversial President. Why not? Sadat was excoriated daily in bulletins, broadcasts and speeches throughout the Middle East as the supreme traitor to the Arab cause; he enjoyed the dubious distinction of being the most hated man among millions of Palestinians, Syrians and Iraqis, and that hatred could easily lash out in Switzerland. "Why is he coming here?"

"Many heads of state come incognito to Zurich—for medical reasons, or to transfer half their national treasury to a private account, to conduct an affair—"

"I don't suppose that is Sadat's reason."

"In Sadat's case it's medical. Recently his doctors diagnosed an aneurysm, which means an abnormal dilation of the wall of the aorta; they told him the damaged segment has to come out, and recommended flying to Switzerland for the operation."

"Have you estimated Sadat's potential for attracting assassins?"

"High, provided they know where he is. They won't. His visit is being kept absolutely secret. It was decided upon in July at a restricted cabinet meeting in Cairo: Sadat informed only a hand-picked quartet of advisers. No one, or virtually no one, will know that he is here—you see that you yourself had no precise idea of Mr. Salah's true identity. He will not be posing for photographers or granting television interviews to American media personalities: as soon as he lands he will be admitted into the Linder Clinic and will stay confined there till he flies back to Cairo. Our job is to deliver him to the operating room, offer prayers that the surgeons are competent and once he is patched up, send him home."

Huebli thought it over. "You make it sound like caring for a houseguest."

"The new antiterrorist brigade will come under your direct command."

Huebli had watched the special brigade of *Grenadiertruppen*, all between twenty and thirty, with previous service in paratroop and armored units, practicing close-combat engagements and mock assaults on skyjacked aircraft at a training camp outside Bern, and come away impressed. By its very existence, the brigade had the power to dissuade. Yet . . .

"Among a hundred high-stepping Arabs arriving on a shopping weekend, a highly trained and motivated Fatah terrorist can slip in with no problems to speak of. An isolated kamikaze act is virtually impossible to fend off unless we get advance warning."

"That's what we have an intelligence service for."

"Our intelligence capability abroad is limited. If something is brewing, we do not necessarily pick it up in time."

"You conduct liaison with the Americans," the major reminded him, "to remedy that."

Huebli relaxed minutely. "You're giving me authorization to notify the Consulate of Sadat's trip?"

"The answer is, definitely no. The risk of bringing the CIA into the picture is greater than the advantage—never overlook the Israeli connection." The major managed adroitly to avoid meeting Huebli's eye while he added, apparently as an afterthought, "However, if the Americans were to discover anything on their own about a projected terrorist attack and come to us with the information, I wouldn't object. We would owe them less that way and simultaneously respect our commitment to hush up the visit."

"They won't necessarily find out about the visit beforehand if we don't advise them."

"How can you be sure? Not only is Sadat taking a whole floor at the Linder, which isn't conducive to anonymity, but an Israeli specialist from Hadassah Hospital in Jerusalem will be on the surgical team. Of course, neither Cairo nor Tel Aviv will be publicizing *that*." The major's voice was as dry as granite. "There are many instances, Huebli, where one should beware, as of the plague, of international cooperation."

"Pay dirt. Break out your best brandy and listen," Ditweiler said when he arrived at Guthrie's apartment that evening and plumped himself down without being invited in Guthrie's favorite chair. "You struck pay dirt, *amigo* . . . maybe. Bauer came out of his shop less than a quarter-hour after you left. Have you ever seen a guy who's just been hit by a claim for ten thousand dollars in back taxes?"

"Yes. My former father-in-law."

"That's how Bauer looked. He checked first to make sure you weren't lurking about the premises; then he hotfooted it to Niederdorfstrasse and hopped into a taxi. . . ."

Guthrie set down a bottle of Martell and two balloons on the glass coffee table.

Ditweiler smirked ambiguously. "Where did he go in such a flap? To the new Botanical Gardens. His contact was already there, waiting: older party, lots of tradecraft. Careful dance away from the foliage and shrubbery to forestall anybody's presumptuous notions about mike-and-wire; footpaths out in the open. But no one can win them all, can he? We got telephotos of both of them from one of the pavilions. After ten minutes, they split. Bauer went back to his shop and didn't budge for the rest of the afternoon. Second squad shadowed the old boy—dignified, erect, nicely dressed, wouldn't be surprised if he charges his clothes where I do, wouldn't be surprised too if he stops to help old ladies across the street: no evasive action, behaving strictly like a law-abiding party out for a respectable stroll, but with quite an eye for the Fräuleins, he marches into a private bank on Blecherweg—and here comes the kicker. It's past business hours, but he enters like he owns it and doesn't come out. Why? Because in fact he does own it— De Wrendt und Kompanie Bankhaus. One of my men elicits this from the guard on duty with a lightweight story about recognizing an old friend from the States who just stepped inside. Guard says can't be so, only person who's been allowed in for the past ten minutes is Herr Generaldirektor Konrad de Wrendt. Our guy bows out. De Wrendt goes back to counting gold bullion." Ditweiler ended his recital abruptly.

"You've been through the traces, I suppose."

"We will, *amigo*." Ditweiler tugged at a mauve handkerchief in his breast pocket and wiped his forehead. "Whew! Evenings in Switzerland are muggier than they used to be." Then he said challengingly, "Of course, it doesn't prove anything."

Guthrie enjoyed this game. "Of course it doesn't. Bauer simply felt a sudden, uncontrollable urge to take a turn outdoors, so he traveled more than halfway across town to the Botanical Gardens in the middle of business hours. He wanted to meet a friend, but he had an urge to do so where the conversation couldn't be monitored. And the meeting itself couldn't wait. It took him no more than a quarter-hour to establish that there's no Jack Garrison registered at the Baur au Lac. That's when he really started to worry. Here's a snooping American who mentions Cologne, has sandy hair and stays in the same hotel room as Marie-Christine. How did he track me down? he wonders, then begins to understand. Perhaps someone took down his car number the other night after all? But if I'm a CIA agent, why do I tip my hand so grossly? What's the point? It's illogical. Bauer is rattled: suppose I turn up again, pry some more? Therefore, he calls his contact for a crash meeting—"

"Very good," Ditweiler said approvingly, and gulped down his brandy. He had delayed his departure for Bern to supervise the operation personally; he had also found time to shave and change his shirt at the Consulate.

"You shouldn't drink that stuff in this weather."

"Of course you should. You're a crude character, Guthrie. I've noticed that before."

Guthrie put down his glass. "It merely proves," he said, playing devil's advocate, "that Bauer has a banker pal."

"Swiss bank presidents don't make brush contact in the park, *amigo*. Now, you mentioned a Third World Committee Bauer belongs to . . ."

"It's pretty effective. The Swiss contribute to it to offset their reputation abroad for niggardliness."

"Weren't some students connected with it picked up near Turin last winter for gunrunning to the Red Brigades? Is that supposed to be a form of disaster relief?"

"Who believes the Italian police? The students were so insignificant that nothing came of it. The committee's reputation wasn't tarnished."

"So what we have, then, as you have so helpfully pointed out, is two pious Swiss burghers, an antique dealer and a banker, who have committed no known crime. Since everything is that proper and unprovable, we'll not confide in brother Huebli at this stage. It would only embarrass him. . . ." Ditweiler's noble face was ruddy from the combined onslaught of heat and cognac. "I know this business inside out. When I think of all the horseshit that's put out . . ." He did not amplify his thought, but continued: "The banks are the bulwark of the system here. No other country in the world, in proportion to its size and population, has so many banks. Monkeying around with a banker in Switzerland rates as sensitive intervention. We've been accused of everything else; let's not take the rap for that. Our task is to score points discreetly."

"Therefore?"

"Therefore," Ditweiler said, "follow up, track back, play out the line . . . but fumble this one and it will be your ass."

He did not pursue the subject, but looked about the cluttered room. "How's bachelor life?"

"Lousy."

"Are you making out with that blonde?"

"Not often enough."

After Ditweiler's departure, Guthrie mixed his own conception of a hot-weather drink—gin drowned in grapefruit juice and ice cubes—turned up the air-conditioning unit, put on a record, kicked off his loafers and padded pleasurably about barefoot retrieving and sorting out various documents and reports about Bruno which he had carried home from the Consulate. His cramped, disordered apartment was strewn with mementos of days at Freiburg and friendships in Vietnam; normally he found it an easy place in which to work, but this evening he couldn't concentrate. He recalled Ditweiler's last question, and tried without success to banish Marie-Christine from his uncalm, leaping imagination. At this moment she was being guard-dogged by two bored members of the station in a breezy chalet above the Lake of Lucerne. In his Audi he could cover the distance in less than a half-hour. Since Starkey's death, his need of her had soared; he had found that out the night before, when, upon arrival at the safe house, he had followed her into the bedroom. Without a word she had shut the door, turned and faced him. Passively, at first, she had tolerated his hands running exploratorily over her sunburned face and fluid hips, but then very quickly she had begun to respond. As he sought and obtained from her a surrender, a warmth and pliancy that blotted out his obsessive memory of the bloody square in Cologne, she had murmured at one point, "When I first met you, I spotted a certain look in your eye, but I wasn't attracted to you at all." Still later, as she lay half spread-eagled over him and traced the initial G across his breastbone, she added, "You may find yourself being happy. Don't you want to be?" When he left three hours later, she had wanted him to stay, and he had foreseen that he would return. On the surface, no problem existed; on the surface . . .

At midnight, his neck clammy with sweat, his shirt unbuttoned to the waist, he set aside his checklist of unelucidated points, which remained intact, as baffling as ever. Where was Bruno? What had happened to him during the missing years 1962–70, between Dieter Koenig's disappearance from Marseille and his reappearance in Paris? What did Seeblick and Rosenthalerstrasse refer to? And to this list of questions could now be added still another, murkier line of speculation: if one assumed that De Wrendt was Bruno's shadowy mentor, what exactly was a reputable Swiss banker doing in the enigmatic and murderous Aurora network?

Part Two

What's to do?
A piece of work that will make sick men whole.
But are not some whole that we must make sick?
That must we also.

—Shakespeare

Chapter Twelve

Two Gentlemen of Zurich

"THE STRATEGY of destabilization—keeping up pressure through repeated attacks on already mushy institutions—is particularly applicable to Western Europe," De Wrendt was saying. "Present-day Europe's trouble is that it has no faith in itself."

Maxim Maisky smiled.

"Since 1914, perhaps it has never had. A banker's office, incidentally, is an excellent vantage point from which to observe failures of faith. I see astonishing examples of it daily."

"How is business at your office? I seem to read more and more criticism of Swiss banks."

"Swiss banking, like most institutions, doesn't possess the virtues it pretends to. Lately we've wallowed in mismanagement of funds, arrests, suicide; we're called hypocrites, usurers, bandits; there are a few too many 'brass-plate' outfits." De Wrendt shrugged. "It has no effect on the balance sheet. People are only too eager to swallow myths. You'd be amused how superstition enters into the disposition of considerable sums of money."

Maisky sampled his consommé Madrilène and lightly wiped his lips. They were dining outdoors on the semicircular terrace at the Dolder Grand Hotel on the forested heights above Zurich; far below, the lake gleamed rarefied and opulent like a black diamond in the clear night. The evergreens roundabout had been warming in the sun all day, and their resinous secretion lingered on the heavy air. Neither man cared especially for the elegant old Victorian construction set in the pinewoods, but it was a convenient rendezvous, away from the city's racket and pollution—and a further advantage was that at this late hour so few tables were occupied that they could talk without taking complex precautions against being overheard.

"You said Bauer wanted a crash meeting?"

"He called me up at the bank. I couldn't very well refuse, although, as it turned out, the request was hardly justified."

"Was he clean when he arrived?"

"Oh, yes, as far as I could determine. It seems an American visited his shop, mentioned Cologne and claimed to have the French girl's room at the Baur au Lac. Quite a lot of nasty coincidences! Bauer promptly panicked. I think I succeeded in calming him." De Wrendt's illusionless gaze lingered on his dining companion. The reasonable assumption, by anyone who might observe them, would be that a Swiss banker and the Soviet Embassy's economic attaché were discussing business together. "Undoubtedly the American is a CIA agent; evidently the Agency has identified Bauer in connection with the botched kidnapping attempt. But what of it? I reminded Bauer that he had been in Zurich, hundreds of kilometers from Cologne, when the assassination occurred, and could prove it. I advised him to master his nerves and, above all, to make sure he's not under surveillance when he comes to my house tomorrow night. I also gave him a good dressing down for provoking an unnecessary crash meeting."

"And can he master his nerves?"

"It is clearly in his own interest. This is an argument Bauer listens to."

De Wrendt's attentive, gray-eyed scrutiny embraced more than the dining room and the civilized, docile lights pricking the hillside. "I think we can definitely assume the French girl tipped the Americans off to the envelope's existence; then someone cleverly interpreted the first notation, which would account for the alert the Germans put out in Cologne."

"Suppose the same person is just as clever about interpreting the other notations?"

"I would say that is highly unlikely."

"Unlikely, but not impossible."

"The operation entails risks, obviously."

"But in your opinion Grand Slam is not compromised?"

"The target is arriving on August 21, per schedule. My contact at the Linder Clinic has confirmed the date. Bruno is safe as of this moment. In sum, nothing is changed."

"What about the girl?"

"She disappeared from her hotel—collected her clothes and paid her bill—and is perhaps being protected by the CIA. However, she has done all the damage she can. At any rate, there is no reason to alter the operational plan."

Maisky considered De Wrendt's long, but far from ascetic, greyhound head and found himself relieved by his unruffled manner and tone.

"I have to tell you that Moscow Center insists on transferring Bruno to Algeria and keeping him there until the uproar about Wadi Khalef subsides. He is to fly out after the debriefing. The arrangements have been completed at the Algerian end."

"He may object to that."

Maisky looked at the banker speculatively. Although Maisky, as head of the Swiss *Residentura* and third-ranking officer at the Soviet Embassy, outranked De Wrendt, he never committed the error of talking down to the older man. "For a number of reasons the transfer is desirable," he said in his throaty Ukrainian tenor. "The Americans lost an agent in Cologne and are going to hunt down his murderer actively. In Algeria our friend can alter his appearance at leisure and familiarize himself with his new cover. It's better for him to cut loose temporarily from Europe." Stolidly, Maisky took his time, so as to marshal his arguments before broaching the next, uncomfortable topic; stolidity was one of his innate characteristics, reflected as much in his laborious pauses as in the deliberate way he ate. "The problem, you understand, is that in the past week or so he's become quite a celebrity. From the start we wished Aurora to have a low profile. It did, until that unfortunate business in Paris."

De Wrendt was sensitive to the distinct strain of implied criticism in the other's voice. "He had no choice in that trap but to shoot his way out. He didn't set out to become a public figure. An ironic twist is that the holdup man the French police were actually after surrendered yesterday in Lyon."

Maisky, however, wouldn't let go. "I expect it was asking too much under the circumstances for your protégé not to gain instant notoriety. But one danger is that all the tawdry publicity could go to his head."

De Wrendt stared about at the few remaining diners on the terrace, and then his impenetrable gaze came to rest on Maisky. "It will not go to his head. And as for the publicity, it can be turned around. If Bruno is going to Algiers, he should hold a press conference upon arrival and make the usual statements about fighting for a Palestinian homeland. You can imagine the French and Germans relaxing, happily convincing themselves that the problem has shifted elsewhere, which is what they profoundly want."

"I don't think we want to give him any more exposure than he has already received. He is an instrument, after all, and not an end."

"Since Paris he's done very well."

"I'm not challenging his record."

De Wrendt hesitated, then spoke in his understated, powerful manner. "Do you know why in the first place I recruited him? There were obvious qualifications—marksmanship, smattering of Arabic, tactical-leadership qualities, disregard of physical danger; and even his past membership in the OAS, which could so automatically inspire people to make the wrong assumptions about his political loyalties. But considerations of that sort always come afterward. I chose him because I could control him, because he is in my debt."

Maisky listened politely, as he always did to De Wrendt: this meticulously groomed man redolent of lime scent and privilege was seldom not worth listening to. But Maisky was already acquainted with the facts of Bruno's original recruitment, and another, quite different preoccupation was gnawing at his ingrained, officious sense of administration. He could not forbear from commenting almost rudely, "You look tired."

"I *am* tired. Running a bank and conducting this career burn up an enormous emount of energy. Once Bruno is safely aboard the Algiers flight, I plan to take a few days' vacation."

"On Ibiza?"

"I go there in August each year. It does my cover good. Security people are always comforted by a recurrent pattern," he declared icily. "Shall we have another bottle?"

Maisky frowned. "By all means," he said. It was unlike De Wrendt to linger at table: he was a professed believer in De Gaulle's dictum that the most important meal in the world should not exceed one hour. In spite of his bronzed complexion, De Wrendt really did not look well: something was fretting at his nerves; Maisky couldn't put his finger on it, but he was sure. He was thinking of De Wrendt's dual, phenomenal careers played out with *brio* over four decades, the details of which Maisky knew by heart, and which had contributed to the near-legend at Moscow Center.

In the late thirties, De Wrendt, as a young man, had descended upon Switzerland from his native Budapest and started work in a large commercial bank near Bahnhofstrasse. Already he was running and tacking, with the Center's dexterous assistance. The Center in those unpredictable days of the rise of Nazism was foresightedly infiltrating a number of sleepers into Swiss society, who would later form the vital nucleus of the celebrated wartime Red Orchestra. At the bank, De Wrendt, one of this group, rose from *aide-gestionnaire* to commercial agent, while the war raged around neutral Zurich. As early as 1952 he was a *fondé de pouvoir* in a small private bank with considerable liquid assets and a sound reputation; by 1957 he was a partner and director; by 1960 he had bought out a senior colleague's share, and four years later the bank bore his name. Simultaneously, his covert career had flourished: by 1942, De Wrendt was operational; he had not ceased being so since, through the hectic ups and downs of the Cold War. At one time running NATO's chief information office, he had also played a sensitive role in knocking off a troublesome and deceitful British diplomatic courier; his most memorable coup, however, had been in stealing the top-secret Emerald file from the International Atomic Energy Agency's headquarters in Vienna during the Six-Day War. Throughout those years, his photograph had been taken only once by a security service. In the photo he had appeared tall, rather stiff of carriage, his persona imbued with the faintly cruel swagger of a Venetian rake in the Doges' time, his expression veiled by dark glasses as effectively as by a domino.

Had the Swiss at one stage or another of his parallel successful careers ever sniffed him out? The attitude of the Swiss toward espionage was extremely ambivalent—merciless when it was directed against their military security, indulgent if it was carried out from their territory against other powers—and it was possible that they had shut their eyes to some telltale sign or other.

De Wrendt had always known how far to go and no further: Switzerland had served as a base for his far-flung operations, but these were never undertaken against Swiss interests; he had meticulously avoided stumbling into that pitfall for spies, espionage against Swiss defense secrets, which could bring the entire nation's wrath thundering down upon the hapless agent who was caught. So for almost four decades he had gone unscathed, a professional with an unblemished dossier, who had achieved impeccable status in Zurich society. His heterogeneous network comprised airport personnel at Kloten, journalists, nervous industrialists who were hedging their bets in the event of a Soviet invasion of Western Europe. Then, with the decline of classic espionage in the late sixties and the burgeoning of international terrorism, he had played a pivotal role in setting up and funding the little-known Aurora network to provide Moscow Center with direct insight into the underground scene, as a base for manipulation and, not least, to outflank the opposition—that was, the CIA. Maisky, who was no beginner at the game, admitted to himself that few illegals he knew could have achieved half as much. This was one reason why he treated De Wrendt's views with unfailing deference.

And yet in spite of the brilliant, durable record, something was wrong—the conversation throughout dinner had acted joltingly on Maisky, and left him deeply disturbed. Although he was fourteen years younger than the man seated across the table, as a case officer in Vienna and Bern Maisky had accumulated a practical, cynical expertise that comes from wet-nursing field agents of all stripes, frightened and overconfident, neurotic and slow-witted. When danger signals went up, he knew where to search for clues to their origin: that afternoon, already worried, he had restudied De Wrendt's personal file, paying special attention to various sources' comments on the banker's persisting domestic problems—his separation from his wife, his antagonistic relationship with his teen-age son.

Then, in the corresponding professional file, Maisky had come upon further evidence of—he hardly knew what to call it: of detachment, notably in De Wrendt's scarcely concealed contempt for the terror tactics to which he paid lip service and which he so skillfully coordinated. As Maisky tasted the wine from the second bottle, the answer suddenly came to him—De Wrendt had been at this game overly long: his twofold, probably incurable ailments were age and satiety. Maisky observed him with genuine curiosity. Shirt and tie from Lanvin, cuff links from Guebelin on Bahnhofstrasse, hair razor-cut and dyed at the Dolder barber's.

A Hungarian Conrad Veidt! During his long exile, the banker had divested himself of the gaudier aspects of Hungarian charm, that effective but insincere and occasionally saccharine charm which is such a trademark of Magyar relations with the outside world, but he had retained a gliding, frictionless deportment, an acute eye for the main chance and available females.

It was easy to conceive how he had wheeled and dealt, enlarged his network and feathered his nest in a war-stunned Central Europe, but the former, Manichean world of contrasting good and evil of the forties and fifties was unarguably dead. How did this banker of sixty-some years feel in the pop world of the seventies where cultures, sexes, ideologies and presumably even loyalties crazily overlapped? Displaced? Adrift?

Analogous ideas were running through De Wrendt's mind. Approaching sixty-two, he viewed the past—his vibrant, uncommon past—as a monstrous cliff cutting off the light on the plain in the middle of the afternoon. Old age is no country for men, he speculated without a trace of indulgence. He had an acute, informed sense of Europe's being on the hinge—in a few years it was inevitable that a Leftist society would be in place. Perhaps he had contributed modestly to the outcome, done his bit. But now he was indeed exhausted to the core. . . .

"Have you thought of retiring?" Maisky asked bluntly.

De Wrendt raised his elegant eyebrows and gave back stare for intractable stare. "Not so long as I can be of use."

Until Grand Slam was successfully terminated, a disposition of the problem could wait, Maisky decided.

Chapter Thirteen

The Eye of the Storm

THE CAR ferry takes a shade under forty-five minutes to cross the Lake of Constance from Friedrichshafen, in Germany, to Romanshorn, in Switzerland. On that warm, windy evening, the last boat arrived on schedule just past 8 P.M. with only ten cars aboard, all of which had ordinary German or Swiss plates save for a Zis limousine that bore yellow-and-green Diplomatic Corps plates and a Chief of Mission's oval plaque bolted to its rear bumper. A kepied Swiss inspector came out of the Customs building at the foot of the landing pier and removed a link chain that was looped across the five exit lanes; then one car at a time drove down the ramp and came to a stop beside the building, where the inspector examined the occupants' passports and checked the number of passengers inside. Choosing an Opel with Frankfurt plates, he made the driver open up the hood, glanced through the interior and then waved the car on. The Zis was the last car to stop. The inspector saluted, took the three dark red Soviet diplomatic passports which the chauffeur had handed to him and cursorily leaned forward to count the occupants. For a second or two he was puzzled. In the rear sat two men: one middle-aged, well dressed and swart; the other a chunky, youngish straw-blond who glanced at him stonily out of light blue eyes and whose face was troublingly familiar. His passport identified him, in Russian and English, merely as an assistant commercial attaché. The inspector was sure that he had recently seen a mechanical sketch of the second man in the papers or on television in connection with an incident abroad, an investigation of a crime or a trial. But he could not recall the exact context, and he was not paid or encouraged to detain diplomats unless specific evidence came to light of illegal entry or flagrant violation of Swiss duty regulations. There was no such evidence, and his memory might be at fault. On the infrequent occasions in the past when he had discovered an irregularity in a foreign diplomat's papers or declaration, it had invariably resulted in a nasty scene and his chief's failure to back him up. He looked again at the passport, and drawing upon past experience, he stepped back and cleared the limousine through the checkpoint.

Ten minutes later, the inspector snap-bolted the chain into place, locked up the Customs office for the night, mounted his bicycle and pedaled home with no further thought for the Zis passenger

The Zis itself had veered left from Romanshorn and was following the shore road eastward. The two men in the rear remained silent until they were in open country. Then the swart man, the Soviet military attaché in Bonn, said in his rudimentary English; "The Customs inspector seemed to recognize you."

Bruno shrugged. He was stiff and irritable after the non-stop six-hour journey from Cologne, and he had no intention of favoring conversation with the man beside him, whom he disliked.

They passed through the sedate old lakeside town of Rorschach without stopping. The Embassy chauffeur continued eastward, encountering little traffic. Between walled waterfront estates they caught occasional glimpses of the gray, sealike lake. The sun was down in the west now, and the farther, German shore invisible. About ten miles beyond Rorschach, under cover of increasing dark, they turned into the driveway of a property bordered by thick, centenary beeches. A two-story gabled house facing the lake rose at the end of the driveway. Lights shone in the windows of a ground-floor room.

For the past quarter-hour two men had been waiting in the salon—De Wrendt beside the semidrawn window curtain, and Bauer, who was massively ensconced in a sofa beside the fireplace. Spotting the Zis, De Wrendt left with his measured, courtly step to unlock the front door. As two of the limousine's three occupants slipped into the hall, he saw that the chauffeur, obeying instructions, had remained with the car and was still seated behind the wheel, where he could survey the long driveway.

"I'm delighted the trip went well." De Wrendt gripped Bruno's hand with genuine affection, while his brain recorded the fact that Bauer had made no move to join them and was critically observing the encounter in dead silence.

"Why shouldn't it have gone well?" Bruno stood in the center of the salon, taut and irate. He wore a nondescript suit of clothes that was his size yet somehow didn't belong to him.

"A drink? I imagine you need a large one." De Wrendt had started toward a maple sideboard, but Bruno swerved impatiently aside from the whiskey decanter and tall glasses.

"I didn't even bother to crawl into the recess behind the rear seat before we passed through German Customs," he said. "I don't believe in these adolescent tricks. Can you imagine a civil servant with enough guts to stop a Soviet Embassy limousine even if he suspected it harbored a terrorist? These bureaucrats are all scared shitless by the threat of a diplomatic incident with Moscow."

De Wrendt grimaced. The congratulatory mood was

shattered. His husky voice was crisp and aloof again. "In your position I wouldn't crowd my luck. Be thankful I planned your escape route. You'd still be in Cologne if it weren't for the considerable help I and others organized in your behalf."

"Cologne?" Bruno snorted. "From the moment I left the cathedral I was followed. Hans-Peter was followed. Wadi Khalef came with a bodyguard instead of his chauffeur. . . ." His pale blue eyes flicked suspiciously over all the people in the room, including the military attaché, who was taking no part in the meeting and plainly was restless with his unwanted role as supernumerary. "Instead of a clean operation"—his metallic, unimpressive voice scratched like flint against the attentive silence—"we had an amateurish, bloody mess."

He's beginning to swagger, De Wrendt thought in dismay, reminded of his conversation with Maisky. He's beginning to behave as though he were on prime-time television. Surveying him, De Wrendt thought, Take away his popgun and there's nothing left but a corner boy. No, he rectified his judgment, that was much too superficial; Bruno had qualities that merited definite respect, those mentioned to Maisky at the Dolder; but indisputably an element of self-glorification was creeping into his conduct. Furthermore, there was no excuse for his arrogance.

"What sort of horseshit is this?" Wheeling his bulk cumbersomely about on the sofa, Bauer had broken his ominous silence. "Whose fault was the mess, anyway?" He jerked his head in Bruno's direction. "To begin with, he puts information down in writing . . . a security breach. Then he entrusts his notes to a Parisian bourgeois slut—a *bourgeoise*, mind you, who never had a political idea in her spoiled life and for whom collaborating with the police is as automatic as buying a new pair of shoes. Then *he* has the gall to complain. . . ."

With misleading conciliatoriness, Bruno glanced down at his shoe tips—probably nothing suited his mood more than a clash with Bauer, De Wrendt guessed. There had been a time when Bruno had expressed what he felt, but over the past decade, at the indoctrination school outside Baku, then at the Iraqi training camp, he'd learned the value of veiling his emotions, especially among comrades. That must also worry Maisky. A terrorist with secret inner thoughts and feelings was no more reliable than an *agent provocateur*.

Bauer glared and bore relentlessly on: ". . . And finally he leaves a bagful of handguns in plain view *on a bed* where the first policeman with the smallest brain is bound to spot it and start asking questions."

Bruno's unfeeling stare settled momentarily on Bauer. That pale, hard body, that bloated girth. Bauer had the possessed glint of a clergyman who was determined to extirpate sin at whatever pain to the sinner; but beneath the severe jowls a perceptible, subcutaneous vein of hedonism trembled: a middle-aged queer who'd gone berserk with grenades and a caseful of ammunition. Six days out of seven he buttered up affluent customers; on Sundays he read the Bible to neighborhood morons, and nights he spent preaching urban guerrilla war. There are only a few people I'd let stand behind me, and Bauer isn't one of them, Bruno thought. Aloud, he observed with deceptive mildness, "I gave that girl my notes for the same reason I slept in her apartment: because she had no contact with terrorist cells. I've used other women in other cities who supplied the same cover. Right?"

"Right," De Wrendt snapped.

"But Marie-Christine leaked the Cologne timetable. To prevent that from happening, I wanted her held where she couldn't contact the police. It wasn't difficult—but the simple matter of hustling her into a car proved too much; she made a fool of an old—"

Bauer's thick face was russet, and his sunken hazel eyes blinked too rapidly.

"—a fool of us all, and she escaped," Bruno modified his

conclusion smoothly. "Where is she now? We don't know. What do we plan to do about it?" He mimicked an effeminate voice while making a point of letting his chill gaze rest on Bauer. "We're thinking it over. Christ! She knows too much about me, and that makes me uncomfortable. Priority has to go to—"

"Priority goes to getting you out of Europe," De Wrendt cut in. "Forget about the girl. Later, possibly, she will have to be dealt with—though after Grand Slam it may not seem so important." He was incensed by Bruno's reaction. Maisky might worry about celebrity going to Bruno's head, but the real danger was his inherent destructiveness, his readiness to lash out at whoever upset his plans: no matter how much one defended the Paris fusillade, it had unarguably contained an element of trigger-happiness. And in Bruno's erratic past there were detectable early symptoms of the same dangerous disease. He imagined himself to be cool, collected and logical, but he wasn't. . . .

"You'll be flying to Algiers as soon as arrangements are completed." De Wrendt uttered the order with flat decisiveness. "Meanwhile, the chauffeur is driving you to Geneva tonight after our business is finished. You'll stay in the bank's apartment."

Bruno's opaque stare switched to him. "What makes you think I want to go to Algiers?"

"It's your old theater of operations."

"I'm not longing to visit it again. Moreover, someone there may recognize me."

"What of it? You shot up a few Arabs, but it was in wartime. Don't you think the Algerians are as opportunistic as anybody else? Now you're a front-line freedom fighter for a cause they endorse and support."

"I'd prefer Libya."

"Only in theory. As soon as you spent twenty-four hours there, you'd loathe it. Everybody with the slightest sense does. We are being extremely careful to cut them out of this operation—it's not meant to be a half-baked vaudeville turn."

Bruno measured De Wrendt's lean, formidable jaw. Some men had the quality—or was it instinct?—of persuasion in their blood. When De Wrendt wanted to, he could be overwhelmingly convincing. "How long am I supposed to hang around Geneva?"

"Forty-eight hours, I should think."

"I don't want it to stretch out. I've had my fill recently of other people's apartments."

"Yes, that's understandable. It won't be longer. The concierge has already been informed that one of the bank's important clients will be using the apartment for a short time; occasionally we *do* put up legitimate clients, so he won't be suspicious. Still, avoid him as much as possible. There are plenty of books and records, so you won't be bored; stay indoors without overdoing it, but when you go out take your meals at restaurants far away, in a different neighborhood each time. I'd prefer to keep you here, but I have a gardener who *is* nosy. Besides, when the signal comes from Algiers we may have to get you on the plane in a hurry, and the flight leaves from Geneva."

Bruno studied the palms of his agile hands. "You'll have to get me a girl."

"I'll see what I can do." De Wrendt's eyes had flickered momentarily in Bauer's direction.

Bruno had noticed the glance. "Him? Are you asking *him* to provide a woman?"

Portentous and immobile, Bauer addressed De Wrendt. "We can probably unearth someone," he rumbled. "Someone who isn't sleeping with the CIA."

Bruno grinned predatorily. "Look, if this son of a bitch is going to keep sniping, I won't take it. Instead of listening to any more of his shit, I'll hurt him."

"Shut up. Don't give ultimatums." De Wrendt's tone was peremptory. He couldn't afford to seem to favor one man over the other. On occasions like this, Bruno's weak points became disturbingly obvious: conceit, insubordination, quarrelsomeness. "Bauer raised a valid point. Why take notes? Why not commit everything to memory?"

Bruno stared incredulously at him. "An imbecile relies on memory. Memory can be unreliable."

"Did you jot anything else down?"

"No."

Bauer was listening deadpan and seemed disappointed by the reply.

Brusquely Bruno confronted the banker. "Am I still in charge or not?"

"Of operational details, yes. Bauer handles administration. The network functions under a split command—you know that."

"Are you faulting my operational command?"

"I am not," De Wrendt said neutrally.

"That's fine, because I don't intend to step down."

De Wrendt was very angry but in control of himself. "No one is asking you to," he said. "Cologne succeeded, but both of you made mistakes. The point is, we can afford no more blunders, and certainly no more of this constant wrangling." The problem had been smoldering for months. Bauer was eager to take over Aurora and embark on an indiscriminate campaign of terrorism in England, Germany and France. With his affected manners and flagrant homosexuality, however, he had had trouble at first being taken seriously. Then his interest had focused on Bernard Rubin, a Jewish real estate promoter in London whose prodigious fund raising for Israel had marked him out as a prime target of several terrorist rings. It was a question of who would get to him first. A month later, Rubin was grabbed from his Bentley outside a Park Lane gambling club under the nose of a bobby. When a ransom of a half-million pounds was paid, he was found in a coma—chained, head shaven, viciously beaten—in a North London cellar, a "People's prison," with a card listing the amounts he had transferred to Tel Aviv and the revolutionary cell's Guilty verdict looped around his neck; it was Bauer who had snatched him, and henceforward his clandestine reputation was made. Physically, De Wrendt found

Bauer repulsive: the man had no hide—if one stuck one's finger between his ribs, it sank into folds of gelatin. But De Wrendt was impatient with his own disgust, for Bauer had qualities. The strength of his position was that he believed what he preached—he was an oracle of wrath whose rolling voice lent his intolerant homilies a certain momentary impressiveness, although his mind, to De Wrendt, seemed a ferment of pseudo-verities or, more precisely, a kettle of boiling water from which a jet of silly notions steamed.

As De Wrendt scanned both men, he knew that enough authority flowed to him to force them to cooperate with each other for the time being. The relationship might ultimately break down, but it had to be temporarily sustained for a simple reason. He needed both of them to carry out Grand Slam.

Chapter Fourteen

De Wrendt's Wife

DITWEILER, AWASH in sweat, came off the tennis court. The club pro had informed him that modern tennis is almost exclusively a matter of serve and volley, and Ditweiler applied this theory with a disciple's fervor, bombarding his opponent with deep, rocket serves, then rushing to the net with a slam-bang assortment of shots. He had just won, 5–7, 6–3, 6–2, and grunting contentedly, he parked his well-nourished rump on the grass. Guthrie considered him with aversion. If I can't beat him, I'd better give up, he thought, recalling how twice he had walked into traps. I should give up tennis anyway and stick to boating. I'm more at home on water than on land. My ancestors must have been fish.

"I thought I'd better tell you orally what I found out," Ditweiler said. "De Wrendt was born Károly Lukács in Budapest in 1917. He turned up in Switzerland in his early twenties, changed his name and subsequently, after making a career in banking, obtained Swiss nationality—doing so was easier in those days. He works twelve hours a day. His bank is solid: it manages trust accounts, acts as executor of wills, participates in bond issues and grabs whatever other business it can. De Wrendt built it up into a fifteen-million-dollar-net-income operation. That's an achievement, but not so much as it sounds. International banking includes some sleepyheads and certifiable morons; when a bright guy turns up on the circuit, the others don't provide much of a match. It's like you in tennis," he added unambiguously. "De Wrendt has a reputation for being tough in his trade, a guy who doesn't refuse to sully his fingers; outside banking hours, he manages to be a friend to all the world. He's a member in good standing of Zurichberg society; living here, you know what that means . . ."

". . . anybody who can afford it," Guthrie murmured.

"He doesn't actually live on Zurichberg; he has an apartment on the top floor of his bank and a summer house near Rorschach, on the Lake of Constance. He has a seat on the board of Oerlikon, the arms makers; he's a patron of the Zurich Art Society and a director of the Linder Clinic—"

"—and he knows Bauer."

"That's blameless, at least on the surface. One item in the traces is less stuffy and relevant. The flag went up on him in '44 as a possible Soviet agent. Something to do with a Nazi military attaché in Bern and a tiny mistake in rendezvous times. A Ukrainian the British were running asserted that Moscow Center had had a hand in settling De Wrendt in Switzerland. But the Ukrainian himself was far from kosher, there was a lot of confusion at war's end and the lead, for what it was worth, petered out or wasn't actively pursued. Ever since, De Wrendt's spent his time—as I should have if I'd had any sense—becoming richer. . . ." Ditweiler scrambled to his feet and swiped at the grass stains on his white shorts. "If he is a Center illegal, he may be one of the few Rote Kapelle agents still alive and operational. Fascinating speculation, isn't it?"

"Does he consort with Maisky?"

"The shlock king of espionage in my burg, you mean? They've been spotted together. Infrequently—nothing to write home to your aunt Tilly about. I wouldn't call it consorting. No conclusive evidence of any unholy relationship. Maisky sees a lot of people in his working day—"

"Maisky runs a lot of people, too."

"True."

Another idea had occurred to Guthrie. "The guns and ammunition in Bruno's tennis bag came from Oerlikon, didn't they?"

"So what? Trying to establish a connection is impossible. Oerlikon sells hardware to a dozen African countries: the possibilities for hanky-panky are limitless." Ditweiler stared beyond the tennis court. "De Wrendt's private life is a mess. Six months ago he separated from his wife; he wanted a divorce, but she's holding out for a cash and property settlement that would tide New York City over for a decade. His teen-age son sides with the mother; incidentally, the son is studying in the States. Since the separation —before too, for that matter—De Wrendt has had a number of girlfriends. They're culled from his milieu—sleek little divorcées, titled mannequins. The romance never lasts more than a few months: it seems he tires of them, not the other way around. His wife's a German; she did a bit of acting before their marriage in 1955, then went back on the stage briefly in the sixties. She's living in Castagnola, outside Lugano. Why don't you drive down there in your Audi? It's a nice drive at this time of year."

"Why do you think his wife will talk to me?"

"Because according to Zurichberg gossip, she's goddamn hopping mad at him. So maybe she'll have something to say."

"Unless, of course, she belongs to Aurora or sympathizes with it. Germany breeds women terrorists the way it used to breed soldiers."

"That's a determination for you to make. Chat her up. The trip won't even come out of your operational funds."

He had thoughtfully replaced the six tennis balls in their box. "What did you dig up?"

"I tracked back on Bauer. In the trade he passes for reputable, but one of his suppliers is a French antique dealer named Pierre Rubinstein, who's considered a crook. Bauer travels frequently to Paris to meet Rubinstein, and makes an abnormal number of calls to him. At first glance they don't seem to have enough in common to justify the heavy traffic. Interestingly, Rubinstein has a son, Jean-Charles, who's had a record as a revolutionary militant since the May '68 riots. The French are taking another look at Rubinstein *père* and *fils*, and monitoring the calls."

Ditweiler wiped his face but for a moment said nothing. August 9, the second notation, had come and gone with no further violence—therefore, it was possible the two other notations on Bruno's list referred not to new attacks but to arrangements within the network; or were Aurora's ringleaders being crafty, and was it the lull before the storm? "Bauer is being careful since your visit. He drove out of Zurich last night but gave my guys the slip. Maybe he was only delivering that Compagnie des Indes dish to a higher bidder."

Guthrie waited for Renata de Wrendt on the terrace of her house. The Italian cleaning woman who had admitted him had declared that the *Signora* was in the rock garden below. Oleanders and mimosa, phlox and alyssum throbbed in the southern light, and the flagstone terrace shimmered with heat. The house itself was a whitewashed peasant cottage similar to those remodeled by painters in the nearby artists' colony of Gandria, and it boasted a spectacular view of rugged slopes tumbling headlong into a small limpid hill lake.

Then De Wrendt's wife appeared—a raven-haired, green-eyed woman in her forties with trim hips and fine, unadorned arms nicely bronzed. She wore a polo shirt over corduroy slacks and had hedge clippers in one hand.

"You're from the American Consulate? Come inside where we can talk." The German accent was buffed over but audible.

Guthrie sat on a large sofa in the breezy living room and noted vases of cut flowers everywhere, pottery and paperbacks. The house's style, like the owner's, was clear and welcoming.

"It's about my son's visa, isn't it?" She drew off her garden gloves, and he remarked her well-manicured nails.

"No, I came about an antique dealer in Zurich named Franz Bauer," Guthrie said. "Know him?"

"Of course. We bought a set of chairs from him. He overcharged us." She manifested some surprise. "Why are you interested in Bauer?"

On a hunch, Guthrie discarded the story he had prepared. "He's probably involved in a terrorist network. They mounted an attack in Cologne a few days ago. . . ."

"Bauer involved? Pudgy, sanctimonious Bauer? You must be joking." She tossed back her glossy black mane. "The notion of Bauer's being a terrorist is funny. I wasn't aware he had political ideas of any sort. Incidentally, why did you come to me? Why don't you go to my husband for information?"

"He's a very busy man, like most Swiss bankers."

Her intelligent eyes sized him up. "I see. You didn't want to go to him. Are you really from the Consulate? I have a feeling about you."

Guthrie was beginning to admire her poise and directness. He could imagine her entrance onstage: she had probably garnered good reviews. "What does your feeling tell you?"

"I'm not sure yet. What else did you want to ask?"

He tried a shot in the dark. "Did you ever meet one of your countrymen from Bremen, a mercenary named Dieter Koenig? Straw-blond, brawny, not too big?"

Renata de Wrendt smiled this time. "How did you find *that* out? Not that it's a secret, but it was a long time ago."

146

"It's important. I'd like to hear everything you know about him."

She shook her head. "I'm not sure that I want to tell you. Do you realize that your manners are awful? You turn up unannounced in my house with no introduction or identification and straight off you begin interrogating me."

"We're trying to run to earth a terrorist network and are hoping to enlist your cooperation."

"Who is 'we'? How do I even know you're with the U.S. Government?"

"You could telephone the Consulate in Zurich for confirmation."

She nodded smartly and rose to her feet. Without going to the telephone, however, she asked, "Do you want something to drink?"

Guthrie relaxed a little. "I'd like a beer."

"I thought you might. I could tell that about you as soon as you marched in."

He followed her exit from the room. Her long, coal-black hair and somber eyebrows were almost Mediterranean. If a Carmen from Berlin were conceivable, she could have played the role—that, or Mutter Courage.

When she returned, she set down a tray with two tall glasses of beer and sipped from one, watching him.

"All right, I'll satisfy your curiosity," she said. "My husband and I met Dieter when we were driving through Spain in 1968. The front-door lock of our car didn't work, so we stopped at a little roadside café outside Tossa del Mar on the Costa Brava to ask where the nearest garage was. The café manager was a neat young German who turned out to be Dieter. He offered to try to fix the lock himself. It proved to be more of a job than he thought; another person would have shrugged his shoulders or sent us to a Mercedes dealer. Finally he got the lock out, repaired it and charged us only the minimum for his trouble. It sounds like nothing at all, but we were both impressed by the way he went about it. So a month later, on our way back, we made a point of stopping at the same café for lunch. My husband hit it off well with Dieter and questioned him about his background. It turned out that he'd served in the Foreign Legion, then drifted down into Spain, tried his hand at this and that, and was barely making ends meet. . . . To make a long story short, my husband asked whether he'd consider coming to Switzerland to work."

"As what?"

"As a bank courier. My husband had had someone else who quit."

Guthrie speculated but said nothing and let her go on.

"Dieter came to Zurich and got a work permit. My husband said to me, 'Of course, he's rough around the edges; he's never had anyone to open doors for him. But he's thorough, quick and ambitious. Let's see what happens if I open a door.' " She finished her glass of beer and set it down on the tray. "My husband did all that was humanly possible: lent him money, encouraged him to feel he had someone he could count on . . ."

"Well?"

"Dieter simply walked out one day the following spring without explanation and disappeared. My husband was so enraged that he never mentioned his name again."

"Where did he go?"

"I got the impression that he left Switzerland."

One key piece of the puzzle was in place, Guthrie thought, but others still lay scattered formlessly about. "What was your opinion of him?"

"Frankly, I didn't always share my husband's enthusiasm. I was never convinced that gratitude was one of Dieter's strong suits. One doesn't mind helping, but one likes a word of thanks."

"Nowadays he doesn't call himself Dieter anymore." She regarded him with interest. "He calls himself Bruno."

"The terrorist in Cologne?" Renata de Wrendt's color changed perceptibly for a second, and her hand strayed to her throat. "I had no idea," she said carefully at last, "but I can't say I'm altogether surprised."

Guthrie reminded himself that she was a former actress who had played roles professionally. "Oh?"

"He has a vicious streak and a temper as flimsy as matchwood. . . ."

"In what way?"

"I don't want to go into it." A flash of remembered anger darkened her luminous eyes, and Guthrie intuitively understood. When had De Wrendt's protégé made love to her? How long had the affair lasted, and who had ended it? The relationship, it was clear, had left a flat aftertaste. "Speaking for myself"—she had abruptly regained her habitual composure—"I wouldn't trust him with an idea, let alone an ideology. Basically he's just one more bloody-minded, mixed-up German, and I know what they're like."

Guthrie made a rapid calculation: 1969 was nine years back; that was when today's terrorists had begun to receive their first training in Middle Eastern camps. Had someone with quiet persuasiveness recruited Dieter Koenig in Zurich and encouraged him to go underground? Had De Wrendt really been so incensed by his protégé's sudden disappearance? Couldn't it be an example of that expert stage management Moscow Center was so partial to? And had De Wrendt's actress wife been aware of it or duped by it?

"How did he become a terrorist?" she broke into his silence.

"That's one of the things we're trying to find out."

"I can't shed any light there." She frowned. "I realize what you're getting at. My husband once helped Dieter, so perhaps there's still a connection? But it wouldn't make sense. My husband represents what they want to destroy. . . ."

Possibly she believed what she was saying, but Guthrie reminded himself of the hurried meeting between Bauer and De Wrendt in the Botanical Gardens, the traces' reference to De Wrendt's elusive past: tenuous threads, yet threads. . . . His guess was that, on one level at least, Renata de Wrendt knew more about her husband's affairs than she admitted.

"I hope you track down Dieter. It may prove something." She directed a fleeting bleak smile at him. "I'm glad that you came."

As Guthrie started to his feet, it occurred to him how resilient this strong-willed, sensuous woman was. Ditweiler's information had hinted at it. "How long have you been living here?"

"Too long. However, for the moment there's no choice." It was the first time she had mentioned the separation. "I moved out of our apartment in Zurich and didn't want to go to our summer house. There is that penthouse in Geneva which I would have enjoyed, but it belongs to the bank and is definitely not at the disposal of the future ex-Frau de Wrendt; it's supposed to be for VIP clients, but my husband also finds it handy for entertaining impromptu lady friends. You've never met my husband, have you? He's brainy, works like a Trojan and is an assiduous lady-killer. Of course, almost all the men in Zurichberg society fit that description." She rose. "My husband's in Geneva right now. However, if you decide that you want to talk to him about Dieter, you'll have to hurry; he's leaving for Ibiza in a day or two."

Guthrie paused. "Maybe you can answer one more question. Does the word Seeblick mean anything to you?"

It seemed that Renata de Wrendt had never missed a cue in her life. At the threshold of the scorching terrace she stopped. "It's funny that you should ask that. The name of our summer house near Romanshorn is Seeblick."

Chapter Fifteen

The Airport Chapel

IN GENEVA it was raining. The silver Ferrari stopped on rue de Carouge. De Wrendt got out with the suitcase and bareheaded walked quickly through the pelting dark to the apartment building. He rode the elevator to the sixth floor and rang the bell of the penthouse.

"We're getting you out earlier than expected," he said to Bruno, who had admitted him.

"When?"

"Right now. Are you ready?"

"It won't take me long to change." Bruno took the suitcase, began to remove the contents and went into the bedroom.

As De Wrendt waited for him, his eye roamed over those objects in the living room which he had collected on his travels—a tapestry from Bali, a lacquered Chinese bowl, a Spanish abstract construction of wood and metal. They were nice pieces, as befitted clients a bank wished to pamper. He noted that his albums of rock and baroque music were stacked intact on the open teak bookshelves, beside the profusion of paperbacks in English and French accumulated by previous transients. He called out, "Any encounters with the concierge?"

"Only when I moved in. Nothing to worry about."

"What did you do with yourself?"

"I waited for the girl Bauer didn't provide."

"There was no time to organize anything."

When Bruno came out, he was clad in an air steward's navy blue blazer with a single gold stripe on the sleeve, white shirt and navy blue trousers. He was too fair, of course, for a typical crew member of Air Algérie, but, De Wrendt thought, he would pass muster: no one in the airport would be curious; these days airlines employed nonnationals as a matter of course.

"Did you go out at all?"

"Once, for a meal. When I came back, the taxi driver kept staring at me idiotically. He got on my nerves, so as I paid him I said, 'I'm Bruno' and walked away down another street. Naturally, he didn't follow me."

At De Wrendt's quick twitch of anger, Bruno bared his teeth. "I'm making it up, of course."

But was he? De Wrendt realized that he could no longer be sure. It was the sort of conceited and dangerous provocation of which the other man was entirely capable. Curtly, he said, "Did you put your other clothes in the suitcase? Yes? Then we'd better go."

Driving down the glistening boulevard, De Wrendt glanced regularly in the rearview mirror. Traffic was light after the shower. He concluded that they were not being followed. "Board the plane right away. Once aboard, stay in the pilot's cabin. In Algiers your contact will be Leonid —he will know how to reach you at the camp."

Bruno made no reply, and De Wrendt had the disconcerting impression that he wasn't interested.

"Did you get that right?"

Bruno twisted his head around slowly and stared at him. "I heard you the first time. Relax."

"You don't seem to be concentrating enough on your departure."

"Yes, I am. I happened to be wondering which has changed more in sixteen years—Algiers or me."

"How would I know?"

"It's the sort of question that occurs to anyone who is not a damn fool."

For a minute or two De Wrendt did not reply. "We all change. And the situation is not the same either."

The tone was so studiedly noncommittal that Bruno turned again to look at him with curiosity.

"You mean that in those days you didn't deal with roughnecks like me, except to filch a few defense papers and eliminate the odd troublemaker. Intelligence services were gentlemanly. Espionage, sabotage, blackmail: in case one was tactless enough to ask, it was all a clever game between educated players."

"We never called it a game," De Wrendt retorted. "Only the English did that. But you have a point. Motivations were possibly less murky; there was no confusion about the enemy. Certainly there were fewer players."

"I wonder why you went to so much effort to recruit me into your snobbish world."

"What makes you think I did? When you came to us, you were really wet behind the ears and were meant to be an occasional agent in North Africa, where you could be of some use. The terrorism business came later. I must admit, you've done well at it and made a name for yourself." His voice was stony with distaste.

Bruno grinned. "It's a growth industry, and I happened to get in on the ground floor."

"Since you're such a success, why can't you get on, if only superficially, with Bauer?"

"That swollen ego yelping about upheaval. Aurora isn't a political movement; it has no popular clout and never will. Our purpose is not to incite riots but to tilt the situation with pinpointed operations like Grand Slam. You said so yourself at one time."

"I still maintain so." But De Wrendt couldn't quite purge a tincture of heretical disbelief from his voice. "I got into this business when I was twenty-three, because I passionately believed in a cause. Now there are so many days when I am no longer sure." Indiscriminate skepticism, it occurred to him, was the end product of a career in Intelligence: it had sifted like grit into every fold of his brain, paralyzing his faith.

The rest of the way to the airport they drove in silence. Upon parking at the far end of the terminal lot, De Wrendt made sure that Bruno, as he got out, had left behind the suitcase with the incriminating clothes.

"I wouldn't worry about the situation at the Algerian end. You'll be there only a few days and have limited exchanges with the people at the camp. They're merely providing temporary facilities." De Wrendt held out his hand. "We'll see you back here in a short while. Good luck!"

"You too," Bruno replied, with surprising warmth. Some of their old friendship persisted.

Inside, he saw by the indicator board in the departure hall that he had ample time. De Wrendt had set him down with an hour and a half to spare. One hour before takeoff, each outbound air crew assembled at a briefing room to pick up whatever special orders concerned them, as well as copies of the flight plan, meteo report, load sheet and operational charts; then they reported aboard their plane. He was to dispense with the first step and go straight through the terminal to the Air Algérie Boeing 727 on the stand. The flight captain and copilot would be waiting for him in the cockpit. On the face of it, he had nothing in particular to fear. No one was looking for him in an Air Algérie uniform—nor did a definite suspicion exist that he was even in Switzerland. He would steer clear of the rest of the crew until he got aboard the plane, but even if an Air Algérie employee noticed him he would not excite undue interest, because last-minute substitutions of cabin personnel were forever taking place. As for the arrival, he would be met on the apron at Dar el Beida, Algiers' airport, by two men, a member of the Foreign Affairs Ministry and an instructor from the camp, and promply led out through a side gate reserved for official visitors. So there was little likelihood of his being spotted there either; if he was, it would matter much less.

With no particular plan in mind he went to the upper level, where the restaurant, coffee shop, chapel, dispensary and duty-free shop were located. He was in no hurry to board the plane before he had to—the two-odd hours he would have to spend confined in the cockpit with two acquiescent but probably taciturn Algerians would seem long enough. He crossed a lounge where some people sat waiting on plastic banquettes. Ahead of him, several passengers were apathetically wheeling luggage carts with the peculiar stiff scurrying walk of people in an airport. At the duty-free shop he bypassed the liquor and tobacco counters and went to the perfume stand. He bought two quarter-ounce bottles of Miss Dior from a woman attendant, who did not ask to see his ticket and boarding pass because he was in uniform. He had no particular girl in mind, but it did no harm to have a gift available should an opportunity arise.

Carrying his small, sealed parcel, he wandered over to the book-and-magazine stall opposite the liquor-checkout turnstiles. He ignored the paperback display and paused before the collection of newsmagazines ranged along the back wall: *L'Express*, *Stern*, *Der Spiegel*, *Newsweek*. Several carried almost identical covers on terrorism in Europe, which showed Wadi Khalef's ambushed car, the chauffeur's and Starkey's lifeless bodies sprawled on the cobblestones in Cologne. He began to riffle through *Stern*, searching for photographs of himself, but the inside pages carried blowups solely of the victims.

Just then, his skin prickled warningly.

He continued to flip the pages over; then he replaced his copy on a shelf and strolled over to the stacks of daily newspapers beside the cash register. He cast a bored glance at the French and German headlines. Then his aqueous blue eyes suddenly focused on the aisle near the magazines. Before one of the revolving paperback racks, a chubby man with chestnut hair combed forward in prim bangs teen-age style over a broad forehead was loitering indecisively with an unopened book in his hand. He was under thirty, could be almost any nationality, and he flicked his hungry, fascinated gaze away from Bruno just a second too late. Motionless, annoyed, Bruno stared past him. The man had immersed himself in his book—it looked like porno removed from the top row. He was wearing a tapered sport shirt and tight corduroy pants on his plump, soft build. A fag, Bruno thought. No detective or intelligence officer could be so clumsy at trying to deflect attention. So he was probably a fag cruising the airport. But suppose that wasn't it? The alternatives stunned him. Had those thousand-to-one odds against his being recognized paid off for some total stranger? Or was it one of Bauer's boys? Had that musclebound shit set someone to spy on him? He was sweating under the collar of his blazer. By lingering in the terminal, he had disobeyed De Wrendt's specific instructions; now it was too late to undo that stupid error, yet he didn't dare head for the flight gate without determining whether he was under surveillance.

There was one simple way of finding out. Making a wrenching effort to master his rage, he trod down the corridor toward the men's room at the far end of the hall. It was empty inside. There was no attendant on duty. Methodically he washed his hands in the bowl and adjusted his tie knot. He didn't like the insistent, unforgiving look in his eyes. He counted to twenty, but no one appeared. He inhaled deeply, swung around and stamped out, colliding in the door with Chubby, who was wriggling anxiously to get out of his way.

Close up, under the fringe of chestnut curls, his face was moon-round and moon-gray, a desolate, flaccid surface split by a nervous rictus. "It's strange, you look like—" the petulant voice whistled without intonation.

Bruno drove his fist without a word into the man's belly

and without emotion watched him stagger backward, clutching his groin.

"Don't proposition *me*, you turd. I know whom I look like," he snarled, and strode down the hall. It was happening just as he'd described it to De Wrendt—an unfunny joke becoming burlesque reality.

He swerved left and came to a passageway that overlooked the departure hall below. Over the constantly reforming groups at the check-in counters he heard the monotonous polyglot drone of the PA system: *"Nous annonçons le départ de . . . Attenzione . . .* Last call: passengers should go at once to . . ." He thought that he heard the word Algiers. Without consulting the overhead clock, he knew that he had twenty-five minutes left. The heat at his neck was dangerously aggravating his edginess. Straight ahead, a sign warned, NO ENTRY BEYOND THIS POINT. There were no passengers in this secluded area, which was occupied by administrative offices. He halted, looked back, and there was the queer stalking him at a safe distance, like a dog cautiously following another of which it is afraid.

He ducked into the chapel just short of the sign. A middle-aged couple came out and smiled approvingly at him. Against one white wall was an altar table adorned with wrought-iron candelabra and two bouquets of fresh carnations. There were carpeting and soft overhead lighting in the rectangular room. It was a nondenominational refuge not only for worshipers but for people who wanted to withdraw momentarily from the airport's turmoil. At this moment it happened to be vacant. Setting his parcel on a chair in a corner, Bruno swiftly positioned himself behind the door and watched the knob. If the stupid, masochistic fag changed his mind and did not come in, he would escape unhurt; if he insisted . . . well, it was up to him.

Breathing lightly, Bruno waited. He could swear that he felt an indecisive presence on the other side of the door. Since entering the chapel, he had utterly forgot De Wrendt's parting admonishment, the plane, Algiers . . .

The knob slowly turned and the vacuous moon face appeared, peering inside. After hesitating, Chubby took an uncertain step forward.

Bruno's right arm snaked out and twined around the inane pudgy neck. A tremor ran through the man's frame as Bruno locked a hold on his windpipe. With his left foot he kicked the door firmly shut.

Chubby wasn't prepared to resist, but then he glimpsed the dead, severe expression in his captor's eyes. Understanding what was going to happen, he opened his mouth, but only a bubbling gasp escaped. He began to squirm frantically, trying to wrest himself free. Wondering what to do with him, Bruno swung him around, kneed him with absentminded accuracy in the crotch, then yanked him backward so hard that he almost snapped his neck, clasping his hand over the man's mouth and receiving his wet breath on his fingers. Disgusted, he relaxed his stranglehold, but a flutter of calculation in the dilated pupils reawoke all his anger, and he choked down unsparingly again on the quivering throat. Then he stepped back and hammered two pile-driver punches at his liver. Back in De Wrendt's pseudo-glamorous penthouse, Bruno had found a copy of Rilke's poems and cursorily glanced through them. A phrase in one sonnet had leaped out with vivid malice: *mein verborgenes Blut*—my crooked blood. It had brought back overwhelmingly the worst days at the foster house, where there was no appeal, and his blind, flailing rage. In those days he had hated the world with an intensity that seemed to predate his birth, suggesting an inheritance of unknown forebears which set his spine tingling. Perhaps he had crooked blood and could do nothing about it. At times, like now, in baleful flashes, he saw his past and future irremediably joined, arid and desperate.

Chubby was slumped against him, limp, passive. "What in hell do you want?" he murmured, almost like a lover, into the queer's ear.

When there was no answer, he hurled him forward, letting go as he did so, and Chubby lurched awkwardly and collapsed to the floor. Bruno noted his doughy color and stood pensive. Suddenly he aimed a short, jabbing kick at his rib cage, and the man doubled up and groaned. Scowling, Bruno squatted beside him and listened to his shallow respiration. He tugged at the frieze of artfully coiffed chestnut curls, and as he had expected, the hairpiece came askew, revealing a dull patch of skull. The wig was part of Chubby's makeup for cruising in the airport—a fag's notion of attractiveness.

Footsteps in the corridor grew louder, then receded, slapping evenly on the tile floor in the direction of the administrative offices, and there was silence again. Scrambling to his feet, Bruno surveyed the shut door. His instinct was to grab his chance and clear out. No one had spied them together. In a sense, he had done the idiot at his feet a favor: with a violent bellyache and possibly a broken rib, he would hesitate next time before accosting strangers and so avoid more serious trouble. At that moment a fingernail brushed Bruno's ankle like a leaf. He jumped aside and glanced down. Chubby had, presumably with immense effort, crawled along the carpet and, squinting up at him with fixed, crazy desire, was clawing repeatedly at his trouser leg to bring him down.

Without expression Bruno considered him for a moment. He stooped and swiped away the bunch of groping fingers. Chubby's colorless lips were moving, tirelessly inventing formulas of supplication, but no sound materialized save for a glassy wheeze. Bruno sighed. It seemed to him that his problem had been resolved. Brusquely his sunburned hands shot out and clamped the man's throat in an inflexible vise, massaging it with a movement he had not used since Algeria when he had been a paratrooper disposing in the anonymous desert of certain recalcitrant Arab prisoners of war.

Seven minutes later, after having smoothed out his blazer and recovered his parcel, he left the chapel. He passed an airport employee who was sweeping cigarette butts into a pan and did not glance up. A trio of genuine stewardesses sauntered past and complacently viewed their reflections in the long window of the cocktail lounge. The airport was quieter at this hour, and the duty-free shop was already shut.

Once on the lower level, he hurried toward the flight gate. He had dragged the roly-poly body to the unlit recess behind the altar table, where it would not be discovered at once; but he had lost so much time that he had not dared linger to empty out Chubby's wallet to determine who he was. In the long run, he thought, it did not matter. Chubby was merely someone who had been unwise enough to get in his way.

Chapter Sixteen

The Night Consul

"Break into a Swiss banker's flat? While we're at it, why not hold up his bank?"

"I'm playing a hunch. De Wrendt's apartment in Geneva is used for transients."

"Listen, his wife told you about Seeblick. You scored points on that. Obviously, the place to start—since you're so eager to effect illegal entry—is his house."

Guthrie shook his head stubbornly. "The notation said August 9: we're three days too late. Whatever Bruno's business was, you can be sure he didn't hang around after it was finished, waiting for us to drive up. Besides, there's a gardener at Seeblick. It's not an easy setup."

"What makes you think the Geneva flat is?"

"I've checked it out. The concierge goes to bed at ten. De Wrendt flew off to Ibiza this morning. I won't be interrupted."

They were in the Embassy office in Bern, and Ditweiler was in a mood to challenge all assumptions. His blunt nails drummed on the desk.

"There's also De Wrendt's apartment in Zurich, over the bank."

"Too conspicuous. He wouldn't allow Bruno to come within a mile of it."

"If you're nabbed in Geneva, how do we wriggle off the hook? Did you ever hear of a third-rate robbery called Watergate?"

"I won't be nabbed."

"Easy to say. What does all this boyish cloak-and-dagger accomplish? What do we—I mean the station—get out of it, so that I can sell the idea back home?"

"If we can't roll up Aurora from the bottom—and we're not having much success on that front—then perhaps we can roll it down from the top. De Wrendt seems to be involved up to his ears—"

"Seems to be. . . . You can't indict a man on appearances. There's one slight new clue that supports your thesis. De Wrendt was in Paris on August 2, the night before the murders. Conferring with Bruno? Maybe, but who can prove it? I'm not saying De Wrendt is lily-white. His bank could be a conduit for payments. It would figure. The smaller and weaker the local Party, the bigger the underground apparatus is an almost invariable rule. It applies in Switzerland: Moscow Center runs a major show here, and De Wrendt is perhaps a spoke in the wheel."

"Fingerprints or other tangible evidence of collusion would help to sweat him."

"Sweat him?" Ditweiler snorted. "What are you fantasizing about? We'll turn the file over to the Swiss at that point and step humbly aside." He heaved his bulk about and gloomily surveyed the bank of telephones on his desk. "There's too damn much hassle all at once. I just took a call from my field team in Lucerne. Your French chick is getting fed up: Alpine scenery, three free meals a day and no action—she wants out. I can't say that I blame her. What's the point of keeping her dangling if we have no use for her? The Swiss are bound to find out that she's still around, in one of our safe houses, and start hollering about infringement of residence regulations and nonnotification on our part."

"She could make a trip to Ibiza," Guthrie said.

"You're full of grand ideas today."

"It would get her out of the country."

Ditweiler looked up sharply. "De Wrendt flew to Ibiza this morning; is that it?"

They were thinking the same thing—that even if the apartment yielded evidence, De Wrendt somehow had to be personally tackled, that the shadowboxing had lasted long enough.

"It's worth trying," Guthrie offered. "We know basically so little about De Wrendt, particularly his relationship to Bruno and Bauer. Who rules the roost? Why, if De Wrendt represents Moscow, is Soviet Intelligence manipulating the Aurora network? I admit it's a stab in the dark, but we have so few options. De Wrendt will be puzzled and worried if Marie-Christine turns up unexpectedly on his island. She was in Cologne, and he knows it by now. He'll have to react, and he may drop a hint as to where he stands and what comes next."

"Our working assumption is that De Wrendt's an old pro. He'd never fall for so obvious a ploy."

"We're not risking a damn thing by trying. He won't have Bauer and his friends about to mount anything fancy. It will be a one-on-one confrontation."

"Have you sounded her out? Suppose she doesn't care to play?"

Guthrie rose and massaged the cramp that had developed in his leg from sitting too long. "She'll want to go. She said that she wanted to be of help. She feels responsible for a lot that happened."

"I'll think about it." This was Ditweilerese for assent. "But it would probably make more sense to insert a full-page ad in the *Neue Zürcher Zeitung*: 'Anybody who knows anything about Bruno call this number toll-free, Sundays and holidays included.' " He was only half joking.

"Meanwhile, I'd like a crack at De Wrendt's apartment," Guthrie insisted.

"Did I ever describe for your benefit my first assignment in Paris? I had to meet a source at a hotel on avenue Matignon. It was our first contact, and he was jumpy as a *cucaracha*. I couldn't take notes for fear of his freezing up altogether, yet he had a lot to tell me. Outside in the street were honchos from three East Bloc services—it was in May, under those marvelous horse chestnut trees—making sure we didn't emplane for Kennedy."

In spite of himself, Guthrie asked, "What did you do?"

"I ordered another Dubonnet."

Knowing that he had been had, Guthrie sighed. "With the info, I mean."

"That's why I'm telling you the story. I memorized every bit of it and returned to the Embassy, and while it still made sense I typed up a twenty-two-page cable. That's what I expect you to do in the event your harebrained scheme to rifle Herr Question Mark's den pays off. On the other hand, if it backfires, bear in mind that you'll probably be up for reassignment home. I don't think you'd enjoy *that*." An engaging grin split Ditweiler's wide features. "You know whom you remind me of? The fellow in the old New York story about the Depression: 'Kid, you can't write poetry and you won't sell apples, so you gotta steal!' "

The flashlight's pin beam played across the darkened living room, exploring restlessly, but it discovered no evidence of recent occupancy. The problem was, he didn't know what he was looking for, except something amiss, something disturbed and out of place.

The thin, high-intensity beam traveled past a hassock, a sofa in sections, fluffed cushions bereft of a single telltale fold or wrinkle. On a Moroccan brass serving table it picked out a deck of playing cards, boxes of Brazilian *cigarillos*, matchbooks with the bank's monogram—but two big ceramic ashtrays nearby had not been used, and the *cigarillo* boxes were still sealed. A desk set, letter opener and pocket calculator were laid out with exacting symmetry on a stainless steel table. If anyone had inhabited the apartment, he had been as neat as a cat and left even fewer clues to his presence.

Guthrie approached the room beyond, which he surmised correctly to be a bedroom. Deep-pile carpeting muffled his steps, but he could hear his own measured breath. A floor-to-ceiling wardrobe closet along the length of one wall caught his eye. With his gloved left hand he slid back the white plywood panel on oiled runners. The interior was astonishingly bare, as though no one had used the apartment in a long while. The center of the room was occupied by a single, immaculately made up king-size bed, neutral and unrevealing as a board. Yet Renata de Wrendt had stated that her husband was in Geneva two nights before. Had he slept elsewhere? or bizarrely moved out all his belongings and gone to inordinate lengths to remove all trace of his passage? and if so, why?

Doubtfully, Guthrie returned to the living room. The interior—to judge by the decor the flashlight had revealed —suggested wealth, acquisitiveness, selectivity. It must have impressed the hell out of the girls De Wrendt had invited up here, if his wife was to be believed. Guthrie drew back the draperies. It also had a view—real estate agents would have burbled over a vista. From below rose the indistinct murmur of nocturnal Geneva. Its visitors made a ritual of staying up late in summer, promenading along the lakefront, through leaf-shadowed squares, on softly illuminated boulevards, as though they could never burn up their stored energy or exhaust the city's resources. Had Bruno used this VIP apartment as his base, slipping out undetected among the August tourists? It was not inconceivable —the state of the penthouse was a shade too spick and span to persuade—but if he had, there was no doubt he was gone, as elusively as he had come.

Guthrie put out the flashlight and stood still, deliberating. He had waited till eleven o'clock to enter the unlocked building; at that hour the concierge's lodge was, as he had expected, shut and silent. Creeping past it on tiptoe, he had ridden the elevator only halfway up and got out, so that the concierge, if he was still awake, would assume that it was a tenant on the second floor returning home. The remaining two flights he had ascended on foot in the dark. As every burglar could attest, a top-floor apartment was the easiest to enter with minimal risk of interference. The door lock could have posed a problem: it was a sturdy double-cylinder, drop-bolt model which, to judge by its unscratched finish, had been installed recently and was certainly newer than the building. It would undoubtedly deter most thieves. Guthrie had waited in the corridor to be sure there was no noise within the apartment; then he had inserted past the wards of the keyhole a skeleton key engineered by the Agency for the specific purpose of violating such pickproof models. The key went in as deftly as a probe; as the bolt revolved, there were two slight clicks, and when he pressed gently on the panel with his palm the door had yielded.

But had it been worth the risk?

Skeptically he ran the flashlight along the open bookshelves beside the window. Dozens of paperbacks in French and German, as well as a few hardcovers, were aligned more meticulously than in a library. One slim volume protruded from its place, not by much, perhaps a half inch; he would not have noticed it had he not been searching so intently for a clue. It was a collection of Rilke's sonnets. Was that De Wrendt's taste in literature or someone else's? Picking up the book by its spine, he cradled it in his elbow and turned over the pages in the beam's powerful light. They bore no annotations—had he seriously expected to find any such providential clue? It was simply evidence that at one point someone had been in the apartment.

He wedged the book back into place, then went into the

vestibule and located the bathroom, his real target. Whoever had occupied the apartment had presumably used the toilet. From one patch pocket of his jacket he drew out a 35mm Swiss-built Tessina equipped with an electronic flash connector; an ultraviolet gel filter was carefully fitted to the flashcube with black photographic masking tape to screen out any other light source. In the dark he set the camera on the floor, then removed from his other pocket a stoppered vial. Everything he would need had slipped easily into his clothes. Miniaturization was a boon for snoopers. The vial contained an ultraviolet yellow dusting powder which, with his left hand, he sprinkled on the chrome flush lever, while the flashlight in his right hand showed him what he was doing. Thank God, he thought, for a hot summer. Sweaty fingers left lots of latent prints on smooth, highly polished surfaces, and when the perspiration reacted to the powder the prints stood out against the background. On exposure to a bright light the prints fluoresced and could be photographed with an ultraviolet filter. The technique was similar to that used by narcotics teams with infrared film to gain evidence in the dark. He put aside the flashlight, knelt, held the Tessina steady four inches above the flush lever—Ditweiler had told him to get as close as possible, provided the entire print would fit in the frame— and then shot a full roll of film, thirty-six exposures, each flash flooding the room in eerie momentary light. After setting down the camera, he scrupulously wiped away the remaining yellow specks of print powder on the lever and floor.

As soon as he had finished, Guthrie straightened up and swiftly passed into the kitchen he perceived on the far side of the vestibule. Dimly looming in one corner was a giant, double-door refrigerator with a freezer. To remove anything from the interior, a person would have to strew thumbprints generously on the handle. He was just getting ready to repeat the dusting procedure when he heard the hum of the elevator ascending from the ground floor.

He waited for it to stop at one of the intermediate landings, but it kept coming, the hum growing louder as it approached the top floor.

He turned off the searchlight immediately and retreated into the living room, his eye on the rectangular doorframe barely discernible in the obscure vestibule. The elevator had stopped, and a man's heavy tread was heading unmistakably toward the penthouse. Guthrie stood between the sofa and the wall, taking care not to be silhouetted against the window, and wondered whether the visitor had a key to the apartment. It might be De Wrendt, back impulsively from Ibiza, but that was unlikely. It was unlikelier still to be Bruno. Whoever it was would need time to open the lock and reach out for the light switch. . . . Edging forward, Guthrie gripped the flashlight's knurled metal barrel in his fist and gauged the distance to the door. As soon as it opened, he would hurl himself at the intruder, exploiting the advantage of surprise, club him and make a lunge for the elevator. It was worth a try. But if things went wrong . . . He had taken the precaution of removing all Consular identification from his papers before starting out for the building on rue de Carouge; however, no matter what name he chose, in the event he ended up being booked at the police station he would have to contact the Embassy. Eventually Ditweiler would bail him out—but Ditweiler would detest being obliged to clue in the Swiss, who would ask merciless questions.

There was enigmatic silence outside the door. Then, to Guthrie's extreme relief, the footsteps receded slowly in the elevator's direction. Motionless, aware of his neck muscles' untensing, he waited in the dark till he heard the shaft door slam shut and the elevator start on its downward journey. The man outside had perhaps been the concierge dutifully making a nighttime round of the building. Perhaps he went to special trouble to check the penthouse whenever De Wrendt was absent; however, seeing no light under the door, hearing no noise within and presumably having no passkey, he had gone away. Whatever the visitor's motives,

Guthrie thought, his heart pumping fast, one alert was enough. The refrigerator door handle might be smeared with additional evidence, but the opportunity would have to be passed up. Either he had already shot a set of prints or he hadn't. Either they belonged to De Wrendt or they were those of someone else who had furtively stayed in the apartment. Unbolting the penthouse door from the inside, he exited into the pitch-dark corridor, guiding himself with his hand along the wall; a subtle gradation in the gloom indicated the stairwell near the elevator.

Though it was past midnight, the building was still warm, a sleepy organism sapped by the day's stunning heat. Guthrie thought with boundless yearning of Marie-Christine. How much nicer to be unwinding beside her at this relaxed hour! She didn't take him seriously. It was inspiring to have boosters. He started down the wide flight of stairs, treading gingerly, adjusting his vision as best he could to the tomb-like absence of light.

He reached the ground floor. The concierge's lodge was silent as ever, but a strip of light was visible under the door. He thought he heard a faint noise like the click of a telephone receiver being replaced in its cradle; the click was muted, but vaguely alarming. As he came outdoors, a feeble breeze caressed his forehead, and he realized that his face was aflame.

His car was parked two blocks away. Under pallid street lights, rue de Carouge extended rectilinear and austere as the Swiss concept of orderliness toward the glow of a traffic intersection, where there were garish neon signs, all-night cafés and a theater. Guthrie hastened along the deserted sidewalk, but he was still fifty yards from his destination when the plate glass of a furniture shop opposite reflected the ominous dazzle of fast-oncoming headlights. He had barely had time to leap back into a doorway to his left when a police cruiser rounded the corner, its tires squealing as it emerged from a side street, its dome light playing on the darkened sculpted facades along rue de Carouge. Down the street he heard the car slam to a halt and a man jump out,

169

and he expected to be confronted in the next instant by a flashlight and a drawn gun. When the sound ceased, he understood that one of the policemen had dashed into De Wrendt's apartment building. The dome light continued its swift, circular flashing, and Guthrie guessed what had happened. No doubt the elevator had climbed to the second floor once too often that night. After some hesitation, the concierge had decided to investigate; but then he had thought better of confronting alone a possibly armed burglar, retreated to his lodge and called the police. With no real choice, Guthrie took stock of where he was: in the recessed entryway to a pharmacy, which afforded almost no cover. The two policemen might drive away after a routine search of the penthouse; or, if they were conscientious, they might decide to poke about the immediate neighborhood. If he stayed where he was, there was every chance that they would discover him—but if he tried to bolt toward the intersection, the second policeman, who was still in the car, would hear the thud of his heels on the pavement. Guthrie hummed thoughtfully, almost soundlessly between his teeth, and, as occasionally happened when he landed in trouble, one of his less preposterous ideas occurred to him. Officially he was a vice-consul from Zurich on an overnight business trip to Geneva, who had no cause to be diffident about his presence on the street. No one had seen him enter or leave De Wrendt's penthouse. There was no reason to loiter like a criminal in the shadows. He edged away from the doorway and strode conspicuously toward the apartment building. As he came abreast of the prowl car, the policeman at the wheel scanned him from top to toe, started to say something to him, then changed his mind.

Guthrie continued along rue de Carouge at a deliberate pace, resisting the temptation to cut down the next side street. Once he was out of sight, he would double back to his Audi. The Tessina with the exposed film was safe in his jacket. Guthrie grinned in the dark.

Chapter Seventeen

The Heat

SIXTEEN YEARS later, North African summers were unchanged.

The little room was stifling. He lay naked on an iron cot without blankets and, too drowsy to turn the pages over, held a battered paperback history of Islam in his hand. A dispirited breeze driven by a table fan stirred the cotton curtains, and a sliver of light danced on the blue-painted wall. The blinds were slightly ajar, and beyond, the sky was silky white. Nearby, they were firing again on the practice range.

The training camp lay thirty miles west of Algiers, between Zeralda and Tipasa, at a short distance inland from the sea. His bungalow stood a quarter-mile up the crushed-stone road from the firing range, and the clear late afternoons were periodically troubled by brief clattering bursts of automatic-weapons fire in the hollow where Polisario volunteers and Eritrean Liberation Front recruits were receiving instruction. The day before, he had wandered down to the range and watched the coffee- and coal-skinned recruits diligently practicing, their faces intense and blissful as they clutched their newly uncrated Czech-manufactured Skorpion machine pistols and raked the life-size cutouts, presumably of imperialist oppressors, erected on the butts two hundred yards away. The East German instructor, who was on loan from his country's secretariat for African operations, had offered to let him speak with the class; he had declined, because it seemed pointless. The recruits' problems were not his; the political situation that confronted them was different from the one he had known when he had received his training a decade ago. The camp itself was bigger and more rationally laid out than the improvised semidesert bivouac in southern Iraq where he had lived for two months under a tent. Plainly more funds were available these days, and the facility had a feel of permanency which the other had not had.

There was another difference: the foreigners were not hermetically segregated; they strolled as they pleased in the evening to the main area where the camp staff and the Algerian police cadres—men and women—who were also there for training were billeted in whitewashed barracks. Although the language barrier inhibited exchanges, contact between the two groups was not discouraged. In Iraq the foreign volunteers had been isolated and considered with glittering distrust. Because they were not Moslems. Here most of the instructors were non-Moslems, and it seemed to matter less. Guerrilla warfare was now a thriving multinational industry that frowned upon religious and racial discrimination. As for the curriculum, it was still essentially the same—field instruction during the day, self-critique sessions, political films and lectures at night—but the material was, naturally, tailored to fit regional needs. Some instructors were brilliant; others were hot-eyed and ineffectual. Ten years ago he had been lucky in drawing a middle-aged, German-speaking Estonian who had spent years in the jails of Farouk's Egypt. A tubby, bald man, he had never lifted his voice, tirelessly instructed his students in the paradoxes of history and given them the benefit of practical tips (based on his own grueling experience) for surviving prolonged imprisonment. One of the lessons he had hammered home was always to keep informed of what went on beyond the walls; another was to count on outside help; still another was to remain alert for opportunities to organize the other inmates politically. The first was the lesson that had made the deepest impression on Bruno.

He flung down the book about Islam and went to the door of the bungalow. It faced west, which was a mistake. Houses in North Africa that were exposed to the afternoon sun's poisonous rays were less valuable than others. There was still no relief from the great heat. At five o'clock, earth and sky were absolutely white: the dazzle from the tamped rock and mica of the roadbed was blinding, unendurable beyond a few seconds. In the late afternoon the country-side became an abstraction in pure immobility: no one tried to exert himself in that fierce light, except, of course, the stalwart freedom fighters at the firing range. On the coast it was the same: the shopkeepers closed early and vanished into secluded back rooms, where they unrobed and made love to glistening chubby girls; the blistering sand beaches were occupied solely by foolhardy Scandinavian tourists, who moved about shirtless and shoeless and rued their imprudence the next day. In the camp, he had gathered, there was a problem with the Europeans. The heat left them gasping, caused them to nibble too much raw fruit and experiment, in defiance of regulations, with smuggled liquor and native fig brandy. At the administration office yesterday, an intoxicated German girl, a former kindergarten teacher from Essen, had exclaimed in disbelief as she staggered wildly into the bleached compound, "The air feels like fire burning in my breasts!"

He returned indoors, took a long swig from a liter bottle of Ain Garcia mineral water on the night table, swirled it in his mouth and spat it into the washbowl. What was he doing again in Algeria? Marking time, growing a mustache, arranging to have his hair dyed, experiencing boredom, waiting to be summoned by Leonid. Having a single bungalow was an unwonted luxury—there were only three in the camp, reserved for VIPs. He had decided to make use of his privacy and leisure to read, but he had discovered that he couldn't concentrate on the print, couldn't think straight, couldn't even be bothered to remember whether sixteen years earlier he had reacted differently to these somnolent, never-ending afternoons. He contemplated with derision a creased, three-day-old German newspaper beside the fan. It carried an interview with a Bremen couple who claimed to have known him as a mutinous pupil in the local *Volksschule*. The tone of their statement was a remarkable mix of reproval and admiration. In spite of his destructive record, he was a celebrity in their eyes. Involuntarily, his imagination reverted again to the past. Long ago, at the time described in the interview, he had nurtured fierce dreams of returning someday to Bremen to strike back at his foster parents, but he had delayed too long and then revenge had no longer interested him; besides, their attitude had forever baffled him: how could he avenge himself upon an enigma? . . . He recalled suddenly another period of his life, when he had first hitchhiked into Spain. There had been a bar brawl over something or other—the Algerian war or a woman; his arm was fractured and he was operated upon in a hospital in Gerona. Hospitals are interludes where one reckons up one's miscalculations. His life until then, he conceded, had been misspent; but what, after all, was a well-spent life? Forearm set in an overtight cast, he had been released after several days, fair, sullen, violent and penniless, with a grudge, and it was shortly thereafter that he had met De Wrendt, and grown to admire and like the man for his far-ranging intelligence and unflagging readiness to help—even though that readiness was bound to an ulterior motive. . . . With frugal movements he kicked off his sandals, stepped into the foul-smelling shower cubicle and dowsed his flanks with water that came tepid in a jerky trickle from the pipes. By the time he was dressed and combed, a subtle alteration was noticeable in the torpid air; as he had expected, the sun was beginning its long decline on the blond horizon. He shut the door behind him and set out along the road toward the camp exit.

His destination was a clay-walled shack just beyond the camp gate run by a Berber who sold figs, grapes and tomatoes. If the owner spoke any French, he would be someone to chat with. Apart from his visit to the range, Bruno had kept to himself throughout the past two days. He had no desire to speak with the Europeans in the camp. Certainly not with the German kindergarten teacher, who was a security risk. There was a thin, sloe-eyed Algerian girl whom he had noticed at work in the administrative office who was probably available. If he stayed at the camp another twenty-four hours he had resolved to try her out.

Ahead, an old man in a worn khaki uniform trudged along the roadside, glancing to neither right nor left, stolidly indifferent to his surroundings, like a town Arab to filth underfoot. Then a gaunt yellow dog with a long, pointed muzzle materialized from the lee of the last bungalow and, barking stridently, raced toward the old man. Pausing, he stooped and pitched a stone through the air. The animal howled and swerved off, limping, toward the bungalow, where it sat down and began to yelp monotonously with no expectation of being comforted. The color had drained from Bruno's cheeks. He didn't hold with mistreating animals. Halting in his tracks, he crouched and silently grabbed a second stone on the ground, tempted to hurl it at the small of the old man's khaki back. But he did not. His fingers unclenched, and the stone dropped beside his feet. The old man wouldn't understand his indignation. Arabs! They were supposed to have twelve centuries of civilization. He thought of the intimidation raids which his OAS commando of deserters had mounted on the streets of Algiers. The raids had not achieved their purpose: the

175

Algerians had gained their bloody independence. What had they done with it? They were still stoning dogs.

Absorbed in his thoughts, he paid no attention to the mud-caked Land-Rover that had overtaken him and braked. Before he could bypass it, a burly Arab with prominent cheekbones and a flamboyant mustache smirked down at him.

"Get in. Free ride to Algiers!"

Bruno studied the driver's wide bister face, his spotless linen suit.

"You don't remember me, friend?"

When Bruno sought to move aside, the Arab bellowed, "I am Fuad Assam! In God's name, what terrible thing has happened to your memory?"

Removing his sunglasses, Bruno thoughtfully scrutinized the driver and shook his head. "I don't know you." His voice grated slightly in the warm air like rusted metal.

"*Merde!*" The Arab tapped his belly proprietorially. "Ten kilos more; I eat better, make more money too: things have changed for the poor village boy from Biskra." He bared his large teeth in a terrific grin of great strength. "You think I'm making it up? I never invent."

"You never saw me before today, friend."

"Dieter: ex-sergeant Koenig of the First Foreign Legion Para Regiment, the tough-assed sergeant we tried to ambush. Instead, you ambushed *me*, you son of a bitch. You're a little heavier in the gut too, but you still have your blond hair and your teeth. Moreover, you are a famous man."

Bruno stood utterly motionless beside the vehicle. He remembered that he had stupidly left his Beretta in the bungalow on the assumption that the camp interior was safe.

"Well, what are you waiting for? No formal invitation! Jump in!"

He climbed wordlessly into the Land-Rover and matched the Arab's crushing handclasp. By now, of course, he did remember: during a surprise house-to-house search of the Casbah in Algiers in 1961, they had captured a thickset young FLN courier and taken him to a back room at regimental headquarters on rue d'Isly. To everybody's chagrin, the courier had endured three days and nights of *interrogation poussée*, which included, naturally, electric shocks to his genitals, without blowing a single agent of his *wilaya*; then he had stood up to the far-from-idle threat of being flung out of an Alouette helicopter at two thousand feet altitude above the boulder-strewn wilderness of the Aurès mountains. The courier's name had been Fuad Assam; his toughness, resilience and realistic acceptance of his likely fate had affected Bruno, who was moved by very little, and prompted him to recall aloud to the regimental commander that the same Fuad Assam had spared a French soldier's life six months earlier during an FLN attack on an infantry outpost near Blida. As a result, the grilling had been suspended and the courier transferred to a POW stockade, from which he had later escaped.

Fuad Assam put the Land-Rover into gear, and it lurched erratically up the steep rise toward the camp gates. "There is a lot of crackbrained gossip in this place. The rumor was that 'Bruno' had arrived. Though I didn't believe it, I planned to look you up: it's always interesting to discover how a decade and a half rub off on a rhinocerous-hided man and his ideas. But I didn't expect to give you a lift like a hippie or a tourist!"

Bruno nodded noncommittally, watching the road level off between slender colonnades of date palms. The camp gates were visible directly ahead. At the checkpoint he would get out and bid Fuad Assam goodbye, then return to the bungalow, and that would be the end of this brief, singular, suspect reunion.

Fuad Assam cast him a sidelong, devious glance. "You're wondering what I'm doing here?"

"Obviously."

"From time to time I'm still a courier, friend." His semi-smile was self-satisfied, crooked and indecipherable. "For our Palestinian brothers, my old friend. It's the same liberation war as sixteen years ago, but it is being waged in another theater. You grasped this basic fact and joined us: I cannot tell you how happy that makes me. What you did in Germany to that pig Wadi Khalef was—"

"—mismanaged," Bruno said.

"What are you talking about? It inspired the masses in all progressive Arab countries. It set an example for *fedayeen* in the camps. 'Combat Zionists and their imperialist allies on all fronts in a continuing struggle': you made it come true!"

Bruno smiled faintly to himself. He was aware that underground pamphlets depicting him as a redresser of wrongs, a freedom fighter in the cause of world revolution, were peddled among Maoist cells, in student clubs and Arab solidarity committees. What high-flown rubbish! He could visualize De Wrendt's frosty grimace.

"Listen, let's have dinner." Fuad Assam reluctantly slowed down the Land-Rover as they approached the concrete guardhouse. "There's a lot I want to discuss with you. . . ."

"You haven't changed."

"How you came to be a revolutionary. Your assessment of the situation. Your opinion of Algeria. I can list twenty important topics for two men like us to explore."

Bruno watched him present an oblong plastic pass with his photo to the helmeted corporal on duty at the wire-mesh gates. Then he showed his own temporary identification card, which Leonid had handed him at Dar el Beida airport. Leonid had made one significant comment during the subsequent drive across the darkened, sleeping countryside: "Within the camp you'll be perfectly safe. Outside, anything can happen." Leonid was wrong: if an unplanned encounter with a former enemy such as this could take place inside the camp grounds, then it was no safer than the exterior.

Fuad Assam stared at him challengingly. "Are you coming with me? There is nothing to do in the camp at night but attend the indoctrination lectures. *I* know."

It was probably true, Bruno thought. He didn't trust a single word of Fuad Assam's, but he appreciated his free-wheeling style. More to the point, he wanted to pin down what he was after. He knew that his own departure in the Land-Rover would be promptly reported to the administrative office, but he had made no promise to Leonid or anybody else to sit tight in his bungalow. There would be a row over his absence, but it wouldn't come to anything. His position was strong: they needed him more than he needed them.

He remained seated in the Land-Rover. "I'm hungry, my old friend. What are we wasting time for?"

They ordered bourek, that fine, redolent, filling dish of meat, onions and fried egg which is stuffed into a flaky crust, and drank full-bodied Mascara wine.

"*B'sahtek!*" toasted Fuad Assam as he filled the glasses to the rim. He noticed Bruno's interested scrutiny. "A Moslem is not supposed to touch this stuff, eh?"

"Plenty do."

"Listen: in '60 when we were in the field near Guelma, we got orders from our sector commander *not* to fast during Ramadan. Of what use are weakened troops? A boy in my platoon, a true believer, disobeyed, fainted from exhaustion and was evacuated. . . ."

"So it made a disbeliever of you."

"Hardly, but I drink all the wine I want. *And* whiskey. *And* anisette. We're not Libyans. This is a Socialist country but not a republic of puritans. I'll show you later. . . ."

During dinner Bruno chewed, dabbed at the sweat on his face and watched the door. He remembered this same restaurant when it was thronged with French paratroopers who had ordered countless rounds of pastis from twilight till curfew and left behind a litter of peanut shells on the bar. Then, the thoroughfare outside had been known as Boulevard Sidi Carnot; now it was named Hassiba Ben Bou-ali, in honor of an eighteen-year-old girl student militant who had died for the Revolution. The restaurant these days drew Algerian men in business suits and emancipated young Arab girls in Parisian dress; no Europeans seemed to patronize it, which was just as well and spoke for Fuad Assam's security-mindedness.

It was Fuad Assam who monopolized conversation. Leaning forward over his plate, stabbing with his fork at the tablecloth to emphasize certain details, he recounted how he had inherited a cousin's firm a year after independence and become an exporter of Berber mats and rugs to France; how prosperous this commerce had made him; how simultaneously he had felt a moral duty to militate in behalf of those Arab brothers in the Middle East who had not yet conquered their own homeland; how, consequently, he had turned to use sales trips to Paris and Lyon to run messages and funds to PLO cells; how he had almost been apprehended by the DST, French internal security, while transporting an attaché case crammed with two hundred thousand Swiss francs and cassettes of compromising tapes. Listening to this recital, Bruno noted that Fuad Assam scrupulously—or perhaps automatically—shunned the term "terrorism" in favor of "guerrilla warfare" and "direct action." Was it delicacy or disapprobation? He did not know, but he noted too that Fuad Assam had not yet embarked upon the grand exchange of ideas that was supposedly a purpose of the dinner. Nor put a single question to him about his own activities. He found himself speculating more and more about this glib, affluent Arab and wondered when he would venture to tip his hand. But when it came time to leave, Fuad Assam still had not. As he unfolded two one-hundred-dinar notes on the table, Bruno let him pay for the dinner, idly conjecturing as to whose money it was.

They went on to a cabaret frequented by Algerian soldiers—a cavernous, smoky pit near the former Place de l'Opéra, where a shrill skit was in progress that satirized the King of Morocco's recent invasion of the Spanish Sahara. The acting was gauche, and there was much declamatory reading in Arab style of impassioned passages; the audience guffawed each time the actor who was playing the King in combat uniform stumbled onstage and was rebuffed by nomad women: this was the part it seemed to enjoy most. Fuad Assam's burnt-sienna skin gleamed through the smoke. The nightclub proved his contention that Algiers was permissive enough to accommodate Western license. Bruno's gaze strayed to the corpulent bar girls lounging in the gloom.

Fuad Assam followed his gaze. "The hostesses in this place are pigs, but if you really want to—"

"No."

"There's one good-looking thing at the camp whose name is Rima. Have you noticed her?"

"Yes."

"She is in the administrative office. She wants to volunteer to fight alongside the *fedayeen*. You should try her. If you want to meet her, I can arrange to—"

"No."

Fuad Assam's virile mustache glistened with droplets of whiskey, and his voice boomed, then plunged confidentially. "Algiers is not what it used to be, eh? I admit that at times I miss Paris . . . Brussels . . . Munich . . . Zurich. However, soon you will be back in Europe . . ."

So, finally, it had come.

"It will be a long time before I set foot in Europe again," Bruno lied casually.

Undaunted, Fuad Assam persevered. "Why are we not talking about you? My contribution to the struggle is minute. Yours is . . ." He let the silence last to suggest that it alone was eloquent enough to convey his meaning. "You'll be at the camp awhile?"

"I don't know."

"Day after tomorrow I'll come to see you. We'll have another conversation."

Bruno said nothing. He's really trying, he thought.

Next morning he was awakened by an Arab boy who said there was a telephone message for him at the administrative office. He walked to the one-story concrete structure, knowing who had sent it. The day was turning out as fiery as its predecessor. A thud at a little distance was succeeded by blast waves reverberating across the dull landscape of sand and stone: the volunteers were training with offensive grenades. As he entered the office, the sloe-eyed girl at the counter smiled at him and handed over a slip of paper.

It was the encoded summons he had been expecting from Leonid.

He returned to Algiers in one of the camp's discolored old Renaults; made sure the Land-Rover was not dogging his trail; got out at the Air Algérie city terminal; loitered intentionally beside the entrance; then, as the stoplight changed, darted across the wide square. Striking up rue Khalifa Boukhalfa, he shoved his way impatiently among the creeping pedestrians as far as the Soviet Cultural Center.

At the reception desk a bullet-headed Russian who spoke indifferent French checked his identity card, kept him cooling his heels while he used the interphone, then indicated Leonid's office at the end of the corridor.

Leonid, in a creased poplin suit, sweating, with a bottle of lemon drink in his frail hand, swerved away from the shut window and confronted him aggressively.

"You left the camp last night without authorization. You went to a restaurant and nightclub: in these insecure, not to say exposed, surroundings you drank—"

"Two glasses of wine. A brandy and water."

"Your capacity to drink is not in question, but your judgment: you were not alone but with—"

Bruno lifted his fair eyebrows. "Is that why you called this meeting?"

"It is not. But your behavior is provocative. I don't need such problems. What do you know about this Fuad Assam?"

"Is he one of your spies? So sly, so nosy . . ."

"What did he want to know?"

"Everything."

"I don't suppose he obtained that. So what did you tell him?"

"Nothing. He wasted his time . . . and incidentally, mine."

"He isn't ours," Leonid snapped. "What gets into you to run these superfluous risks? This is a Socialist country, admittedly, but nevertheless it attracts numerous politically unreliable elements."

"Even this Center may have some," Bruno observed.

Leonid ignored the remark. "Fuad Assam is connected with the Palestinians and ferries their funds abroad, it seems. Still, we'll check him out."

"I was about to suggest it. These revolutionary Arabs don't trust outsiders. Why should we always buy their story?"

"And all the more reason for you to stay away from them."

With a twist of distaste Leonid set the sticky bottle out of reach on his desk. He found himself drinking all the time in the Maghreb's debilitating heat—far too often for his good, yet he couldn't stop. He was under pressure back home to produce results that justified the Cultural Center's budget. This *blondin* with the inflated reputation was not making his task easier.

"Probably you judge my cautious attitude excessive? There is more justification for it than you imagine. The German police arrested your colleague Reindorf yesterday."

Bruno blinked twice: it was his only outward reaction to unfavorable news. Finally he inquired, "How did it happen?"

"The secretary at the Jordanian Embassy who was his mistress panicked and identified him for the police. His

183

description was broadcast on German television; quite by accident an old man spotted him in the street, far from his usual neighborhood. It's bad enough to be at the mercy of such mishaps without prompting them," Leonid said sententiously.

"Why don't you calm down?"

"When you are safely out of Algeria, I shall. How much did you tell Reindorf about Grand Slam?"

"That jellyfish? No more than I told Fuad Assam."

"But he could divulge your escape route . . ."

"Only as far as Romanshorn—a dead end, as far as the interrogators are concerned." Beneath his impassive exterior, he was tingling with anger. He had foreseen that the Cologne operation would end in Reindorf's arrest—and it was clear that under questioning Reindorf would crack . . . or had already cracked. Who had recruited him in the first place? Bauer. . . .

"That brings up another matter." Leonid ran a limp hand through his damp hair. "On the night you flew out from Geneva a man was found choked to death at Cointrin Airport. The murder is still unsolved. It appears that the victim was a known homosexual."

Bruno's suppressed rage made him more imperturbable than ever. "Why should I know anything about it?"

"I'm not implying that you do. But it means, of course, that the police are running a computer check of all passenger and crew movements through the airport that night: not a welcome development for your ultimate safety, I would say. If the trail grew too hot, it might have some effect on the Algerians' hospitality." Leonid was plainly not disposed to pursue that pessimistic line of thought. "Fortunately, we won't be depending on the Algerians much longer. Grand Slam has been moved up by forty-eight hours. Consequently, you will be leaving here earlier than expected. Since you seem to be so restless at the camp, you will be pleased, I imagine."

Bruno scowled at him, his sunburned, peeling face

glazed with suspicion and impatience. "As you very well know, Grand Slam's timetable *cannot* be changed. Whose idiotic notion is this?"

"The target's," Leonid retorted tersely. "Sadat is arriving in Switzerland two days ahead of his original schedule. There is no time for you to alter your appearance here; it will have to be done at your next stop. You are flying out tomorrow."

Bruno nodded brusquely and turned toward the door. In spite of the heat he felt the same preliminary iciness, the *froid intérieur* before an attack, which he had experienced in Reindorf's apartment in Cologne. "So much the better," he remarked.

After he had left, Leonid went to a small refrigerator in the pantry and distractedly opened another bottle of sweetened lemon drink. At times, in this alien country, he caught himself daydreaming crazily of cold, sweeping, regenerating winds.

Chapter Eighteen

The Ibiza Approach

IT WAS a positive identification. Without comment, Guthrie nudged the flimsy from Paris across the report-littered desk to Ditweiler, who read the message through in a glance and clicked his teeth ambiguously. "You should be working at Justice," he remarked.

"I'm not trying to build a case against the guy."

"Sure you are. But who can blame you? The prints smeared all over his john are Bruno's—it says so right here: '. . . conform to those lifted by French police in the rue Chateaubriand apartment.' Furthermore—where is it? here we are—we've got the minutes of Reindorf's interrogation from Bonn: 'Escape route Cologne—Autobahn to Frankfurt—Stuttgart—Ulm—then south on trunk road to Friedrichshafen. . . .' Reindorf claims he didn't know the game plan beyond, but it's not that difficult to figure out. There's a regular car-ferry service from Friedrichshafen to the Swiss side of the lake. With diplomatic plates you drive aboard the ferry; no one at Customs or Passport Control dreaming of asking indelicate questions, not if the passengers are certified Soviets, which impresses all the yokels. Then you settle down with maybe twenty fellow passengers to enjoy the nice crossing while a certain fair-haired tourist —sorry, terrorist—in your car makes damn sure to keep out of sight: that's not asking too much of him for forty-two minutes. Then you land, and naturally the neutral Swiss aren't so crude as to take a second look at who's in the vehicle or the vehicle itself when you brandish those useful diplomatic passports. But then to avoid compromising the Swiss fraction of your network the trail must peter out, so you dive for cover quick. By happenstance, comrade De Wrendt's celebrated summer estate Seeblick, which befits a senior member of that snob outfit, the KGB, is only a few miles' easy drive from the ferry terminal. Am I jumping to rash conclusions?"

"A pattern emerges," Guthrie insisted.

"Yes, you couldn't ask for a more conveniently located safe house. I wish our safe houses were that conveniently located."

"De Wrendt is running Bruno or at the very least organizing his support. That's what the fingerprints prove."

"Sure." Ditweiler removed his glasses and looked paler. "Too bad you went to so much trouble breaking and entering—and almost getting busted, I might add—to make your point. It's become of strictly academic interest." He shoved a photocopied two-page report at Guthrie. "I've been doing all the reading. Now it's your turn."

Guthrie studied the two off-white sheets, noting that they had been cabled from Algiers station to Langley, then disseminated to Bern and other Western European stations.

"Who's the source?"

"It's a pure fluke. We picked him up several years ago as part of a penetration effort of the PLO and found that he was on a regular circuit. He draws a retainer to brief us about his travels: what sort of goodies he's bringing in, to whom, where. Nothing ambitious: he's too low on the totem pole to have access to the juicy stuff. Now, this isn't his sort of assignment at all, but there you are: having heard that Bruno's in town, he takes it upon himself to ferret out his old enemy-in-arms for a class reunion with lots of nostalgia for the good old days in the torture chamber, and lo and behold! at first crack he locates him, succeeds where a half-dozen services with money, communications and computers at their disposal are still witlessly chasing their own tails—"

"Is he any good?"

"No, according to Algiers station. He's a goddamn rug merchant, for heaven's sake. But we go with what we've got. Right?"

Guthrie set down the report. "This tells us Bruno's in Algiers. Fine. For the moment he's out of circulation and harmless. But how long will that last?"

"For argument's sake, why not indefinitely? What makes you so sure?"

"Rosenthalerstrasse isn't in Algeria. His network is in Europe. Algiers is merely rest-and-relaxation; what happens when the holiday is over? What's he after? The third date is August 21. It means something: he didn't jot it down for fun."

"Damn right he'll be back on our doorstep," Ditweiler said. "I was just testing your reflexes, *amigo*."

And making sure of a consensus for the next move, Guthrie thought.

"You'll be happy to learn that under interrogation Reindorf yielded another tidbit—Bruno in Cologne, it seems, bragged about a forthcoming 'bigger operation.' Unfortunately, he stopped short of furnishing details. It would be nice to catch up with him beforehand."

"Diplomatic channels," Guthrie said promptly. "Paris or Bonn or both demand his extradition from Algeria."

"Are you kidding? The procedure takes time—weeks, not to say months. He'll hop it as soon as the word leaks out."

"Of course, there's an extreme solution. Fuad Assam seems to have access, so why not provide him with a gift for his friend? Cinchonine or some such?* Do unto Bruno as he does unto others." Starkey's death was still vividly present to Guthrie's memory.

"Great minds always think alike," Ditweiler said. "The suggestion was made in Langley and rejected out of hand by the Director. It's a fact that we're no longer in the execution business. More to the point, a project like that often boomerangs, and we certainly can't afford a stink in an Arab country. Besides, Fuad Assam isn't *that* close to him: if you read the report, you noticed he mentions the subject's extreme suspiciousness. So where does that leave us? Langley, in reply, drafted one of those eat-your-cake-and-have-it cables urging Algiers station to maintain contact and determine Bruno's plans and movements while 'protecting its source and proceeding with caution.' Maybe Fuad Assam will elicit the information; maybe he won't." He shuffled through the papers on his desk and pushed another flimsy sheet toward Guthrie. "I've asked to get all of his take on a priority basis."

"Are we sure that we're his only clients?"

"We're funding that rug-export business of his: there's no problem about his loyalty. But what beats me is the phrasing of his report, the undertone of veneration. He actually seems to adore a lousy Kraut paratrooper who went around not so long ago shooting up Moslems on the street. All Arabs are alike: they're in search of a father figure with an automatic rifle, a guerrilla with charisma, the—pardon the expression—terrorist with the mostest." Ditweiler went to the window and surveyed the untroubled skyline of Bern. "And how about that place's record?" He was referring to Algeria. "They extend unbounded hospitality to Carlos, Abou Daoud, the skyjackers of the Japan Air Lines plane. With Carlos they were cute. They put him on a Belgrade-bound plane in the middle of the night dressed up as an

---

* Cinchonine: an antimalarial drug, an overdose of which can cause cardiac arrest.

Arab TV technician on his way to cover a conference of nonaligned nations. However, he was spotted by a German at the airport; we found out and tipped off Belgrade. The Jugs denied everything, claimed it was a case of mistaken identity and personally put him on another plane to Baghdad, where we lost him. If you're a bona fide terrorist, you can count on cooperation getting into and out of countries like Algeria. I don't know why. Of course, they're among the Palestinians' strongest supporters. Perhaps it enhances their sense of self-importance. In return for Soviet aid, it's also likely that they receive orders from Moscow to furnish backup. No wonder Bruno chooses to hole up there."

"It's also a handy place to fly out of if you've got business in certain swinging capitals: Interflug to East Berlin, Libyan Arab Airlines to Tripoli, Aeroflot to San'a."

"So?"

"So we may lose him the way we lost Carlos." After a moment Guthrie said, "Fuad Assam is simply one approach; thankfully, we have another. . . ."

"The Ibiza approach."

"I keep coming back to De Wrendt. I'm convinced he's the key. Once Bruno stops trotting around the Third World and reenters Europe, who will be heading the reception committee? De Wrendt. So we stick with him to lead us to Bruno. Meanwhile, during the time he's on Ibiza we mike-and-wire his apartment over the bank—"

"We do nothing of the sort. Geneva was more than enough—De Wrendt's no dummy: as soon as he learns someone broke in, he'll know what it means. You have a good operational brain, but don't let yourself get carried away." Ditweiler sat down and rubbed his jaw meditatively. "Have you heard from your lady friend?"

"Yes."

"No contact yet?"

"She expects to make contact tonight."

"I hope she justifies the money we're spending on her."

Ditweiler searched Guthrie's face for a reaction. "No regrets about sending her into action?"

Guthrie scowled, the freckles leaping out on the ruddy bridge of his nose. "She won't get into trouble," he boomed.

Marie-Christine had flown into Ibiza on a Sunday morning, her eyes as profound as the waters below. As the plane made its approach, she looked down and studied the deepening shades of green that succeeded one another marching from the shore to the inland mountains: sea green, vine green, fir green. Abruptly a white blot of a house came into view on a hill; then more and more habitations appeared on the plain. This rocky speck of a Mediterranean island was a miniature of mainland Spain: tawny cultivated fields, terraced olive and almond groves, rugged mountains brooding in the deceptive distance.

She went straight by taxi to Santa Eulalia del Rio, a resort village fifteen miles north of the airport where her hotel room was booked. The room had a wide terrace with a spectacular view of a white sea foaming in the sleepy sun and surf fingering the shore like lace. Hotel rooms on Ibiza were unobtainable in August, but Guthrie had managed. When he really wanted something, he worked overlong to get it.

She unpacked, changed into the vaporous summer clothes she had hastily bought in Zurich for her stay and walked along the shore. Small waves were rolling gently landward, green when the sun emerged, unfurling with parade-ground precision on a sand beach. The dry path wound between cactus and sea pines, past a new apartment building, a blue-and-white-striped ice cream bar, a jetty on which children sat barefoot watching a little boat from up the coast enter the placid bay.

Santa Eulalia del Rio (it had once been a fishermen's village) boasted a wide *paseo* that extended from the water's edge to an arched, whitewashed two-story town hall from

191

whose balconies laundry shone in the blazing sun. In an adjoining side street was the diminutive bar Guthrie had briefed her about. She found it without difficulty. Through a bead curtain she could make out a clot of midday habitués gathered in its cool depths where the sunlight seemed seldom to penetrate. Satisfied, Marie-Christine returned to the *paseo* and sat down at a table. It was Ibiza's high season. She considered the parade of jeans, T-shirts and sandals in the main plaza; the procession of Land-Rovers, tiny SEAT cars, motorbikes dusted by the island's fertile red soil; the profusion of fishing skiffs, sailing dinghies and inflatable rafts bobbing lazily at anchor inshore. Sipping a glass of *rosado* wine beside a hedge of oleanders, Marie-Christine felt drowsy, warm and happy in the beneficent heat. She wondered what the place was like out of season and if she would enjoy it as much then.

After which, reluctantly, she thought of her assignment and wondered whether she could carry it out without making a fool of herself. "He has a son almost your age," Guthrie had remarked. "He's separated and temporarily alone. His taste runs to classy blondes, to your type . . ." "My type?" At this, Guthrie had made an elusive gesture. "His curiosity about you will be triggered by other factors. As soon as he finds out that you're the girl who put up Bruno in her apartment, a lot of danger signals will flash through his mind. Automatically it's going to occur to him that this is a setup. He'll check you out discreetly, but it isn't so easy to do on Ibiza as on his own turf. When he determines to his own satisfaction that you're alone, it's going to be hard for him to resist making an approach. He knows you were in Cologne with me—but what happened afterward? You dropped out of sight and never returned to Paris. Where were you in the interval, what else did you tell us? He'll want answers; well, so do we, and this may be a shortcut to them: specifically, where is Bruno? what operation is scheduled on August 21 . . ." They were standing close together in the living room of the chalet above Lucerne. It was the first time she had seen him in four days, and in this period she had had a great deal of opportunity to ask herself questions about him. Without intending to, she had revealed some of her state of mind: "I wonder if you're acquainted with a realistic French saying—remorse is better than regret."

"Is that supposed to mean you're sorry we went to bed?"

She had shaken her head.

". . . because I don't think you realize how I go crazy thinking about you. I didn't come here just to talk about Ibiza. The two things are totally separate: you and me— and this situation."

"Are they?"

"In my mind they are."

She had smiled and brought his face down to hers. "I'm glad of that. I wouldn't want to be thought of merely as an operational gimmick." But when he had begun to do more, she had interrupted him. "Go on, tell me about your banker."

"Later."

"No, now. You've made me curious."

"You can't get into trouble. De Wrendt will be alone on Ibiza. The people he's staying with aren't part of his network."

"How are you so sure?"

"They're banking friends. He's their houseguest each summer. He makes certain not to mix his overt and covert activities."

"Do you want me to do it?"

"It would help. It's merely a case of playing along an older man."

She couldn't refrain from smiling humorlessly to herself at this description of her mission.

"If he approaches you, he'll go out of his way to be charming. So will you—and ask innocuous things. About how long he plans to be on Ibiza, for example. Possibly about Seeblick, but only if he mentions it first."

"You haven't answered my question," she had pointed out.

"What's that?"

"Do you want me to go?"

"Hell, no, I'd prefer to keep you here, but there's clearly no one else we can send."

"I'm so flattered."

"The hell with it. Don't go."

"I think you're more eager for me to go than stay—so I'll do it as a favor for you," she had said matter-of-factly, "on one condition. That I can came back whenever I feel the situation is slipping out of my control."

Now, Marie-Christine rose from the sidewalk table and went back down the shore path to her hotel. I wonder what De Wrendt will be like, she thought.

That evening she arrived early at the bar. Run by an Irishman, it catered to the English-speaking resident colony but had latterly been invaded by other foreigners. Three shallow steps led down to an agreeable room furnished with wicker chairs and low tables, potted plants, oils and watercolors by island painters, posters for gallery exhibitions and guitar concerts affixed above a mantel. For the moment it was not crowded. Two Belgians happily traded sailing stories over a dozen bottles of beer. In a recess a young English couple played intense backgammon. De Wrendt was nowhere to be seen. Marie-Christine ordered a Bloody Mary at the bar and sipped it. In her white cheesecloth shift and wedge cork heels, with her rippling honey hair and satiny shoulders, she was the best-looking girl present. There was one gypsy-complexioned girl with fabulous almond eyes who might compete, but she left almost at once with her escort. Then the bar began to fill up as though a ritual were being observed. She overheard snatches of jubilant conversation: "It's an Ibiza fiddle," a sunburned man declared with pride. "People don't come to Ibiza for the beaches," exclaimed an angular, harsh-faced woman with an odd accent, but what it was they came for was lost forever in the increasing din of voices.

In no time Marie-Christine was joined by a tanned young German with a blond beard who began to speak to her in guttural English. He was making enormous money out of selling houses, he told her. After finishing his gin and tonic he disappeared, and the stool was claimed by a stout man in damp tennis clothes who turned his back resolutely to her. Then the German boy reappeared and with polite insistence reclaimed his place. It was all quite casual and a bit chichi, redeemed by a certain anarchy: the atmosphere the bar secreted was simultaneously that of a London art-show opening and a bus station at the end of the line in Afghanistan, and Marie-Christine saw how it might appeal to De Wrendt's eclectic taste.

At that moment she saw him nimbly stepping down the flight of stairs behind another man and three young women. They waved to several people and made for the alcove, now unoccupied, at the far end of the room. De Wrendt's austere, distinguished head and gaunt, elegant figure were easy to recognize. "He's getting on, but he still looks like the Duke of Windsor," Guthrie had said, which was almost true, save for the shape of his head. De Wrendt was the sort of European man, Marie-Christine noted with a mixture of approval and impatience, who in the evening sallied out flanked by stylishly attired, clannish, faintly contemptuous women. Was he ever alone? *Be natural*, Guthrie had advised her. *Let things run their course.*

The German boy stood a round of drinks and began putting questions to her without realizing how transparent his purpose was. Where was she staying? Was she alone? She set down her glass and let the silence dwell between them; then the conversation strayed off to other subjects. At last, she grew tired of the game and said, did he want to know why she had flown to Ibiza? A gunfight had occurred in her Paris apartment during her absence ten days ago. Her nerves were shaken—she needed a complete change. . . .

Doubt was mirrored clear and large in the German's kindly dark eyes, but she wouldn't let him escape. . . . The Swiss police had interrogated her at length; however she couldn't help them much in their search for Bruno. The German boy's skepticism yielded to puzzlement. Was she the French girl who—?

By this time the standees congregated two deep around the bar couldn't help overhearing her. Guthrie had briefed her that on Ibiza gossip was an industry. She told the German boy a bit more; then with a friendly tap on his bronzed forearm she broke off and left.

She had done her best for that evening.

From her hotel room an hour later she direct-dialed a number Guthrie had given her in Zurich. When his voice sounded, she was suddenly weak with relief.

That had been the evening before. Now all day a relentless south wind with a smack of desert fierceness had blown across from Algeria, one hundred eight miles distant, kicking up whitecaps in the bay.

When Marie-Christine reentered the bar at the same hour, it was filled to capacity, but to her relief the German boy was absent. As she gave her order, the barman's expression was welcoming. Her story had established her. She felt confident, but her heart was beating uncontrollably fast.

Then De Wrendt was soundlessly at her side. She hadn't seen him enter; this time he was unaccompanied.

"It seems you're the girl in the Bruno affair," he said directly. "I recognized you."

"You overheard me mention it here last night."

"Indeed. But your photo was in our Swiss papers."

"Who are you?" she demanded.

"My name is De Wrendt. I live in Zurich. However, I spend a part of every summer on Ibiza." His educated accent had barely a Danubian hiss.

Marie-Christine's eyes settled for a second on the thick silver-blond hair and firm skin scraped gray around his chin and determined mouth. He could indeed have a son almost her age, she thought. He was also much handsomer than she had expected.

"A part of every summer? I was able to manage a few days only."

"How sad for me. You are undoubtedly the most attractive young lady here."

Force him to move, Guthrie had said. But how? The solution came without her seeking it.

"May I join you? I am alone this evening." He had ordered a gin and tonic. "Do you know anything about this island on which you've landed? Real estate promoters call Ibiza a dream island. It was indeed that until the promoters arrived."

"Then why do you come?"

A facsimile of a smile accentuated his distinctive features. "Many reasons," he answered equivocally. "How did you discover this bar? Few newcomers to Santa Eulalia do."

"Oh, word gets about," Marie-Christine said. "By the way, what makes you assume this is my first time on the island?"

"I have an astonishing memory for good-looking faces."

She frowned and moved infinitesimally away. "Do you always come on this way?" Under De Wrendt's thin, glistening coat of conceit, she realized, there was, of course, more—substantial accomplishment as well as, she suspected, a Magyar gusto for pleasure and affluence. Guthrie, at bottom, had sketched only a two-dimensional figure, whom she still had to decipher.

De Wrendt seemed in no way disconcerted by her coolness. "My friends with whom I am staying are putting out wine for a *fiesta* at their farmhouse tonight. A number of the people you see here are invited. Why don't you come along too?"

Marie-Christine's pulse tripped. *Reel him in slowly*, Guthrie had said.

197

"I'd better not. My vacation schedule is simple: beach, two drinks at most, early bedtime. A real rest."

De Wrendt's shrewd eyes held hers. After a moment he said, "Then perhaps we can arrange something tomorrow?"

Realizing that her gamble had paid off, Marie-Christine smiled. "Let's play it by ear," she said sweetly.

Chapter Nineteen

The Stepping-stones

RENATA DE WRENDT'S voice on the telephone was unexpected. Her tone was brisk and blank. She was in Zurich for the day and wanted to have lunch with him. Guthrie proposed meeting at the Storchen. Then, after hanging up, he canceled a prior appointment.

When he arrived she was already seated on the upstairs terrace, wearing a silk bandeau around her raven hair, and she waved to him.

After a dour spring, midsummer had touched off an explosion of foliage, parasols, flowers. The jade-green Limmat flowed soothingly past the hotel. It was one of those luminous August days when cloudless skies seemed everlasting, and Zurich was at its most appealing. Like a well-engineered watch, life here did not race ahead of itself but advanced methodically and dependably.

"You're looking cheerful," she said.

"It must be something I drank last night."

"Something has happened which I think you should know about." She had inspected the menu indifferently and ordered almost nothing to eat. "I'll make it as short as possible; I abhor long explanations. When you came to see me, I mentioned my son. For years his closest friend in Zurich was a boy named Karl Sutter. He's serious and conscientious. The day before yesterday he paid me a visit. I hadn't seen him in more than a year, and I found him extremely disturbed. He's supposed to be studying geophysics at the Polytechnic University here, but when I asked him how his studies were progressing he said that he hadn't been near the University this past semester—he was locked up for four months in an Italian jail and got back to Switzerland only forty-eight hours ago. Are you following this?"

Guthrie nodded. A girl in a featherweight white dress was crossing the footbridge over the Limmat, and her flowing honey hair reminded him of Marie-Christine.

"His troubles began last fall when he responded to a campus appeal for volunteer fund raisers to assist drought-stricken African countries. He met one of the organizers, who was Franz Bauer—"

Guthrie looked at her sharply.

"Yes, Bauer. He interviewed Karl and told him that he'd applied too late but invited him to attend a debate on Third World political and socioeconomic problems at a nondenominational chapel . . ."

"In Oerlikon? On Friedheimstrasse?"

Renata inspected him with suspicion. "Yes. How did you know?"

"I go there to prayer meeting," Guthrie said.

"I'll bet you do. You're just the type. Well, Karl went. There were students, young teachers, neighborhood reformers—a fraction of the 'concerned public,' I suppose you might call them—specialists with maps, charts and statistics. Karl participated in the debate, and as a result, through Bauer, he met one of the specialists, a German by his accent. Several weeks later, after they became better acquainted, this man told him about another, more restricted study group that was pursuing a parallel goal. It

200

turned out to be about a dozen people of all ages who met at a woman professor's house in Rapperswil and discussed ways of aiding oppressed Third World peoples. Karl got a chance to air his views, which are very progressive; he had the impression that he was being judged. One evening the woman in charge suggested that he stay on after the others had left, and she told him about a two-day confidential seminar in a mission house just outside Zurich which belonged to an organization called the African Fellowship Center. The seminar would deal with other ways of helping than fund raising. Karl was ripe for it—ripe was her word. She stressed that he shouldn't inform anybody about the invitation: if the ultraconservative Swiss press found out, they might sabotage the seminar with prejudiced coverage. Late one evening Karl was picked up outside the Hauptbahnhof and driven to the mission house. There he met a Frenchman, whose name was—"

"Forget the name for the moment; it's a blind. Keep talking, but pitch your voice so that it doesn't carry. We don't want the entire restaurant sharing this little story."

Under the stricture in his voice Renata colored and began to retort, but then changed her mind and moved her handsome head slightly so that as she spoke, this time less audibly, she seemed to be studying the idly flowing Limmat below.

"On the very first morning of the seminar, the participants, who were mostly students—about ten in all—were told about support networks throughout Western Europe whose humanitarian purpose was to assist oppressed minorities with funds and equipment. These networks couldn't operate in the open as they wished because of Fascist police repression; therefore, there was some risk, but it was worth taking for a morally defensible goal. Then the students heard lectures on practical methods to stay out of jail and survive in reactionary regimes. Finally the organizers got down to brass tacks, and Karl and several others were asked whether they had the courage to pass from words to action. . . ." Renata paused. She said defensively, "There was never any mention of terrorism."

"Naturally."

"By the time the question was put to Karl, the answer seemed obvious. He wanted to contribute to a better world. He couldn't achieve that by selfishly sitting in a University auditorium all day while countless fellow human beings in the developing nations were being exploited by the West and deprived of self-determination. He was assured that whenever he chose he could back out, that whenever an assignment seemed too dangerous he could reject it—"

"The promise was in writing, I presume."

She laid down her fork and regarded him angrily. "I don't like your sarcasm. Are you trying to understand?"

"I'm trying to dredge up a minimum of indulgence for that idiot."

"I acknowledge that he was naive. The pattern seems clear now, but perhaps it wasn't so apparent while it was happening. First he carried some funds across the frontier to a small cell in Milan, which was 'fraternally linked' to the Zurich organization—the African Fellowship Center or African Missionary Fellowship; they never used the same name twice. The assignment was child's play, since *importing* currency into Italy is perfectly legal. Then he took in a suitcase full of leaflets and booklets—underground propaganda literature printed in Switzerland. Eventually he was asked to drive a car to Turin with a crate of stolen Swiss Army machine pistols concealed under the back seat. He was caught and sentenced to six months' imprisonment. The Italian police told him the hardware was intended for the Red Brigades and wanted to know about further delivery timetables. Karl was beaten up, but refused to inform. To his astonishment, one day he was prematurely released, escorted to the frontier and strongly advised not to show his face in Italy again."

Guthrie weighed her story in his mind, then said, "And then he came to see you?"

"He didn't want his parents to learn what had happened.

So he hitchhiked to my house, and I'm the only person to whom he told his story. He always used to talk freely with me, you see. As I said before, he's upset and confused: in his cell he had plenty of time to ask himself questions—"

"Such as?"

"He suspects he was being played for a sucker from the start. And of course he was, as I pointed out without sparing his feelings. The upshot is, he's hoping to return to the University with no one the wiser; he doesn't think the Swiss police will bother him if he steers clear of further involvement."

"Let me get this right. He's been back forty-eight hours and he's sought no contact with his study group or the African comrades?"

"Contact is the last thing he wants. He's dropping activism, at least temporarily, he claims. But they may not let him alone." Renata shook her hair to one side. "I hesitated about phoning you, but because Bauer is connected with the fund raisers I did." She stared straight at him, hardbitten and forthright. "Do you want to meet Karl?"

"Why should I?"

"I thought you were interested in terrorism. And perhaps, incidentally, you could talk some sense into him?"

"What did you tell him about me?"

"I haven't mentioned you so far. He doesn't like Americans in general."

"There are plenty I can't stomach," Guthrie said equably.

"He's in town, at the University, trying to enroll at this late date in a summer course. I can call him up if you like."

"Do that. Make an appointment for later this afternoon."

Guthrie signaled for the check, speculating on her purpose. She hadn't once mentioned De Wrendt, he noted. Didn't she have the remotest suspicion of his role—or was she still covering up for him? Guthrie asked suddenly, "Did you come up all the way from Lugano to tell me about Sutter?"

"I came to light a fire under my laywer," Renata said, her

eyes green as the river below. "My husband's on Ibiza, no doubt enjoying himself with a new fair lady, while I spend the summer carefully watching my pennies. Enough is enough."

The Consulate files—both active and inactive—contained no trace on Karl Sutter. At five o'clock Guthrie went to the Federal Polytechnic University.

Around the school buildings bikes and motorbikes were parked in orderly rows. As he proceeded up the campus, he spotted a ripped poster on a wall. IRAN TODAY: 40,000 POLITICAL PRISONERS, TORTURE, EXECUTIONS, it read. FIGHT FOR FREEDOM AND DEMOCRACY! It was easy to understand what was chafing at Sutter's sense of justice and decency. And who, Guthrie thought, irritated with his own position, could fault him for that unselfish attitude?

Guthrie sat down on a concrete bench near the *Mensa*, the University cafeteria. He felt the still-warm afternoon sun through the back of his linen jacket, and envied the students in jeans and sandals who were lying on their stomachs on the grassy slope reading. No one in his vicinity seemed to be over twenty-five. Birds swooped overhead, and the traffic on nearby Remistrasse was subdued. The workaday center of Zurich seemed distant, though the Altstadt's tiled roofs were aligned just below. The leisurely atmosphere recalled his own optimistic studies at Freiburg more than a decade ago. When he had returned home at semester's end, his uncle Paul had exclaimed, "Jim, I'd give up all my property and titles to be in my twenties again, on a motorbike, free to go where I pleased." His uncle had been right, except for the motorbike—a Cadillac was always his style.

Then Karl Sutter emerged from the cafeteria and sauntered over, easily identifiable by Renata's description. He was lank and rawboned, and looked somewhat older than his age and verged on being handsome-featured in a cross and disconsolate way. A seemingly permanent frown striated his forehead.

"I'm not a policeman, I'm not a journalist," Guthrie said. "This is simply a casual chat."

"You're from the American Consulate; that's worse."

"What are you afraid of? We're not going to ask you to salute the Stars and Stripes or sign up for a subscription to *The Wall Street Journal*. I'm interested in hearing about your experiences as a fund raiser."

Sutter shrugged. "It's over. I made a mistake, that's all; everybody does at some moment or other. I am not so interested in talking about it." His English was markedly throaty in the characteristic Swiss-German manner. "I do not know why Renata discussed my activities with you."

"She seems to think you haven't learned your lesson."

"What lesson? My basic ideas are still the same," he rejoined quickly. "I take exception to extremist methods, but the objective is valid."

He had youth's unfair advantage in his favor, Guthrie thought—that was to say, resiliency: he had bounced back from his misadventures with no obvious bruises to his stamina or ego.

"What objective are we talking about?"

Sutter turned his flat, uncooperative gaze on Guthrie. "You live in Switzerland; can't you see for yourself?" He was a bit vain and self-important, not impervious to the momentary status his implication in a terrorist network had conferred on him.

"The bourgeois establishment? Since I navigate in it, I'm aware of its shortcomings," Guthrie said. "Shall we say for a start selfishness, lack of imagination, smugness?"

But Sutter wasn't heeding him. "Since you don't seem to know, the objective is to end oppression everywhere. Without a civil war that is probably impossible."

Guthrie blinked. In his experience it was absurd to demand sagacity or realism of students. Their tumultuous universe of impulsive allegiances and limitless theorizing ought to be declared off bounds, he thought, to politicians, dope pushers and secret services. But it wasn't. Everybody fished in these teeming waters.

"So what did you accomplish by smuggling a few handguns to some urban guerrillas in Italy?"

"Down there is a sick and rotten society," Sutter exploded, waving not toward Italy but toward Zurich's center. "Swiss firms sell millions of dollars' worth of arms to dictators; therefore, I thought, why not supply the other side with a few?"

"The guns were confiscated, and you lost most of a semester in prison."

"The hypocrisy here stinks. We prattle about human rights, but rich crooks from abroad get residence permits while foreign workers are expelled. We boast about direct democracy, but this is the republic of the rich: Swiss bankers manipulate the money market . . ."

That's not all they manipulate, Guthrie thought, recalling De Wrendt, and it hardened his resolve.

". . . the Swiss sense of tidiness! I think that means especially tidy profits. Lenin said of us, 'The Swiss are the parasites of parasites,' and he was merely stating the obvious."

"What does the situation here have to do with Namibia, where the guns were theoretically supposed to end up?"

"The problem is international. There are abuses and atrocities in Chile, Brazil, South Africa, so it is only right that those fighting neoimperialism should join forces."

"You didn't even know who was financing the African Fellowship Center. The connections aren't as simple as they seem. The threads lead back to people you never heard about. . . ."

"Too bad," Sutter merely said.

"The guns went to the Red Brigades. You were gullible, and they exploited that."

"Once. Not twice."

"You concede, I hope, that collaborating with them was an error of judgment. . . ."

"Every cause acquires extremists who are destructive."

"Let me get this right." Guthrie spoke carefully. "If pushed, you might agree that terrorism and urban guerrilla warfare aggravate the situation instead of improving it—that they play into the hands of the bourgeoisie's most reactionary elements?"

Sutter stared at him moodily, and after a moment's reflection he nodded.

Their conversation lasted another three-quarters of an hour. Finally Guthrie put it to him baldly, just as had the organizers of the seminar, he imagined, in that respectable mission house on the city's outskirts, and after another fifteen minutes of clashing and prodding he had obtained Sutter's agreement to recontact Bauer.

"It's important because it may forestall another attack. By chance you can be of enormous help. . . ." The idea had occurred to him during his lunch at the Storchen.

"All by yourself, you spotted my potential?" Sutter inquired with a smart-aleck inflection that made Guthrie want to hit him in the mouth. "Or did Renata and you confidentially discuss that too?"

"No way. I don't intend to tell her. And I'm also warning you not to. She stays out of the picture. Don't underestimate the danger of penetrating that group. What's Bauer ostensibly up to nowadays?"

"His committee currently has an aid team in Mauritania."

"That's cover. He'll be leery of you for good reason—because the Italians perhaps managed to turn you around in prison. That premature release after four months won't sit well. You'll have to sell him on the idea that you're a tough nut, too tough for the Italians to crack—that in your cell you figured out that the *only* way to react to police brutality and neo-Fascist violence is through counterviolence."

"I'm not doing this to help you but because they're wreckers."

"Be very careful with Bauer."

Sutter chose to misunderstand and smirked. "I'm not his type."

Guthrie watched him amble off—rangy, limber, more down-to-earth in some respects than he'd anticipated—across the wide, balustraded campus terrace. The University was Sutter's real element. Remove him from it and he floundered into mischief. Beginning with a praiseworthy desire to supply aid to a drought-stricken sub-Saharan country, he had ended up in a Turin prison cell—it was a typical student odyssey of the seventies. Along the way, the views uttered had become more truculent, the meetings more secretive: stepping-stones to a dizzying commitment.

Guthrie shook his head. He had spent considerable time recently inciting people to cooperate, to spit out what they knew, to spy: Marie-Christine, Renata, this student. He did not relish his role. Under other circumstances he would have forborne from pressuring them; but there had been, as usual, no real choice. Just as he had had no time for a drawn-out dissection of Sutter's motives, capabilities, weak points. This recruitment was being slapped together in a way that would cause Wells, who ran Counterintelligence in Langley, to shudder. Still, it might pay off; it might— who knew?—yield bigger dividends than a penetration according to the book. It was a toss-up.

Chapter Twenty

East Wind

"MAHMOUD ALI MALIK, the chief of the Egyptian Air Force, has vanished," the Division Chief said.

In Langley it was morning. Emmett White had arrived at his office at 8:30 A.M. and was considering the dense traffic on the Dolly Madison Highway visible beyond the leafy treetops. Most of the traffic was inbound for Washington past the entry road where the overhead sign proclaimed for all the world to know: CIA. Out there was a brave world of open secrets and spendthrift oil consumption. So be it, he thought.

The Division Chief continued: "Sadat dispatched Malik to Cyprus at the beginning of the week on a fence-mending liaison mission. He flew into Nicosia on schedule, pumped hands, visited a couple of air bases and closeted himself all day with Defense Ministry types. Next morning he left the Egyptian Embassy, where he was staying, and hasn't been seen since. Our station got a hint about his disappearance from a local source. The Egyptian Embassy doesn't know what he's up to, the Cyprus police claim they don't have a clue and Cairo isn't talking. Of course, conspiring is a way of life for Malik: he may simply be huddling in a mountain hideout with his Soviet chums for some therapeutic soul-searching; he's done it before and surfaced twenty-four hours later, all brag and double-talk."

"Malik is merely a minor irritant—"

"He's certainly an irritant, but he's popular in the mud-walled villages of the Delta and the Upper Nile. His notion of sound statesmanship is to stage a coup, accuse us of duplicity, invite Russian missile technicians back in and order a preemptive dawn strike against the Knesset. Sadat confided to the Ambassador that he was sending Malik out of the country for a while to lessen his scope for plotting. That seems valid."

"What's the fever-chart reading in Cairo?"

"Sadat in complete control. The legal opposition is—well—limp. The illegal opposition is splintered, and the mae-stro plays one bunch of malcontents off against another so deftly that they're never sure whom to blame when they're carted off to jail. There *was* a rumor about a health problem —back pains, I believe—but the Information Ministry put out a denial that sounded plausible."

"And the Palestinian brethren?"

"Much as they'd like to, they can't get at him."

"What is Sadat's own timetable this month?"

"Stick to his summer villa outside Alexandria while the heat lasts. No major peace junkets until he flies here later next month."

"Are we hearing from the Israelis? They keep track of Malik's movements."

"We're awaiting a report in a couple of hours."

"Personally I think Malik, like all these flyboys, doesn't have much up there. However, let's stick with it."

Later in the morning, White reconsidered the problem. Malik's propensity for troublemaking had to be taken seri-ously for a fundamental reason. Whatever precarious sta-bility existed in the Middle East at this moment hinged to an alarming extent on one man's peace efforts. If Sadat were to disappear from the scene . . .

There was a cove De Wrendt had discovered that was inaccessible by road and where not a human habitation could be seen. The boat lay at anchor off a sandstone cliff at the nameless *cala*'s mouth. Its deep waters sparkled ultramarine and changeable tints of green—lime, emerald, turquoise—with splashes of other iridescent hues. Occasionally a kayak or a runabout from nearby Cala Mastella ventured into the inlet, but otherwise its peace endured undisturbed. At the base of the cliff were two irregular kidney-shaped slabs of stone on which lizards darted, hunting for morsels of food. The boat, which De Wrendt had borrowed from his friends, was a twenty-one-foot Glastron cabin cruiser with twin engines that produced 140 horsepower and slept three in the forward cabin. For the past half-hour Marie-Christine had reclined motionless on the afterdeck and watched scarflike clouds trailing across the flawless sky.

Now she sat up as De Wrendt prepared to go over the side with his mask, fins and knife. He executed an arrow dive like a man thirty years younger, and vanished into the sea. When he reappeared, he adjusted his mask and kicked out toward the cliff; a few yards from the rocks he made several more dives, remaining under longer than Marie-Christine had expected, and then he swam back. She scrambled to retrieve the plastic bag that he held up, which contained sea urchins. By the time he had hoisted himself aboard over the transom, she had begun to slice them open, cradling them lightly in her palm as he had shown her, to avoid being stung by the tapered needles, and then she set them out with a half-lemon on a plate. He toweled himself dry, went below into the cabin and returned with a bottle of Spanish champagne, two plastic glasses and ice cubes from the gas refrigerator.

"Mmm. I'd go anywhere in this boat," she said after she

had finished tasting and drinking. "Around the world, if possible."

"I take it, then, you don't regret having come out today."

"No regrets," Marie-Christine smiled.

It was her first date with him. They had sailed out of Ibiza port in the late morning and cruised slowly north along the raw, rockbound coast, passing small sand beaches crowded with bathers and stopping once to swim off an unpopulated, crescent-shaped pebble shore. A tame south wind had blown so gently as to be of no consequence. Then it had died altogether, and now, at midday, heat haze clung like a vaporous web to the glass pane of the quiet sea.

"Tomorrow I'm flying back."

"Oh," she said blankly. "Isn't that unexpected?"

"I had planned to stay longer." He didn't elaborate on the reason for his departure.

"I'm sorry."

De Wrendt studied her curiously. "Are you serious?"

"I'm becoming used to this life."

"It's so fortunate for me that I should have met you—"

"Oh, come on, now," she said. It was when he spoke like that, adding dollops of whipped cream to the cake, that she had no trouble in believing he was Hungarian.

"No, no, I mean it. Recently my life has been a mess. Then you unforeseeably turn up, and I have the feeling it's fantastic luck and shouldn't end merely because I'm leaving Ibiza."

"It's not nearly so simple as you imagine."

"When a relationship is worthwhile, it seldom is."

She knew that she ought to change the conversation, although she didn't want to. What she had just told him wasn't a lie; the truth it implied bothered her. He was far more attractive and impressive than she had been led to believe. He had not yet made a pass at her, but, she sensed, it would come shortly, and when it did she wouldn't feel altogether like discouraging him. Guthrie had put her into this predicament. That dissembling Irishman was merely using her—practically putting her into De Wrendt's bed. If it wasn't pimping, it came awfully close. If Guthrie desired her for himself, he wouldn't act that way, even in a good cause.

"Why, after so many years, did you want a divorce?" she asked suddenly.

De Wrendt considered her quizzically. "Is it of such overwhelming interest to you? I needed a certain freedom which very few marriages could afford. And it was exacerbated by other things. In Zurich I have a quite undeserved reputation as a lady-killer. There were one or two little flirtations that upset my wife."

"Was *she* ever unfaithful to *you?*"

"Not really," he said too promptly.

"What vanity!" she scoffed.

She was, De Wrendt thought, as appealing as tart cider. He fancied her very much. If the cruise had been following form, they should already be below in the convenient cabin, where he and whoever his partner of the moment was forgot that their bodies were wet, the bunks were narrow, the air within was close, the light outdoors bright and throbbing. He guessed that she would accept, but thus far he had refrained from inviting her because he could not swallow his mistrust of her very presence on Ibiza. If he had survived for so long, it was by never confusing priorities. Women offered, as the saying went, the "adventure of adventures"—but adventure, no matter how tempting, could certainly be asked, politely, to wait a bit until one or two basic doubts were resolved. And yet he wanted her more than he had wanted a girl in a long time.

"What are you thinking about?"

"You know." He rose and came up to her and, drawing her up to her feet, turned her face upward to his mouth. She responded slowly at first. I should never have come out here with him, she was thinking. Then she was pressing desperately into his lean body. Why not? Why not? the eternal question sang in her mind.

"You are so lovely . . . I want to . . ." His voice was inescapable beside her.

Marie-Christine felt the strong sun wrapping her shoulders and caught a glimpse of the glittering sea as it slipped off the shining rocks.

"Go on. What do you want?" she said.

"Isn't that clear? You. No one else. You."

"Are you sure?"

He glanced at her, surprised. "Of how I feel? Yes."

As he sought to lead her to the companionway, she swerved aside. "But I don't think I want to."

"Yes, you do."

"Oh, damn you."

Later they lay in the cabin without speaking. Finally he broke the silence. "In a way, one must admit, we met through Bruno. . . ."

It brought her back altogether unwillingly to reality. "I'd rather talk about us."

He ran his hand lingeringly through her blond hair. "Why don't you come back with me tomorrow?"

"I can't. There's no point to it." She sat up and touched his lips. "But it was nice."

"Nice enough, certainly, to repeat."

"In Zurich you may have second thoughts."

"Would I ask unless I wanted you to be with me?" I shouldn't have become involved, not with her, he was thinking, yet I do not regret one instant.

Naked, she shivered suddenly. The wind entering the cabin had grown chill. De Wrendt rose from the bunk with a sigh. "I'd better have a look above," he said.

When he came on deck, grayer clouds were moving in from the horizon and the boat was pitching noticeably. He heard a light footstep at his back and found that Marie-Christine had joined him. "We're getting an east wind." He pointed at the direction in which the foaming waves were running.

"Well?"

"On the radio they mentioned the possibility of a storm this afternoon; we'd do well to head about."

He turned the starter switch, idled the engines and went forward to haul up the anchor. Then, as he brought the boat about into the wind and began accelerating to full throttle, he motioned to her to stand beside him in the cockpit. "It's going to be rougher than I expected," he shouted. He was sorry that the interlude in the cabin was over, and out here in the blowy cold he wondered whether the mood that had swept over them both could be recaptured.

The bow slashed into the oncoming rollers; she gripped the bulkhead and was drenched by spray. In the distance a sailboat was running downwind under the overcast as it made for port before the storm broke. The Glastron's speedometer needle hovered at twenty-five knots, and De Wrendt was zigzagging to quarter the waves. As the wind tore at her hair, Marie-Christine found that she was enjoying the unsettled weather, primarily because of her confidence in his ability to handle the boat. Already, when they had cast off that morning, she had noticed his very real eagerness to set the shore behind. She had commented upon this: "You like it out here, don't you?" "I have my own boat on the Bodensee and am on it as often as possible," he had replied matter-of-factly.

They were several hundred yards off the uninhabited island of Tagomago, which rose sheer like a fortress wall to port, when the engines faltered and they lost speed. De Wrendt eased the throttle forward, then back, to no avail; the engines spluttered powerlessly and died. "Take the wheel and keep us on that point," he shouted, indicating a reef rising before the island. As Marie-Christine handled the wheel, she found that the boat was being buffeted more than she had suspected by head seas. Glancing aft, she saw that De Wrendt had removed the deck seat and casing and was kneeling beside the two engines with a toolkit at his feet. "The fuel line is choked," he yelled. "It's nothing serious." She nodded and strained to make out the reef over the top of the blurred windshield. Apart from the distant sailboat that was sticking to its course, she saw no other boats on the water.

The charcoal smudges on the horizon seemed no nearer, and even the riotous wind had abated; the ominous difference was in the swells, which were lead-hued and running high, lifting and then tumbling down with casual destructive force. Tagomago seemed miles away, separated by unfriendly waters. Struggling to keep the wheel from wrenching out of control, she heard De Wrendt call out, "I'll have it fixed in no time." Beyond, the horizon line soared and plunged with giddy regularity. She was becoming hypnotized by its predictable rise and fall. Losing way, the boat had come broadside to the wind and was rolling.

When the first inimical queasiness stirred in her stomach, she fought it down, turning her eyes up to the stable sky. It must have been the sea urchins, she thought, and felt a faint spasm of revulsion. "Just another few minutes," De Wrendt cried. He had undone the two clogged filters and was washing them out with gas from a jerry can. She gulped down a lungful of cold air and made an attempt to ignore the heaving hollowness in her stomach. It was because they were at a standstill, she thought dully as the wheel kicked out of her grasp. Without warning, the bow lurched violently to starboard; a cataract of water poured across the gunwale, sloshed around her legs, streamed down the companionway and flooded the cabin. She clutched the wheel and twisted it back, feeling the hull quiver like a horse. Suddenly the sea's roller-coaster antics subsided, and in the lull she tossed her head back.

"It's fixed. We can go now," De Wrendt bellowed beside her as she gratefully relinquished her place. He switched on the ignition, and the two engines throbbed reassuringly.

As he brought the boat back on course, engine-oil fumes wafted forward to them, while the wind moaned once again. The cabin cruiser plunged ahead and smacked down hard into a trough, reared and collided into another roller.

A fresh tremor of nausea swept up into her nostrils, and her skin tingled in a rash of sweat. Vomity liquid erupted uncontrollably from her mouth. Blindly Marie-Christine stumbled away from the cockpit and leaned far over the side. She heard De Wrendt's warning cry too late. At that moment the boat swerved to port; the wet deck slipped away under her; she snatched at the rail and with a gasp went overboard.

The water's contact shocked her into acute clarity. As soon as she surfaced, she saw dead ahead, but smaller and farther off than she had expected, the boat and De Wrendt at the wheel. He had put hard about and was approaching her at reduced speed downwind. He was energetically pointing, and she made out, then lost from view in the waves, the life jacket he had tossed into the sea. It was bobbing perhaps forty yards out of reach. Waving to him, she struck out to retrieve it. The sky glinted black and silver in the offing; the billowing water all about was gray, but decidedly warm.

What must it be like in winter? the irrelevant thought crossed her mind. Be calm, she commanded herself. The boat had executed a sweep to starboard and come about into the wind again, and she raised her arm so that De Wrendt could keep her in sight. She was tiring in the swells more quickly than she had thought possible. She spied the orange life preserver atop a cresting wave apparently being blown toward her; but then it floated away and she gave up any hope of overtaking it.

De Wrendt was close now, maneuvering the boat to come up from leeward beside her. She could see the aluminum propellers shearing the water powerfully and the spreading frothy wake. She gathered up her force and kicked out over the remaining distance. The hull was perpendicular to her, and almost motionless; the engines' roar subsided in neutral; De Wrendt appeared above midships and threw out a line. She grabbed it and to her horror felt her legs swinging helplessly in the current toward the still momentarily slashing propeller blades.

As she let go the line and thrashed away, De Wrendt shouted at her. She looked back. The blades were no longer whirring, but she was breathless and beginning to feel numb. De Wrendt had flung the line to her again; had tied a bowline in it so that she could secure the loop under her armpits, and he was urging her to make an effort. Cautiously she swam forward, and after she had fastened the line around her body he hauled her up as high as the gunwale. Finally she half-slid, half-plopped onto the deck, fearing crazily for a moment that the boat would capsize.

As she looked at her legs and thought of the flailing metal, Marie-Christine shuddered.

After a while, she quieted down.

"I don't know what would have happened to me without you," she said, huddling into one of his sweaters, while De Wrendt throttled the boat full forward.

"It's all right now," he said. "But I should have kept closer watch on you."

Marie-Christine cast a sidelong glance at him. All the way back to port, she was silent and thoughtful.

Chapter Twenty-one

State of Play

FUAD ASSAM sat in his showroom on rue Ben Mehidi in downtown Algiers, enduring with stoicism the heat and flies and bawling of a radio in a neighboring shop. He saw no quick or easy way of fulfilling his assignment. Ascertain Bruno's plans and movements during the next week! He had not seen Bruno again after the night in Algiers, and suspected that he had vanished from the training camp as abruptly as he had arrived. His bungalow, at any rate, was shut and padlocked, with no sign of life about. One couldn't, for example, just stamp into the camp administrative office and inquire about Bruno's present whereabouts. In present-day, Socialist Algeria, unwonted inquisitiveness could have dire effects. Bruno himself had furnished no hint as to where he was going or what he was up to—indeed, he had eluded those topics, it seemed to Fuad Assam's worried mind, with more than ordinary distrust. Yet a man didn't simply turn up in a semisecret guerrilla training camp without a purpose and sponsors. Fuad Assam could recall no names being disclosed during their dinner or later at the cabaret. Then suddenly he wiped his forehead and placed his fists squarely on his carved fruitwood desk. One name *had* cropped up—or, to put it more accurately, Bruno had in a way responded to one name: that of Rima, the sloe-eyed secretary employed in the administrative office. Motionless, Fuad Assam indulged in some realistic speculation. Bruno, to judge by his behavior that night, had clearly wanted a woman, but the portly, over-perfumed bar girls in Algiers' few surviving nightclubs weren't to his taste. Where else could he turn during the short time he had? A brothel—but only if he had returned to Algiers. More likely, to the girls in the camp, as did the other European volunteers. Young Arab girls were flattered by a foreigner's attentions, and there was no nonsense anymore in a liberated Socialist country about segregating sexes. And of the half-dozen girls at the camp, Rima was the one who had seemed to appeal to him.

Fuad Assam grunted and got up. He paused only long enough to tell his wife that he would be gone the rest of the afternoon, and to check that his linen suit was impeccable.

The drive out led past sunny vineyards, tawny wheat fields, glimpses of unspoiled sandy seacoast, But Fuad Assam had no eye today for scenery. The girl would have to be tackled with circumspection. She was a Socialist militant who had got her job at the camp, he had heard, as a reward for zealousness in Party affairs; he remembered some reference to her activity as a student propagandist for Al Fatah. Luckily, on the strength of his own record and frequent presence at the camp, he was identified by the staff as politically reliable.

Consulting his watch, Fuad Assam drove at a steady, moderate speed and arrived, as he had intended, about ten minutes before the administrative office shut at 6 P.M. He parked the Land-Rover in a lot within sight of the office and passed several minutes checking the spark plugs and the battery's water level. A few employees—those who caught a bus to Algiers—were already leaving the camp.

Then he spotted Rima. She was alone and walking toward the whitewashed staff barracks a short distance away at the far end of a row of eucalyptus trees.

He fell into step beside her.

"I am Fuad Assam," he said.

Rima glanced at him in surprise. She was a slender, matt-skinned girl not much older than twenty, with a swaying walk and large, coal-dark eyes that needed no shadowing for accentuation.

"I've seen you before," she said. "You are with the Palestinians."

"And you are Rima, the camp's most attractive and competent secretary."

When she smiled, she showed white, uneven teeth.

"I am looking for my friend with whom I had an appointment," Fuad Assam said. "He did not come. I went to his bungalow and found it empty. I mean Bruno. Is he all right?"

The smile went out. "Why should I know?" she asked shortly.

"Because you keep a record of all the transients."

She had begun to walk more rapidly toward the barracks. "You should ask the Director during office hours."

"I'll explain why I asked you. When I saw you, I thought, There's the girl whom Bruno wanted so badly to meet. . . ."

She stopped short. "Did he tell you that?"

"He asked me your name, what you did at the camp, whether I would introduce him to you. He was trying to find a way to make your acquaintance."

"He found a way. He isn't shy." Rima frowned. "I wish he hadn't talked about me. What else did he say?"

"Listen, I haven't seen him again."

"Is that really why you wanted to speak to me?" Her breasts were melon-round and well defined under her nylon blouse, and she had a dusky, sullen quality which was very appealing to Fuad Assam. These emancipated, educated young girls were very unlike the females in his household.

He grinned and took her elbow. "Come and have a coffee with me." He indicated the camp canteen near the barracks.

"I don't have time." But indecisively, she did not move away. "How good a friend of his are you?"

"*Jarra!* I saved his life during the War of Liberation!" It was a version of the story Fuad Assam had told often.

"I hope you're not as big a liar as he is. He said that he was in love with me and wanted to take me out every evening. He gave me Paris perfume. I didn't want it. He insisted, instead of saying simply that he wanted to go to bed with me. He is like every European I have ever met. . . ."

Fuad Assam felt untouched by this indictment and breathed more lightly.

"He left the camp early yesterday." She scanned his face thoughtfully. "If you are his friend, how is it he didn't tell you?"

"He should have." Fuad Assam decided he had learned as much as he could, but nevertheless persisted. "Let's sit at the canteen."

"I can't. I have a date. I have to dress to go out this evening." She was still disturbed by her recollections. "I went out with him and let him take me to his bungalow. Then he disappeared next morning without saying goodbye."

"He is not always like that. Where did he go?"

Rima contemplated Fuad Assam sternly. "Why are you asking so many questions?"

"Because I want to contact him!" The little bitch probably knew his destination but wouldn't say, Fuad Assam reflected. Then inspiration came to him. "I wanted to pay him money I owed."

She shrugged. "That is not my problem. Your famous friend has a neocolonialist mentality and is a racist. Why does he come here anyway—just to show off or to hide? If you really want to know, he went to Mauritania."

"You are misjudging him."

Rima returned to her room in a cross temper. Discussing

222

Bruno had upset her. Then another cause for worry began to gnaw at her. All information about Bruno's movements was classified secret at the camp files. She was convinced that somehow she had been misled into talking too much by this gross Fuad Assam. She had suspected him, at first, of wanting to flirt with her; she still thought so, but something else was behind his insistent questioning. After mulling over her doubts, she decided to cover herself by reporting the incident to the Algerian Socialist Party's district delegate.

Mauritania . . .

Guthrie read over twice the Algiers station's lateral cable, which had reached him via Bern in the morning. When he finished, he drew no particular conclusion. Bruno would sit still in Mauritania, he was persuaded, no longer than he had sat still in Algeria. They were a terrorist's way stops, of no real significance, water holes useful primarily for refitting, rearming and refinancing. Bruno's ultimate destination could be anywhere in the world, and it was futile to speculate on it. One tiny fact had become Guthrie's only fixed compass point in the whole affair: Rosenthalerstrasse on August 21, the third date scribbled on the sheet of paper. If a new operation was in the wind—and Bruno had boasted of it to Reindorf—it was reasonable to assume that Bruno would be back by then. And August 21 was now only four days off.

The morning passed with no news from Marie-Christine. By noon her call was ominously overdue. Her last contact had been thirty-six hours earlier, when she had informed him succinctly of De Wrendt's change of schedule. Why was De Wrendt returning to Zurich prematurely? Once again, there were a hundred possible explanations. "He may be handing you a line or testing you. Stay put and see whether he actually leaves. At any rate, he'll smell a rat if you leave too." Guthrie had expected her to protest and accuse him of being illogical by asking her to remain after the quarry had fled—what French girl could resist the pleasure?—but she had unpredictably shown no fight, curtly acquiesced and hung up. Probably he had erred in sending her on a wild-goose chase: her trip to Ibiza had produced nothing but this one piece of ambiguous information. She was fed up, and who could blame her? He was concerned about her mood and her security. At their last encounter in the safe house above Lucerne, she had implicitly charged him with using her. He had denied it, but wasn't it so? He would never again entangle her in gambits that were definitely none of her concern. *For a boy with an alleged brain*, a loud caw, his uncle Paul's, resounded out of the past, *you have a knack for overreaching yourself!*

From his office at the Consulate, Guthrie despondently watched the weather spoiling over Zurich. Rain had been threatening since early morning; sky and lake were the same color of slate. Clouds hung unpromisingly over the amphitheater of hills beyond Kilchberg. It was a foretokening of Zurich's notorious *Hundewetter* as summer faded toward its end. There was no word either from Sutter, he thought. However, Sutter would need time to regain the confidence of those upstanding fund raisers and militants who swarmed so purposefully around the nondenominational chapel in Oerlikon. Give it time. Pray that you have time.

For once Guthrie found himself idle. He recalled that he wanted to buy a lug wrench for his Audi and lay in some gin at the apartment. The problem of international terrorism wasn't going to be resolved in the next hour. He rose and strode grumpily out of the Consulate without a word to his secretary, persecuted by a puritan sense of sinful inactivity.

A thin, stubborn rain was seeping down on Bahnhofstrasse, like a solvent laying bare the city's inherent grayness. He parked the Audi but found that he couldn't advance on foot through the congested center of town, where sopping pedestrians were standing patiently behind police lines. Columns of chanting student demonstrators were filing past the Hauptbahnhof with a petition to be delivered to the Rathaus. The dripping marchers held aloft banners and cardboard signs protesting the delivery of Swiss arms to South Africa. Guthrie wondered if Sutter was participating in the march-past; once again he understood the student's moral dilemma and worried about him. I'm becoming Switzerland's champion worrier. What are the symptoms of paranoia? Ditweiler must know. He had three lines out, Guthrie thought. Probably it was fanciful or plain lunatic to postulate a hidden relationship between them; yet conspiracies were by definition a web of invisible threads spreading out into far corners. Unraveling them—tracing them back to their source still more so—depended on patience. Thus far he had established solely that Bruno had hastily decamped for Mauritania. . . . He stood stock-still, bareheaded in the rain. According to Sutter, Bauer's volunteers were organizing relief in drought-stricken Mauritania.

Abandoning his errands, he hurried back to his car.

At the Consulate he ransacked his file-card index until he found the telephone number he wanted. It belonged to a young Sicherheits-Polizei officer detailed to Passport Control at Kloten Airport, for whom Guthrie had done several favors in the recent past.

"I want to have a list of flights that arrived from Mauritania in the past forty-eight hours," Guthrie said when he had him on the line. "There can't be many, so it should be easy to check out."

"We're busy now, but I'll have a look later and call you back. Anything else?"

"Who was on board—nationality, birthplace, destination: whatever is on the landing cards."

There was no point in involving Huebli unless the call produced results. It was, after all, only a hunch.

Three hours later his contact phoned.

"I went back over a week's records. There are no sched-

225

uled flights from Mauritania to Kloten. However, Air Mauritania runs a service from Nouakchott to Dakar, where passengers can catch a Swissair flight that operates three times a week from Rio to Geneva and Zurich. Yesterday a fairly large group that was booked through Zurich boarded the flight in Dakar and occupied all the available seats. The group consisted of two doctors, several nurses, two soil specialists, a food-distribution technician, whatever that means—the rest are listed as drought-relief volunteers, all with Swiss passports."

"Is the group connected with the Third World Committee?"

"I believe so." The voice was breezy. "Do you want their names, addresses and so forth?"

"I'll put my secretary on the phone and she'll take the information down."

"I happened to be on duty when they landed. When you phoned, it had skipped my mind."

"Well?"

"Nothing out of the way. They all disembarked in Zurich. All their passports were in order. We waved them through."

Volunteers returning from strenuous unpaid duty in the African desert wouldn't excite suspicion; they would arouse approval and sympathy, Guthrie thought.

There was a pause. "According to the manifest, one passenger was added to the original list—"

"Who was that?"

"A paramedic by the name of Walter Frey. I checked him through myself."

"Blond, stocky by any chance?"

"No. Dark-haired, I'm sure of that. Sturdily built, yes. Not more than forty, probably a bit younger."

"What address did he put down on his landing card?"

"Let's see. Here it is—Hotel Victoria in Basel."

"Was he alone? Did anyone meet him?"

"No idea. That's not our department." The voice pursued: "Of interest?"

"Routine checking," Guthrie said austerely. "Could you do one more thing for me? I assume the same group flew out to Dakar in the past month or so. Was Frey with them?"

"You're lucky. Airport management keeps the manifests two months back. I'll run through what they have."

Guthrie went into the adjoining office and instructed his secretary, a girl from Milwaukee who spoke Swiss German, to call the Hotel Victoria and leave a message asking Walter Frey to contact the Third World Committee.

She came into his office several minutes later. "They have no Herr Frey staying there. No reservation was made in that name."

The phone rang again sooner than Guthrie had expected.

"I found the outbound manifest," the breezy voice reported. "The same group took off from Zurich in mid-July. Frey was not aboard."

"Many thanks."

Guthrie sat back. Bruno was finally beginning to make mistakes. It *was* Bruno, he was sure of it. Fuad Assam's latest report had made no mention of dark hair. For good reason. Bruno's hair had probably still been blond when he'd flown out of Algiers. But in Nouakchott he could have attended to that—had his hair dyed, as well as collected a Swiss passport from an accomplice, before picking up the Rio–Dakar–Zurich flight. Reentry made easy. A last-minute addition to the relief group, an unfamiliar face, would excite no astonishment: the other homebound volunteers would assume he'd been working at another desert site. It was as simple as that. Simple and virtually foolproof. Guthrie paused to weigh the implications. At this moment, if his hunch was right, Bruno was back in Europe, somewhere in Switzerland, preparing to go over to the attack again. Guthrie buzzed his secretary. "Phone De Wrendt Bankhaus in town. Tell them you're the executive assistant of a major Stateside textile manufacturer who's doing business overseas and is thinking of opening two accounts, one corporate, one personal. Ask whether the Herr Direktor-General can receive him personally."

"It's past closing time."

"Someone is counting up the loot and will answer."

She had learned not to argue. After a while she buzzed him back. "Herr de Wrendt returned from holiday yesterday. An appointment can be made with him in the morning."

"Tell them we'll call back, then forget it."

Guthrie glanced at his watch. It was 5 P.M. Now it was becoming clear why De Wrendt had cut short his vacation. To welcome home his favorite terrorist. De Wrendt was back. Bruno was back. One piece of the puzzle still didn't fit. Still no word from Marie-Christine. What was she doing —sunbathing? sulking? Never employ a girl agent, make do without. Let Women's Lib sue him next time if it wanted to. With or without her help, he was going finally to nail that s.o.b. So far the tug-of-war had undeniably gone in Bruno's favor, but now with one determined yank . . . Guthrie's scalp tingled as he deliberated over the state of play. The threat embodied by Bruno's presence was like a storm that had been persistently circling overhead without breaking; now there was every reason to believe the lull was over.

Part Three

The urban guerrilla's only reason for existence is to shoot.
—Carlos Marighella,
late Brazilian radical

Chapter Twenty-two

The Patient

THE LINDER CLINIC stands in a nicely wooded park in a
placid, prosperous suburb of Zurich. Neat lawns and meticulously tended flower beds flank a flagstone walk that leads
to a low, wide four-story building. At the rear, the equally
decorative grounds slope restfully past the Nurses' Residence and a tennis court to the lakeshore and the walled
estates of affluent Riesbach. Although the clinic has only
sixty rooms, it works with some one hundred and eighty
doctors, and Mercedeses, BMWs, Porsches are conspicuous in the visitors' section of the parking lot. The prospec-
tus emphasizes that the clinic is not bound by the rates
applied by health-insurance groups; and an initial deposit
of fifteen hundred dollars is required upon admittance. To
the Linder come Persian Gulf emirs, Italian film directors
and Swiss bankers' wives, who have their babies in its
famed obstetrics department. If the Linder is not Zurich's
biggest private clinic, it is certainly its most expensive.

The fleshy, gray-featured man who was admitted that
afternoon was assigned, as he had demanded, a quiet sec-

ond-floor room with a view of the lake, near the elevator and the staircase. A few days earlier, he had turned up—middle-aged, foppishly groomed—at a Zurich doctor's office with a vague referral from one of the doctor's provincial colleagues, and identified himself as Felix Hassler, a manufacturer of microelectric components who lived in Sankt Gallen. Specifying that his appendix had already been removed, he had complained of intermittent abdominal pains, lack of appetite, chills and nausea. To the doctor it had sounded like gastrointestinal upset, but a preliminary examination had turned up no significant disorder. It could be this or that, perhaps gallstones. "Let's find out, shall we, Herr Hassler?" the doctor had declared, which was exactly the reaction the patient had meant to induce. Herr Hassler had made a point of remarking that he could not absent himself from his factory for prolonged tests. Because of this —and since he was obviously able to afford it—the doctor, who worked with the Linder Clinic, had proposed hospitalizing him for several days so that a cardiogram, X rays and gallbladder study, as well as routine blood and urine work, could be carried out in a minimal period of time. A further advantage was that, depending on the availability of beds, Hassler could set an admission date at his convenience—which was also what he wanted.

After being admitted—too late for any tests to begin till the following day—Hassler, once he was alone, minutely inspected his room. It had a private terrace with wicker garden furniture, a color television set, a telephone on the night table, a private bath and toilet and a clothes closet: this last feature, from his point of view, being its most important adjunct. He went over with care the visiting hours, mealtimes and other house regulations set forth on a plastic sign affixed to the door, and was happy to note that the information in each instance corresponded exactly to the details that De Wrendt had provided. He saw that he had missed tea, which was served between 15:30 and 16:00; now there was a long interval till dinner at 18:30, during which he was unlikely to be disturbed. Unhurriedly he disrobed, put on fresh pajamas and a dressing gown.

About a half-hour later there was a light knock at the door and a tall, gangling Swiss from the nondenominational chapel on Friedheimstrasse entered the room. He carried a tan sponge-vinyl two-suiter case with polyurethane trim and chrome-plated locks, which he stowed immediately in a corner of the closet where Bauer's clothes were arrayed.

"Did you have any trouble getting in?" Bauer asked.

"No. They gave me a visitor's pass without asking my name. But there are already quite a few security guards about."

"Naturally. Mr. Salah arrives day after tomorrow. Patients are being transferred out of his wing. The surgical floor will be closed to visitors as of tomorrow evening."

When a nurse arrived shortly afterward with a thermometer, Herr Hassler was alone again. He inserted the thermometer into his anus, then stared at the closet. There was nothing unusual about a relative or friend's bringing in a suitcase that contained a patient's personal belongings which he might require during his stay. No one who came into the room, not even the orderly who cleaned up, would investigate the luggage. After placing the thermometer on the night table, Bauer rose from his bed and went out onto the terrace. Three stories below, at basement level, by the ambulance entrance to the clinic, was a parking lot reserved for doctors, patients and visitors. A beige Opel had just backed out from one of the visitors' spaces and was moving up the ramp to street level, past a sign that read, SLOW DOWN. Bauer watched the car turn sharp left and disappear in the direction of downtown Zurich; satisfied, he waddled back to his bed.

Grand Slam was under way.

That night they had had a farewell dinner in a small, secluded *fonda* near Santa Eulalia, lingering late over their

233

cognacs as a Dutch hippie plucked at a guitar and the howling wind slashed the Mediterranean into blue-black ribbons. Toward the end of the meal, Marie-Christine had announced that she too was returning to Zurich the next day.

"I'm so glad." De Wrendt had looked up and smiled, and she had seen what he must have been like as a younger man. "Why don't you come with me to Seeblick?"

"It's sweet of you to ask."

"I'll ask again."

She had considered. "Come for how long?"

"As long as you like."

"I'm thinking it over."

So they had flown together, bound by a complicity of unspoken feeling, and landed at Kloten, where his silver Ferrari was waiting in the parking lot. Why was she doing it? She was attracted by him, pleasurably aware of his desire for her. During the drive past Frauenfeld her anger persisted with Guthrie, who had neglected to mention that De Wrendt might be a man she could fall for. Guthrie had assumed—why?—that she would be immune to any emotional impact during her stay on Ibiza. Already, before dinner at the *fonda*, she had reached a decision. De Wrendt had saved her; perhaps she couldn't repay him, but she would no longer spy on him. Let someone else do it. Behind her aviator sunglasses, Marie-Christine's green eyes flashed. She didn't like the role Guthrie had foisted on her; especially after what had happened on the boat, she felt cheapened by it. Guthrie's treatment of her had been shabby; De Wrendt's, by contrast, had been . . . as it should be.

It was late afternoon when they reached Seeblick. She saw the name painted on a small signpost beside the driveway, then the gabled stucco house itself, facing the lake. The grounds were separated from the next property by a row of high Canadian poplars, and taller, older beeches lined the driveway. But it was the garden that charmed her

—it was like a Renoir garden, with apple and pear trees, dahlias and rambler roses, and the declining August light that streamed through the glossy foliage imprinted fanciful geometric designs on the lawn. Intuitively she had imagined his house to be like this.

They carried their baggage into the front hall, and then Marie-Christine's heart stopped.

A man had stepped out of the salon and barred her way. It was Bruno, his thatched hair dyed an unrecognizable shade of tobacco.

She whirled about too late as De Wrendt locked the front door firmly behind her. Marie-Christine started to speak, then bit her lip and stared at Bruno, her eyes very wide.

"How long has it been? Two weeks—three?" Bruno's tone was cordial—falsely cordial. "Probably you never expected to see me again. How wrong you were, Marie-Christine. . . ."

She couldn't take her eyes off him. This was the encounter she had dreaded since the night of the attempted kidnapping, and now, with a bad dream's inner fatefulness, it was finally taking place. She was afraid of her reactions—of succumbing once again to that unreliable terse voice and self-confident manner. With an effort she turned to De Wrendt.

There was little trace of embarrassment in his attitude. "I'm not a strong believer in coincidence. As soon as we met, I gathered what your assignment was."

"Assignment? What are you talking about?"

De Wrendt ignored her question. "We're going to keep you here for a while. In a sense, it's for your own sake." A glint of something else appeared on his austere face. "After all, you did agree to accompany me. Without your cooperation we could never have brought you here."

"The only way to get me here was to lie. Everything you said and did on the boat was a lie." Her voice, Marie-Christine realized, was unnatural and hollow.

"I'm sorry," he said coldly. "They weren't lies, but unfortunately, I am dealing with priorities. You'll stay till there's no danger to any of us."

Where was the shifting borderline between what one did and what one felt in life, and how—De Wrendt mused—did one make another person aware of it? He admired this girl's behavior—she was quick, courageous, didn't break up or beg for pity under stress—and he knew that he didn't want to lose her. Later, if all went as planned, perhaps . . . But especially now, and in front of Bruno, he could express none of his deepest feelings.

Marie-Christine's frantic thoughts were focused on escape. Unwillingly she recognized that it would be difficult. Seeblick's garden was walled about, while the only neighboring house seemed unoccupied: she'd caught a glimpse of weeds growing up in the driveway, shuttered windows . . . This was what happened when you behaved on impulse. Some girls could get away with it, but obviously she wasn't one of them. She took up De Wrendt's ambiguous phrase: "Till there's no danger? And when will that be?"

"Don't ask so many damn-fool questions," Bruno interrupted her. "I'm detailing two men to guard you around the clock. The holiday is over, Marie-Christine. Understand that?"

They had put her in an upstairs room that overlooked the lake. The window was nailed shut, but by standing near the casement and gazing down she could see in the failing twilight a striped awning drawn over a flagstone terrace at the house's side and a garden swing near the kitchen. The lawn extended to the irregular shore and formed a small, landscaped promontory, or lookout point, with stone benches and flower beds. Seeblick was certainly not sinister in appearance; to the contrary, it smacked of decorousness; from outside, no one would ever dream that it harbored a hostage: to catch a glimpse of her from below one would have to approach the property along the shore, and it was deserted. Conscious of the guard's presence in the corridor behind the locked door, she sat down on the single bed, opened her handbag, fished out a pack of cigarettes and lit one with trembling fingers. Then she stared at the books of fiction aligned within reach on an adjoining table, but she was far too demoralized and terrified to concentrate on rows of printed words.

The door lock clicked open and Bruno entered. He glanced unhurriedly about, like a warden inspecting a prison cell for its escapeproof features, and only after a moment deigned to address her.

"I misjudged you," he observed. "You can't keep away from trouble. Meddling in Cologne—snooping on Ibiza—"

"—and lending you my apartment." As soon as the words burst out, Marie-Christine regretted uttering them, but she was relieved by one discovery: no matter what his mood, his hold on her was broken. That macho charm she had once admired seemed to her not only spurious but ridiculous; it had not survived the past few weeks' carnage.

"Chérie, you have to answer some questions." Bruno's deceptively calm expression was unchanged. "In Cologne your American boyfriend kept his head down, but one thing I never cleared up: how good a shot is he?"

"How would I know something like that?" she retorted, angered.

Bruno smiled wanly to himself. "For his sake, if we ever meet up, he'd better be damn good. Last contact with him?"

Marie-Christine considered. She anticipated the moment when Bruno's exaggerated, unnatural composure would shatter, and she had no desire to hasten the moment. "Twenty-four hours ago." The truth could no longer matter much.

"Well, now he won't be hearing from you. He must be thinking, did you bungle your assignment or run off with another fellow?—which is precisely what you did. Does he know that you're promiscuous?"

Marie-Christine gazed at him and said nothing.

"There's a weakness in your character," Bruno continued. "You're lazy and influenceable."

"Is that what you came to tell me?"

"I thought we should have a talk. I'm not sure whether to sleep with you or shoot you, *Liebchen*."

"Try neither," she said promptly.

"We made out pretty well together." His glistering humor was short-lived. "No one's had time to deal with you because of more important business, but maybe later I will," he said moodily.

With sheer relief she watched him leave. The unfamiliar dull brown hue of his matted hair made him seem thicker and coarser, like an older and plainer brother, a blurred copy, of the paratroop sergeant she had first met in Paris. But he still tended to swagger, she noted: it was solely his appearance, not his instincts, that had changed.

She nervously lit another cigarette and watched the insubstantial smoke swirl and dissolve against the nailed window. It was night now over the broad, featureless lake. A telephone shrilled somewhere directly below in the house; then the noise ceased as a man's voice answered. It wasn't De Wrendt's, and she wondered whether he had driven back to Zurich and his cover there, which she had jarred. She realized now why they were running the risk of sequestering her. *More important business* . . . the next operation was imminent, and she had to be isolated until it was over. The conversation below had ended, succeeded by dense, fathomless silence that spread through the house. Although it was of no practical immediate assistance, she made a mental note that the phone seemed to be located beneath her room, at the foot of the staircase.

Two hours later one of the guards entered with a tray of food. He was tall, in his twenties, with a ragged blond beard. He looked about and sniffed the stale air saturated with cigarette fumes.

"You smoke too much," he observed.

"It's stifling in here," she agreed promptly. "Why can't you open the window a crack?"

"I'll bring a fan. You can let it run during the night."

She did not want him to go away immediately. "Wait a moment. What's your name?"

"So that you can identify me to the police later?" he said, surveying her derisively.

After he had left, Marie-Christine sipped the lukewarm tea but left the plate untouched, although she was ravenously hungry. If they distrusted her, she distrusted the house's occupants and their food still more. She was yearning for another cigarette, but her pack was almost empty. Finally the silence and uncertainty overcame her resistance and she lit the last cigarette, inhaling profoundly. She was cheered by the guard's parting reply, which implied that they weren't planning any action against her immediately —there was still time to try to devise a way to get out of this nightmarish, self-sprung trap. But she had no idea where to begin.

She finished the cold tea, stripped off her dress and lay down on the narrow bed. It occurred to her that a flaw in her upbringing or character impelled her to be used by men who didn't give a damn about her and never would. There were two in this house—the old spymaster and the younger terrorist.

She came awake and abruptly remembered where she was. The fan had stopped whirring, and the room was oppressively close. It was still very early. Through the window, gaudy bars of color were visible against a pearl sky as the sun tinged the lake's rim.

She slipped on her dress and moved soundlessly on bare feet to the door and listened; then, hearing no noise, turned the knob. As she had hoped, the guard had forgot to lock it after bringing the fan. She opened the door gently and peered into the dim corridor. Legs thrust out, the guard was fast asleep in a wing chair set under a framed lithograph on the wall.

She edged past him toward the staircase and began to descend the shallow steps as cautiously as a cat, mindful of the slightest creak. Once in the hall, she had trouble at first discovering the phone; then she spotted it on a round inlaid table in a recess near the stairwell.

Heart in her mouth, Marie-Christine lifted the receiver and heard the faint, reassuring dial tone. Would Guthrie answer right away? She glanced up fearfully, but saw no shadow in the staircase. Just as she poised her finger to dial, however, a chair squeaked, a muttered exclamation followed and a man's feet sounded on the floorboards heading toward her room.

She swiftly recradled the telephone and moved away toward the living room.

"What in hell are you doing there?" the guard barked, hastening down to the hall.

Glowering, he motioned to her to reascend the flight of stairs.

"I couldn't sleep. I was looking for some cigarettes," Marie-Christine murmured. He hadn't seen her near the phone. There would be another opportunity, provided that she bided her time. And provided that Bruno's operation wasn't already terminated.

Chapter Twenty-three

The Informer

GUTHRIE HAD arrived first, and as soon as he spotted Sutter's blue-jeaned figure ambling up the embankment he left the handicrafts shop where he had been waiting in the doorway and made for the next coffee bar, halfway up the block. Within a few seconds Sutter pushed open the door and sat down opposite him. The tiny coffee bar's proximity to the Café Select made it relatively safe: Sutter's classmates, being more conservative in their habits than they cared to admit, haunted the Select and would not dream of entering this rival café.

Guthrie watched young women moving past the window along Limmatquai, their brushed hair gleaming in the sun, their bronzed legs shining. He felt Sutter's morose eyes resting on him and his extreme inner tension, but he did nothing to put him at ease. A source must always be forced to feel dependent.

"I went back to the chapel on Friedheimstrasse the same evening. There was no meeting, but Bauer was there, fatter and holier than ever." Sutter had ordered coffee and a bun but was staring at his cup with distaste.

"That's very good."

"Why should I be blabbing to you I don't know. . . ."

"You're not doing it for me. I told you before to put that idea out of your head."

The waiter had vanished into a back room; they were alone, immersed in a reassuring, peculiarly Swiss hush, an almost palpable absence of pressure and haste.

Sutter nibbled sullenly at his bun. "Bauer didn't seem overjoyed to see me. He said he'd heard about what had happened near Turin, that I'd been reckless to become involved with extremists. He said that in the meanwhile he'd severed his connection with them. . . ."

Guthrie smiled but forbore from comment.

"He asked about my plans. I took him by surprise when I said that in my cell I'd come to realize the hopelessness of trying to survive under a brutal, illegal system of police repression. Bauer wasn't very much interested. What did you tell the police about the Third World Committee? he wanted to know.

" 'I didn't mention the Committee,' I said."

"Did Bauer buy that?" Guthrie asked. His gaze was focused on Sutter's face for a hint of contradiction or weakness.

" 'If the Italian interrogators are as tough as you claim, how did you manage *not* to refer to the Committee?' he asked.

" 'They're tough but inconsistent,' I told him. 'They kicked me around twice but then lost interest.' "

Guthrie nodded.

"I told him I didn't plan to stop militating merely because one shipment went wrong. Repeated attacks were necessary—that was what they emphasized at the Fellowship Center mission house. I quoted it back to him. He thought it over awhile, grunted and said that if I felt that way I should recontact the study group. He happened to have their new address, he said."

"That's fine," Guthrie said. "It's much better than I expected."

"Next evening I went to the address Bauer gave me, an apartment on Frohburgstrasse in Oberstrass. Obviously he'd called ahead. The atmosphere wasn't friendly. Who was the chief police interrogator in the Turin jail? What did he look like? How much had he already known? They ordered me to come back the following night—"

"At the same address? Frohburgstrasse?"

"Yes."

If they had seriously distrusted Sutter, Guthrie was thinking, no second meeting would have been in the cards; the study group's members would have vanished without a trace into Zurich's bizarre political underground: the African specialist, the woman professor of Rapperswil, the whole pack.

"You weren't supposed to attend a second meeting without prior clearance from me."

Sutter pushed aside his cup and swore. "Well, I went anyway last night," he muttered, "and I met him."

"Him?" Irritated, Guthrie said, "You mean Bauer?"

"I don't mean Bauer. Bauer's dropped out of sight." Sutter lifted his reproachful eyes and said without enthusiasm, "Bruno."

Guthrie expelled his breath slowly. "I don't believe it."

"You'd better believe it. When I arrived, he was at the apartment. Of course, he didn't come up and say, 'I'm Bruno,' but I immediately recognized him by his build and damn North German accent; he resembles his picture in the papers, although his hair is dyed brown."

"You're absolutely sure?"

"I'm not on a trip, not drunk, I'm not putting you on."

"It's very, very important. . . ." Guthrie did an unusual thing and let his own coffee grow cold. "Who does he claim to be?"

"Someone called him Frey. He left after a few minutes."

It was at this point that Guthrie nearly ordered Sutter to break contact permanently with the group on Frohburgstrasse. Unleashing an amateur to spy on Bauer was risky but feasible; on Bruno, it was suicidal. Guthrie watched the

243

anarchic Swiss traffic lumbering down the *quai*. So his assumption had been correct and it was Bruno who had flown in from Mauritania, and as recently as last night he had been tantalizingly close, in the sedate district of Oberstrass, no more than ten minutes' drive away. But why had he surfaced so brazenly and prematurely when August 21 was still three days off? Then it struck Guthrie that he was uncritically accepting the third notation in Bruno's handwriting as a bona fide premise when it was perhaps no longer meaningful. Suppose that at one point it had really corresponded to the date of a new attack but had then been changed? As soon as he stopped to reflect, further, unsettling questions sprang to the fore. What was the reason for Bauer's mysterious loss of contact with the study group? Where was that bitch Marie-Christine? It was more than forty-eight hours since he had heard from her, and he now regarded her assignment as terminated.

"Do you want your coffee or not?" he snapped.

"Coffee isn't good for anyone," Sutter replied inanely, while munching the bun with every appearance of being famished. A shower of sugary crumbs fell onto his lap, but he made no attempt to brush them away.

"Apart from putting you on probation, what was last night's meeting's purpose? And who exactly attended? How many were they?"

"Eight people all told, including the woman professor from Rapperswil. They kept dropping hints—nothing definite, you understand—about getting ready for another operation, maybe in the next day or two."

"Is that all they said? No time? No location? No target?" Of roughly one million inhabitants in Zurich, Guthrie was thinking, how did I choose as my source this imbecile?

"I couldn't damn well ask, could I?" Sutter retorted, a trace of anger for the first time lacing his voice. "Tonight another meeting is scheduled to go over the details. I don't know where; they'll let me know before it happens, and spell out my role then."

Guthrie leaned across the table. "Listen carefully. As soon as you find out the basic plan, I want you to call this number. Whatever develops. By midnight tonight; I repeat, *tonight*: tomorrow won't do. I'm none too happy about these hints they're dropping so freely: you'll have to step sharp in case the meeting's a phony and you're being set up; perhaps even more so if it's legitimate. Okay? *Einverstanden?* Then get off your butt, God damn it, and go!"

Guthrie watched him scuff passively down the embankment, an uncomfortable member of a turbulent generation. He ought to have ordered him to break contact, but it was a luxury he simply couldn't afford. He felt justified in committing Sutter to battle, but was embarrassed that his edginess had prompted him to be so short; he had no way of foretelling that before another day was over, his conduct at their last meeting would be a cause of enduring remorse.

He seriously hesitated about embarking on the next move. Tactical liaison with the Swiss security service was as fraught with pitfalls as a performance on the high wire. Morever, since the demarche involved disclosure of operational details, it could not be undertaken without Ditweiler's specific authorization. Reluctantly, he called Bern.

"Do you really know what's going on out there?" Ditweiler growled into the scrambler.

"A bit. Not enough."

"Let's assume the Swiss track him down on the strength of your information. They need oil and don't want the fallout from Middle East terrorist plots: what's to prevent them from taking the easy way and expelling him? Then where do we stand?"

"They won't react that way if it involves a terrorist attack on Swiss soil. That's original sin. They'll crack down hard. And they may already have picked up a few tremors on their own—who knows? At this point they probably want to match notes as badly as we do."

"You're lucky to have me as chief scoutmaster. Go

ahead." The assertive voice paused, then gathered force for a final thrust. "Guthrie, don't forget: not everyone gets two bites on the cherry."

He found Huebli in his office at police headquarters on Kasernenstrasse.

Huebli appeared harried and overworked, but for a police official whose resources were spread too thin, his reaction to the essential information, it seemed to Guthrie, was admirable. "Do you have any more than the fact that Bruno may be in Switzerland planning an attack?" The question was put with granite calm. There was no excitement and, above all, no exasperation in Huebli's voice.

Withholding Sutter's name and the identity of his airport source, Guthrie gave him a detailed rundown of the material.

"I see. How recent are these reports?"

"The oldest came into my possession twenty-four hours ago."

Huebli considered him with interest. "Why didn't you break the good news to me then?"

"The material was extremely sketchy. Until we had confirmation from another source we didn't see the point of disseminating it." It was eyewash, of course, and Huebli certainly knew it to be such; but it was irrelevant whether Huebli at this stage bought such a specious explanation: what mattered was his readiness to cooperate.

He rubbed his broad, ugly nose, and the corners of his mouth twitched back. "We have a Swiss student's vague word that an attack is going to take place. But if it does, we have no precise idea of the intended target. Obviously we can't throw a safety cordon around every statesman, diplomat, industrialist or other potential terrorist victim on our territory. Bruno was perhaps in Zurich last night, but who's to say that tomorrow he won't be in Madrid or Milan?"

"Do the reports correspond to any early warning you have?" Guthrie asked.

"Wait here a minute." Huebli rose with alacrity and started for the door. "I want to take a pee."

And also clear things with your boss, Guthrie thought.

When Huebli returned, his olive face was expressionless; he locked the door, then ordered his secretary on the interphone to refuse incoming calls for the next ten minutes. Was their conversation being taped? Guthrie wondered. That too was irrelevant.

"This information is for your Agency alone," Huebli began, solemnly enough. "By disclosing it I could lose my job. Sadat is arriving here anonymously tomorrow afternoon for surgery at the Linder Clinic under the cover name of Mr. Salah."

At this juncture Guthrie's respect for Huebli soared. Had the roles been reversed, would he have entrusted a foreign colleague with such vital information?

"Sadat . . . Damn it, are you sure? Say it again just so it sounds right." But even as Huebli opened his mouth, Guthrie had accepted the basic fact and was thinking, So that is it. I wondered what was drawing them all—Bruno, De Wrendt, Bauer—so powerfully to Zurich, and now I have an answer I didn't want. They've raised the stakes; they're not gunning for dime-a-dozen ambassadors anymore. Sadat: the jackpot.

"Tomorrow afternoon, you said?"

Huebli nodded.

"The time and date fit. Mr. Salah . . . a pseudonym isn't going to fool this gang. You realize that?"

"The Government isn't happy about his presence, but had no reason to say no to the request." Huebli went on stolidly: "We have no indication whatever of a forthcoming attempt upon Sadat's life. But of course we do not rule out the possibility."

"Is the Linder Clinic on Rosenthalerstrasse?"

"No. Why?"

"It was a notation in Bruno's papers."

Huebli laid his swart hands palms down on his desk. "I

believe there is a street with that name in Zurich, but I would have to make sure. In German-speaking countries it's quite common. What else? Spit it all out."

Guthrie hesitated, then told him of Bauer's position on the Third World Committee and his connection with Rubinstein in Paris, the study group in Rapperswil and the African Fellowship Center.

"Now, that *is* interesting. Bauer is evidently at a higher level in the organization than your anonymous student. A Zurich businessman," Huebli mused. "We can squeeze him hard. You really should have come with this information much earlier. What else have you left out?"

"I can't think of anything," Guthrie said, suppressing all reference to De Wrendt. I'm as devious as Ditweiler, he thought, but I can't give away De Wrendt's name yet. De Wrendt is too important, he has too many influential friends: spring the trap prematurely and he'll squirm free.

"Under the circumstances, all we can do is reinforce the already considerable security we have planned for Sadat's stay," Huebli said. "He can't have both—anonymity and security—so the former is going to be sacrificed whether or not it pleases him. I'll also put Frohburgstrasse under surveillance. Your source is attending another clandestine meeting tonight—is that correct? That's promising: if they're going to attack tomorrow, they can't wait longer to divulge how, when and where to the comrades. You'll keep me advised, of course?"

"What is Sadat's exact ETA?"

"Sixteen hundred hours tomorrow aboard a regular Egypt Air flight from Cairo. Mr. Salah and party are in first class by themselves."

Twenty-eight hours left. More than ever, it occurred to Guthrie, upon whom the irony was not lost, the battle's outcome rode upon the unruly shoulders of a twenty-three-year-old recently jailed arms smuggler.

"What in hell is wrong with our Cairo station? How is it we learn Sadat's itinerary from Zurich? And why does

Sadat behave in this irresponsible way? If he comes to grief, he asked for it. Let him flit around Europe without asking our advice under a comical alias inviting assassins."

The new Director continued with fluent blandness: "I met Sadat the last time he was over here. . . ." Stoically Emmett White waited for the rest of the story. "He asked me what I thought of Qaddafi. I told him my opinion. He clapped me on the back and invited me to stay with him."

They were in the Director's airy office. He was a four-star general who had been selected for the post after the President's two priority choices had vehemently turned it down. There had been some trouble about Senate confirmation and with still-active remnants of the CIA old guard who disdained the newcomer's lack of field experience. White, who liked him, considered him with sympathy tempered by impatience.

"The Israeli report arrived." White steered the conversation toward the practical. "They traced Malik to a beach house in Limassol; it's a local KGB facility. Two Soviets paid a call on him yesterday; they stayed three hours, but the Israelis had no mike-and-wire. He's had no other visitors."

"Has their report gone to the Egyptians?"

"There's reason to assume so."

"Let's see. Malik has surreptitious contact with the Russians on Cyprus, which is the KGB's Middle East headquarters. Meanwhile, Zurich picks up several leads about a terrorist attack Bruno is planning tomorrow, on the day Sadat is due to land there—well, it would obviously suit Moscow to replace Sadat with someone they control, and Malik is a likely successor to Sadat anyway. Would Moscow be above nudging events in that direction provided it thought it could get away with a power play? I don't think so. Authorize Cairo station to warn Sadat of a possible attempt upon his life in the next twenty-four hours."

"The Swiss have already transmitted a warning."

"Coming from us, it will carry ten times more weight."

"May I suggest something?" White hesitated. He had to

249

tread lightly with the new Director. "Our message should go to Sadat personally or no one at all."

"Are you afraid of a leak in his entourage?"

"Except for us, everybody who shouldn't seems to have been clued in to Sadat's travel plans: Malik, the Russians, the commando that assassinated Wadi Khalef. Surely there's a leak. Send the warning through Egyptian official channels and it may never be delivered. Bruno's network is, at the least, far-flung and efficient." White removed from a ring binder a photostated info copy of a priority report from Algiers station.

The Director read it and handed it back.

"Who was he?"

"A rug exporter. Algiers ran him on a low-level, intermittent basis. When they put him on Bruno's trail, they urged him to exercise extreme caution. Apparently he didn't."

"Nasty way to die."

The Director rose and looked out the panoramic window at the Washington skyline just visible in the distance. "You're right: Cairo station should request a crash audience with Sadat personally."

"Sadat can still cancel his flight to Zurich."

"But knowing him, I wouldn't bet on it," the Director said.

Chapter Twenty-four

Searching for Sutter

THE TELEPHONE call aroused Guthrie from fitful, troubled sleep. He glanced at his watch, saw that it was past eight, and his first thought was *It's Sutter*.

But it was Marie-Christine's almost inaudible murmur— so light and weightless that at first he assumed she was still on Ibiza—penetrating into his consciousness with unmistakable urgency: "I'm at a house called Seeblick, do you understand? I've been trying for three days to call you. They're holding me. Bruno just left."

And that was all. Wide awake now, Guthrie dressed rapidly; he had overslept after waiting up vainly till three for Sutter's call. It had been a long, unsatisfactory vigil—was Sutter hopelessly unreliable, or had something ugly and irrevocable happened to him?—and in the meanwhile other bleak meditations had chafed at Guthrie's mind, making the darkness outside seem still more inimical. At midnight, the Consulate duty officer had dialed his apartment number and paraphrased the contents of a coded cable just received from Algiers. Fuad Assam's repeatedly stabbed body had been washed ashore on a beach by Tipasa, where the police had identified it. One more death: whoever came imprudently close to Bruno suffered a swift, tragic end: Starkey, Fuad Assam, probably the homosexual at the Geneva airport. Thus, as the night passed without word from Sutter, Guthrie had begun to dread the news that the morning might bring. "People aren't disposable like cigarette lighters," Marie-Christine had said to him accusingly at one point. Amen.

He gulped a cup of bitter coffee in one corner of his untidy kitchenette, drew gratefully on his first cigarette of the day, thought that he shouldn't smoke so much and reflected on the phone call. God, how he missed Marie-Christine! And how he had misjudged her motives. She had managed to utter only four short sentences, but she had packed maximum information into them. By instinct he would have driven out to De Wrendt's house at once, but then he reconsidered. Since she was being held hostage, nothing would befall her until after the attack was carried out. Bruno had to be stopped beforehand, and then everything would fall into place and Marie-Christine could be freed. With Bruno, the toughest of the lot, out of the way, captured or killed, and his operation in a shambles, the other members of the network would be less inclined to put up a last-ditch fight: they would probably scramble for shelter, but if they took her with them—well, it was not unheard of to negotiate a hostage's release in return for safe passage. He hoped it would not come to that.

What a gallant way of doing things, he thought drily. You asked a girl to stick her neck out on a half-baked mission, and her reward for loyalty was Wait till we can find time to cope with your small problem of being held in an isolated house by a group of murderous fanatics; we have bigger fish to fry and hope that you will understand; if you don't, tough shit. Intelligence work was an eternal, demeaning, nerve-racking balancing act between long-range benefits to the Service and short-term losses for individuals.

Guthrie crushed out his cigarette, went and rummaged in the bottom of a battered cedar chest where he stored his extra hi-fi equipment and found a 9mm Parabellum Browning semiautomatic he had not needed in months. He stepped out of his apartment house and squinted into the fierce sun. The day showed every sign of turning into the sort of scorcher when every Zürcher who could hied off to the lake or the pools in the surrounding hills. It required lurid imagination—or firsthand experience with Bruno's single-mindedness—to conceive of the prevailing summer peace being bloodily shattered in a few hours. Yet if Sutter was right, the Third World Committee zealots who clustered about Bauer, and who preached liberation and disorder, equality and extermination in the same breath, were planning to go over to the attack today or tomorrow. The notation August 21 had led him astray, Guthrie thought. He should have made allowance for the operation's being moved up or the date's not referring to it directly. How much time was left? Probably very little. It was no wild fantasy to deduce that Sadat was on a collision course with his would-be assassins, unless, Guthrie thought—unless he could obtain Sutter's final report.

Inbound traffic was already slowed down; he'd never find a parking place for his Audi at police headquarters, Guthrie realized, and hailed a taxi. Perhaps Sutter would materialize abruptly, of his own volition, but Guthrie didn't think so.

"All right, let's find out what became of him."

They piled into Huebli's shabby vintage Fiat and drove fast to Frohburgstrasse. Guthrie thought, I just blew Sutter's cover and now I may blow my own. Nothing in this case corresponds to the field-book rules they swear by at Langley.

"After our talk yesterday I checked out the Frohburgstrasse lease." Huebli kept his eye on the chaotic traffic. "The apartment is rented in Bauer's name, but he doesn't live there. He's vanished from his home, and his antique shop on Neumarkt is shut indefinitely; no one in the neighborhood knows where he is."

"He hasn't been near the study group either." Watching the sun bathe the modest stone houses of Oberstrass, Guthrie kept his mind free of further hypotheses. There'd already been too many.

"In one way your tip about Bauer produced quick results. We telexed the French police, who finally got around to raiding Rubinstein's apartment. They found a jumbo-size cache of stolen passports and arms. Both Rubinstein and his son are in custody. The Aurora commando is beginning to come unglued . . . but, of course, Bruno is still at large."

And therefore capable of striking, Guthrie reminded himself.

As they approached Frohburgstrasse, Huebli said, "The surveillance squad went on duty last night but reported no activity whatever. I'm not expecting much."

"Nor am I."

The house number they had belonged to a drab, dilapidated building bracketed by an auto-repair shop and a Laundromat. Huebli left the car in the next block. As they returned on foot, he stopped and entered a grocer's across the street, then came out accompanied by a thickset man in a gray poplin suit who declared laconically, "Nothing new."

The study group's apartment stood one flight up an uncarpeted staircase steeped in the vagrant reek of onions and stopped drains. Huebli rapped sharply three times on the narrow paneled door. When the knocking aroused no sound within, he grunted, "We'll talk to the *Hausmeister*."

They found him in his neglected rooms behind the staircase, a soiled wisp of a man with a Chaplinesque sorrowfulness about his eyes. No, Herr Bauer's friends had come and gone two days before but had not returned. No one was in the apartment; it often remained empty for weeks at a stretch.

"We'll take a look," Huebli said.

The *Hausmeister*, limping, got his extra key and clumped back upstairs with them. The small parlor was dingy, dark, cluttered with valueless furniture. The air within was stale but inoffensive; the hallway's sour stench of cooking and dishwater didn't emanate from here. And as they poked through two other depressing rooms, another fact became obvious: Bauer's guests had carefully left no debris in their wake—not a smudged glass, not a scrap of paper, not a cigarette butt.

"What are they like?" Huebli barked.

"Proper. Never making a disturbance. Young men of good family with correct upbringing—"

"Queers."

The *Hausmeister* pursed his lips. *Proper* in his mouth, Guthrie thought, reflected the lavish tips which the janitor had undoubtedly received to look the other way each time one of those discreet revolutionary sessions took place.

"Always the same *höflich* young men? You got to recognize them?"

"There was a German the other night I never saw before—"

"Description?"

"Dark-haired, sturdy, not so well mannered."

Standing in the middle of the seedy parlor, Huebli said, "This is hopeless. We're wasting time. Last night's meeting, if it took place, wasn't held here. Should we go to—?"

"Yes," said Guthrie. "He gave me his home address. It's worth a try." But he felt thoroughly deflated, convinced that they would arrive likewise too late: the others had too much of a head start.

Accompanied by the thickset man, they tore down Winterthurerstrasse in the Fiat, silent and preoccupied.

Sutter lived in a gray stucco house on Stapfer-strasse, a short uphill walk from the University, in a neighborhood of student boardinghouses. The entrance was on the side, and an electric button operated the door but there was no interphone. Receiving no response to the button marked SUT-TER, Guthrie pressed one marked BECK and was admitted at once. As he raced up the unlighted stairs with the others following closely, he thought, Anybody could get in. On the next-to-top floor there was only one room, and the door was slightly ajar. Guthrie shoved it open and stepped inside. To judge by the room's condition, they hadn't overpowered him as easily as they'd expected. Sutter, surprised, must have put up a desperate struggle; but like Fuad Assam and Starkey, he had woefully underestimated Bruno's tenacious sense of survival, Guthrie thought, surveying the wreckage. Chairs were overturned; textbooks lay strewn around a crushed lampshade on the floor; a curtain drooped, ripped from its rod, beside the window where he had perhaps tried to shout for help. Heubli was silently contemplating the telephone cord yanked out of the wall socket; then he turned his attention to a walnut armoire set against the wall. A few denim clothes were still draped on hangers inside. Of Sutter himself there was no sign anywhere. Addressing the thickset man, Huebli said, "Hofer, talk to the other tenants and try to get an idea of when it happened."

They moved to the kitchen, where a light was still on. "It must have been before midnight," Guthrie said, thinking of Sutter's overdue call. "They were already suspicious of him, and somehow he blundered. They followed him back here from wherever—"

"Any notion where else they meet?"

Guthrie shook his head. An idea was forming in his mind —a bizarre, tricky plan to offset Bruno's thrust that might pay off. To carry it out, however, he would need to be unencumbered, free of Swiss scruples and inhibitions. Huebli was competent, a valuable colleague in a crunch, but he couldn't be asked to transform his mentality and violate rigid police rules.

Lost in thought, he watched Huebli plug the telephone cord back in, get the tone and begin to dial a number.

"Emil?"

"I'm putting out a *Grenzalarm* for Bruno and Bauer," Huebli said to Guthrie.

"It won't do any good. They haven't left Switzerland—not yet." He saw by his watch that it was eleven o'clock. Sadat was due at Kloten Airport in five hours.

Huebli considered Guthrie's bluff, freckled face set in frustration and concern. He liked this American and realized what he was thinking.

"You know, Sadat will be exposed to maximum danger, as I see it, for only a few minutes at the airport, so this is where we are concentrating our personnel. From Kloten he'll be rushed to the clinic in an unmarked car with a fore-and-aft escort of two likewise inconspicuous cars. The ride takes no more than twenty-five minutes, and the actual route will be decided upon at the last moment, avoiding the downtown sector. A terrorist commando would find it extremely difficult to position itself along the correct route at the right time."

"The whole damn trip is unnecessary and hazardous. Sadat!" Guthrie exploded, biting off the name like an expletive. "Last night the Agency warned him of the danger and advised canceling his flight—"

"He's maintaining it because he has faith in our ability to handle his visit here," Huebli declared with a strange, Swiss combination of pride and vexation. "Personally I wish he had chosen London or a German hospital, but it is true that his anonymity will make the job considerably easier. The press doesn't know he's coming, nor does the public; only a few trustworthy members of the Linder staff are aware of his identity—"

"But Bruno's gang undoubtedly knows exactly who Mr. Salah is. What about security at the clinic?"

"There we are dealing with a static situation: on the perimeter, armed guards; restricted parking; no deliveries and no admittance of visitors an hour and a half before Sadat's scheduled arrival; screening at the main entrance of everyone who *is* admitted. As soon as his car drives up, he'll be hustled inside through a side entrance, which means that

257

he won't be outdoors more than a minute or so, the absolute minimum. Once he's indoors, our worries are reduced. Both Egyptian and Swiss security are staked out throughout the surgical floor, so that no one can approach within a hundred yards of his suite without proper identification. One or more of his personal bodyguards will be constantly on duty in the *Vorzimmer* just outside his bedroom. All medical staff who have a reason to come into contact with him have already been screened. You know, the Linder has had long experience caring for VIPs and shielding their privacy; for us, this is a bonus."

Guthrie's skeptical glance roved about the ransacked, empty room. He was remembering that Wadi Khalef in Cologne had had a bodyguard too, and that the German police had been alerted, but he refrained from bringing these facts up.

"As for the larger picture . . ." Was Huebli as confident as he sounded? ". . . in the event Bruno is counting on outside reinforcements, we are naturally maintaining surveillance of all Palestinians and their known agents arriving by air, rail or road. To date, the frontier posts have reported nothing suspect."

"The infection is already here," Guthrie said simply.

Hofer had returned to the room.

"The top-floor apartment is vacant," he announced. "A woman lives alone in the apartment below this; she heard what sounded like a fight up here and locked herself in. On the floor beneath her are an elderly couple; they were already in bed when they heard a lot of commotion—furniture being overturned and so forth: they decided it was a wild student party, considered phoning the police to complain, but then, about eleven forty-five, the racket ceased and they changed their minds and fell asleep. The ground floor is occupied by a younger couple who went out to dinner and returned around midnight. They heard the front door slam shortly afterward and a car drive away—they assumed visitors were leaving."

"But they heard no sound of a struggle?" Guthrie asked.

"No."

"And the *Hausmeister?*" Huebli asked.

"There is no *Hausmeister*. A janitor acts as caretaker in charge of maintenance and collecting the trash, but he lives down the street in another apartment house."

"The racket stopped a quarter-hour before midnight," Guthrie mused aloud, "but the car drove away only after midnight. What happened in between?"

"I doubt anyone in the building can supply the answer," Huebli said.

They were halfway down the staircase when Guthrie paused. Huebli and Hofer, who were following him, saw it almost at the same moment—a small russet splotch on the floorboard beside the door of the elderly couple's apartment. On the way up they had missed it in the dark. Guthrie pressed the hall light button and they proceeded down the stairs more attentively. On the last landing they found two more dried spots of blood, then several more at the side entrance. Outdoors, a cement walk ran parallel to a ragged boxwood hedge that delimited the house's grounds. Guthrie followed the walk as far as the street but found no other splotches; then he returned and continued around to the back of the house, where three stone steps led down to the basement. Conscious of the heat, the stillness, the summer mildness roundabout, he stopped, staring at a larger, rust-colored smear on the lowest step.

He pushed the unlocked basement door hard, barged in and, snapping on the light switch, looked about. A spade shovel, a pile of old magazines and a discarded bicycle tire stood gathered in one corner beside some stacked hardwood boards. Overhead, heating ducts and hot-water pipes ran along the ceiling. Sutter's lean body was rolled over motionless sideways on the cement floor between a large oil burner and the far brick wall, his nose and upper lip puffy and dark, his jaw stark white. From a gash beside his left eye filaments of blood had coiled down his cheek and run behind his ear. Blood that had spurted from his nose had soiled his checked gingham shirt. His wrists were lashed behind his back with wire, and a man's handkerchief was stuffed into his mouth. Kneeling beside him, Guthrie ascertained that his breath was still emerging in grating sighs. The worst of the beating had probably been administered after he was subdued and defenseless. As Huebli and Hofer came up behind him, Guthrie gently prodded Sutter's rib cage.

"He has at least two broken ribs, no doubt considerable internal bleeding and I don't know what damage to his eye."

"Use the phone upstairs and get an ambulance over here right away," Huebli said to Hofer, then for a moment was silent. "Given their usual methods, they let him off lightly," he observed.

Guthrie rose to his feet and avoided staring down at Sutter's figure. He could imagine how the student had been slammed back and forth against the brick wall to raise those raw, bluish bruises. They were Bruno's furious graffiti, his eerie method of self-liberation. Guthrie found himself remembering the two dead French policemen with the astonished expressions, Starkey's supine frame on the cobblestones of Cologne, the homosexual who had been savaged in Geneva. He wondered when, in this affair, he would be able to feel another emotion than blank, simmering anger.

"I don't think they intended to let him off," he replied. "After Sutter was jumped upstairs, they dragged him down here to sweat him at leisure and find out how much he'd revealed; they were probably just softening him up when the ground-floor couple chose that awkward moment to come home. Since they lived directly overhead, they would have heard Sutter if the interrogation was too rough and he began screaming. It wasn't the side door that the couple heard being slammed, but the basement door."

"You're probably right. They were running no risk by leaving Sutter behind: he's in no state to tell us anything."

". . . And he was our only valid lead." Guthrie had an

abrupt, bleak vision of Bruno striking again and escaping with impunity, as he had in Cologne.

"What are you going to do now?" Huebli asked, watching him closely.

"I don't know," he said. It was a lie. He knew exactly what he was going to do as soon as Sutter was safely hospitalized and Huebli was shunted out of the way. He had exposed too many other people to danger, involving them in the hunt without sufficient consideration for their vulnerability. Now the time of acting by proxy was over.

Chapter Twenty-five

The Orderly

IN THE early morning, both men strolled about the Zurich-horn casino's deserted grounds. The first outbound steamer for Kusnacht and the lower reaches of the lake had just hooted and chugged away from the landing pier. Sloops, catamarans and catboats were moored in the basin, but their owners were not yet about. At this hour, spot surveillance of the site without being conspicuous was virtually impossible.

"Bruno went to Rosenthalerstrasse first thing today, and Bauer is in place," De Wrendt said. "There is really nothing more to do but wait." He added, "Waiting is always intolerable. Once, believe it or not, while the outcome was uncertain I shot thirty-six holes of better-than average golf. On another occasion, I made a substantial placement in convertible bonds for one of the bank's best clients." With lifelong relish he sniffed the tart breeze wafting off the lake. "When it is over—"

"Within a quarter-hour of the first alarm we have to reckon with the Kanton antiterrorist brigade's being committed in and around Zurich," Maisky cut in. "Bruno and Bauer must be well on their way by then. Did you impress that on them?"

"They will be. Bauer will go to France and lie low. As for Bruno, his escape route remains the option we agreed upon. At Seeblick yesterday I gave him a passport and thirty thousand schillings for his temporary expenses in Vienna. That should be more than enough."

"What about the Aurora commando's communiqué?"

"One of Bauer's volunteers will call up the AP, Reuters and Agence France-Presse offices and instruct them where to find it—in plain envelopes left with the concierge at the Baur au Lac and Atlantis. That was Bruno's idea and I approved it. But in my opinion, the action will speak for itself: everyone will grasp what Sadat's assassination implies in the Middle East without the help of Bruno's prose."

"Everything seems to be under control." Maisky looked at the opposite shore, which, with its villas and cypresses, blurs of jade verdure and sunny slopes, had a mellow Tuscan air. "Your role, one might say, is terminated. From the start we committed ourselves to support: support of a special sort, true, but nothing more; when the PLO representative first contacted you, that was made abundantly clear."

When pressure mounted, De Wrendt noted, Maisky sought refuge in formal, contractual language. He should have been a lawyer. He had a lawyer's passion for demarcating responsibility.

De Wrendt himself remained silent.

"I can sense uneasiness seeping out of every pore. That's unlike you. What is it?"

Generations of justified skepticism had contributed to the making of De Wrendt. "Everything," he replied.

Maisky restrained a gesture of impatience. "Specifically?"

"I told you about the Swiss student the CIA recruited who almost managed to infiltrate Bauer's cell. He was neutralized in the nick of time. What other surprises are in store? The Americans are being too quiet, too passive. By now, with the Swiss police's assistance, they must have put two and two together. That's what they have computers for."

"You mean Sadat's trip? We're assuming it's no longer a secret, or at most a *secret de polichinelle*. Obviously they realize Sadat is targeted; perhaps they even expect an attack today. I understand there's been a last-minute tightening of security. But this dutiful deployment of men and matériel rests on a naive expectation that a terrorist attack against a target of Sadat's stature will break new ground, escalate to a record degree of nastiness. All security services instinctively assume that the adversary will commit the newest, slickest and latest technology available, because they themselves feel safer resorting to it. What are they fearful of at this point? Probably a ground-to-air-missile attack against Sadat's plane. Or something even more fanciful, like germ warfare at the clinic. So they'll devise spectacular countermeasures; it's a bit reminiscent of doctors' girding to combat a sophisticated virus strain while the patient is stricken with a common cold. They are going to be woefully disappointed by our unimaginative ways. . . ."

"In the last analysis, this operation hinges wholly on Bruno."

"—whom you handpicked for the job." Maisky's ample cheeks gleamed in the pale, transparent light. "It was an intelligent choice. Would you have entrusted the assignment to a high-profile Palestinian thug who would be gunned down before he came within a mile of his target, and could compromise your entire network into the bargain? No, I don't agree with your misgivings. If anyone can liquidate Sadat, Bruno will."

"When I recruited him, he was controllable. A hardnosed, opportunistic ex-paratrooper adrift in Spain: there was nothing complicated about his character. He had good sides, too, which I respected. But give a man like that ideological motivation, funds and weapons, and you gamble with disaster."

264

"The trouble with Bruno is, he's a bit of an idealist," Maisky remarked astonishingly.

"An idealist?" De Wrendt snorted, and for once his manner became jeering. "An idealist with an automatic rifle."

"You outdid yourself praising him when we had our last dinner. Isn't your attitude now exaggerated?"

It was one of Maisky's stock euphemisms, and De Wrendt spotted it as such at once. What Maisky really meant, no doubt, was—aren't you being overcautious? losing your grip?

Maisky's anxiety was legitimate. Brilliant operations required a streak of daring. However, what he lacked was not boldness but belief. Time was, during the war's gloomiest days, when Moscow Center's interests had loomed paramount in his mind and he had run breathtaking risks in behalf of a cause to which he subscribed without demur. But more than thirty years separated him from those unquestioning and rousing days. What had begun as a rivulet of doubt in the early sixties now flowed deep and wide and irresistible through his being. After so many years his career in the Service was, after all, only a job—a skill, a technique or, worse, a routine with which he could no longer break. He had lost some of his faith coincidentally with growing older, just as he had lost a vital contact with his wife and son, and at times he compared himself mockingly to a lapsed Catholic who still mouths prayers he scarcely expects to be answered and continues to haunt churches in a state of sullen disbelief because he can think of no better place to be.

Nettled, he replied, "Is it exaggerated to demand honesty? Bruno is a liar."

"In what way?"

"The homosexual's death at the Geneva airport—"

"How can you be positive Bruno killed him?"

"All the evidence points to him: the time, the manner; besides, an Air Algérie steward was spotted with the victim outside a men's room shortly before the murder." De

Wrendt's face was blizzardlike. "He denies it, of course. He's begun lying even to me. After this operation I won't use him again."

"To date he's carried out your orders."

De Wrendt saw the futility of pursuing the exchange and said, "There's still another matter to be settled. The girl—"

"I've been running that over in my mind ever since you returned with her from Ibiza. If we turn her loose, she can identify you." Maisky was merely repeating what they had already said before, to gain time and force De Wrendt to make a suggestion which he did not want to make.

"I wish there were an alternative solution."

"Naturally. That's understandable." Maisky's broad Ukrainian features were bureaucratically unaccommodating.

"I saved her life on Ibiza."

"You told me about that."

"She's an admirable girl."

"I don't doubt it."

If Bauer had done his job properly, De Wrendt mused, we would have been spared a great many headaches. "I'll have to find a way to persuade her not to talk," he said. "It won't be easy, since she has no reason any longer to trust or even like me."

Pure chance was responsible for Renata de Wrendt's still being at the Hotel Storchen. She had planned to leave the day before for her house in Castagnola, but when her lawyer had encountered difficulties in making an appointment with De Wrendt she had reluctantly postponed her departure.

"I'm coming over to see you right away. It's urgent and concerns Sutter," Guthrie informed her drily on the phone, and scarcely waited for her reply. He had stopped off at the Consulate only long enough to make the call and check incoming cables. One was an info copy of a message

Langley had flashed to the Cairo station, and another was Cairo's subsequent, rapid reaction. Guthrie read both with special interest, memorizing their classified contents for eventual use.

Then he set out for the Hotel Storchen.

He blinked as he stepped into her room. The plastic venetian blinds were lowered against the white glare of the high afternoon sun. A television set opposite the bed was tuned to a panel discussion. She switched it off and confronted him without amenity. "What's happened to him?"

Without surprise Guthrie observed the strain on her face. Even in that dim light the effect of his news was noticeable. Between his phone call and arrival, she had had time to dread the worst.

"I'm going to see him." Renata began to gather up her handbag after he had told her, while Guthrie speculated on the real relationship between this robust woman and that gaunt, restless student. Was her pronounced solicitude intended for her son's best friend or her young lover?

"They won't let you in at the Kantons-spital. I just spoke to the doctor in charge of the emergency ward. Sutter's on the critical list."

Her somber eyes blazed. "At the first opportunity you persuaded him to spy."

"Did he tell you that?"

"Yes."

"Obviously he told too many people."

"I asked you to talk some sense into him, not nudge him into a trap."

"He was warned about the danger."

"He isn't mature enough to take a warning of that sort seriously. Suppose he dies?"

"He won't," Guthrie said offhandedly. He recalled the caked blood around Sutter's tumefied eye, the dead-white skin, the broken ribs, the sadistic pummeling by those expert meat-chopper hands, and all of a sudden he was beside himself with fury. "Forget your own needs and oh-so-

267

tender emotions for a moment. There's been too much covering up and tiptoeing genteelly around the truth. How about laying the blame where it belongs: on the goon who roughed up that kid? Herr and Frau de Wrendt are too honorable and elegant to consort with a wanted terrorist— or are they? He was your husband's protégé in the first place; a relationship of dependency like that doesn't necessarily wither with time. You once described dear Dieter as a mixed-up German whom you wouldn't trust with an idea, yet his operations have a specific political purpose. Well, then, where do the ideas come from? Who inspires him and gives the orders?"

His flare-up had smothered her own anger. "You're always insinuating that it's my husband, when it's not true! My husband hasn't seen him in years. I've already made that clear." She set down her handbag and sat on the bed.

Guthrie eyed her unindulgently. "You mean you trotted out a number of facts and withheld others."

"When you came to my house, I didn't want to speak to you at all," she said inconsequentially. "I shouldn't have."

"One reason being your knowledge that your husband is a Soviet agent."

Renata made no attempt to avoid his flat gaze. "Of course I know what he is. You don't think a woman can live twenty years with a man and not realize something like that. After our marriage, in fact, Moscow ordered him to tell me. I was terrified, but—"

"But found that you could live with it."

"Yes."

"Did he discuss his operations with you?"

"Are you out of your mind? I made sure not to ask."

"Then why are you so positive he hasn't seen Bruno in years?"

"I was simply quoting him," she said with lassitude.

"For your information, he secretly met Bruno less than two weeks ago at your house Seeblick. With his help, Bruno hid out from the German and French police in that Geneva penthouse you find so attractive. Did your husband have something quotable to say about that too?"

Renata de Wrendt stared at him, subdued. "No, he didn't."

"He also has contact—clandestine contact—with Bauer, who, let me remind you, played a key role in recruiting your young friend Sutter as an arms smuggler to the Red Brigades."

"Was I supposed to guess?" For the first time she showed fight. "We live apart, which means I'm unaware of my husband's involvements and am not responsible for them—whether it's his lady friends, bank loans or secret meetings."

"The question is, how do you react once you're made aware?"

"If you're asking my opinion of terrorists, I think they're mad."

"That statement costs you exactly nothing," Guthrie said. "Bruno is going to kill someone today, here in Zurich, unless he's stopped in his tracks. I need your cooperation. I want you to persuade your husband to drop whatever he's doing and come to your room right away."

Renata de Wrendt's eyes never left his. "Why do you want him to come here?"

"Don't bother about why. Just do it."

"It's a trap of some sort, isn't it? Your specialty is drawing people into compromising situations so they can be manipulated. I'm not going to help you no matter what imbecility my husband is planning. I want nothing more to do with him, but I find detestable your assumption that I'd trick him."

Her reaction, Guthrie thought, was not so very different from those of dozens of other potential recruits whose cooperation he had exacted solely through pressure. He didn't relish leaning on her, but there was really no choice. "Do you want your son to continue studying in the States? Have you thought about his visa? It can be revoked, you know."

For a full minute she contemplated his ruddy, determined face. "I see. In the end you're no different from
Bruno, Bauer, the rest of those hoodlums. You're tainted
by their methods."

It rankled as much as when Marie-Christine had implied
the same about him in Lucerne. "That's a brainless gener-
alization. We're not pursuing the same goal at all: they're
after blood; I'm not." He saw that this logical argument had
little effect on her. "If you stop to consider, there's another
reason why you should cooperate. The Swiss will throw the
book at your husband when the documented evidence of
his complicity comes into their possession. And I can
promise you that it will . . . today . . . if we don't forestall
the attack. They don't appreciate terrorism on their territory, least of all by an alien from Eastern Europe who's
acquired their nationality and should be grateful for the
favor: he'll face a half-dozen charges, beginning with conspiracy and ending with espionage." Suddenly the glibness
quit his voice and he was leveling with her, rather gravely,
a bit superiorly. "It's not because he's an illegal, you know.
We could live with that; we do elsewhere. But terrorism is
another ball game entirely. In the last analysis, if you still
feel loyalty to him as you claim, it's a question of saving
him from himself."

"I want time to think it over," Renata said.

"No, that's what you can't have. To help him, you'll have
to call the bank right away."

"If he's there . . ."

"Then, if not, find out where he is. When you do, tell
him that he can have a divorce at once, on his terms, if he
comes over here to see you. But it has to be today, this
afternoon: in half an hour. . . ." He gave her no opportunity to interrupt. "Of course, you won't follow through; it's
just a ploy to attract him. Dial his number."

Renata's lips compressed at his tone: like Sutter, she resented receiving orders.

Guthrie had forehandedly saved one argument in the
event of last-ditch resistance on her part. "Fighting terror-

ism is ultimately a problem of willpower. Abject capitulation is no more effective than it was against the Nazis. You, as a German, should understand that."

"Oh, I want to stop it. I never thought of Dieter as anything but a perverted romantic. But I don't want to be in this room if my husband comes."

"I'm sorry, but I can't let you out of sight."

She hesitated, then rose and went to the phone on the bed table. Guthrie listened while she appeared to have difficulty getting through to De Wrendt. "Even if he's in conference, I want to speak to him," she insisted. It was foreseeable, Guthrie thought, that De Wrendt had arranged to be in a board meeting on this particular afternoon: it was perhaps the most airtight—and certainly the most respectable—of alibis. When he finally replied, Guthrie gathered that he was balking at an impromptu meeting. Then Renata made her offer and after another moment hung up. Almost regretfully she said, "He'll be right over."

The orderly strode into the Linder Clinic through the ambulance entrance on the parking level shortly before 3 P.M. He was a dark-haired, husky man clad in hospital whites who merged imperceptibly among the other orderlies reporting for the afternoon shift. That no one had ever seen him before failed to excite curiosity, for in clinics the size of the Linder there is constant coming and going of personnel, and it is assumed of an unfamiliar employee that he is working on another floor or in another department. Nor was he obliged to present a pass or an I.D. card at the door; even the most security-minded medical institutions train their vigilance on visitors, not staff. Then there was another, obscurer reason for the indifference to his presence. Orderlies, as the drudges of the hospital world, are forgettable: while they toil, no one takes notice of them. Doctors and nurses expect them to turn up at wrong or inconvenient times, be bizarre, do less rather than more of their assigned duties.

Making his way along the dim basement corridor, he

passed X-ray rooms, a massage room, a hydrotherapy room, and reached the laundry. A row of aluminum hand-carts heaped with fresh bed linen for rooms vacated at mid-day stood parked along one wall. He took the first cart.

"Is this for West One?"

"You're early." The nurse in charge was a stout, middle-aged woman who was replying to a call on the house phone and awaiting her relief. He had known that unless he was exceptionally fortunate in his timing and found the laundry empty between shifts, he would have to contend with her.

"I want to get it done." He couldn't suppress his German accent completely, but the Linder these days employed underpaid foreigners in menial jobs—Italians, Spaniards, even the odd German.

The nurse lifted her eyebrows. "I haven't seen you before."

"I'm on Floor Two."

He wheeled the cart out into the corridor toward the elevator feeling the nurse's doubtful glance and bracing himself for the squawk of her raised voice at his back. But nothing happened.

Though he did not know it, the nurse was on the point of telephoning to the Administration office upstairs to inquire about him, but she was distracted by her relief's arrival. Almost immediately the two women began to gossip about the identity of the VIP who was due in within the next hour on the surgical floor, after which the nurse forgot about the orderly entirely.

By midafternoon, hospitals and clinics have shaken down and attained a sort of cruising speed following the morning's industrious bustle, and there is less traffic between floors. Using the elevator, the orderly reached Herr Hassler's room without speaking to anyone, drove the linen cart inside, swiftly locked the door from within and smirked.

Bauer surveyed him critically from the bed. "You're one minute early."

With the windows almost completely shut the room was quiet, and no sounds on the floor reached them except for the elevator's occasional laborious hum. Bruno glanced at the wall phone, the bedside emergency button, the plastic sign hooked to the bedstead which read, NOTHING BY MOUTH AFTER MIDNIGHT. "It's certainly an ideal existence for a rugged athlete like you," he observed, his eyes resting without indulgence on Bauer's corpulent body propped up against the Linder's rectangular pillows.

"We have fifteen minutes before the nurse comes with the bloody tea." Bauer had swung his hirsute legs out of the bed and begun to unbutton his pajama jacket, revealing a gray, equally hairy torso. "Is that enough time for a media celebrity like you to get into position?"

There was something mushy and revolting at the core of Bauer's being, like lumber that has been allowed to stand too long on the ground, Bruno thought, but he did not reply. He went to the clothes closet, returned with the tan vinyl suitcase, placed it on the bed, unstrapped it and inserted a tiny key into each of the twin recessed chrome-plated locks. Folded inside lay an extra-large-size dun tropical worsted suit, a shirt and tie. Wordlessly he handed the clothes to Bauer; then from the bottom he drew out three black plastic sealed bags of dissimilar shape and size and set them on the floor. Hands moving deftly, he made room on the cart's lower deck for the three bags, stowed them side by side and heaped up some of the bed linen to conceal their presence. The remainder of the bed sheets and bath towels he added to the pile already on the upper deck.

By the time he had finished, Bauer was dressed in the dun suit. He tossed his suit of pajamas into the suitcase and returned it to the clothes closet, where it would be inconspicuous. There was still no movement in the corridor.

"You're leaving nothing behind?"

Bauer grunted. "Only an unpaid bill and Herr Hassler's clothes."

"You go first."

Bauer opened the door. Diagonally opposite his room was a small pantry with a sink and hot plate where one of the floor nurses was busy preparing afternoon tea. She did not look up, and he stepped quickly out. When the nurse arrived within the next quarter-hour and found Herr Hassler's bed empty, she would set down the tea tray on the bed table but give his whereabouts no second thought; his tests were finished and he was ambulatory: she would assume that he was in the day room or solarium. His absence would be noticed only at dinnertime, at 6:30 P.M. There was no real difficulty about skipping in this way. Every hospital had fantastic tales of patients who for one reason or another rose from their beds and casually slipped out into the street without being intercepted. The sole danger as far as he was concerned was the nurses' station at the end of the corridor. He shuffled off in the opposite direction, to the elevator, and pressed the DOWN button. Should the charge nurse glance up, from that distance she would see only a visitor in an unfamiliar dun suit leaving Herr Hassler's room. The elevator arrived almost at once and was empty. He jabbed the basement-level button.

As soon as the door slid open, he set off heavily down the long corridor. He passed a set of unmarked double doors on his right and, recalling De Wrendt's description of their purpose, shuddered: patients who had succumbed in the clinic were transferred through that unpublicized exit to a waiting hearse. Shirt collar wet around his fleshy neck, and arms, like those of many fat men, akimbo, he marched faster, legs pumping sturdily, past a room where two white-shod attendants were setting a plaster cast on the leg of a woman lying on a gurney bed. At the ambulance entrance he came out with relief into the dazzling sun. NO PARKING stanchions were up in the visitors' parking bays today. Two armed security guards patrolled the courtyard, making sure that the temporary ban was respected. Seeing Bauer, one of them started forward but then turned back: the guards' job this afternoon was to screen inbound visitors, not those leaving the building. A policeman was on duty at the SLOW DOWN sign. Bauer trudged up the ramp without being challenged, turned right and came to the end of the block, out of sight of the clinic's main entrance. In the next side street, parked at the curb, was the same beige Opel that Herr Hassler's tall visitor from the nondenominational chapel on Friedheimstrasse had used for his reconnaissance two days earlier. The door on the driver's side was unlocked. Bauer got in and waited.

Bruno wheeled his cart from Herr Hassler's room into the empty corridor. This afternoon the clinic had pressing concerns elsewhere, and few staff were about. But then, to his intense annoyance, a young nurse emerged from the pantry with a teapot and blocked his way, frowning. "Have you just come from Herr Hassler's room?" she asked.

His ice-blue, slightly protuberant eyes raked her for a second with calculated insolence.

"Did you hear me? I asked you a question."

"I thought the room was empty and the bed had to be made up," he retorted loudly.

"That room is down the hall. Can't you get it right?" As she walked hurriedly away, he shrugged and slammed his cart toward the elevator, a slight frozen smile on his lips.

He waited patiently before the shut door, reflecting that Bauer had probably just reached the basement level. As soon as the elevator arrived, he pressed the top-floor button; the cabin started, but then stopped bumpily at the next floor, where two doctors entered. Taking no notice of him, they continued their conversation. When the elevator reached the top floor, Bruno let them get out first. Damn obtuse fools.

Down the corridor was a conference room reserved for staff and committee meetings, which was unoccupied, as it generally was afternoons. Without being seen, he steered the cart inside and bolted the door. Then he swiftly set to

275

work, aligning the black plastic bags on the floor. They contained the disassembled, dull, greased parts of a 7.62mm Belgian-built FAL light automatic rifle, which he arranged in a semicircle around his feet. Mass-produced, the FAL is in use in thirty countries around the world, including NATO member nations, Israel, Libya, South Africa and Australia, its widespread adoption being due, at least in part, to the fact that it weighs no more than nine pounds and can be field-stripped and reassembled in a minimum of time without tools, springs or screws. A rookie could learn to do it in the dark, he thought furiously as, squatting, he guided the gas assembly and breechblock into the receiver's open rear end until the recoil spring was compressed.

There were other reasons why he had chosen a FAL for Grand Slam. Being so popular, it would be difficult to trace. And then he fancied the idea of using a Western weapon against Sadat, that cat's-paw of the West. From the last bag he withdrew a twenty-round box magazine and inserted it into the housing. He set the lever to Safe; then, after a second's hesitation, he clamped a four-inch flash suppressor over the FAL's steel muzzle. This done, he replaced the assembled rifle in one of the black bags, into which it almost fitted, laid it diagonally on the cart's lower deck and covered it with some of the bed sheets and towels he had used before; after which he took the two remaining crumpled plastic bags and tossed them into a wastepaper basket by the conference table. He unbolted the door, left the room and proceeded with his cart past the doctors' lounge to Central Supply. At the door, a sign over a red bell said, RING FOR SERVICE. He checked his watch and glanced through the glass pane. The nurse in charge was off at this moment on her coffee break. Gently he pushed the door open and, removing the plastic bag with the rifle, parked the cart just inside.

Then he sprinted unobserved to the nearby fire stairs.

One flight up, at the head of the stairs, on the inner side

of a steel door a metal plaque warned, FIRE EXIT—DO NOT CLOSE, and the door itself was indeed partially open. Concealing himself in its angle, Bruno stood motionless and looked out upon the Linder's flat tarred roof. A brickwork elevator housing and a concrete water tank partially obstructed his view, but after a moment, as he had anticipated, a Swiss detective, a walkie-talkie slung from his shoulder, moved into sight. He was a medium-sized man with straight gray hair in a brush cut, and his back was turned to the fire stairs as he stared intently through a pair of binoculars at the houses opposite. They were older buildings with mansard roofs, which had rendered impractical assigning other security guards there. Satisfied, he lowered the binoculars and began walking away past the roof's low coping. Bruno set down the plastic bag, softly closed the door and crept forward, keeping the water tank between himself and the detective. It was better to dispose of him now, since sooner or later he would have to be neutralized.

Utterly still, Bruno waited, conscious of his vulnerability on the exposed roof. Then the sound reached him, at first faint, soon insistent and loud, intensifying so that there could be no mistake—the aggressive drone of an oncoming Alouette helicopter flown by the Swiss *gendarmerie*. He hugged the tank's wall, listened as the blades' disorderly racket grew deafening, saw the insectlike fuselage dart across the roof and fly on, and slowly exhaled his breath. From above he had been invisible in the tank's shadow. A second later, the heavy tread he was waiting for approached in his direction and he heard a burst of staccato, static-ridden splutter. The Swiss plainclothesman's brief, low replies into the walkie-talkie were quite audible. He was apparently no conversationalist, and abruptly the exchange ended.

Take him now, Bruno thought. Edging forward, he perceived the man's broad back and sprang, getting an immediate stranglehold on his neck. As the detective stumbled backward, Bruno crouched to support his weight, kicked him hard in the calf and pulled downward with all his force to bring him to the ground, then as nimbly as a cheetah leaped on him and, driving his upraised arms aside, went with his experienced fingers for his throat.

Chapter Twenty-six

The Unforgiving Game

DE WRENDT HAD not seen his wife since June, when a meeting at her lawyer's office had ended acrimoniously. He was irritated by her latest call—the conditions she had set sounded suspiciously like an ultimatum—but he was curious about her change of tactics and had agreed to meet her to avoid being disadvantaged through a point-blank refusal. *She can't mean what she said. I'll stay twenty minutes,* he thought. It occurred to him that she had furnished no satisfactory reason why the meeting had to take place at her hotel.

He left his Ferrari at Strehlgasse and strode across Weinplatz to the Storchen. Out of instinct, his eye reconnoitered the sunlit square, but he detected nothing alarming.

Automatically he checked his watch and the sky. Perfect flying weather: the Egypt Air Boeing would be landing in about fifteen minutes. Everything connected with Grand Slam was ready—for better or worse. *Why for worse?* To De Wrendt's intense displeasure, he was oppressed by a sense of failure and ruin that was irrational but which he couldn't shake off: it left him stiff and testy, disdaining Bruno's prevarications, his wife's willfulness, his own negativism. "The eternal problem in this profession," Maisky had once observed—"the problem is the danger of agents like yourself falling under the spell of their cover—confusing lies with truth." Had this happened to him in a broader sense than Maisky intended? Around the outer edges of De Wrendt's pessimism danced and undulated the lithe, provocative figure of Marie-Christine. She had set demons loose by coming to Seeblick so willingly. He was attracted to her, he realized lucidly, because she incarnated a future to which he could lay no valid claim.

At the Storchen's entrance he paused. In the past he had brought numerous young women to this hotel, but at this distance in time he couldn't even recall which was which: their names had been as evanescent as their perfume. Feeling cold and defeated, estranged from the sunny world about him, he went up to his wife's room, knocked peremptorily, heard her familiar, clear voice and stepped in. Three men he had never seen before in his life confronted him, barring his escape.

It was Guthrie's first face-to-face encounter with the banker.

"I wanted a confidential meeting with you," he noted tersely.

"And just who are you?"

"Let's say I'm from the American Consulate."

De Wrendt's alert gray eyes settled on his wife, who sat erect and impassive in an upholstered chair beside the bed. She seemed to be neither listening nor participating. "You were out of your mind to do this," he declared to her.

She threw her head back. "I did it for your sake."

"My sake!"

"Sit down," Guthrie said.

De Wrendt remained standing. "I have no reason to be here, and I want the door unlocked."

"Whenever you like you may leave, but I don't think you'll choose that. You've been identified as a member of Soviet Intelligence—"

De Wrendt considered his immaculately laundered French cuffs, and a ghost of a smile illumined his lean greyhound head.

"There's nothing to smile about so patronizingly in your position. We should have had this talk earlier; a couple of lives might have been saved, though I doubt that's an argument Bruno appreciates."

"You're wasting your time, which is your affair, but also mine, and that is considerably more valuable."

Guthrie's voice was suddenly sharper. "This is my case; I know it inside out. No bluff, right? Seeblick, your house, crops up in a terrorist's secret notes; the same terrorist's escape route from Germany leads, by an odd coincidence, to Seeblick. Then photo evidence comes into our possession of his thumbprints in your Geneva penthouse while you're off on Ibiza—"

"This is absurd." It was as though De Wrendt were discussing a bankrupt client's application for a loan renewal.

"The Swiss police won't think so."

"The Swiss police are far likelier to listen to my explanation than your fanciful assumptions."

"Not when a terrorist attack is about to take place against a foreign head of state for whose security the Swiss Government is responsible."

"It sounds like the sort of fantastic spy fiction I never read."

Renata de Wrendt cut in unexpectedly. "He's trying to give you an opportunity to back out while there's time," she said to her husband.

"His main source of information about me seems to be you."

"The Police and Justice departments will investigate you," Guthrie continued implacably, "and bring indictments for espionage on behalf of a foreign power, association with an illegal terrorist group, incitement to homicide, harboring a fugitive from the police"—De Wrendt's gray eyes switched back unwillingly to Guthrie—"what else? I have no doubt that when they audit your books they'll discover regular payments to suspected terrorists and sympathizers. They'll close your bank, revoke your citizenship and toss you into jail on a twenty-year sentence."

De Wrendt cleared his throat lightly. "You mentioned before that you weren't bluffing. I would say you are." His eyes wandered to the locked door guarded by the two men from Ditweiler's surveillance team. "Since I have no choice, I'm going to wait here till your delusion of conspiracy—or fit of megalomania—wears off and then return to my office." He was thinking, Almost forty years' work destroyed by a conceited roughneck who could find nothing better to do than scribble incriminating notations and smear his thumbprints all over my apartment.

Guthrie went to the window and, raising the blind, looked down at the sluggish-flowing Limmat. De Wrendt's native composure and hard-shelled professionalism were as formidable as he had feared. He could not afford the time needed to break him down by degrees: it had to be all at once through a chink in that urbane armor, or not at all. It seemed probable that the banker, after so many years of deep cover, had only one remaining allegiance—to Moscow Center, which dominated his vision, blotting out nation, regime, ideology.

Guthrie turned around.

"No matter what happens to you, the operation won't benefit your service. . . ."

For the first time a gleam of attentiveness flashed in the depths of De Wrendt's gray eyes.

"It would naturally be to Moscow's advantage if General Malik came to power should Sadat be incapacitated or killed. However, Malik is no longer in a position to take over. Israeli Intelligence tracked him down on Cyprus, and the Cypriot police have orders to prevent him from flying back to Cairo. The Egyptian Government made the request. Both the Vice-President and the Prime Minister this morning alerted all loyal Army and Air Force officers. In the event Malik did manage to get off Cyprus, he would be arrested as soon as he landed in Cairo. His coup is over before it began."

De Wrendt smiled mirthlessly. "Another ludicrous bluff. If Sadat were assassinated or removed from office, who can predict what would happen in Egypt?"

"You're the one who's gambling his future on that prospect. Because if someone from the Aurora network so much as scratches Sadat, we deliver our material about you to the Swiss police—there's nothing unpredictable about *that*." The information on Malik had turned up in the exchange of classified cables between Langley and Cairo which Guthrie had found waiting on his Consulate desk that morning. Without this one lever, he thought somberly, they would be deadlocked. "The game ends here and now, with or without your cooperation; the effect on your cover and career—that depends on you."

The room had become singularly quiet. Imperturbably, De Wrendt sized up Guthrie. Renata de Wrendt remained silent and attentive, fascinated by the showdown's outcome. The breathing of the two members of Ditweiler's surveillance team was low but audible.

"Do you think I trust what you tell me?" De Wrendt asked, and suddenly the room's atmosphere was different, more businesslike. It was De Wrendt's first unmistakable step toward negotiation. Don't let him wriggle free now, Guthrie thought. Get him by the gonads, never let him go.

"Who asked you to trust me? Phone up Maisky at the Embassy in Bern. By now he'll be aware of the situation."

"Very well. I shall call your bluff." De Wrendt's tone grew caustic. "Incidentally, I don't share your hand-wringing concern for Sadat's fate. He's played into Israeli hands like a weakling or outright traitor. Were some mishap to befall him, how many Arabs would really mourn? In his own country he'll be forgotten as quickly as Farouk."

Guthrie was incensed by De Wrendt's bland assumption that between them assassination required only the most fleeting justification. "You're so complacent. The only question that ever causes you to lose a night's sleep is whether such-and-such an operation will succeed. Morally you're as blind as a bat. Now phone Maisky!"

Without another word De Wrendt sat down on one of the hotel's straight-backed chairs beside the night table. He felt Renata's somber eyes upon him, but his glance by-passed hers and rested on the plain, oyster-toned wall-paper. If I could get out of here with dignity, bow out in orderly fashion, end with a small measure of self-esteem . . . Of the confusion of ideas racing through his mind, one predominated: contrary to Guthrie's opinion, he had experienced moral disquietude over terrorism. Bruno had seemed to him to be one of the breed of new barbarians who were not trying to storm the city but were unfortunately already inside it; trigger-happy, technique-obsessed, steeped in ignorance. In contrast with their behavior, he had sought to practice fortitude and rectitude as conscious guideposts of his life . . . but in the unforgiving game being waged in this hotel room, neither carried weight. It was a one-way world, in which one never reversed an action but merely refined upon it. Aware of everyone's watching him, he reached for the phone.

"Where are you?"

Security was no longer a consideration, De Wrendt decided bleakly. "I am with three gentlemen from the American Consulate."

"How does it happen you are in such company?" De Wrendt's plight clearly perturbed Maisky less than the operation. "What is it they want?"

De Wrendt gave his report.

"I have been trying urgently to reach you for the past half-hour at your bank." Maisky sounded oddly awkward. "What you learned is essentially correct. Malik, like a fool, let himself be trailed by the Israelis, who alerted Washington and Cairo. The anti-Malik faction in Cairo has mobilized two armored brigades and several jet squadrons to resist a coup. A quick, bloodless move is now obviously out of the question, and it was the only one we were prepared to support." There was silence, and De Wrendt wondered whether Maisky was hastily reading an incoming cable. When he spoke again, his voice was remote and impersonal. "Therefore the Center has decided that Grand Slam has become meaningless. You have to cancel it at once."

"At this point I doubt that I can," De Wrendt said angrily.

"You still have a short margin of time. Do it however you can, with whatever means are necessary." The stress in Maisky's voice fell like a rockslide on the last four words. After an instant he added, "The Americans want to stop the operation?—well, so do we. They are offering a deal that protects you and us?—then snap it up!" He seemed to be anticipating De Wrendt's ultimate argument. "You insisted yourself this morning that he's become untrustworthy, a liability—that you had no further use for him. Well, draw the conclusion!"

De Wrendt laid down the receiver with care, consulted his platinum watch, smoothed back his hair and focused his full attention on Guthrie.

"The operation has to be canceled. I need your cooperation," he snapped.

"It depends on what you tell me."

"What precisely do you want to know?" The unavoidable truth struck out at him with dull force, like the flat edge of a sword blade. Maisky was right: canceling the operation was the sensible procedure. There was an earthy Hungarian saying: When you walk in shit and can't scrape it off, throw the shoe away. And indeed, only hours ago he had argued that Bruno had to be dropped—but outright betrayal was something else again.

"Where, when, how"—Guthrie began to spell out the

285

terms concisely—"is the attack scheduled? Where is Bruno at this moment? Where is Bauer?"

"You ask a damn lot of questions," De Wrendt growled.

"You're stalling. We already know a lot; now let's have the rest."

"First I need a guarantee that whatever bears on my involvement with the Aurora commando will not be released to Swiss authorities."

Guthrie nodded.

"He can count on that?" Renata intervened. "It won't go wrong? It won't be like your arrangement with Karl?"

She was still obssessed by Sutter, Guthrie thought furiously.

"Why shouldn't it be binding?" he said to her. "We've struck private deals before with the opposition. It would be stupid not to respect them."

Guthrie considered De Wrendt. He looked haggard and aged. The banker's long-playing balancing act was coming to an end: one betrayal would spawn further betrayal. Guthrie had witnessed the indecent process before, but he still could not altogether quell his repugnance. "We're wasting time," he said.

De Wrendt leaned back against the flimsy chair's back rest and sat unbending, his elegant hands locked in his lap; the tip of his pale tongue ran over his fine, prim lips: whether he was disquieted, outraged, resigned, it was hard to guess. "Grand Slam is supposed to function as follows. . . ." His voice had regained its husky, studious modulation.

As Guthrie listened, his anguish mounted. The plan was simple and ingenious, capable of succeeding. He no longer doubted that De Wrendt for once in his life was leveling: Grand Slam was a bravado operation exactly cut and tailored to Bruno's deadly talents. . . .

"In twenty-five minutes?" Guthrie shouted, interrupting De Wrendt's impassive recital. "Are you telling me the attack will take place in just twenty-five minutes?"

"That is correct. When Sadat arrives at the clinic," De Wrendt repeated with obstinate precision. "You must either let me go or get there yourself."

Stunned, Guthrie calculated. By this time Mr. Salah's motorcade was picking up speed as it left Kloten Airport. Huebli and his security team were likewise en route to the city. If he phoned ahead, there was no one at the Linder Clinic whom he could alert without losing precious minutes explaining. . . .

"Will Bruno obey your orders?"

"At this point I doubt it."

Guthrie jerked his head around furiously. "What will he do?"

"Smile and open fire on Sadat."

Guthrie turned to the door. In fifteen minutes—twenty, at most—he could be at the clinic. His gambit had succeeded, but Sadat would nonetheless be very dead unless De Wrendt's information could be exploited without the slightest delay.

Renata de Wrendt had sprung to her feet. "You're going to kill him in cold blood. . . ." There could be no doubt whom she meant.

"Don't let either of them out of this room until I come back," Guthrie instructed the two men.

De Wrendt was also moving toward the door. "I'm going. It's my responsibility—"

"A little late to discover that."

As Guthrie stormed down the stairs alone, it struck him that his chances of stopping Bruno in time were one in a thousand. They were odds his uncle Paul would have grabbed.

Chapter Twenty-seven

The Roof

HE WAITED, with the walkie-talkie he had seized suspended from his neck, on the flat tarred roof of the clinic, alone. He was hidden behind the brick housing of the elevator machinery, where he had dragged the detective's body, and without stepping out of the housing's shadow he could see the parking area below, the ramp and the street. Beside the SLOW DOWN sign the policeman on duty had just waved away two passenger cars and a delivery van. In the yard two security guards lounged near the ambulance entrance, their eyes fixed on the empty street. As Bruno watched, two plainclothesmen in dark summer suits came out of the clinic and joined them. Beyond the parking-lot wall extended a row of one-family stucco houses, each set in its own quarter-acre oblong plot, then a beer garden; farther off rose the new wing of a large public hospital where most of the neighborhood inhabitants who could not or would not afford the Linder's rates went for medical treatment. To Bruno's right, only one building adjoined the clinic, the recently completed glass-and-steel headquarters of a Zurich insurance company. It had a flat roof that was flush with the Linder's and separated from it by a two-foot-high stone parapet. Danger could materialize from either that direction or the fire stairs. There was no other access to the roof.

He undid the black plastic bag at his feet, removed the rifle and, folding the bag into quarters, stuffed it into his white trouser pocket. He pressed the FAL's release stud, and the bolt drove forward with a thin, sharp, definitive click, chambering the first round. The rifle felt dry and reliable in his hands, with just the heft he wanted. Satisfied, he set the change lever at Single Fire, then moved it all the way over to Full Automatic Fire, changed his mind and brought it back to Single Fire. The magazine contained twenty rounds, but by the time the first two rounds were expended Sadat would be dying or dead or he would no longer be in range.

He raised the stock tentatively to his right shoulder, being sure to keep the long metal barrel away from the coping and out of the sunlight, sighted through the rear aperture and low-mounted front scope and adjusted the graduated rear sight to fifty meters. You could hit a bird with a BB gun at that distance, if . . . From the moment Sadat emerged from his car he would be in motion, and his bodyguards would be too, running backward and forward, screening him intermittently from view. Moreover, under his lightweight suit Sadat would no doubt be wearing a bulletproof vest, as he did whenever he traveled abroad, whether to Jerusalem, Paris or Washington. Thus, he would have to be dropped with a plunging shot to the head. The bullet will rip through his temple and, given the angle, it will exit through the nape of his neck, shattering bits of skull bone on its passage.

Bruno looked up. The parking area lay bathed in bright illumination, and the hard, angled shadows would not reach the ambulance entrance for another half-hour. There was not even a premonitory hint of a breeze. Sadat would be sidelighted. The conditions for precision fire were as favorable as anybody could demand. A second bullet should really be superfluous, but to make absolutely certain he would squeeze off another round.

Lowering the stock, Bruno glanced at the insurance-company roof but saw no movement. The dead detective's assignment had apparently been to survey both buildings. From time to time the elevator motor started up in the housing and he heard the steel hoist cable running as the car ascended or descended; and he waited attentively for the noise to cease. Twice, when the car stopped on the surgical floor just below, his flat, unsparing gaze shifted to the steel fire door, his body tensed and he prepared to bring up the rifle barrel. If someone came up the fire stairs with the intention of exploring the roof and managed to force the door open, he would be staring straight into the rifle's muzzle. But thus far no one had appeared.

In the street below, three motorcycle policemen were keeping the approaches to the clinic clear; another group was posted for the same purpose before the insurance company's headquarters. By this time Sadat's own security men were undoubtedly swarming inside the Linder, in the basement, on each landing and throughout the surgical floor, sanitizing the area through which he would pass. They were counting, of course, on speed and anonymity to minimize the risk during the transfer from his car to his clinic suite; as soon as the motorcade raced up to the ambulance entrance, they would hustle Mr. Salah indoors before anyone had time to identify, much less attack him.

Bruno squinted up at the brilliant arc of sky. The same *gendarmerie* helicopter would surely return, hovering over Sadat's route; but the team aboard would find it virtually impossible to spot a lone figure who hugged the elevator housing's brick wall and remained motionless in its shadow. And if the helicopter whirred up after he opened fire, it would be too late for Sadat. As for himself . . . it would clearly be more than time to hightail it off the roof, but

Grand Slam's timetable included a final surprise to facilitate his retreat.

You were still wet behind the ears when you came to us, De Wrendt had said to him with urbane condescension. No longer, Bruno thought unsmilingly. De Wrendt—he swallowed hard. De Wrendt was changing faster than anyone could have foreseen. At their last two meetings, the banker had flared up in fits of picayune criticism. Bruno suddenly thought of those sand castles children build on a beach, which, apparently intact but already infiltrated by rivulets of seawater, abruptly collapse. The image vexed him. To consider De Wrendt as a monument undermined by age and doubt was pernicious, for as soon as he did he could no longer sustain the slightest respect for him. He had never believed in coddling the old and infirm.

Through the aligned sights he gazed down frowning on the magnified gray parking lot. Or, as he preferred to think of it, the battleground. In less than ten minutes the Middle East peace drive was going to be dealt a traumatic blow here from which it would not recover. Terrorism could alter history with one meaningful operation. As his tremorless fingers flexed around the pistol grip, Bruno was aware of the sun's dancing warmth on the back of his broad head. He wasn't happy. He was experiencing some other emotion. Over some undetermined period in the past he had renounced as a goal conventional, acceptable happiness. So many people squawked fatuously about a human being's aspiration to happiness as one of life's prime purposes. What balls! This moment was more exhilarating and elevating than their trite concept of joy. And all at once he knew what he was experiencing: vindication. This moment balanced the past and, in a sense, annihilated those meager, emotionally empty years. There was a symmetry to be discovered in his presence on the roof. This was where he should be at this moment: some conjunctions in life are foreordained.

A brackish taste filtered into his mouth, but that was all

right. It sprang from simple concern about carrying out the operation with all the ability he could muster: concern, curiosity, excitement—but definitely not fear. Fear was the demeaning thing he had smelled in his foster parents' home in Bremen long ago, when he had harrowing and disabling visions of abandonment and disorder from which there was no salvation. But growing older, he had managed to shed his panic. At this moment, accordingly, he was not afraid, though concerned; the colors and forms in the street below passed before his sights remote, almost abstract.

A subtle change in the parking lot alerted him that it was time. The policemen and security guards had stopped chatting and were bunched together, squinting into the sunlit street. A gust had sprung up, and it ruffled Bruno's dark brown hair. No helicopter was visible in the sky. The summer-afternoon silence was abruptly interrupted by a fierce, almost incomprehensible outburst of orders at his chest. He grabbed the walkie-talkie with his left hand and growled, *In Ordnung* into it, knowing that the static would smother his accent. Body's weight displaced slightly forward onto his left leg, stock wedged into the hollow of his shoulder, he cradled the rifle in his left palm.

As the taxi braked in the cleared area before the Linder's main entrance, Guthrie glanced up at the roof, but saw only a television rotor antenna and a round water tank set back from the low stone decorative coping. No activity was visible up there—which, of course, meant nothing. He was conscious of superficially unimportant details—the radiant afternoon, the brooding silence, the trafficless street. Before he could get out, a helmeted motorcycle patrolman ran up on foot, waving energetically to the taxi driver to keep moving. Guthrie drew out his dark blue diplomatic passport. Suppose he shouted, "There's a terrorist on the roof getting ready to murder Sadat—and another member of the network in a car parked around the corner"? The patrolman, being leery of foreigners even with diplomatic status, would react slowly, ask damn-fool questions and seek to unload the problem on his superior. . . . Guthrie dismissed the idea and looked out for Huebli. Huebli would not lose vital time hesitating, but he was nowhere in sight. The motorcade itself had plainly not yet arrived; the cabbie had covered the distance from Zurich's center in a providential burst of speed. The patrolman returned the passport, saluting, and stepped back. Restraining an urge to sprint, which would bring every policeman and bodyguard in the area converging on him with gun drawn, Guthrie hastened up the flagstone walk to the main door. Inside, he recognized at once the palpable atmosphere of expectancy that precedes a celebrity's arrival—hushed, tense, slightly disbelieving. Half of the clinic's staff seemed to be congregated by the Admissions office. Two plainclothesmen moved forward, and Guthrie showed his identification again. "Herr Huebli is on the surgical floor. You'll have to show your passport to the Egyptians up there," one of them replied to his question. They assumed he knew the incoming patient's nationality, perhaps his identity. No one was making a serious effort any longer to maintain Sadat's incognito. Still not running, Guthrie strode swiftly to the elevator at the far end of the hall, feeling the 9mm Parabellum's weight in his jacket pocket. The plainclothesmen were not suspicious of American diplomats and had not considered searching him. Suppose I were the assassin? Couldn't a bearer of a diplomatic passport be bent on a deadly errand? What sort of laxity and snobbishness exempted diplomats from suspicion?

Just as the laminated elevator doors slid open to admit him, the unnatural silence in the lobby ended. A Swiss police captain with tabs on his tunic began to bark concise orders into a walkie-talkie held up close to his mouth, while three security guards converged across the hall and took up positions by the front glass double door. Simultaneously, a couple of tall, thick-hipped Egyptians burst out of the Administration office, their service revolvers bulking conspicuously under their tight silk suits, and rushed toward the emergency staircase. The motorcade was evidently arriving and might already be in the parking lot. Till now Guthrie had entertained a vague, desperate hope that somehow he could not only locate Huebli but bring him into the picture in time—share with him the information he had pried loose from De Wrendt, about what was happening in and around the clinic at this weird moment: Bruno on the roof, stalking Grand Slam's victim; Bauer awaiting the kill in a beige Opel around the corner; Bauer's volunteers standing back in reserve throughout the neighborhood, to be committed at the necessary moment, though for what exact purpose Guthrie had not remained long enough at the Storchen to find out. But it was already too late to enlist Huebli's aid; on this malefic day, it seemed, nothing was going to work out the way he hoped. Probably Bruno could no longer be stopped in time. I tried, God knows I tried, he whispered savagely to himself, with no one about to register his sudden deflation as the cabin bumped to a halt at the top floor.

Guthrie darted out and stormed down the sterile white corridor, not quite sure whether his involvement still mattered. To a bewildered young nurse who came out of an X-ray room, he bawled, "Which way to the roof?" She took in the unsmiling American, pointed automatically to the fire stairs farther on and at once regretted her folly as he lunged in that direction.

By the time she had hurried off to report his presence to the charge nurse, Guthrie was pounding up the staircase, heels clattering loudly on the iron steps. One flight up, a red metal sign plate screwed to the wall read FIRE EXIT—DO NOT CLOSE, but the blank steel door was shut. Guthrie halted. Gently he turned the knob, regretting that he had not crept soundlessly up the stairs. The door was not locked, but it did not budge, and reluctantly he released the knob. Although the motorcade had evidently arrived, he had heard no gunfire. Perhaps De Wrendt had lied and

Bruno was not really out there. The door might have been shut by negligence. The risk of banging it open was stepping into a withering, deadly fire.

A small window protected with wire mesh was let into the wall beside the steel panel. Climbing over the staircase banister, Guthrie edged out on the narrow concrete ledge that protruded above the stairwell and peered through the rectangular panel. His eye encompassed the water tank, the television antenna and a chimney, but at first he made out no one on the flat deck. He was about to turn his gaze away when a fleeting glint of sunlight on metal beside the brick elevator housing captured his attention. It had lasted less than a second, but told him what he wanted to know.

He glued his eye to the window, fascinated. There in the shadow—recognizable in spite of the thatch of dyed dark brown hair—was the assassin, clad in a hospital attendant's white jacket and pants, as De Wrendt had said he would be: the same chunky, agile figure who had lurked with murderous patience in the doorway of the photographer's shop in Cologne while waiting for Wadi Khalef's Mercedes to drive up. Close up, Bruno looked bigger than he had then. Poised beside the brickwork, he was staring with grim absorption along an automatic-rifle barrel equipped with a flash suppressor at the courtyard below. And Guthrie registered the fact that in Bruno's taut, totally concentrated stance at this moment there was a strangely depersonalized and inaccessible quality which imbued him with a fanatic's dangerous remoteness. No longer acting as an individual, he was the fatal embodiment of a cause.

Guthrie felt his spine grow cold as he drew out his gun. The elevator housing stood about twenty yards away. He would have to be damn sure to jump backward and open fire right away, before Bruno could turn his lethal-looking rifle around. Whatever happened, he promised himself, it was not going to be a replay of Cologne—this time he had a weapon and he would not be a defenseless target board like Starkey. He got a steadier grip on the Browning, moved sideways against the sign plate, pressing his left shoulder to the door, and then with all his force he slammed into it. As it flew outward, he regained his balance and dived, but almost as though the push had set off a chain reaction, two flat, sharp reports cracked out, one almost on top of the other, and echoed with seemingly infinite variations of pitch off the housing's naked brick walls.

In a crouching stance, Guthrie fired a fraction of a second too late, just as Bruno whipped around and trained his rifle muzzle on him.

Bruno had heard the elevator cable straining again but paid it no particular attention. He was too busy now observing the lead car's descent down the ramp. As it drove up and halted at the ambulance entrance, its occupants—three youngish men, all Swiss—leaped out and swiftly formed a protective semicircle around it. Beyond, the second car, a simonized Mercedes sedan whose stylish black flanks caught the sun, came into view, slowing up to make the turn and enter the parking area. Bruno frowned. The Mercedes was too showy to be anything but a decoy; someone was being clever and pulling the classic security stunt of switching cars in mid-trip between arrival and departure points. A moment later he was proved right. The Mercedes wheeled off to the left and disgorged another trio of bodyguards—darker, quicker, nattier: Egyptians—who fanned out in an outward-facing perimeter. Staring up briefly at the roof, they moved to the ambulance entrance, their gun hands straying to their hip holsters. *Now*, he thought as the last car rounded a corner and drove down the street in a burst of speed, *this is the one*: a gray workhorse of a vehicle with honorable dents and nicks on its coachwork, a Renault. The sun had moved fractionally overhead; light glinted on the FAL's blued sights for a second until he stepped back a quarter-pace, never taking his eyes off the courtyard.

The Renault, surrounded by security men, had come to

a standstill. From its interior emerged Sadat, stooping, then jauntily straightening up with an actor's awareness and a politician's sense of public exposure. He appeared thick in the chest: under the navy blue suit he was definitely wearing a bulletproof vest. A lithe, gray-haired man, the clinic director, was already at Sadat's side, guiding him forward. The thoughtful famous head swam into the scope's circle. The moment's overpowering excitement caught Bruno by surprise. Stunned, he had an intense sense of history on the hinge. He let his finger rest passively a split second on the trigger curve. My role is insignificant. I am an instrument. But I have become part of fatality, a historical process. The prominent, clay-colored temple, a frieze of ridged, steel-gray hair, a fragment of arching eyebrow leaped magnified into the scope.

He went cold as a blade all over; a numb, chill fury drove him: even to save himself he couldn't have held back when, with wild untimeliness, the fire door banged at his back. Welded to his rifle, he squeezed off two rounds and with satisfaction saw Sadat stop short and lurch stiffly backward like a drunkard. However, Sadat did not collapse, and Bruno realized dully that the interruption at his back had made him raise the FAL's sights infinitesimally on the first shot, that the second shot had been too high, stupidly squandered.

A bullet whistled past him in harmless fury. Whirling, he made out a crouching figure in the doorway—the intruder into history—who had fired at him and missed, then ducked out of range. In a blind rage Bruno fired back, heard a rising angry clamor of commands and panicky cries in the parking lot, a fusillade of vengeful gunshots from below; but the Egyptian bodyguards had seen no flash and were firing meaninglessly in the roof's general direction with no clear idea of where the potential assassin was. He drove the lever over to Full Automatic and fired protectively again at the area of the fire door. Then, as the bullets ricocheted with a high, protesting whine off the steel panel, he tore headlong across the roof and sheltered behind the water tank, trembling. It was fifty feet to the insurance-company building's roof, another seventy to the exit that led down to street level where Bauer was waiting in the beige Opel. Hunching over, he ran for the parapet, weaved to one side, heard the crack of a bullet very close to his body, made a running jump over the low wall, reached the exit door and yanked it open. A single idea was thundering through his head. It was no accident that someone had appeared so inauspiciously on the roof: he had been set up. Furiously he spun about, saw his solitary unknown pursuer dashing toward the water tank and fired off another burst.

The beige Opel's window on the driver's side was rolled up, and Bauer, cramped into the plastic-covered seat, sought unhappily to contain his impatience. From time to time with finical movements he rearranged his dress and ran a comb through his sparse hair. Then all at once, around the corner, he heard two dry, flat reports, ragged and unexpected, so close-spaced that one seemed to be a premature echo of the other. Promptly he turned the key in the ignition and braced for pandemonium in the street. He had no doubt that at this moment Sadat was dying or already dead. For another second the deceptive calm persisted, as though the shots were too trifling to merit attention or upset the afternoon torpor; then, still out of sight, a profound uproar burst and swelled like that of a spreading riot. Heavy gunfire, patrol-car sirens, shouts fused, fell off and resumed. Two Swiss policemen, who took no notice of the Opel, raced toward the parking lot. All of the security forces present in the area were being sucked toward the scene of the assassination, away from the side streets. Bauer glanced at his platinum wristwatch. In another fifteen seconds Bruno would spurt out of the insurance-company building's side entrance and scramble into the Opel; Leduc and Jaeggi from Frohburgstrasse would cover his retreat, then clamber into the rear. The route out of Zurich was imprinted on Bauer's mind: first through Hirslanden, then Hottingen and a little-traveled road to Dubendorf. Long before the highway police could coordinate the manhunt by radio and helicopter, the Opel would be one-third of the way to Seeblick. At a crossing before Wils, there was a winding lane concealed by rolling pastureland from the main road. It would require three minutes to switch car plates. Suddenly Bauer heard a pistol shot on the clinic roof, followed by rifle fire, then dead silence.

Shifting his weight nervously, he tore open the glove compartment and removed a loaded Swiss Army automatic, which he placed within easy reach on the adjoining front seat. Out of the corner of his eye he saw two men step forward from an apartment-building doorway where they had been waiting for the past half-hour. Leduc and Jaeggi. The two members of the African Fellowship Center each held a grooved oval metal object in his upraised hand. Bauer's breath came faster. Seven seconds more . . . the scenario was proceeding without a hitch. Then he heard once more unmistakable, sustained automatic-rifle fire high overhead, seemingly on the insurance-company building's roof, and his uneasiness began to yield to panic. Something was seriously wrong up there. The unthinkable possibility sped through his mind: Bruno had botched Sadat's death —weeks of painstaking planning and infernal risk for nothing . . . A tide of fear began to flow like bile through Bauer's abdomen and oozed into his toes, sickening and paralyzing his obese, stiff body. He gazed wildly and unseeingly about, sure that they were all done for. Before he could control his reflexes, he had plunged out of the car and was preparing to detach himself forever from Grand Slam by scampering away as fast as his stout, unheroic legs would carry him down the hazardous street.

Bruno lunged out of the building and, panting, caught up with him.

"Where in hell do you think you're going?" he screamed.

"Get back into the car!" He no longer had the rifle; with his fist he grabbed Bauer's voile shirt and twisted it back.

Bauer gaped at him stupidly, unable to utter a word.

"What are you waiting for to get out of here? Where's your gun? What are you doing without one? I'm going to kill you with your own gun!"

Bauer had got his voice back and was roaring as lustily as he could. "You're finished—washed up. . . . You bungled it, you miserable bastard, as I knew you would. I'm not helping you any longer. We'll form a new commando without you. . . ."

The Opel's motor was still running.

Bruno pushed Bauer backward off the curb, clutching his collar while jerking him viciously from side to side like a mutinous soldier.

He's really going to kill me, Bauer thought, and drove his thick arms upward to try to break free.

"I shot Sadat," Bruno whispered into his startled face. "But you sold me out, you prick. I *order* you to get behind that wheel and drive!"

Bauer spluttered, "Leduc and Jaeggi—"

"Fuck them. We're taking off without them. Why are you taking time to argue with me?" All of a sudden a tight, frozen smile cleared his face; he shoved Bauer aside and ran toward the car alone.

Bauer hesitated, wondering whether he should, after all, race after him. As he stood indecisively on the sidewalk, two policemen rounded the corner at a run. It acted as a signal for Leduc and Jaeggi, who stepped out into the street. The gas grenades flashed accurately through the air and exploded at the policemen's feet, instantly emitting a dense grayish-yellow cloud which billowed upward to second-story level.

The Opel was already moving, gathering speed, while Leduc and Jaeggi hailed it desperately. As the smoke surged toward him, Bauer cast a last, harried glance at the car. He had waited too long. Eyes stiff-lidded and smarting, he retreated coughing and cursing toward the insurance-company building's side door.

Sweat streaming from his forehead, Guthrie fetched up at the head of the darkened stairs and barely avoided tripping over the automatic rifle Bruno had jettisoned in his flight. Guthrie kicked it aside and peered down the stairwell, listening but hearing nothing, unsure whether Bruno had a handgun and was planning to ambush him on one of the landings. I'll still take him, he thought. He started to tiptoe down the stairs, heard voices shouting down below, began to run and, as he reached the ground floor, saw smoke curling through the open door and sniffed the characteristic apple-blossom odor of chloracetophenone. Suddenly he understood the role Bauer had assigned to his volunteers during the secret meetings at Frohburgstrasse. Then through the smoke screen he made out a man's indistinct figure lurching toward him, detected a glint of metal like a pistol barrel, thought that after all he wasn't too late and fired point-blank.

He saw the heavy figure topple sideways. Gasping, he backed off from the stinging gas up the stairs. Out in the street, scattered shots resounded, faint and increasingly remote. Finally the acrid fumes thinned and he rushed forward. He saw at once that it wasn't Bruno. He recognized Bauer's inanimate body sprawled astride the doorway, sunken eyes fixed no longer self-righteously but expressionlessly on the near wall. On the antique dealer's outflung arm glinted the same platinum-link watch bracelet he'd worn that afternoon in his shop on Neumarkt. There was no gun lying beside him.

Footsteps pounded up to the door and two policemen with guns drawn glanced in, their faces edgy with tension. As Guthrie carefully lowered his own gun and pointed it downward, Huebli materialized, extraordinarily pale, and ordered them away.

"Sadat's wounded but alive," he snapped. "One bullet

struck his shoulder; the other went wild. They brought him into Emergency right away. We were lucky—no thanks to this bastard." Somberly he stared at the large figure recumbent beside his feet. "It's Bauer, isn't it? We just collared two of his reformers in the street. How did it happen?"

"Later, Huebli—later you'll get a full report."

Guthrie was already rushing past him outdoors. The tear gas was dissolving and drifting harmlessly upward. He had never seen so heavy a concentration of police vehicles in a Zurich neighborhood. Prowl cars were in position at either end of the street, their radios bawling and their dome lights flashing incessantly in broad daylight. Onlookers had converged from houses and offices around the clinic.

But the getaway car had vanished.

Huebli joined him, and Guthrie guessed at his emotions, which must be like his own. Once again Bruno had escaped, which meant the search had to start again, which meant that Marie-Christine was anything but safe—but this time, Guthrie thought with icy fury, calculating the time necessary to drive to Seeblick, I know where to look for him.

Chapter Twenty-eight

A Farewell to Tradecraft

RENATA DE WRENDT avoided speaking to her husband, who seemed to be observing a focal point of defeat in the limitless distance beyond the hotel window with that streak of Hungarian fatalism which so displeased her.

Finally, however, she broke the silence. "You always assumed there was everything to win and very little to lose—when in fact it was just the opposite."

De Wrendt's eyes flicked toward his watch. It seemed ages since Guthrie's departure, though in reality only twenty minutes had passed. In another few minutes Grand Slam would be over—but here at the Storchen they wouldn't learn about the outcome immediately: they were no longer an essential part of the operation's mechanism. And if Guthrie had managed to reach the Linder in time, what then? To his dismay, De Wrendt realized that Bruno's fate, Maisky's *volte-face*, Sadat's life and death no longer moved him. The world had closed in with terrible cynicism, belittling his career, reducing his objectives to concern for his own skin.

"How did you let yourself be blinded so by illusions of power?" Renata asked harshly.

Illusions of power. She was right: he would have done well to stick to his basic tradecraft instead of becoming entangled in this endless labyrinth of terrorism. But she was wrong about his involvement: he was withdrawing from the game for good if Guthrie honored his part of the deal.

The two Americans from the Consulate sat on small chairs beside the door, one smoking a cigar, the other distraitly cracking his knuckles from time to time.

"Any objection if I listen to the radio?" De Wrendt inquired of the smoker.

The American eyed the small transistor set on the night table and nodded.

De Wrendt found a Zurich station that was playing a festival of pop music. All programs would be interrupted by a special news bulletin, he thought, as soon as Sadat fell back under Bruno's fusillade and collapsed.

His wife watched him critically. "You're hoping that it's going to happen."

He shook his head. "No. It would be a pity now if—"

"If what? If Sadat dies? If Dieter escapes? Which is more important?"

"It's all become utterly pointless." De Wrendt contemplated her levelly, his bony head as austere as early-Gothic stonework.

"He's a thug," Renata exclaimed with sudden vehemence, "but you never admitted that."

"Of course he's a thug," De Wrendt said. "In this trade we can't employ only parfait knights. Do you imagine the other side is so virtuous?"

The Americans were paying no attention to their conversation, which was in German.

The hollows in her husband's ascetic, lean face seemed more conspicuous of late, Renata thought, eroded not by illness but by moral dilapidation; his defenses had been up so long and successfully that whatever of value he was protecting within had withered. Did he still have aspirations? If so, to what?

"There's no feeling inside you—that's always been the problem," she said aloud.

Whether a retort was forming on his lips she never knew, for at that moment the pop music ceased without explanation. "President Anwar Sadat of Egypt has just been assassinated"—the announcer's voice interrupted the program loudly with uncontainable excitement—"while on an incognito trip to Switzerland." The bulletin was followed by static. Outside the hotel room, the summer light seemed unbearably bright and revealing. Conscious of calamity, the two Americans approached and leaned over the radio. Appalled, Renata hoped that the static would continue: she didn't want to hear more. Fascinated, she couldn't tear her remorseless gaze away from her husband's face.

Then the Swiss voice was on the air again, modifying the original announcement. Sadat had been shot but not killed; he was thought to be out of danger. Police forces were pursuing the assassin. . . .

"He got away." Far from harboring triumph, De Wrendt's voice was slack with defeat.

"Not for long. Not this time, please God," Renata exclaimed.

The two Americans continued to listen to the broadcast; the smoker, the heavier of the two, shook his head. They both understood German, De Wrendt noted as an idea formed in his mind. He rose, went to the window and addressed his wife. "Ironical, isn't it? I drove a bad bargain—to no purpose. . . ."

"What do you mean? Sadat is alive; without your information, he wouldn't be."

"But Bruno's escaped. My private deal with that American is now worthless."

"I don't see why."

"His objective was to capture or kill Bruno as well as to

305

save Sadat. There's no reason why he should honor the deal now. In his place I wouldn't."

Renata noticed that her husband had dropped his voice and slipped into Swiss German. She looked at him narrowly. He abhorred the local Zurich dialect and never used it with her. She still didn't grasp his intention. The Americans, intent upon the news bulletins coming over the transistor radio, had not yet registered the fact that he was speaking in a monotone, his head turned to the window so that he couldn't be overheard.

". . . As soon as that fellow meets with his Swiss colleagues, he'll spill all he knows about me; perhaps he already has. I have only one chance left. . . ."

Renata stood likewise beside the window and sought to keep her voice under control. "You can't escape from here."

"With your help I can. Ask for coffee, and don't meddle in what happens."

"You're known everywhere. Where can you go?"

"Never mind. It's the only favor I'll ever ask."

Before she could answer, the smoker interrupted them. "Speak German or English," he ordered, glowering at De Wrendt, "and not that stupid *Kalbsdeutsch*."

"Excuse me," De Wrendt said.

Heartsore, Renata steadfastly studied her husband. He had seldom asked favors of her before, it was true. And now it was up to her whether he got his last chance. Everybody was entitled to that: if Bruno, then why not her husband? She was responsive less to what he was demanding than to his tone—those cadences of fatigue whose source she didn't care to dwell on. To what extent am I to blame for what he became? In a marriage there were no frontiers of responsibility; or if there were, the lines of demarcation were always fudged. She felt an impulse to cry out, "I'm sorry that I lied to trap you," but the words would not take shape in her mouth. As she met her husband's eye, all she could bring herself to do was nod.

De Wrendt bent over the night table to adjust the tuning of the set. Next to the radio stood a candlestick lamp with a parchment shade and solid pine base. Unseen, with a quick tug he pulled the cord from the wall socket.

Renata spoke up. "We've been in this room since three o'clock. Can we have some coffee if we're going to be held here longer?"

"You want room service up here? You must be kidding," the heavier American replied.

"Frank, there's a vending machine down the corridor," the other said.

"Then go and get a coffee for the lady. You want one too?"

De Wrendt nodded. The more encumbered the American was, the less agile he would be.

As soon as they were only three in the room, he said, "I can't seem to get this right." He had deliberately turned up the volume; an outburst of static obliterated the announcer's voice. The thickset American approached and bent over the set. Seizing the lamp by the shaft, De Wrendt raised his arm and brought the lamp base down with full force on the back of the American's neck. The light bulb shattered into a spray of glassy slivers. The American grunted and slumped against the end table, then, as De Wrendt clubbed him again, slid headfirst to the floor, where he lay inert.

Petrified, Renata watched her husband stoop over the American, collect his gun from his shoulder holster, then quickly replace the lamp and crumpled shade on the table.

"Is he dead?" She had trouble articulating, and her hands were suddenly cold.

"Of course not. The blow wasn't to the head." With extraordinary nimbleness De Wrendt had already posted himself beside the door. "Stay where you are, so that he sees you when he comes in."

It seemed to her inconceivable that the sound of shattering glass had gone unheard by the other American, but then she remembered: the vending machine was at the other end of the corridor.

"Don't worry, the worst part is over," De Wrendt murmured as though he were reassuring her after an illness.

The door opened inward and the younger American entered the room, bearing a cardboard coffee container in either hand. The bed hid the sprawled body from his view, but his reflexes were fast. "Where's—?" he began, pivoting as he spotted Renata, alone.

De Wrendt had kicked the door smartly shut and was training the gun on his chest.

The American stood quite still, continuing to hold the two cups and evaluating the situation. "I can't put my hands up."

"You don't have to," De Wrendt said, then spoke to Renata. "Take his gun and keep him here as long as you can."

She did not like getting near that tense, hostile body, but the American was at a disadvantage with the two containers of steaming coffee still absurdly in his hands. With some groping she managed, while her husband closely covered her, to locate the gun in a hip holster and snatch it away.

"Is it on Safety? Put it on Fire," De Wrendt ordered.

She obeyed him, found it was easier than she had expected to keep a man at bay with a pistol.

The American was watching her. "Don't worry, lady. If you knew how to shoot, I might jump you—but never mess with an amateur is my policy," he said.

De Wrendt had pocketed the thickset man's automatic. "In twenty minutes call the manager and report that two foreigners broke into your room and threatened you with assault," he told her. "Let them talk their way out of that." In the doorway he turned back with a remnant of his former stylishness. "Thank you for your loyalty, Renata."

Then he was gone. She had a presentiment that it was over, that she would not see him again.

It was, in a sense, the divorce he had sought.

Chapter Twenty-nine

The Lake at Night

IT WAS past six o'clock when Bruno drove onto the coast road and spied the immense lake. All day the temperature had hovered in the high 80s, and heat still lingered on the air, but now a noticeable breeze had risen. Beyond Romanshorn he perceived the tilted white triangles of sailboats competing on the cobalt-blue water and, closer inshore, a school of slim wind surfers. While there were still pleasure boats out there, he would take De Wrendt's powerboat and cast off—according to plan—but wait till dark among the other boats before making a run for Bregenz. It was risky, but feasible. He had to assume that the harbor police had already received the first telex flash. In the two hours of remaining light they would organize a patrol or two and keep an eye peeled for unfamiliar craft; they might even bestir themselves to alert Austrian authorities farther down the lake. But the *Seepolizei*'s main responsibility, with so much traffic on the water in summer, was to save people from drowning: they weren't trained to search for fleeing terrorists, and De Wrendt's boat, in any case, was well known in the region and would pass unsuspected as long as it appeared to be on a normal outing. In Austria no action would be taken till orders came down from a higher level. Terrorists were a political liability—no government wanted to handle that hot potato if it could be avoided. The Austrians were surely hoping that Sadat's would-be assassin had gone to ground in Switzerland, or had escaped to Germany or France—to anywhere, indeed, but Austria.

As he passed Rorschach, he relaxed infinitesimally. In another ten minutes he would gain Seeblick's park and ditch the beige Opel behind its stone walls and dense foliage. Since Zurich he had stuck grimly to his own itinerary, instead of Bauer's, which he could no longer trust, and stopped only once, on a country lane near a village whose name he didn't know. He had pulled out his poplin Windbreaker and pants from the trunk, stripped off his telltale hospital whites and flung them behind a thorn hedge. Then he had unscrewed the plates from the car, discarded them in underbrush that grew just off the lane and replaced them with a new set bearing a Geneva number. Few vehicles had passed on the nearby highway, which he could make out curving through the valley. In midsummer so many Swiss were on vacation abroad that the roads were relatively free —and the cooperation required between the various cantons in this decentralized country had delayed the setting up of roadblocks. . . . Grand Slam was a disaster, but he might still emerge intact from the wreckage. He had the money and the Austrian passport De Wrendt had handed to him twenty-four hours earlier, and Bauer's 9mm Swiss Army pistol was conveniently within reach on the front passenger seat.

He switched on the car radio and picked up a résumé of the afternoon's continuous news bulletins. A team of Linder Clinic doctors had extracted a single 7.62mm bullet fired by a NATO light automatic rifle from Sadat's shoulder. Egypt's President had survived the audacious attempt on his life and was in no danger; his condition was officially described as stable. The Swiss Government had presented excuses to Cairo. Sadat's would-be assassin had been identified by Swiss authorities, and although he was still at large, a nationwide dragnet was being organized to capture him. Within minutes of the attack, another man had been felled by gunfire as he approached a building next door to the clinic; police had identified him as one of Bruno's confederates, a Zurich antique dealer.

He switched off the radio. Sadat was alive and Bauer dead. Bad luck in one case, good riddance in the other. But altogether so bloody, bloody stupid and avoidable. There was no excuse for muffing a plunging shot at fifty meters— he had been as familiar as humanly possible with the rifle, the layout, the target. Under more difficult circumstances he had picked off an enemy at three times that range; but this time, because of that unbelievable last-moment intrusion on the roof, he had fired a fraction of a millimeter too high. I was set up. I thought it was by Bauer, but apparently I was wrong. But if not by Bauer, then by whom?

Seeblick was within sight: the high stone walls overgrown with creepers, the unobtrusive signpost, the gravel driveway. Then the house itself, which he had left early that morning, appeared, harmoniously proportioned, discreet and elegant, the image of its owner. Bruno braked the Opel to the right of the side terrace, but then he remained seated a second longer, eyes shut, letting the tension drain out of his muscles. If not by Bauer, then by whom? Abruptly he remembered Marie-Christine. It was not that he had ever entirely forgot her awkward presence in the house, but he had set it aside as secondary, a minor problem De Wrendt had arbitrarily created and which would have to be resolved in due course. But now, as he pocketed the Swiss Army pistol and hastened to the front door, he also remembered how things had gone wrong too in Cologne because of that girl, and his jaw whitened with fury.

As he burst into the salon, Marie-Christine took stock of the danger to herself. Bruno's bloodless face bore the taut, censorious expression that crept into his features just before he flew into a deadly rage. It revived her worst memories of him, of the tight, cocky figure stamping down the streets of Cologne unresponsive as a robot to the concept of pity.

"I'll watch her." He avoided her glance at first and examined the room as though he had never set foot in it till the two guards had left. "Before clearing out," he snapped, "I plan to find out what happened."

Misunderstanding him, she began, "Someone shot Bauer, according to—"

"*What happened?*" he bellowed into her face, his lips trembling so uncontrollably that she expected him to foam. "On that island? When you were screwing him, did he spill it all?"

She had backed off, and vigorously shook her head.

"You're lying in your teeth. He liked you and gave everything away. I was set up and you did it."

"No, it wasn't possible. I came here straight with him," Marie-Christine said rapidly. Bruno couldn't possibly know about her furtive early-morning phone call, only its effect, she thought.

"You snotty Paris whore . . ." He was working himself up to a pitch of frenzy, and she had to think quickly of another argument to appease him. "You got the information to that American, who knew exactly where to look for me—"

"De Wrendt never told me!" she screamed. "No one did."

"That American came running straight up to the roof. I had time to think about it on the way here. It wasn't Sutter who told him; that *Spitzel* asked too many questions last night about where I would be, but he didn't find out. Still, to make sure, we fixed him. Therefore it must have been—"

"Wouldn't it have been safer to stop you before Sadat ever reached the clinic?" Marie-Christine cried. "Would any sane person have run the risk of letting you get onto the roof with a rifle?"

Bruno blinked vaguely. "I don't know *how* it happened. I'm interested in *who*. Because whoever did it—"

"It was Bauer," Marie-Christine said, gaining confidence.

"No. He would have dodged down the street as soon as he came out of the clinic and left me holding the bag; he wouldn't have hung about waiting for me to be wiped out. I know how Bauer would have reacted." His blue eyes were once again set and lifeless, but the effect was different, queerer now that his hair was dyed. "Before you meddled in Cologne, we had no trouble. What business was it of yours, anyway? The Middle East doesn't mean a thing to you. Why didn't you run your boutique and keep your nose out of it?" he ranted.

Dumbfounded, she stared at him. He'll never let me get away alive now, she thought in despair. It's too late.

He had turned around. Marie-Christine heard the sound at the same moment with inexpressible relief. Any interruption was preferable to this. Through the window she recognized the silver Ferrari rolling up the driveway.

"Don't·move at all." Bruno was aiming a large Army pistol at her. "I don't know what you two are up to. I'm in a bad mood. I don't know what I'll do next. I'm not trusting you; maybe I no longer even trust him."

Years ago De Wrendt had laid aside an escape passport and money in an unused dresser drawer in his house for an emergency, but as time had passed and his cover had strengthened in Zurich, their existence had become almost unreal. He had a house, a wife, a son: these were the real basics, as the jargon went to describe a spy's equipment, and they anchored his life firmly. Counterbalancing this attachment was a career in shadow, obedience to a remote bureaucracy whose headquarters he had never so much as entered: it didn't weigh sufficiently to tilt the scales. He had organized others' crash exits, but for himself he had foreseen no such calamitous departure. Now without warning this complacent assumption lay overturned, smashed. I'm no better than the seediest small-time agent scrambling for shelter, he thought, and drove faster.

He would abandon the Ferrari at Seeblick, board a train and merge among the Austria-bound summer tourists, whose passports were at best cursorily checked. Later he would decide whether to recontact the Center. It wasn't important; his value to them was ended. An image of the two women who had mattered in his life, one dark-haired, the other blond and young, intruded into his thoughts and weirdly overlapped, becoming one. Impatiently he banished the image. At this moment he had a primary obligation to himself alone, comparable to that of a man swimming unaided in the lonely sea, which was to survive.

He turned up the car radio. There was no mention of Bruno's capture. What could Bruno's reaction be to devastating last-minute failure? And to betrayal? What would any person's be? Bruno had never been the same since Cologne: the notoriety he had known had aggravated his slickness and uppityness, exposed his underlying lack of realism. He had always been wanting in the saving grace of cynicism needed to be effective in the secret world. All of De Wrendt's premonitions about him had proved correct.

As the Ferrari swept up Seeblick's gravel drive, De Wrendt spied the beige Opel parked beside the side terrace. Bruno had got this far and might already be aboard the boat. If he vanished into Eastern Europe with the Center's help, it would simplify things, provide a relatively tidy solution. . . . But as De Wrendt entered the house, Bruno's raised voice could be overheard. I was a fool, he thought, to imagine that I could avoid a showdown.

He strode into the salon and frowned. "Put down the gun," he ordered. "She won't scratch you."

"She's capable of worse." Bruno nevertheless slowly lowered Bauer's pistol.

"You were supposed to get out fast as soon as the operation was terminated. What are you doing here?"

"Finding out what went wrong."

"What went wrong . . ." De Wrendt's voice grated unnaturally. "You missed your target. There will be no more opportunities like that one."

"I didn't miss without a damn good reason," Bruno shouted, and De Wrendt noticed his quivering nether lip. "That American zeroed in on the roof looking for me. I was supposed to be *his* target, and it came damn close to succeeding." He jerked his head at Marie-Christine. "When I came here from Cologne, I said, 'She's a liability, get rid of her,' but you had other ideas. . . ."

Since De Wrendt's arrival, Marie-Christine had stood paralyzed beside the wall, making no motion that would provoke Bruno.

Glancing at her, De Wrendt realized with immense serenity to what extent his infatuation with this French girl had amounted to a banal case of might-have-been. If nothing else, she had unwittingly but mercilessly revealed to him his true age. Love, with its illusions and imperfections, its absurd camouflages and untimely enlightenments!

"He's blaming me for Sadat's still being alive," she said hurriedly, with no attempt at irony.

"She obviously had no part in what happened," De Wrendt said with total calm. "How could she, when she was locked up in this house for the past three days? There'll be time later to dissect the operation, *but not now*. Do you think the police are hanging about to analyze what went wrong? Give them a little more time and they'll be here—"

"They don't know about this house," Bruno said sullenly.

"They know," De Wrendt intoned with incurable weariness.

"How?" Bruno's protuberant blue eyes focused on him, spellbound; suspicion seeped from him like electricity from defective wiring.

De Wrendt expelled his breath slowly. He felt the way he thought of Europe—an old whore that had reveled too long. "If anyone was set up, it was I, not you—by my wife, the Center, everyone."

"What in hell is that supposed to mean?"

"I told the CIA. I received an *order* to tell them. Grand Slam was canceled before you pulled the trigger. Does that penetrate? From the start it was a high-risk operation—and thanks to your fumbling it became wholly meaningless. Fingerprints smudged over my apartment . . . notes scribbled in an envelope . . . guns stuffed into a tennis bag . . . the puzzle is how we survived at all." He was quite steady, in possession of himself, relieved to have got rid of his unendurable burden.

"You *told* them? I don't believe it." Bruno's unblinking gaze did not quit him.

De Wrendt looked vaguely about the familiar salon; he was far too exhausted to argue. "Then don't believe me. Stay here if you like. As for me, I have several items to collect, after which—"

"It's not in your character," Bruno declared stubbornly, grasping at a scrap of certitude out of their mutual past. "For some reason you're still trying to protect her. . . ." He had moved toward the door, blocking De Wrendt's way.

There comes inevitably a moment when a sick tree falls and a hollow relationship collapses. It seemed to De Wrendt that he had always known, though he had tried to deny the evidence, that his association with Bruno would culminate in this shabby debacle and settling of accounts; but the zigzagging trail itself, which had led via Cologne and Algeria to Seeblick, had been unpredictable.

"You gave away the escape route too?" Bruno was untypically subdued again.

"What do you think?" De Wrendt said shortly. "I had no choice."

"How did you manage to come here? Why did you bother?"

De Wrendt shrugged. He refrained, however, from uttering a word. Whatever he said, he realized with acute clarity, would fuel Bruno's feeling of being irremediably trapped.

"I'm not buying it. You two are up to something: I can feel it. When I follow my instinct, I'm always right." He scowled at them, uneasy and baffled. They were lovers leagued against him. He had always believed that infatuation could cause people to be cunning and base. He felt relief that he had never succumbed wholly to a woman, not once in his life; that his own wits were clear and unaffected.

"Are you going to stand here and endlessly squabble? Use the one opportunity you still have, man!"

Bruno was looking beyond De Wrendt at Marie-Christine. "We'll leave together, and take her with us. She'll finally serve a purpose. They'll hold their fire for her sake."

"No," Marie-Christine blurted out with ungovernable fear.

Bruno twisted his head savagely. "No?"

"I am the one who still gives orders. No one is leaving with you," De Wrendt enunciated coldly. "I'm not, she isn't . . ." His right hand dived toward his pocket. Helpless, Marie-Christine saw the Swiss Army pistol leap upward in Bruno's large fist. "You and your crazy bloodthirsty methods of changing society! There's been enough—"

De Wrendt's last word went unuttered as two earsplitting reports reverberated through the room. He took a tentative step away, seeking to free his own gun from his fashionable clothes. Then he tripped forward and almost languidly pitched onto the rug, where he stared out with the momentarily surprised look older men sometimes have for the outer world round about them.

"God damn him!"

For another instant, though Bruno was yelling at her, Marie-Christine stared fascinated at De Wrendt's fallen body. She was overwhelmed by morbid curiosity about his motives. Had he behaved so recklessly in her behalf? No, she couldn't bring herself to believe in his altruism. In the split second before he had died, however, De Wrendt had seemed to revolt against his lifelong choice of slippery ma-

317

neuver—and the revolt had impelled him to make the mistake of reaching for his gun. It was the first unprofessional act of his exceptional career. There was never time for me to discover what it could have been like between us, she thought. I *did* like him very much. And now she was being hustled out of the house without even a chance to mourn —not my lover, but my captor.

"God damn him! Damn him!" Bruno repeated, white around the mouth, nudging her toward the door with the blunt pistol barrel. Unresistingly she obeyed, wondering whether she was still capable of taking a step forward. "I didn't want to shoot him. He shouldn't have drawn—"

"Stop it!" she screamed into his colorless face.

It aroused him from his brief daze. "Probably I shot the wrong person." He prodded her again between the ribs. "Now, move!"

With a final, incensed glance at De Wrendt's prone figure, Bruno opened the door and motioned to her to start down the somber hall toward the back entrance. The house was utterly still except for their footsteps on the tiles. Marie-Christine wondered what had become of the two members of the African Fellowship Center. Had they already cleared out before the gunfire?

Guthrie observed the silent house from behind a tall barberry hedge near the driveway. He noted myriad details— the last daylight filtering through the garden's glossy dark foliage; the blinds of an upstairs bedroom drawn against the summer sun that was now setting on the western horizon in a garish stain. His attentive gaze returned to the silver Ferrari parked beside the Opel. How had De Wrendt managed to break free from his captors? Renata, he thought. She was a woman who would stick to her husband while fighting him tooth and nail. The house's silence was enigmatic and forbidding. Then a branch crackled underfoot and Huebli moved cautiously up alongside the hedge.

"The house next door is shut for the season," he murmured. "I have two men stationed there; the others are staked out along the side wall and the row of poplar trees."

"If they're still inside, Bruno won't surrender. He'll make us dislodge him. But they're probably gone—with Marie-Christine," Guthrie added curtly.

"In either case, we'd better get a start while there's still some light."

Guthrie nodded. Back in Zurich, he had had trouble persuading Huebli not to phone the nearest *gendarmerie* barracks with an order to surround Seeblick. Huebli had dug in his heels; the Swiss were incensed—it was their affair now, an affront to their national image—and his superiors would have little patience with whoever meddled in the manhunt. Finally, receptive to the argument that someone might bungle the instructions and endanger Marie-Christine's life, Huebli had compromised, alerting a *gendarmerie* detachment to stand by but make no move until he arrived on the scene.

"We'll go first," Huebli said now. "My men will cover us but withhold fire. How many people do you reckon are in that house?"

"This was their operational base, but most of the commando is probably still in Zurich. Assume four or five."

"You have no chance of getting in alone."

"She doesn't stand a chance otherwise. He won't hesitate about shooting her if he thinks he's cornered. Let me get her out and then you can take him."

Huebli grunted noncommittally. "Provided you don't take forever." He eyed the two cars. "Whom does the Ferrari belong to?"

"A man named De Wrendt."

"Isn't that the bank—?"

"The house also belongs to him. I'll explain later."

It was then that they heard two dull, unmistakable thuds.

Below was a private cove, and there De Wrendt's boat, a twenty-one-foot half-deck fiberglass runabout, was riding in

319

the water, anchored and secured by a bow line to a mooring ahead. The breeze had not abated and swells were building up, smashing furiously against the retaining wall's piers. Bruno stared down at a wooden ladder that acceded to a small platform supported on piles driven into the lake bottom.

Covering Marie-Christine with his gun, he said, "Go ahead."

She made a last attempt to dissuade him. "I'll only be in the way."

He grinned ominously. "For a while I need you."

She clambered down the ladder and went aboard the pitching boat, her blond hair whipping about her cheeks. The key, she saw with resignation, was already in the ignition. Following her aboard, Bruno motioned to her to sit down in one of the twin cockpit seats. With no visible concern he put his gun away under his Windbreaker, then turned on the starter switch and, letting the engine warm up, began to check out the fuel tank, oil-pressure gauge, light switches and bilge and blower controls. He fished out a checked golf cap from his pants pocket and jammed it over his ersatz dark hair. Marie-Christine recognized the faded cap from Cologne and wondered what it signified to him that he had held on to it so persistently through so many vicissitudes. A good-luck charm? He'd already enjoyed more than his share of that.

Bruno raised his eyes. In the west the light over the lake was already ivory, and he realized that he had lingered far too long. He still found it almost impossible to believe that De Wrendt was dead. He felt a whiplash of deprival and grief more unbearable than he could imagine, searing and acute, which he had not experienced in years. Had De Wrendt betrayed him? If he admitted that, then what became of his respect for the man?

Dusk was spreading rapidly across the vast restless lake. Families with children had made port; only a few powerboats purred in and out between sailboats anchored for the night. As he cast off, Bruno paid no attention to the craft on the water; his eyes, set and dangerously obsessed, were fixed on the promontory at the end of Seeblick's lawn. He's completely unbalanced, Marie-Christine thought with a shudder.

Guthrie, crouching, dashed toward the Opel, expecting a pistol to crack from one of the unlit ground-floor windows. He fetched up hidden behind the car's fender. The ambiguous silence had resumed. The gunfire was inexplicable, unless Bruno had just disposed of his hostage. Then another explanation occurred to Guthrie. It was possible that Bruno or one of his lieutenants had fired deliberately to draw him nearer and was cold-bloodedly observing him. The shortest distance to the house was across the flagstoned side terrace, but it was also the most exposed. Even in the fading light, a figure racing across the open space toward the kitchen would present a ludicrously easy target. The longer but safer approach was to work his way up behind the silver Ferrari, which was parked halfway between the Opel and the house, then gain a corner of the building that formed a blind angle no one within could guard and finally steal up to the front entrance facing the driveway. He conceded that he was afraid. Damn right he was afraid. He sprinted and reached the Ferrari without drawing fire and paused. Steeling himself, he made a dash for the stucco wall and flung himself around the corner. In the cryptic silence he edged gingerly toward the double door, bent over, his gun trained on the entrance. I'm too late, he thought. Again.

Then Huebli's patience failed him. Out of the shadowy orchard on the property's boundary, from behind the thick old beeches and the clipped hedge materialized a platoon of *gendarmes* in battle dress, machine pistols drawn, swarming in a broken run across the lawn around the front and side of Seeblick.

As soon as he saw them, Guthrie kicked the door, and it

flew inward. Whoever had last entered the house had neglected to lock it.

Before the others, he reached the living room and discovered the body sprawled on the rug. The floor-to-ceiling draperies were partly open; enough twilight penetrated the interior to make identification easy. He couldn't restrain an indecent feeling of elation; he had been so convinced that both shots were intended for Marie-Christine that he had braced himself to cope with grief and guilt. The relief flooding through his veins left him almost callous to the dead man at his feet.

"De Wrendt?" Huebli said, arriving on his heels.

"He must have died instantly while we were talking outside." Conscientiously, Guthrie tried to balance his emotions to admit some commiseration for the fallen banker. "Rich, unlucky bastard. But I don't think we could have changed the outcome: sooner or later—"

"You mean you were expecting this?"

"No, I wasn't. But once Bruno figured out who betrayed him, the rest was inevitable." It occurred to Guthrie that Renata—if it was Renata who had facilitated her husband's escape to Seeblick—had not aided but doomed him. A thump of boots resounded on the staircase and overhead as the platoon spread through the house searching, but Guthrie heard nothing else.

"They didn't get away in the cars," Huebli said.

"Along the shore?"

"No, I have some of the detachment posted down there."

"De Wrendt had a powerboat. Bruno was going to use it after killing Sadat."

As they rushed out to the promontory, the young commander of the *gendarmerie* detachment ran up after them. The house had been completely searched, he reported; whoever else had been in it had vanished, probably along the lakefront.

Guthrie stared down at the empty cove where the discarded mooring line trailed in the water like an ultimate taunt. Along the Swiss coast the pastel afterglow had waned, and the distinction between distant and intermediate mountain ranges in the west was blurred. Far off to the north, insubstantial lights pierced the mist—the winking lights of Wasserburg, in Germany. Guthrie, peering eastward, could make out only the motionless silhouettes of small craft peaceably tied up inshore.

"A helicopter won't do much good," Huebli said. "By the time it gets aloft it will already be pitch dark."

"I'm not going to let him bolt once again. We know where he's heading—"

"Do you mean over there? He'd be mad. The Germans won't stand for it a second time."

"No, downshore to Austria, it's nearer. . . ." He didn't bother to add: toward the east, into the concealing darkness. "We still have a chance . . ."

"Assuming his boat can attain a maximum speed of thirty knots, in a half-hour he'll be in Austrian waters. I'll phone ahead to their nearest harbor-police base in Hard, but I don't expect miracles. They'll want to do things their way; they'll demand information I don't have. We have a *See-polizei* base between here and the frontier—if I can talk to someone with a bit of intelligence, I may get action. . . ."

"If we could find a boat ourselves, it would be simpler."

Simultaneously they had the same idea. Turning away from De Wrendt's cove, they started to run along the indented shoreline. Two hundred yards farther on, the property adjoining Seeblick began. A three-story chalet rose up from the beach, its shuttered windows facing lakeward, its high poplars rustling nervously in the evening breeze. Huebli had mentioned that the owner was absent, but the owner had a boat, and it rode at anchor within the shelter of a stony outcrop that formed a natural breakwater. Huebli drew up at the concrete pier, hesitant.

"We'll only be borrowing it," Guthrie said. The boat was an Italian-built triple-screw racing powerboat with a long, pointed bow and a tiny cockpit.

Swiss rectitude temporarily bested, Huebli stepped aboard and began to examine the ignition.

"I could use a flashlight," he said after a moment. "Let's see—ah, here we are." He had found one stashed away among rags and a can of engine oil in a recess beside the wheel.

As Guthrie watched him, Huebli set to work, efficiently and in silence, first unscrewing the three ignition switches, then peering underneath the instrument panel at the wiring and finally shorting two of the wires. Instantly the power was turned on.

"I've had to do it to my own boat when my wife misplaced the key," he explained, almost apologetically.

Reversing until they were well clear of the dock, Huebli headed the powerboat into the wind. A last-quarter moon was ascendant over the immense phosphorescent reach of water, but if De Wrendt's runabout was out there speeding into the inky distance, it was not to be seen. The racing boat's three inboards churned evenly and uninterruptedly.

"With the power we have, we may be able to overtake him," Huebli murmured.

But Bruno had at least ten minutes' head start, Guthrie thought.

"Take the wheel," Bruno ordered. "Maintain the same course and speed. Are you smart enough to do that?"

Marie-Christine nodded. She moved over to his seat in the cockpit and kept watch on the speedometer and compass. Without explanation he went aft and stood staring back at the almost invisible shore. On the crest of a low hill a castle reared up against the moonlit sky. He calculated that they were standing off more than a half-mile from land. They dropped a wooded cape astern, and he sighted the glow of Altenrhein, the last Swiss town of any size before the frontier; soon he would set course northeast by east for the final run into the Austrian sector of the upper lake. Moonbeams stabbed the tremulous froth of water

the angry shouts of the sloop's crew were snatched away by the wind and the boat was already too far. She saw its receding jib and mainsail still profiled against the sky, and resigned herself to watching her last chance of rescue becoming smaller by the second and finally vanishing into the night. Guthrie hadn't turned up. He never would now. She had tried to bolster her rock-bottom morale by counting on a supreme effort on his part, but she had been mistaken. God, this isn't believable, she thought.

Then suddenly she tensed. There was another dark object low on the shimmering water, at first barely visible, then reappearing and growing slightly larger. It was a powerboat, and it was streaking toward them out of the west without running lights too. Bruno's attention was fixed on the compass and the expanse of water ahead; plainly he hadn't become aware of the second boat yet, but within seconds the throb of its inboards would become audible on the wind. Turning to face him, she put her hand behind her back and groped in the dark until she felt a smooth long, round wooden pole. The boat hook was horizontally secured to the gunwales by two straps with press studs, which she unsnapped. She knew that she was going to need a weapon soon with which to defend herself.

"Why don't you say something?" he suddenly bellowed.

"I thought you wanted me to keep still," Marie-Christine retorted.

"I know what you're thinking."

"Do you? Why did you kill him?"

"Why? He pulled a gun on me. He invented the whole myth of Bruno but wouldn't accept the fact or face the consequences." Bruno frowned at the undefined night. "I looked up to him for years. If he hadn't fallen for you, we could have . . ." He did not end the sentence. "Maybe I made a mistake shooting him. Who knows?"

"He should be farther along. He lost time somewhere," Huebli said at the wheel. His hand moved to switch on the forward spotlight.

327

"Not yet," Guthrie said, restraining him. "Let's see what he does. He hasn't seen us so far."

"Now he has." The runabout had just veered violently to starboard in an explosive geyser of spray and was fleeing in a long reach across the lake: an elongated gray blur that lifted, then nosed and thudded into the swells with almost delirious relish.

"He should have stayed on course," Huebli muttered.

"You didn't warn me. Now I *am* going to kill you," Bruno yelled. He cast a rapid glance back at the pursuing streak, slight and V-hulled, to his weather side. In the darkness he judged it to be ten boat lengths away . . . nine. . . . The forms aboard were abruptly quite visible. He threw the wheel hard over, and as the boat careened and slammed down, he yanked out Bauer's pistol from his belt.

Marie-Christine backed away hastily from him, brandishing the boat hook and praying that she wouldn't stumble.

"Why are you moving, you bitch?" he screamed, trying to aim the pistol with one hand as he clutched the wheel in the other. "What are you doing with that pole?"

In a daze she flung the hook awkwardly at his stocky figure just before he fired.

Since she felt nothing except blank terror, she knew that the shot had missed. As for the boat hook, it had fallen short at Bruno's feet, with a clatter. She was defenseless now, and he was still there, twisted about, studying her intently and making no further attempt to maintain a coherent course, concentrating on aligning the raised gun on her profiled body.

Then each detail on deck—the stainless steel fittings, the windshield, the instrument panel—leaped into view in an unnatural dazzle harsher than daylight.

Without a word Bruno rushed up to the stern rail. As he shoved her aside, Marie-Christine realized that she was no longer in danger from him; he had quite simply dismissed her from his mind. On his youthful face she made out an exultant expression that no doubt would have dismayed De Wrendt—a rapt, expectant expression which idealists and dreamers wore when they went into battle.

Finally, Bruno thought, facing the other boat across the tossing opaque water. It was the enemy that had hounded him as a boy: they had been after him ever since and would never let him alone. He had been wrong; he was not free, no more than before De Wrendt's death. For a moment his brain commanded an overview of all that he had known and resented since his remote boyhood. *There has been no beginning and no end to pain; my particular life was inconceivable without it, like a birthright.* The idea was as blinding as the spotlight his pursuers had trained on him.

"Is he crazy?" Huebli muttered.

They were closing fast on the runabout, which was curving to starboard on a pitching race to the far, indistinct shore.

"Slow down. Be careful. I don't want her to be in my line of fire," Guthrie whispered, then ducked down in the cockpit as Bruno's gun hand pointed unerringly at the spotlight.

As it shattered, Guthrie glimpsed Marie-Christine diving to one side, and then heard the low-pitched, brief, lethal ting of a bullet singing dangerously close to his ear. On his knees he slithered down the deck and paused. Taking a chance, he peered into the unhelpful dark. Bruno had not budged. Clearly outlined against the runabout's rail, he stood obstinate and aggressive, in place, positive of his indestructible right to be there.

"Where are you, Guthrie?" he bawled abruptly. "You can't get away from me this time. . . ." Without transition he swerved, and Guthrie guessed rather than saw the gun's barrel uncannily moving on him, and had just time to hurl himself down again to the deck boards as the report detonated. He felt eerily calm: it was a sentiment not at all of being invincible but simply of being superior to the other man, provided that he could wait him out and avoid being reckless or otherwise stupid. He was even glad that Bruno had challenged him by name: it put a fitting personal touch on the long up-and-down seesawing chase.

"I can stay here all night," Bruno bellowed, then illogically fired without a target, this time into the dark empty space around the powerboat's stern.

Now I am going to take you, Guthrie thought. Bracing himself on one knee and suspending his ragged breath, he drew careful aim on the erect, stubborn figure in the poplin Windbreaker and golfer's cap. He squeezed the trigger, heard an exclamation, saw Bruno whirl in rage, then slump against the gunwale.

"He's down!" Huebli shouted over the motor's roar.

Guthrie had the same impression, but a tiny inner voice commanded him to keep out of range. Behind him, Huebli made a swift sucking noise between his teeth. Bruno had struggled back to his feet, staggered forward and was lifting his Army pistol. . . . It isn't possible, Guthrie thought with incredulity; he's hit and should be stunned, doubled over . . . how much pain can he tolerate? But Bruno continued to glance about, left hand clasped protectively to his damaged waist, holding his fire and sniffing the wind for a scent of his enemy.

He doesn't even care about Huebli, who is visible; it has to be me or no one, Guthrie thought coldly. This is what it has been building up to since I first interfered with him on the streets of Cologne. Counting soundlessly in his parched throat, he waited—for what exactly he didn't know. Then beneath he felt a gentle surge of water against the hull, which began to respond, turning . . . putting him for a second out of Bruno's line of fire. It is going to be his last opportunity; even terrorists run out of luck. He leaped into a crouching stance, saw the near chunky silhouette—too close for comfort, but as clearly as he desired—and fired twice again.

As the other boat came about, Bruno seemed to lunge

aside but somehow misjudge the distance and step straight into the twin withering blasts. With a last, hoarse cry, as his gun thudded to the deck, he pitched headlong into the boisterous water, vanishing like a diver, only to reappear floating face upward, dark hair awash and pale lips drawn back over his bloodless gums in a permanent baleful rictus. Then all of a sudden, as though his brain were still functioning and had emitted a final, furious order, his body plunged without surrender into the lake's depths.

It was only later that Guthrie realized he had kept firing viciously—like Bruno at Wadi Khalef—into the moonlit wash long after it became meaningless.

Then Huebli was maneuvering the boat alongside the fugitive runabout. Marie-Christine had scrambled forward, had cut the ignition and stood midships waiting to be picked up—too stiffly, her reaction numbed till later, murmuring audibly over and over, "If you hadn't come . . ."

Guthrie felt weariness rather than triumph. He had saved this vulnerable girl whom he had missed so much from becoming Grand Slam's ultimate victim. And he had put away a rabid killer who was a public menace. But it had been touch-and-go throughout, the outcome unpredictable until the very end; and some aspects of Bruno's behavior rooted in his past—for example, his pitilessness, a form of hopelessness—would remain forever unaccountable, which left Guthrie dissatisfied. It occurred to him that he and his enemy had never exchanged a meaningful word, traded only shots on the Linder Clinic's roof and across the Bodensee. Except in moments of destruction, he hadn't known Bruno at all—those moments that were the peaks of his short, wrathful life—and somehow Guthrie regretted this.

The wind was subsiding at last and the lake was regaining its profound quietude. Huebli broke into Guthrie's thoughts. "Someone—that is, me—is going to have to do a lot of explaining," he said. "We're in Austrian waters."

Chapter Thirty

Summer's End

GUTHRIE SAW Marie-Christine off at Kloten Airport.

"I'm finally returning to Paris on my own passport," she said.

"Pleased?"

"Mmm." She looked sideways at him. "Don't look so relieved. You're not rid of me so easily." Her thoughts spanned the period since he had first shown up at her hotel room. "I was so angry and upset with you on Ibiza. But I've changed. So," she added critically, "have you."

"In what way?"

"More modest. Perhaps a bit more reflective?"

"It won't last," Guthrie reassured her. "I'll be my old impulsive, boastful self in no time. As for you . . ."

"Yes?"

Guthrie cast a glance at this slim girl who had strayed perilously far—in part it was his doing, of course—into the terrorist world. If she had survived, it was due to what exactly? Her loyalty? No way. Her yearning for adventure? To the contrary. Then to a valuable strain of flexibility?

"I wish you weren't leaving."

"Truly?"

"I keep discovering you—and losing you. . . ."

"Irish exaggeration. It isn't as though I were going far."

They crossed the main hall, crowded with tourists ending their vacations, and a question that had been bothering her occurred to Marie-Christine.

"Did you ever find out the third notation's meaning?"

Guthrie guided her down the corridor. "The morning of the attack, Bruno went to a hospital-linen-supply firm to pick up his orderly's uniform. The address was 70 Rosenthalerstrasse. If we'd known that beforehand . . ." But his thoughts were no longer on Grand Slam: it was over and done with; so was his temporary career as a terrorist hunter, he hoped. He knew without having to be told by Ditweiler that sheer luck had played a part in the outcome. If he had not reached the roof in the nick of time . . . if Bruno had not got into a row with De Wrendt at the end . . . Marie-Christine had described the last moments at Seeblick and told him about Ibiza. Wondering what had really happened there between them, he had asked, "How did you feel about De Wrendt?"

"He saved my life."

On that subject, he had sensed, it was all he could get out of her. Some loose ends are best left so.

"Stay," he said now.

"Why?"

"Why do you think? Because I'm asking you to."

Marie-Christine shook her head, then said quickly, "When you come to Paris you may stay in my apartment."

Guthrie started; saw that she meant it; reminded himself that he wasn't superstitious, at least not always . . . and with an astonishingly cheerful heart led her to the gate.

*

CAIRO, Sept. 1—President Anwar Sadat of Egypt flew back here today after being released from a Swiss clinic where he underwent successful abdominal surgery.

Upon arrival in Switzerland almost two weeks ago, Mr. Sadat was the target of an abortive terrorist attempt upon his life.

A spokesman said the Egyptian President would fly on schedule later this month to a summit meeting with President Jimmy Carter and Israeli Premier Menachem Begin at Camp David, Md.